Secrets Don't Sink

Secrets Don't Sink

A Chattertowne Mystery

K.B. Jackson

LEVEL
BEST BOOKS

For Jeffy J, my cohort in life's shenanigans and rigamarole

Chapter One

My resolve weakened with one brackish whiff of the river. Pressed against the Chattertowne City Hall building, I clutched my satchel to my body and cursed my boss under my breath.

"I could live on canned soup and boxed macaroni if I had to," I mumbled to myself. "No job is worth this kind of stress."

I'd circled the block three times in search of a parking space before I'd finally spotted reverse lights. On my approach, an old red truck with white-walled tires and a classic rounded frame had emerged from an alley and cut me off. The driver had thrown the brake, jumped out, and slammed the door behind him. As he'd stormed across the street, I'd readied my hand to lay on the horn, but the glower he'd thrown in my direction had stopped me cold.

Now, the mere thought of walking around the corner to the marina spiked my anxiety even further. I'd been frozen there for at least twenty minutes already, trying to psych myself for the daunting task ahead. Having aquaphobia while growing up in a riverfront town had never been easy, but for the most part, I'd managed to avoid getting too close. Sure, I'd missed out on summer rafting trips and pool parties, but that was preferable to having a panic attack in front of all my friends.

My phone buzzed with a call from my sister Vivienne.

"You must have a sixth sense."

"How so?"

"I've been trying to decide if I'm going into the marina office to pay Mr. Anderson's overdue rent on his boat slip or if I'm quitting my job instead.

Thoughts?"

Employed part-time at the *Chattertowne Coastal Current* newspaper to create content for the around-town section of the generously called Events and Lifestyles, typical topics of my pieces included things like Zeb Brandt's antique tractor collection and Jennifer Rohrbach's prizewinning dahlias.

"Audrey, when you finally decide to get therapy, be sure to start with your poor work boundaries and quarter-century-long overreaction to my unexpected little swim."

"You nearly drowned."

My mind flashed to a faded memory of my baby sister being pulled from the water. I could still visualize my mother's angry expression as she scolded me for letting her out of my sight.

Viv made a dismissive cluck. "But I didn't, and I haven't let fear keep me from living my best life. You shouldn't either."

I stopped myself from challenging her definition. Getting fired for sleeping with her married boss didn't sound like her best life.

"Anyway, I'm calling to find out what happened when you got in to work today," Viv said. "Did anyone give you a hard time about Tasha's party?"

Earlier that morning, I'd snuck into the office hoping to avoid any co-workers who'd witnessed me uncharacteristically let loose at our receptionist Tasha's birthday party over the weekend. After belting out a slightly tipsy and mostly inaccurate rendition of "Bohemian Rhapsody," Sandros, the IT guy with a unibrow and a penchant for frou-frou drinks, had cornered me for an unwanted kiss that left me with an aftertaste of appletini and regret.

"Tasha wasn't at her desk when I got in, so I left a peace offering of maple bars at her desk and scuttled into my office. Unfortunately, Darren sauntered in right behind me and dropped a couple snarky comments before chuckling all the way back to his office."

Darren Benson, the *Current's* newest—and only—Business and Finance reporter, had cunning blue eyes and plump pink lips, which he kept perpetually formed into a smug smile. He liked to pair his signature Burberry plaid scarf with casual condescension.

2

CHAPTER ONE

My irrational attraction to him fit the same predictable pattern as most of my previous disastrous entanglements, where I found myself drawn toward a man despite knowing his good looks would never be enough to offset his arrogance.

"I don't like that guy," Viv said, not for the first time.

"I'm well aware."

I waved at Ms. Truman, one of my mom's good friends, as she passed. She gave me an odd look in return.

"Darren stopped me in the hallway after our morning meeting and asked me to lunch," I said.

"Audrey." Viv's disapproval dripped through the phone. "You're not going, are you?"

"I told him I can't today, but I probably could tomorrow."

She made a sound akin to a cat coughing up a furball. "I'd rather go to the dentist."

"That reminds me. You need to reschedule your dentist appointment to get that filling done. You don't want your teeth to rot out of your head. Oh, and take your car in for an oil change before your engine seizes up."

"Oops, sorry, gotta go!"

"Viv–"

Click.

I squinted at the phone and sighed. I didn't mean to be an overbearing nag, as Viv sometimes called me, but her laissez-faire attitude hadn't served her well. I'd even moved home from Portland to help her put the pieces back together following her latest romantic scandal.

I slipped my phone into my jacket pocket. Across the street at one of Chattertowne's ubiquitous antique stores, a woman monitored me from the window. Apparently, shimmying along the building with my back practically suctioned to the brick wall was suspicious behavior.

"Audrey?"

Chattertowne's city manager Holden Villalobos squinted at me as he held open the door to City Hall with his broad shoulders. As a teenager, Holden had been scrawny, but maturity had turned him into an attractive mix of

3

The Rock and Cristiano Ronaldo.

He wore black nylon jogging pants and a white T-shirt. Both the shirt and the man were covered in perspiration.

"Hey!"

I went to hug him, but he stopped and held up his hands.

"Trust me. You want no part of this right now." He laughed and took a step back, shifting the gym bag strap that hung at an angle across his chest.

"What…why…what happened to you?" My voice trailed off like the beads of sweat currently rolling down his swollen biceps.

"You caught me at the end of my lunch workout. Normally, I don't meet with constituents in my gym clothes. What are you doing here? You're not actually going near the water, are you?"

"I'm still trying to decide. When I applied for this job, I knew it was for a puff piece reporter, but I had no idea I was also going to be Anderson's errand girl. He asked me to make a payment on his boat slip rental."

Holden gave me an appraising look. "I can take it down there if it's going to give you a panic attack."

I shrugged. "If I don't look directly at the river, I'll probably be okay. Thanks, though."

"I'm sure you'll be fine, but if I don't get a text from you in an hour, I'll come looking for you. Oh, shoot, I just got a new phone. Let me give you the number."

He dropped his gym bag onto the sidewalk and squatted to rifle through it. He shifted a pair of khakis and a navy polo shirt to the side.

"Going on a trip?"

"Nope. Just my work clothes. I didn't want to get them sweaty. I'll change back into them once I get to my office." He stopped digging through his bag. "You're a reporter. You got paper and something to write with in your purse?"

"It's a satchel, not a purse."

He blinked at me.

I reached into my bag, retrieved a yellow Post-it notepad and a pen, and handed them to him. He was still squatting as he scribbled his number on the pad. My quads ached on his behalf. When he finished writing, he stood, ripped off the top sheet, slapped it against my upper arm, and handed me the pad and pen.

"Thanks." I peeled the sticky note off my sleeve.

Holden's cell phone rang. He picked it up and frowned at the screen, hesitating before answering. "Yeah." His brows furrowed deeper, and his gaze darted around like a pinball. He pointed at the phone as if to say, "I gotta take this," gave a head nod and backed away.

I waved, but he'd already turned toward City Hall. I stared at the paper with his number and then at his broad retreating frame. I shoved the notepad, pen, and sticky note into the front pouch of my bag.

I couldn't help but wonder what the call was about, but I had bigger issues to consider, like whether I could get myself all the way to the marina office without somehow plunging into the water.

I took a deep breath and slithered around the corner, limb by limb. At my first unencumbered sight of the docks, a full-body shiver came over me.

"People go near water every day and live to tell the tale."

I rolled my shoulders back, lifted my chin, sucked in some air, and took one cautious step.

"I'll survive," I whispered.

Step. Deep breath.

I hummed the disco classic "I Will Survive."

Step. Deep breath.

The heavy breathing made me lightheaded and blurred my vision.

My humming intensified with each step.

The scene came back into focus just as the scowling man who'd stolen my parking spot thundered in my direction, nearly plowing through me as if I were invisible.

Stocky and about sixty, he was fair-skinned with a dark bushy mustache, a ring of brown hair circling a bald crown, hunched-up shoulders, and hairy balled fists.

He didn't say excuse me or in any way acknowledge my presence.

Cursing my boss again, I surveyed the docks for any other potential obstacles. My shaking hand shielded my eyes from the sun, trying to eke its way through the clouds.

About thirty yards ahead, the sign for the marina office shone like a beacon. Beyond that was the Port Authority building, and from there, the pier branched into a maze of boat moorages, or what I liked to call *no man's land*.

Vessels ranged in size from dinghies in small slips to cabin cruisers in medium berths to cargo ships nestled against the outer rim of the docks. There were two enclosed docks, but most of the boats were out in the elements with only their canvas covers to protect them.

Positioned along the banks of the Jeannetta River, which funneled into Puget Sound about twenty miles west, Chattertowne was close enough to the Pacific Ocean to be a busy access point for fishing and transport. It was also near enough to smell like brine and have a boardwalk splattered by shorebirds.

Taking another deep breath, I willed my feet to move, carefully navigating through the gauntlet of droppings until I vaulted myself through the door of the marina office like at the finish line of a marathon.

Inside, the lobby was lined with several chairs, but only one was occupied. A young woman with long black lashes, a turned-up nose, and braided bun atop her head greeted me from behind the counter with a smile. She wore a red-and-brown wool patchwork poncho.

"How can I help you?"

"Hi, my name is Audrey O'Connell. My boss, Nicholas Anderson, asked me to make his rental payment for his boat slip." I handed her the check. "I guess it's a bit late, and he's worried about penalty fees."

"I'll see what I can do. Do you need a receipt for him?"

"Yes, he insisted, actually. Thanks."

"Gimme a sec. I'm already working on something for her." She indicated the visibly pregnant woman waiting in the lobby. "It'll be a few minutes before I can get the payment entered and print out the receipt. I'll see if I can override any late fees which have been assessed." She headed into the back with the check.

The hard-plastic gray chairs were reminiscent of my elementary school days. I'd expected the marina office to be more nautical, maybe have some rope art or one of those tripod spyglass lamps. Instead, stained utilitarian carpet met with dingy gray walls. A corkboard held advertisements for marine services, boats for sale, and slip sublets. It was more DMV, less yacht club.

I turned to the pregnant woman. "Have you been waiting long? These chairs can't be comfortable for you."

The woman snickered. "Honey, I'm having twins. I haven't been comfortable in six months." She stretched her legs in front of her, revealing she wore pink slippers.

The clerk returned to the counter and nodded at the woman next to me. "Mrs. Faulkner?"

The pregnant woman attempted to hoist herself out of the chair. When she failed to get enough leverage, I offered my hand in assistance.

She blushed and smiled at me. "Thanks. Last week I made the mistake of testing out one of those giant bean bags, and it took three salespeople to pull me out of it."

She waddled up to the counter, where the clerk handed her a paper.

"Lance said he'll give you a call as soon as a covered berth becomes available. In the meantime, check out these thirty-foot uncovered slips and see if any of them will work temporarily. Here's a map of the marina, with all the slips numbered."

Mrs. Faulkner nodded and thanked her. She waved an exhausted goodbye to me as she schlepped her giant belly out the door.

"I haven't forgotten about you," the clerk said to me. "I'll have your receipt ready in a moment."

"No problem."

After about fifteen minutes, she came around the corner waving an envelope. "Here you go! Sorry for the delay. Our computers are running slow. My boss says we can waive the late fees just this once."

I took the receipt. "Thanks so much. I know *my* boss will appreciate it."

I stepped into the chilly air and scanned the boardwalk. A small crowd had gathered just beyond the Port Authority building. I couldn't see much from my vantage point, but it looked like someone was lying on the ground.

I groaned. On the one hand, it was my job to investigate the goings-on in Chattertowne. On the other hand…water.

I blew a resigned sigh.

Shimmying along the building to gain a better view, my initial thought was it was it must be a CPR training doll, but as I edged closer, there was no mistaking the long-legged figure for a mannequin. Kelp vines snaked around wet jeans, and bruised hairy ankles protruded from scuffed black leather work boots.

I counted to three and lunged for one of the support beams, clinging to it like I'd done with Mama on my first day of kindergarten. A woman standing nearby jumped at my sudden intrusion and glared at me.

"Is that person okay?" I asked in an exaggerated whisper.

"No." She pulled her tan trench tighter and pursed her lips. "He's not okay."

"Do you know what happened?"

She grimaced. "They pulled the guy out of the river. What he was doing in there, I have no idea."

I hugged the post and tried to calculate how close I'd need to get for a better look while still keeping a safe enough distance from the edge of the dock. It was important to factor the sturdiness of each of the looky-loos into the equation. One klutz with flailing arms was all it would take to send me into the river. Not only didn't I know how to swim, but as soon as I hit the water, I'd have a panic attack and sink straight to the bottom.

A Port Authority officer attempted to control the crowd, but they'd encroached, disregarding his attempt at a perimeter.

I glanced at the woman in the trench coat. "Could you do me a favor?"

She eyed me with a narrow gaze. "Depends."

"I'm a reporter for the *Coastal Current*. Any chance you'd be willing to take my phone and snap a photo of the victim?"

"Why can't you? It's your job."

"I have a slight fear of water. More than slight. Debilitating would be more accurate."

She pursed her lips. "Do I get credit if you print it?"

"Sure."

I had no intention of submitting the picture to my boss. I only wanted to be able to write an accurate story.

I watched as the woman dodged a rotund man as he swayed back and forth, and a little boy darting around like a pinball. She stood on her tiptoes and held my phone aloft to get a better view of the scene.

After a few minutes, she returned and handed the phone to me.

"I took video instead."

"Thanks so much."

"Caroline Gates." She pointed at the phone. "Caroline with a C."

I nodded and pressed play on the video.

As I watched the camera zoom in on the face of the man lying on the docks, a tidal wave of grief crested over me. My lungs struggled to catch a breath, and I felt like I was drowning myself. A strangled cry lodged in my throat. I stumbled backward and fell onto the splintered planks.

The woman rushed over to me. "Are you okay?"

I shook my head.

"Did you know him?"

I nodded. I tried to swallow but gurgled instead.

Time might change a person, but familiarity always remained.

"Marcus. His name is—was—Marcus."

Chapter Two

Splinters poked through my pants as I rocked side to side on the dock. I held the post-it note in my trembling fingers. My tears smudged what Holden had written so I made my best guess and texted what I hoped was his number.

It's Audrey. Come to the docks. Hurry!

I pulled up the video again and stared at the lifeless face of my former boyfriend, Marcus Washburn.

Earlier that morning, I'd stared warily at Marcus's unopened message as it taunted me from my Facebook inbox. It was a ritual I'd repeated several times in the days since I'd received it, unsure whether to even open it, much less respond to it. Exes were exes for a reason, and bringing one back into my orbit, particularly a married one, brought many potential landmines with it.

None of that mattered anymore, though. That message contained the last words he would ever say to me, and I suddenly, desperately needed to know why he'd reached out after so many years. I opened my phone and clicked on the message.

Hey Audrey,

Long time, huh? I hope this isn't too awkward, but I heard you're back in town, and I could really use your help with something. I'm working on something pretty big, and you, being a reporter and all, well, I could use your digging skills. Whether you choose to help or not, please keep this on the down-low. My wife would kill me if she knew I reached out to you. Also, you should know you can't trust anyone in this town. I've been stirring a hornet's nest, and it's already gotten me in some trouble. If you choose not to respond, I'll understand. As always, I want only the best for you. I'd be lying if I said I didn't still look for you wherever I go. Old habits die hard, I guess, but I'm perfectly capable of keeping things strictly professional, I promise. Let me know if you're willing to meet so I can explain in person. I'm not comfortable discussing what's going on any other way. You never know who might be reading or listening.

Marcus

What investigation could he possibly be doing? What did he mean by being in trouble? Had he always been so paranoid?

I clicked on his Facebook profile. In the dozen or so years since I'd last seen him in person, Marcus's black hair had become flecked with silver. Though only thirty-two, his skin sagged from the fatigue of a difficult life, and dark circles rimmed his heavy-lidded brown eyes.

He'd posted photos of his wife and kids, three boys ranging in age from preschool to about ten. His wife, Renee, had a scowl in almost every picture, perpetually miserable, angry, or both. Renee and I had never been friendly, not because I'd once dated her now-husband but because her animosity toward me went all the way back to some unresolved middle school drama. She hadn't outgrown her less-than-sparkling personality.

No wonder Marcus didn't want her to know he'd messaged me.

Sirens wailed in the distance, and my phone buzzed with a text from Anderson.

"Any luck?"

I glanced in the direction of Marcus's body lying mere feet from me. Nothing about the situation felt lucky. I'd exited the marina office and stumbled into a nightmare.

Shock had robbed time of all meaning, so although it felt like an hour, it was probably only a few minutes later when I heard urgent footsteps pounding on the boardwalk.

I looked up as Holden approached me from behind the Port Authority building. He'd showered since I'd last seen him, and his hair glistened. His sweaty workout clothes had been replaced by the khaki pants and collared polo shirt he'd carried in his bag. His frenzied gaze darted from me to the crowd and back again.

I stood on wobbly legs as he came near. Without hesitation, he opened his arms and pulled me close. My heart thumped, and my shoulders shuddered with each hyperventilating gasp.

"Audrey, are you okay? What happened?"

My response came out with a stuttered whoosh. "I…I came to see… pe…people were crowded around…Mm…Marcus. Holden, it's Marcus. Ma-Marcus W-Washburn."

"What do you mean? What about Marcus?"

"He's…he's not breathing. He's blue. No, purple. Sort of grayish. He's d-dead. Oh, gawd, Holden, Marcus is dead." My teeth chattered as I babbled.

His arms went slack around me. I pulled back to scan his face. He'd donned the guise of a public official.

I wiped my tears from his polo, brushing his chest with my fingertips. When he'd pulled it out of his duffle bag earlier, the shirt had appeared black, but now stretched across his body in broad daylight, it looked navy blue.

"Stay here, Audrey." His tone left no room for rebuttal.

I stood with leaden feet anchored to the spot, swaying like a buoy in the eye of a hurricane.

Holden gestured for the crowd to back away from the body, and they complied. The Port Authority officer gave him a smile of relief and gratitude. He'd done what he could to contain the crowd, but his efforts had been disregarded for the most part.

Holden pulled out his phone and made a call. While speaking to whoever was on the other end, he crouched next to Marcus and gently pressed two fingers to his throat. He dropped his head and rubbed his eyes. He stood again when several Chattertowne policemen rushed down the gangplank toward the scene.

One of the officers wasn't in as much of a rush. She ambled over to Holden like she'd just dismounted a horse following a long ride across the prairie. She leaned in and whispered something to him. He shook his head

12

in response, and she pulled away, grim-faced. She ran her hand across the top of her head, shorn in a military-style buzz cut.

I plopped to the ground like a deflated balloon. I'd known it in my gut, but the confirmation still felt like a terrible blow.

Marcus was dead.

Marcus, who'd sent me a message saying he was in trouble, but I'd ignored it, blowing him off like an annoying gnat.

I tried to focus on my breathing but found it difficult to fill my lungs. The air smelled like rotting seaweed, making deep breaths quite unpleasant. Panic, adrenaline, and grief clashed in cacophony with the beat of my heart.

Holden squatted in front of me, his warm brown eyes searching mine.

"Audrey." Angst and concern shadowed his face. "Why don't you go sit on that bench over there? I've got to talk to these guys for a few more minutes, and it can't be comfortable for you to be sitting on the ground. I want you to wait for me so I can walk you to your car."

I nodded, and he pulled me to my feet. I stumbled over to the bench and slumped onto it, noticing too late the pool of melted chocolate ice cream.

"Who eats ice cream outside in February?" I scowled.

It was petty, but somehow focusing my anger and irritation at the thoughtless person who'd left behind a mess gave me a momentary respite from grief.

Since the police had taped off the scene, it was harder to get a clear glimpse of their activity, and the crowd began to thin.

I glanced across the river to where a cargo ship was anchored, stacked high with blue, orange, and red containers looking like giant LEGO bricks. I began to read the information on their sides to distract myself, like counting sheep, but less relaxing.

It didn't work.

Unbidden memories of my past relationship with Marcus floated to the surface.

We'd dated briefly after high school. Once the initial flutter of romance had subsided, I'd known we weren't meant to last. I had ambitions and dreams of leaving Chattertowne, while Marcus made it clear he was content to stay forever. His aspirations began and ended with creating the family he'd never had growing up. He'd wanted me to set aside my dreams to become his wife and mother to his children. I felt too young to settle down and suffocated under the weight of his vision for our lives together. Sometimes I wondered if he was looking for me to be a mother to him since the one he'd had was incapable of being what he needed.

The breakup was brutal. If he'd yelled and called me names or said what a terrible person I was, I wouldn't have felt so guilty. Instead, he'd just looked sad and lost. I'd even considered punching him in the arm to see if I could get him angry at me.

Angry.

Jerking upright and nearly falling off the bench, I waved at Holden who was standing next to the female officer. When he spotted my theatrics, he said something to her, and she gave me the once-over.

He jogged over to me. "What's up?"

"I just realized I may have seen something."

He sat next to me and slanted his head to give me full attention.

"Well, maybe it's nothing, but it could be something," I said.

He tucked his chin, arched his eyebrow, and pursed his full lips.

"There was a man. I saw him this morning when he cut me off."

He blinked. "A man. Can you be more specific? Cut you off in what way?"

Despite obvious skepticism, he was actively listening and so focused on me that I found it difficult to maintain eye contact. I attempted to find something other than his mouth or eyes to focus on—a mole, a blemish, even a freckle—but his tan skin was nearly flawless other than the half-inch scar slicing through his right brow. How did he get the scar? Judging by those lips, probably kissing someone he shouldn't have.

He impatiently cleared his throat. "Audrey?"

"Oh, uh, I was waiting for someone to pull out of a spot in front of City Hall...by the way, parking's the worst down here. You really should do something about that."

He briefly squeezed his eyes shut. "It's on my list. Tell me about the man, please."

"Well, he busted out from an alley, pulled in front of me, and took my parking spot. I was about to honk at him, but the look he gave me...the glare...." I shuddered at the memory.

"What does this have to do with Marcus? One mean look and bad manners isn't cause for suspicion."

"You'd have to have seen him. Anger radiated off him." I paused. "Do you think Marcus's death was an accident or something more nefarious?"

Holden sighed and rubbed his neck. "I don't know anything for sure yet, but I'm thinking he didn't just fall in and drown. He has a large gash and signs of blunt force trauma on his head. The injury could've happened after he fell in, but my guess–and, at this point it's only a guess–is he fell in *because* of the head injury. Whether he hit his head by accident or someone hit him on purpose, I don't think we'll have those answers for a bit."

"You know, his dad...."

He nodded. "That thought did occur to me."

"What thought occurred to you?"

Holden stood and acknowledged the officer with a head nod. "Kimball, this is Audrey O'Connell. She was also a friend of Marcus Washburn's. The three of us go way back, to high school."

Kimball loomed over me. She wasn't tall for a police officer, 5'6 or so, but she had girth. Not fat, just sturdy.

"If you have information that might aid the investigation, Ms. O'Connell, you should share it."

I blinked up at her. "D-did you grow up in Chattertowne?"

"Sort of. I went away to boarding school for a while." She folded her arms and splayed her feet. "Why?"

"I figured if you had, you'd have heard the stories about what happened to Marcus's dad, David Washburn."

"Probably but refresh my memory."

"Marcus's dad went missing when he was a baby. His car was found abandoned down here." I indicated the marina parking lot. "By itself, it wouldn't have created much of a stir. However, it happened only a few weeks after Jimmy Chatterton was found floating in the Jeannetta River.

My mom told me even though Jimmy's death was ruled a suicide, once David disappeared, most people in town believed the two events must somehow be connected. At the time of his death, Jimmy was under investigation for possible criminal activity related to the port, and David worked down here."

Holden gestured toward me. "Audrey, explain why you think there was something suspicious about the man you saw earlier besides his scary vibe and bad parking manners."

"You saw a man. What man? Where?" Kimball narrowed her eyes.

"Yeah, well, after he stole my parking spot and had the audacity to glare at *me*, I ran into him again. Literally. No, more like he ran into me. Over there." I pointed toward the corner of the building. "I didn't see him coming until he was practically on top of me. I had to jump out of his way to avoid getting knocked over."

"He was leaving the scene quickly?" Holden folded his arms across his chest.

"Well, I don't know if he was *leaving the scene*." I made air quotes. "He was headed back toward where he'd parked, and he seemed even angrier than the first time I saw him."

Kimball shifted her feet farther apart and rocked back on her heels. "Can you describe him? What about his car?"

"He was driving an old red pickup truck. Not like the rusty work trucks of the farmers drinking at Jim's Saloon, but a collectible classic. He was short, I'd say five-four or five-five at most, with a heavily receding hairline and a nasty scowl."

Holden grimaced, released a soul-weary sigh, and muttered an expletive. He shook his head and sighed again.

Kimball's face was unreadable. One of the other officers called her name.

"Duty calls. Thanks for the info. I'll be wanting your official statement in the next day or so."

She jogged back to where Marcus's body still lay on the ground.

I shivered and pulled my jacket closed. Holden joined me on the bench and wrapped his arm around my shoulders, drawing me against him. His warmth and scent brought comfort like a wool blanket and a thermos of spicy tea after a chilly walk in the woods. It was a vast improvement from the putrid odor of decaying fish.

At one point, another officer, Charlie Jacobs, came over to speak to us. Apparently, he and Holden had both pledged Omega Psi Phi at Washington State University.

Charlie asked me, "Did Holden ever mention he used his fraternity paddle to pry open an old window in the back of the Creamery and stole a box of Cougar Cheese tins? This dude, man."

Holden held up a finger. "Allegedly. Nothing was ever conclusively proven."

"Back to the matter at hand." Charlie pulled out his notebook and cleared his throat. "So, Audrey, describe to me what you saw earlier."

I repeated my story about the angry little man for the third time that day. Charlie jotted a few notes, took my phone number, and told me someone would be in touch to set up a full interview to take my statement.

As Jacobs walked back toward Kimball, an official-looking woman marched down the docks with two young men following close behind.

"Who's that?" I asked.

"That's Daphne Pierce. She's the coroner. She's also Kimball's ex," Holden said.

Daphne approached Kimball, who stiffened at the sight of her. The interaction looked icy. They exchanged a few words, and then Daphne examined Marcus. She directed the men who'd arrived with her to encase his body in a black plastic bag.

One of the Kohler boys, Seth, had come to oversee the removal of the body. The Kohler family owned the only funeral home in town, a multi-generational business run by Samuel Kohler and his two sons, Seth and Abel. Seth, the eldest son, had a long, solemn face which reminded me of a basset hound.

The Kohler family was a prime example that the pull of family obligations was never to be underestimated. Seth had once aspired to be a chef, but instead of creating culinary masterpieces, he had to babysit a corpse. Every day he bore witness to both the culminating moments of lives well-lived, and the tragic end of hopes and dreams left unfulfilled. The latter, I supposed, served as a constant reminder of all Seth had given up out of family loyalty and perceived duty. He spent the bulk of his time in the presence of death and carried with him the sorrowful resignation of a man who'd relinquished control over his own life.

I gasped when they lifted Marcus onto the stretcher, and Holden tightened his grip on my shoulder. The wheeled gurney thumped hauntingly over each plank of the boardwalk as it carried his body under the yellow caution tape, past the lingering ambulance chasers, toward the waiting aid car.

Holden pulled me to standing. He let go of one hand while still holding onto the other. We followed the somber march of the officers and coroner staff escorting the body from a respectable distance. Red lights flashed ahead on the street, but there was no siren and no rush because there was no life to save.

Just before we reached the street, Darren rounded the corner of the City Hall building and came to a screeching halt as he caught sight of us.

"Audrey?" He glanced at our hands, and his eyes flashed.

I released Holden's grasp. "What are you doing here?"

"I've got a police scanner app on my phone for breaking news. I heard they found a body, so I ran right down."

"You ran? You haven't even broken a sweat."

He shrugged. "I stay cool."

"Wait. Did you say you have an app for breaking news…in business and finance?"

"You'd be surprised." He glanced at Holden and then back at me. "Speaking of surprises, what are you doing here?"

"Anderson asked me to bring a check to the marina office for his boat slip rental. That's when I saw…" The words caught in my throat.

Darren grabbed my arm, pulling me to him and away from Holden. "I'm sorry you had to witness that."

We'd never hugged before, and although not an entirely unpleasant experience, it was awkward, particularly in front of Holden.

"You ran all the way over here from the paper?" Holden remained locked onto Darren's previous statement.

"I was in the area." Darren reached his hand out to Holden while keeping his other arm wrapped possessively around my shoulders. "Forgive me for being rude. Darren Benson. And you are?"

Holden hesitated before gripping Darren's hand. "Holden Villalobos. We've actually met before, Benson. At the Chamber's Christmas party."

"He's the city manager," I said.

Darren's jaw clenched and released. "Mmm, yes, I vaguely recall. You have that lovely fiancée. Emma, is it?"

"Emily." Holden's chin jutted forward.

"Right, right, Emily. Beautiful, sweet girl. You're a lucky man."

"I was just walking Audrey to her car."

Darren squinted at him. "Thank you for looking after her, but I've got her from here."

If I weren't so emotionally drained, I'd have given them both an earful. Pissing contests were neither impressive nor endearing.

"Audrey?" Holden tilted his head and cocked one perfect eyebrow.

I released a weary sigh. "Give me a call if I need to talk to anyone or answer any more questions."

Holden stared at me, blinking slowly. "Got it." He turned to Darren. "Nice to meet you. Again."

"Likewise."

I didn't believe either of them.

Darren rubbed my back. "Your eyes are red, you're a mess, and you're in no condition to drive. Why don't you ride with me back to the office?"

"That's not necessary."

"At least let me take you to dinner."

"I don't know."

"Audrey, I want to help."

I pulled away from him. "Fine, but I don't know what kind of company I'll be. Are you going back to the office right now?"

"No, I'm headed into the police station."

"Why?" I couldn't hide my irritation.

"To get more information on the investigation."

I blinked at him. "You write about the stock market. Mortgage rates. Free Seahawks poster at the credit union when you open a new account."

"As a citizen, I also want to know if we have reason to be concerned about safety in this town."

His assertion didn't ring true, but I didn't have it in me to probe further.

"Whatever." I waved my hand. "You do what you've gotta do. Pick me up at my apartment. I'm gonna drop off Anderson's receipt and head home."

"Great idea. I'll come by around seven."

"But...." I called after him, even though he'd already entered City Hall. "I never told you where I live."

When I got into my car and slumped into the driver's seat, what remained of my facade shattered. Heaving, wracking sobs overcame me as shock gave way to grief. I pulled up Marcus's last message on my phone, carefully reading and rereading each word in search of any clues. What seemed at first glance to be mild paranoia now had an ominous and foreboding tone.

One question loomed over me. If I'd read it earlier, would I have been able to stop what happened to him?

Tears squeezed from the corners of my eyes as I closed them. Marcus's face appeared in my mind. Not the bloated grayish-purplish-bluish mask of death, but the face of his youth when he'd look at me with heavy lids and his gentle, lazy smile that couldn't quite hide his desperation for love.

I'd been unable and unwilling to give him the love he needed and wanted.

Despite all the challenges he'd faced in his life, Marcus had remained optimistic, hopeful, and a bit naïve.

I couldn't help but wonder if perhaps that was what had ultimately led to his demise.

Chapter Three

I stood in the doorway of Anderson's office, fiddling with the strap on my satchel.

He looked up at me with his steel-gray bloodshot eyes. "Oh, Audrey. I didn't see you there. Come on in."

My boss was the embodiment of a classic newspaperman cliché with his gruff demeanor, teeth stained yellow from years of coffee and cigarettes, cragged jowls, and red bulbous nose.

I plopped onto one of the overstuffed red leather chairs facing his desk, which was cluttered with papers. To my right was a large free-standing globe. Hidden within it was a Waterford Crystal decanter filled with Woodinville Bourbon Whiskey, a fact I'd discovered a few months prior during my first week at the paper when I'd been informed my duties included going to the liquor store to restock his booze stash.

Like most of his employees, Anderson had another job. He taught English part-time at Chattertowne High, where he'd been my advisor on the school paper.

He glanced at me over his readers, perched low on the bridge of his nose. "I heard about what happened down at the marina. I don't suppose you got any photos."

I blinked at him, trying to decide how to answer. I didn't think he'd publish a shot of Marcus in that condition, but I couldn't risk it. I gave a technically truthful answer. "No, sorry, no photos."

"That's unfortunate. Next time I hope you'll be more on top of it. How about my receipt? I never got a text back from you. You remembered to pay my rent, right?"

"Oh, erm, yeah."

I reached into my satchel and pulled out his receipt. It was creased in several places and had a streak of pink across one corner. I held it to my nose and caught the sticky scent of my strawberry lip gloss. I set it on the desk.

He crooked his head as he looked at the crumpled paper. "Thanks." He glanced at me. "I know it couldn't have been easy for you, going down there."

"That's an understatement."

He cleared his throat. "How's the Kupit series coming? We're only a couple weeks or so away from the due date for the first installment."

The Kupit Festival was Chattertowne's annual spring fair held in Founder's Park. Vendor booths, activities and contests, food trucks, and a parade highlighted the weekend's events, along with a rickety traveling carnival on the baseball fields. It was a pretty big deal, even for a two-7/11 town. Kupit was an anglicized version of the Lushootseed/Puget Sound Salish word *kʷit,* meaning "go down to the water's edge."

"I've been having trouble getting anyone from the Chamber of Commerce or City Hall to cooperate. All I've been getting is the standard stuff we print every year. I want this year's series to be special."

"Have you talked to Peg?"

I tilted my head and stared at him. "Who's Peg?"

"She's in charge of the festival."

"It doesn't say that on the festival website."

"She's not officially in charge, but as the heart and soul of the Chamber of Commerce, she likes to control everything." He guffawed. "And I mean everything."

"Probably would've been useful information when you gave me the assignment."

He looked down his nose at me. "Look, I know you've had a rough day, so I'm gonna let the attitude slide this time. It's your job to find sources. You should've learned that on day one in your journalism classes. I know they expected that when you worked at *The Oregonian*."

"You're right." I blew out a breath. "I apologize. It's just that I've been out of the area a while, and it would have been helpful to know there's an unseen puppeteer running the show. How do I get in touch with Peg?"

"Peg's old-school, hates email, refuses to get a smartphone. Your best bet is to head over to City Hall and talk to her face-to-face. I'll give you a tip, though. Don't come to her without a peace offering. You want her to cooperate; you're gonna have to put a little effort in. Grease the wheels, so to speak."

"Are you talking about a bribe? You want me to bribe a city official to get information for a propaganda piece for her own event?"

"No government conspiracy here, just a cantankerous bureaucrat with a fondness for pastries. Grab some of Abigail's marmalade scones, maybe throw in a cinnamon roll to get her in the right frame of mind. When Peg's hungry, she's stubborn as hell. Actually," he grunted, "Peg is always hungry and stubborn. I should know, I used to be married to her." He scoffed and shook his head. "Bribing officials."

Although my tiny apartment in Portland had been no Taj Mahal, Viv's spare room was a drab and dreary testament to how my life had stalled.

I suspected the butter-colored walls were once white but had yellowed over time, imbued with nicotine from past residents. The aged synthetic Berber-style carpet was firm and unyielding. Its foam pad had been flattened under decades of foot traffic and carried a permanent whiff of the previous tenants' pets.

The faulty thermostat vacillated between scorching desert and frozen tundra, but the building super Herbert hadn't seemed much in a hurry to do anything about it.

By the time Darren arrived, it was in sweltering mode. I'd donned cutoff sweats and a tank top, removed my makeup, and pulled my hair into a messy bun. I'd have been mortified to be seen in that state, but the day's events had sapped me of any pretense, and the crying jag in my car had left me emotionally numb.

I held a flute of Moscato, my second pour. Darren gave an appraising look but didn't comment on my haggard appearance or the glass.

"I don't feel like going out after all. I thought maybe we could order in. I've started on the wine." I slumped onto the sofa.

"I see that." Darren shut the door. "Geez, it's hot in here." He shrugged off his jacket and walked to the thermostat. He tapped the plastic cover. "It's set to seventy-one but feels like a hundred and ten."

"It's broken. Or possessed. There's Moscato on the counter if you want it."

His grimace was my answer. He made no mention of my unsophisticated wine palate or that my apartment looked like that of a starving college student with mismatched thrift shop furniture. I was too buzzed to be embarrassed that I was a thirty-something woman living out a Macklemore song.

The sole exception was the sofa, a treasure among trash that cost her former boss a whopping four thousand dollars. An impractical silver velvet with tufted cushions, dramatic claw feet, and antique brass nail head trim, Viv said it was the best thing that came from their ill-fated tryst.

Darren joined me, our legs close enough to touch but not quite. "Are you okay?"

"Not really."

He watched me. "Don't you want to talk about it?"

"Not really." I sipped the sweet wine and stared at the wall behind his head. Its blankness was an appropriate metaphor for my emotional condition.

"This isn't only about seeing a dead body today, is it?"

"Nope." I took a larger swig.

"How well did you know him? Marcus, I mean."

"We used to date."

I was too depleted to play coy, too spent to be irritated at his thinly veiled fishing expedition.

"Was it serious?" He continued casting and reeling, oblivious to the fact he didn't have to try that hard to get the information. I was like trout in a catch-and-release pond.

I shrugged. "It was serious-*ish*. I was nineteen. He was eighteen." I took a sip. "Marcus was a nice guy, but he had a lot of issues. Unmet childhood needs, fear of abandonment, an inability to deal with emotions–his or anyone else's—it was more than the relationship could bear."

"So, you haven't seen him…lately?" Darren shifted, his jaw clenching. "Was something still going on between you two? Romantically?"

"No. He's married. Shoot. *Was* married. I guess you could call us friends, sort of. You know." I waved my glass, wine sloshing. "The way you're friends with people you used to know back in the day but now only interact with on social media. You see their posts, maybe click a like on occasion."

"When was the last time you heard from him?" Clench.

"He sent me a message a few days ago, but I didn't read it until this morning. He was worked up about something. Said he needed my help." I stretched my feet before curling them underneath my legs.

Darren stiffened. "What do you mean? Help with what?" Both his gaze and his tone darkened.

"He said he was in trouble. I got the impression he wanted to say more about it, but…"

"But what?"

"I don't know, Darren. Maybe he was being paranoid. Maybe he was in trouble. Like, trouble-trouble."

The smirk he wore wasn't attractive, and I added it to my growing list of strikes against him. "Trouble-trouble? What does that mean?"

"Like with bad guys."

"Darren choked out a harsh laugh, and I chalked another strike.

"It could be what he meant." I jutted my chin.

"Audrey, come on. The guy was messaging his beautiful ex-girlfriend. His biggest trouble was a jealous wife." He crossed his arms.

"What do you know about his wife?"

He paused. "I don't know specifics, Audrey. I just know women."

"Hmph." I yawned, annoyance giving way to wine-induced fatigue. "You know, I saw this man leaving the marina in a rage. It could be unrelated to Marcus, but the dude looked mad enough to kill someone."

"He was leaving the scene?"

"You sound like Holden."

His nostrils flared, and his jaw clenched. "Tell me about the man."

"He stole my parking spot and then had the nerve to glare at *me*. The next time I saw him was about thirty minutes or so later, and he was on a rampage. It's probably just a coincidence. The police want me to give a description of him anyway. If it's nothing, fine. If it's something, maybe it can help solve what happened to Marcus."

Darren stayed quiet for a moment before shifting both his position and his temperament. "How's your research going for your article? Find anything interesting?"

He reached his hand to massage my neck. It was a presumptive move that I hadn't invited, but his kneading fingers elicited a groan of pleasure, and my eyelids grew heavy.

"Gah. That feels good. I've had a headache all afternoon, and I don't think this sweet wine is helping."

"Audrey." His fingers tightened as he squeezed the back of my neck. "Did you find anything interesting in your research?"

"Um, I might have a lead."

He dropped his hand. "What kind of lead?"

"Well..." I yawned again. "I need to talk to Peg at the Chamber of Commerce. People have been strangely resistant and defensive about my questions regarding Chattertowne's buried history."

"Buried history?"

"I can't shake the feeling this town is hiding something." I let my lids drift shut. "Either I'm pushing up against bureaucrats who enjoy being difficult for no reason other than the inconvenience of everyone else, or it's a stonewalling technique designed to protect information they don't want to get out."

After several moments without a response, I opened one eye to look at Darren. His expression was enigmatic.

Finally, he said, "I'd like to help you solve this. Any detail you uncover, no matter how small, may be helpful. You'll tell me if you find out anything interesting." Before I could respond to his request, which sounded more like a command, he slapped his thigh. "Hey, you seem pretty worn out. I'm gonna take a raincheck. Lunch tomorrow?"

"Mmkay." My eyelids drifted shut again.

In my haze, I sensed the warmth of a fleece blanket draped over me. Despite already being overheated, I was too exhausted to protest.

Darren kissed my forehead. "Sleep well."

I nodded but didn't open my eyes, even when the door clicked shut.

Chapter Four

The next morning, I woke to the smell of coffee. I'd slept on the unforgiving sofa, to which the kink in my neck attested. Sometime during the night, the thermostat had switched back to arctic mode, and I was tightly cinched in the blanket Darren had draped over me. I stretched my arms over my head.

"Hey. Sorry, I tried not to wake you." Vivienne handed me one of the two mugs she was holding before sitting cross-legged on the sofa.

"I needed to get up anyway."

"I couldn't believe it when I got your text last night. Everyone at the club was talking about what happened to Marcus. Are you okay? Of course, you're not okay. Your ex-boyfriend was killed practically before your eyes!" With one hand, she held her mug near her chest. With the other, she twirled a strand of her short platinum hair like she'd done since she was a toddler.

"Okay is a relative term at this point. If I can stay in denial for a little longer, I should be able to make it through the day. I have a ton of work, and my deadline's approaching." I hesitated. "You wanna hear something strange?"

"Always." Viv sipped her coffee, her cat-like eyes and tawny brows peeking over the brim.

"Darren came over last night."

"That is strange."

"No, that's not the strange part."

"I wish I could be happy for you, considering you've had a crush on him for months, but you know how I feel about him." Viv scrunched her nose like she smelled something unpleasant.

"You don't even know him! Besides, I don't know if I'd call it a crush. I find him aggravatingly attractive, or maybe it's attractively aggravating. Either way, I haven't quite figured out what I think about him. He's both flirtatious and unbearably haughty."

"He's a walking red flag."

"Eh, I'd categorize him under yellow flag behavior with unknown motives."

"Trust me. I'm an expert on this. My file is regrettably thick and filled with guys like Darren."

"I'm quite aware of that, having helped you deal with the aftermath of those relationships."

"Your file isn't exactly thin either," she said.

I sighed. "Continuing. Yesterday, Darren showed up at the docks right as they were loading Marcus's body into the ambulance. He practically insisted on comforting me. It was awkward."

"Why was he there?"

"I asked him that. He said he'd heard about it on his police scanner."

"Like the one Dad listens to, so he always knows why the sirens are blaring around town?"

"I guess. So, then he gets rid of Holden—"

"Wait. You were with Holden Villalobos when Darren showed up?"

"Yeah, long story, not relevant to this."

Viv's gaze narrowed.

"It's not. Anyway, after he got rid of Holden, Darren insisted on taking me to dinner. When he got here, I was already on my second glass of wine and not up for going anywhere. He stayed for a bit to talk and then he left, but we're doing lunch today."

"After all this time of him sending mixed messages, he decides to make a move in the middle of you discovering your ex-boyfriend is dead. You're right, that is strange."

"That's not the strangest part either."

She arched her left brow.

"Last night, he got all weird when I told him I'm looking into Chatter-towne's past and running into resistance."

"Weird, how?"

"He demanded to know every detail I uncover for my story."

"Maybe he's curious."

"And…he mentioned Renee being jealous of me." I scanned her face for a reaction.

"So?"

"I didn't tell him what Marcus said in the message, and he hasn't lived here long enough to know our history."

Viv tilted her head. "Hmm. You're sure?"

"I'm positive. I didn't even read Marcus's message until yesterday, and I haven't mentioned him to Darren before last night because I had no reason to do so. When I called him on it, he said something about typical reactions of women, that he simply assumed she would be jealous of an ex."

"What's your gut telling you?"

"My circuits are fried right now. I'm not sure I could place a Starbucks order in my current state, much less accurately analyze the behavior of the most enigmatic man I've ever met."

"If something feels off to you, pay attention to it."

"On that note, I'm going to hop in the shower."

"What's your day like today?"

"I'm headed to City Hall to meet with a woman at the Chamber of Commerce; then I have lunch with Darren. How about you? Did you make that dentist appointment?"

"I forgot. I'll do it this afternoon."

"Viv," I scolded.

"Audrey, I'm not a child."

I sighed, choosing not to argue the point. "Are you working tonight?"

"I've got back-to-back performances."

"If I get done with all my stuff at a reasonable time, I'll head over there for the second show."

"I'm adding a few melancholy classics, like Dorothy Moore's 'Misty Blue.'

Seems appropriate for the somber mood in this town right now." Viv ran her fingers through her hair.

"Good choice." I stood and stretched.

"Hey, Audrey?"

"Yeah."

"Keep your head on a swivel today. If there really is a killer on the loose, and they know you've been getting messages from Marcus, you might be in danger too."

I hadn't considered the possibility, but Viv's warning sent a chill down my spine.

I entered City Hall holding a white pastry bag.

"Hi, I'm Audrey O'Connell with *The Coastal Current*. I'm looking for Peg."

An emaciated woman, whose nameplate identified her to be Joan, glanced up from her computer. She appeared to be in her fifties with dyed black hair cut in a severe style, which I found unflattering against her sharp angular features. She gave me a wide-eyed and pitying look. "Peg's on the third floor. Three twenty."

"Thank you."

"The pastries from Abigail's were a good move," Joan called after me.

Just as the elevator doors were closing, a large hand reached in to stop them. They reopened and Holden stepped inside.

"Hey!" His face lit with a broad smile at the sight of me. "Fancy running into you again so soon."

He gave me a brief hug. His scent was intoxicating, an unusual combination of pheromones and nutmeg.

"I'm here to talk to Peg about the Kupit Festival."

He grimaced. "I hope you brought her something sweet."

I raised the paper bag to indicate my offering. "You're the third person today who's warned me not to come empty-handed."

Holden smiled. "Peg knows this town inside and out. She's an invaluable asset. Thus, we've all learned to work around...ohhh...let's call it her complicated personality."

"Maybe I should tie a rope to my ankle before heading into her office. That way you can drag out my lifeless body after she eviscerates me." I winced. "That was in poor taste. Sorry."

"You're fine. Don't worry; she doesn't have quite *that* much power. Lead with the...what exactly did you bring?" He lifted his chin to peek into the bag.

"Marmalade scones from Abigail's." I held it open for his perusal.

"Perfect. Lead with the scones."

The elevator opened to the third floor, and I reluctantly stepped into the hallway. "This is me."

The elevator door began to shut, but Holden blocked it with his massive shoulder. His intense gaze zapped through me. The elevator buzzed a warning.

"Say a little prayer for me."

"You've got this. Come by my office when you're done. Two-oh-four." He smiled again and stepped back inside.

"I will."

The doors closed. It was then I realized he'd ridden with me to the third floor even though his office was on the second.

In room 320, I found a woman behind a substantial seventies-era oak desk scowling at a piece of paper. Short reddish-brown permed curly hair matching the ruddy color of the walls framed her pale, round, freckled face.

I tapped the doorframe, which was the same honey-colored oak as her desk. The office didn't appear to have been updated for at least three decades. The woman's eyes, so tiny their color was indeterminable, squinted at me from behind coke-bottle-thick glasses.

"I'm looking for Peg?"

"What do you want?" Her smoker's voice had the timbre of a longshore-man.

"I'm Audrey O'Connell. I work for *The Coastal Current,* and I'm doing a promotional series leading up to Kupit."

"O'Connell. James and Claudine's kid?"

"Yes. Mr. Anderson...you know, your ex...."

Peg's eyes narrowed further.

"He, uh, he said you were the best resource—"

"What's in the bag?" Peg interrupted with a growl.

"Oh!" I stepped forward. "It's marmalade scones from Abigail's. Would you like one?" I held the bag tenuously in front of her.

Peg snatched it from my fingertips and peered inside. Her expression was like a skeptical cat who'd been proffered irresistible treats. She reached in and extracted a scone, consuming the pastry in two large bites, followed by several minutes of quiet chewing and low humming. She pulled out the other scone and put it to her lips. "What do you want from me?" She took another large bite. Marmalade oozed from the corner of her mouth.

"Like I mentioned, I'm working on the Kupit Festival series. I emailed several people in hopes of getting some real insight for this year's festival, but I didn't really get far with them. I was told you've really got your thumb on the pulse of—"

Peg waved her hand in dismissal. Her cheeks bulged with scone, and her lips were covered in crumbs and sticky orange jam. Rustling in her top desk drawer, she removed a multi-sheet packet stapled together and thrust it at me. The packet contained several pages of names, phone numbers, and emails, along with scheduled activities. It also now had marmalade smudges in the corner.

"Thank you. I did print a copy of this from the Chamber website, but I'm looking for something a little different. I was curious who you feel is the best resource for digging into early town history. I was hoping to get into greater detail, maybe resurrect some stories lost to time. I don't want to regurgitate the same spiel as every other year."

Peg eyed me warily and continued chewing for a moment. "You're not trying to dig up dirt, are you?"

"What do you mean?"

"I think you know exactly what I mean. You've been gone a while, working for that big city paper. I'm sure they paid really well for any scandals you uncovered. That's not how we do things around here. We protect our own."

"I grew up here. I am one of your own."

"Are you?" Peg's puckered mouth tightened further. "I know your parents, Audrey. Hell, I know everyone in this town. I love this town. I was born here. My parents were born here. My grandparents were born here, and their parents before them. There's nothing about this town I don't know, and whatever I don't know, I don't wanna know, and I don't want anybody else to know either. Got it?"

Her eyes glinted with warning. On the wall behind her head hung a framed lithograph of Lucy pulling the football out from under Charlie Brown, which I suspected might be her life philosophy in comic form.

"I understand, but if there are remarkable stories in the archives, I'd like to bring them to light. I swear, I'm not looking for scandal. I believe there's more to Chattertowne than the standard stories that get dragged out every year. My goal is for people to be more excited to come to the Kupit Festival because of my articles. That benefits everyone, especially the Chamber of Commerce."

Peg's eyes constricted until they appeared nearly closed. "You'll want to talk to Mildred Driscoll at the library. She works in the city records and archives department."

"Got it. Thank you for all your help." My tentative smile wasn't reciprocated.

"Remember, Audrey." Her voice held an unmistakable tone of warning. "This festival's a celebration of town history. It's about preserving tradition, not destroying it."

I nodded.

"I mean it." She pointed her finger at me for emphasis and then peeked into the bag once more. "No cinnamon rolls?"

I located room 204 by following Holden's booming voice. The door was already cracked, so I opened it just enough to poke my head into his office. He was on the phone but smiled and waved me in with his free hand.

"Art, you and I both know how this thing needs to play out." His tone was firm but not unkind. "I'll give a little. You've got to give a little also." He covered the phone and mouthed, "One more sec."

I smiled and nodded as I took a seat.

Unlike Peg's office, Holden's had been updated. His walls were a sophisticated dark gray, and his shelves were black. On his mid-century walnut desk, a large purple crystal geode acted as a paper weight. An autographed football was perched on the top shelf, with several smaller picture frames propped on the one below. The others were cluttered with motivational books, binders, and a few novels. His Washington State University diploma hung next to the doorway above a rosewood Omega Psi Phi Fraternity keepsake box. Below that were four empty mounting clips. Conspicuously absent were any photos of his fiancée Emily.

"That's more like it." Holden nodded, even though the man on the other end couldn't see him. "I knew we could find a way to make this work for both of us. Shoot me an email with the revised proposal, and I'll get it approved at the next council meeting." He waited for a response and winked at me.

Normally I detested winkers, but for some reason, Holden proved to be an exception.

"You got it, Art. Talk to you soon."

He turned his attention to me after hanging up the phone. His appraising smile was not without effect.

"I see you survived your encounter with Peg."

His smile grew wider, revealing straight white teeth. He leaned back with hands clasped behind his head in repose.

"Barely. She's not one to trifle with. I think...I think she threatened me." A nervous laugh escaped my throat.

He leaned forward, his smile disappearing. "Threatened you? What do you mean? What did she say?"

"Nothing specific. It was her tone more than anything. She told me to leave certain things in the past, and the implication was if I didn't, well...."

"Things? What things?"

"That's what I don't know. It's not like she said or else. I don't know how to explain it. I'm probably being dramatic, making a fuss about nothing."

"Hmmm. Well, I guess the only thing to do is leave it alone."

"I guess…" My voice trailed off, along with my eye contact.

Holden chuckled. "That wasn't convincing."

"Hey, I'm not gonna go looking for trouble, but if something comes up while I'm researching, I'm not gonna ignore it either. Frankly, her attitude makes me more curious about what secrets Chattertowne is hiding in its archives than before I spoke with her."

Holden sighed and shook his head. "Be careful, okay? We still don't know what happened to Marcus, and I'd hate for something to come back to bite you in the rear." As soon as the words left his mouth, an awkward electricity permeated the room. "So-to-speak."

I stared into his deep brown eyes. "Nope. Wouldn't want that." I reluctantly broke eye contact. "Well, I won't keep you, and I've got somewhere I need to be."

I turned to leave but stopped when I noticed an open door in the corner of his office.

"You have your own bathroom?"

He smiled sheepishly. "Perks of the job."

"That explains why you showed up at the docks with wet hair. You showered." Immediately my cheeks felt warm with embarrassment.

"Your face is bright pink. You're not picturing me in the shower, are you?"

"Oh, look at the time! See ya, Holden!"

His chuckle echoed behind me as I scurried out of his office.

Chapter Five

I shifted my phone from one ear to the other while Mr. Barnette—the owner of a local windchime business and one of the *Current's* advertisers—droned on about social media marketing techniques he'd learned during some online seminar. I found it difficult to concentrate on what he was saying. Thoughts of Marcus and what had happened to him swirled with my confusion over Peg's veiled threats, Holden's flirtation, and Darren's sudden interest.

I sighed, which caused Mr. Barnette to pause.

"Everything okay, dear?"

"Oh, yes, sorry. You were saying you want the article to mention the driftwood you use is hand-picked from the beaches at Ocean Shores and that all your posts contain the hashtag Ocean Shores driftwood."

He launched again into a long-winded explanation, but I was still only half-listening.

I opened my Facebook app and re-read Marcus's message, looking for any clues about what he'd been trying to tell me. I heaved another deep sigh in frustration.

"...so, do you?"

I snapped back to attention. "Sure, okay."

I had no idea what I'd just agreed to.

"Great. Come by later this week, and you can pick out whichever windchime suits you best. I have a feeling you're gonna like the one I fashioned to look like a mama owl with three baby owls. You kind of have to squint and look at it sideways to see it's an owl, but you'll get the general effect."

Darren poked his head into my office. "Ready for lunch?"

I checked the clock on my computer. It was already three minutes past noon. I covered the receiver.

"Sorry, I lost track of time," I whispered.

"I'll wait for you in the lobby."

I ended the call with Mr. Barnette on a promise to visit his workshop to pick out a windchime. I didn't have the heart to tell him I lived in an apartment without a balcony or patio.

Standing and stretching my arms above my head, I smoothed my maroon-and-navy-plaid flannel shirt and ran my fingers through my long dishwater-blond ponytail.

A critical glance in the full-length mirror hanging on the back of my office door revealed the stress of the previous twenty-four hours had taken a toll. My hazel eyes were rimmed with smudged mascara and dark circles. My outfit wasn't the most flattering to my five-foot-six-inch frame, which my mother described as "large bone structure." I pulled my ponytail forward and contemplated taking my natural color lighter or darker.

Maybe I'd go red and really spice up my life.

I shook my head and chuckled, knowing I wouldn't.

One unfortunate spur-of-the-moment department store makeover with a heavy-handed cosmetics rep had convinced me neutrals were my friend. My biggest fashion risk to date was wearing glittery mauve toenail polish encased in closed-toed flats with a coordinating backless dress under a sweater to my cousin's Bat Mitzvah.

Darren was perched on the edge of a chair in the lobby; his face contorted into a concentrated scowl as he glared at his phone.

Tasha raised an eyebrow and gave me a wicked smirk. I had a vague recollection of making a declaration to her about my infatuation with him at her party the previous weekend.

Darren dropped his phone into his briefcase and jumped to his feet. He slid on his overcoat and grabbed the black leather case by its braided handles. "Ready?"

"Yep."

He ushered me toward the elevator with his hand firmly on my lower back. "I thought we'd walk to Martini's. I have a hankering for their deep-fried artichoke hearts."

"Sounds good."

The air was mild for a late-winter day in the Pacific Northwest. Nevertheless, I shivered and rubbed my arms. If Darren noticed, he didn't acknowledge it or offer his coat.

Once inside Martini's Restaurant, we were escorted to a table near the back. The waiter placed a basket of bread and a bowl of olive oil and balsamic vinegar on the table. He attempted to hand me the menu, but I waved him off.

"I already know what I want. I'll have the chicken strips and the Riesling." I put on a self-deprecating smile. "I know. I've got the palate of a four-year-old mixed with a nineteen-year-old sorority girl." I snorted and covered my mouth.

Leaning back, Darren perused the list, ignoring both my snort and my attempt at a joke. "How's the Chilean Pinot, and does it pair well with the sea bass?" He had the air of someone who knew the difference between acceptable Pinot and unacceptable Pinot.

"That's one of my favorite pairings, sir."

"All right, I'll try that and an order of tempura artichoke hearts to start. So, Audrey." Darren dismissed the server by turning his attention back to me. "How are you feeling after the events of yesterday?"

"I'm still trying to process it. I think I may be in a bit of shock."

"Totally understandable." He tilted his head and blinked three times. "I wanted to revisit our conversation about the Kupit series." He picked up a piece of bread and raised it to his lips but paused before taking a bite. "As I said, I'd like to hear what you're planning, maybe offer some help."

"I appreciate the offer, but I'm sure you've got better things to do than discuss social hermits and their yearly spring pilgrimage into town to ride the Ferris wheel and consume their weight in cotton candy and deep-fried foods." I ripped off a small piece of the bread. "Did you know *Podunk* is an Algonquian word? I discovered that while researching local tribal history. Too bad it isn't Salish. It would've been a more apropos name for the festival."

Darren leaned in with his forehead creased. "Are you looking into Chattertowne's Native American history?"

I dredged my bread through the oil and vinegar. "Of course."

"Why?"

"Because it's important." I popped the bread in my mouth.

"What have you found so far? What else are you digging into?"

"I don't see the point of retelling the same stories and doing the same type of articles that have been done every other year."

His gaze flickered, and his brows curled toward each other.

"Nothing interesting ever happens in Chattertowne, anyway," I said. "I've been covering events and lifestyles for a few months now, and the most exciting story I've submitted was a dispute among council members as to whether they should stick with incandescent light strands for the Main Street Christmas tree or switch to LED. I'd wager most residents have little knowledge of our actual history. Not the flag-waving Americana cutesy small-town feel-good history, but the real story. The full story."

Darren drew back with his eyes wide like he'd caught a glimpse into the past and didn't like what he saw. "You'll tell me if you find anything... interesting." His statement landed less like a request and more like a command.

I fought the grimace forming on my upper lip. I was notorious for having a terrible poker face and didn't want my sour expression to start an argument in the middle of the restaurant. The arrival of the waiter with our wine glasses and appetizer was a much-needed tension-breaker.

"How about we change the subject," I said. "Tell me something about yourself. We've worked together for four months, and I think this is the longest conversation we've had. I don't really know anything about you."

Darren sighed, rocked his head from side to side, and rolled his shoulders back.

"I guess you could say I had the typical Eastside childhood. Private clubs, private schools, baseball scholarship to MIT."

"Wow. MIT. That's impressive."

"Is it?" He took a sip of wine.

"Yeah. It is. So, what does one study to become a financial reporter?" I tossed an artichoke heart in my mouth. It was crisp and buttery on the outside, warm and soft on the inside. "Ooh, good choice on the artichoke hearts." I started to lick my fingers but stopped when I caught a glimpse of his disdain.

"They're best when dredged through the aioli," he said after a brief hesitation. "With the appetizer fork."

He nodded toward the tiny three-pronged forks in the center of the table. I made a show of picking up a fork and stabbing another artichoke heart. Unfortunately, this one was blazing hot. I fanned my open mouth with my napkin and contemplated spitting it out. Darren's horrified expression put an end to that idea.

"I got a dual degree in Economics and Computer Science," he began, not acknowledging the scene I's just made. "I had no intention of becoming a journalist, financial or otherwise."

"Do you..." I swallowed the rest of my searing bite. "Do you have any brothers or sisters? Does your family live nearby?"

"I'm an only child. My dad's a stockbroker. I lost my mom to breast cancer a couple years ago."

"Oh, Darren, I'm so sorry. I wouldn't have brought it up if I'd known. What was her name?"

"Maddie." He spoke with a hushed reverence. "It was really tough for several years once she got sick. After she died, I was pretty burned out at my, uh, corporate job. That's when I decided to come to Chattertowne. I moved here a couple months before you came to work at the *Current*, so about six months ago now. I was hoping to start over, find myself, put some things right in my life."

"That's funny. I left this place to find myself."

"What do you mean?"

The server arrived, and I waited for him to place our entrees on the table

41

before answering. "Thank you."

Darren gave a nod of approval at the sight of his fish. "You were saying?"

"I moved to Portland to work at *The Oregonian* in hopes of becoming a legitimate journalist."

"What brought you back here?"

"My parents still live here, and my sister, Vivienne. She's twenty-seven and has a history of questionable choices when it comes to men. Her most recent incident involved getting caught making out in the office stairwell with her boss by a coworker who decided some minor extortion was preferable to reporting the relationship to HR."

"Yikes."

"Yeah. Long story short, they all got fired, and Viv could no longer afford her apartment on what she makes at her back-up gig as a singing waitress at Nautilus. I'm living in her spare bedroom while we both figure out our next steps."

Darren raised his left eyebrow. "So, what, you just quit your job, packed your apartment, and moved home to babysit your grown sister?"

"It'd be easy to blame Viv, but the truth is I was barely treading water in Portland, slogging my way through the ranks of the paper, but my salary wasn't enough to keep up with the cost-of-living increases. When my mom called to say Viv was up a creek without a paddle, I only had three weeks left on my lease, so I gave notice at my job and apartment that day."

I decided not to mention how much my decision was also influenced by lingering guilt from when I'd failed to look after Viv, and it had nearly cost her life.

"*The Oregonian* to *The Current*. That's quite a demotion."

He flaked his fish with his fork, apparently oblivious to how his insensitive statement had landed and the hypocrisy of it as well. I swallowed my annoyance for the sake of a peaceful lunch.

I cleared my throat. "Of course, when I got a degree in journalism, I imagined rocking the world with political exposés, not fluff pieces on driftwood sculptures in the park, the McCormick's Alaskan cruise, or who could spit a cherry seed the furthest. Farthest? Anyway." I waved my fork in circles. "I'm grateful for the opportunity, but I sure hope it's more a stepping stone than a brick wall. What about you? From what you've told me, you're seriously overqualified for this job."

"I don't see myself staying for long." His mien darkened, and he aggressively swigged his wine. He pulled his napkin from his lap and dabbed his face. "Let's make a toast." He lifted his wineglass and thrust it toward me. "To special new friends, Chattertowne, and to getting exactly what we want."

I held up my glass, "And to Marcus, may he rest in peace."

Darren's lips twitched. "To Marcus."

Chapter Six

The Chattertowne library was situated in the historic district. Once shaded by a six-hundred-year-old Douglas fir, the tree had fallen in a winter windstorm about ten years earlier. Moss carpeted the north-facing portion of what remained of the trunk, and the center rings had rotted away. Over the years, many couples had etched their initials encircled in hearts.

The building itself had a Spanish tile roof and rough sand-colored stucco sides, which were completely inconsistent with the neighborhood's traditional architecture. A wall of six-foot-tall opaquely tinted windows faced the sidewalk. The two buildings connected to form a courtyard area complete with a marble fountain, currently dormant for the winter, and a large maple flanked on all sides by holly bushes. A flagless pole stood nearly dead center, and a weathered twenty-foot banner drooped from beneath the eaves advertising the summer farmer's market every Tuesday afternoon from May through September.

As sleet plopped onto my windshield, summer seemed interminably far away.

A plaque hung over the entrance with Roman numerals MCMI, marking the building's dedication in 1901. The library had received a historical grant, so the interior of the building had recently been remodeled with designer colors, modern paintings and sculptures, and a row of state-of-the-art computers lining the far wall.

Cranky old Mrs. Rothschild, the librarian, was nowhere to be found, possibly tossed out along with outdated PCs and dusty encyclopedia sets.

In her place behind the counter was a petite girl with vacant doe-eyes and a lavender pageboy haircut, young enough to have never known a world without Google.

"Hi, can I…help you?" she asked hesitantly.

"I'm looking for any information you have on the early days of the town. I'm writing a Kupit Festival story for *The Current*."

"The current what?" The girl bit her lower lip.

"*The Coastal Current*, the newspaper. I was told the city archives are kept here."

The girl furrowed her perfectly arched painted brows in thought and typed something into her computer. After a few moments of staring at the screen, she glanced around the room, bewildered.

"Is something wrong?"

"Well, I'm not quite sure how to help you, and my supervisor isn't in today. Can you come back tomorrow?"

"That doesn't work for me."

"Oh. Well, maybe you could try over there." She anemically indicated a bay of books underneath a sign reading "Non-fiction, History."

"I'll give it a try, thanks."

Mrs. Rothschild may have been lacking in personality, but she'd known the library like the back of her hand. Sometimes new wasn't always improved.

The history section contained a diverse range of books, from a five-hundred-page tome on the Babylonian Empire to a recap of twentieth-century presidents and their pets. There were general guides on the area, but not what I was looking for. I returned to the desk.

The girl greeted me as if for the first time. "Hi, can I help you?"

"I was told Mildred Driscoll might be able to assist me in my research. Can you tell me where she is?"

She bit her bottom lip again. "What are you researching?"

"Chattertowne. Kupit Festival. Where's Mildred's office?"

"Oh, Mildred's downstairs. Did you want me to go get her?"

"Nope, that's okay. I'll go to her. How do I find her downstairs?"

45

"You go down…the stairs." She slowed her words and then shook her head.

At the bottom of the stairs was a long hallway. Toward the end, a sign reading *Records* hung above an open door. Despite the building's refresh, it smelled dank and dusty. I repressed a sneeze.

A petite elderly woman sat at a desk behind the counter. Her white hair was set in an old-fashioned style typically achieved by sleeping in rollers, and her glasses hung from a silver chain around her neck. She wore a sunny yellow cardigan and appeared to be at least eighty.

"Mildred?"

Her face lit at the sight of me, and she sprung to her feet. "Welcome! How can I help you?" After hearing a brief explanation of my quest, she clapped her hands. "Why, that's marvelous!"

"Do you only have records here, or do you also have historical artifacts?"

"We have several items, even from before the early days of the Chatterton family settlement."

"How long ago was that?"

"Mid-eighteen-hundreds. Jonathan Chatterton signed the declaration for the official founding in eighteen-sixty-one. There are photos in the museum as well, dating back to Chattertowne's pioneer era."

"We have a museum?"

"Well, not an official museum, exactly. That's just what I like to call it. We have a few things on display down the hall for field trips and such. For a while, they were housed in the pioneer village behind the shopping center on the east side of town."

"I remember that! I visited there in the fourth grade. Why were they moved?"

"The village required volunteers and depended upon donations. Eventually, the project couldn't be sustained. The buildings were abandoned, and the artifacts were relocated to the basement in City Hall. When the library re-opened after the remodel, it made more sense for them to be here near the records department for me to oversee. Sadly, hardly anyone ever comes here." Mildred scurried around the desk. "Follow me."

She led me down the dimly lit hall.

"O'Connell. Are your parents James and Claudine, formerly Claudine Bristow?"

"Yes, do you know them?"

"Not directly. I know of them. I mean, it is Chattertowne, after all." She smiled and pulled a large keyring out of her pocket, and unlocked the door, which had been labeled *Archives*. "There are still a few things at the old location in a storage closet, but the best stuff is here. Please be careful when examining the older artifacts. The cases are locked, so holler at me if you need help opening them for a closer look."

"Thank you so much."

She shut the door behind her.

The room held wall-to-wall antiquities and historical trinkets. It smelled like old fur coats and the musty leather of a saddle stored for decades in the corner of a damp barn. There didn't appear to be any rhyme or reason to the way items had been organized and displayed.

Framed photos hung on the walls. Most were sepia or black and white, but some were faded Kodachrome. One caught my eye, and I leaned to get a closer view. Five men stood in front of City Hall wearing polyester leisure suits in hues ranging from baby blue to mint. The label read "Mayor King and the City Council 1976." Lining the wall were several similar photos featuring different styles and eras, all on the front lawn of City Hall.

Two large cabinets were filled with books, while several waist-high glass display cases contained relics labeled with the donor family's name.

Hanging from the wall above the cabinets were wooden snowshoes laced with an animal rawhide, a stretch board used for drying lynx and coyote, and a large bear trap, all apparently donated by the Robinson family.

The first case had a *Saturday Evening Post* magazine from 1913 donated by the Holmquist family, a gentleman's cane, spectacles, and a derby hat from 1875 donated by the Kohler family, straight edge shaving tools, and a fiddle with home-made bow constructed from a twig.

The next case contained a small camera collection with a couple Brownies and a larger accordion-style donated by the Harvey family, along with several metal toy cars, aged paper money, two corn husk dolls, and a tin of marbles.

On the floor between the two cases was a large bell from the old Lutheran church, which had sat vacant for years after a new worship hall was constructed on the other side of town. Recently, the church had been converted into a gallery run by my former middle school art teacher and his husband, who apparently had no need for a four-foot-tall brass bell.

In the far cabinet were sail-making tools, a froe for splitting cedar shakes, a tenon cutter for building log furniture, handmade broad axes forged in the late-1800s, Salish arrowheads, baby moccasins, and a beaded woman's saddle constructed of elk antlers, rawhide, and fringed buckskin.

A large knife had been shoved to the right side of the case on the bottom shelf. The plaque read, "Hunting knife of Jonathan Chatterton donated 1995 by Peter Chatterton." I jotted Peter's name in my notebook. Who better to interview than a member of the founding family? I hoped he was still alive and could offer some insight.

Moving on to the bookcase, I ran my finger across the spines. Wedged between an old copy of *Huckleberry Finn* and an outdated atlas was a thin booklet of less than seventy-five pages. Easing it off the shelf, I turned it over in my hands. The paper cover had yellowed, and the print had faded with age. It was partially detached, there was a russet stain in the lower left corner, and the lower right edge was curled. The book was titled *The Unvarnished History of Chattertowne, Part One.*

Chapter Seven

After getting Mildred's consent, I tucked the small book into my satchel and headed back to the *Current* office.

I'd settled into my chair, ready to take notes on the book, when a text message from Holden came through.

Hey.

Hey. How are you?

I lifted the book out of my satchel and set it on my lap. His response came within a minute.

I was gonna ask you the same thing.

Trying to keep myself distracted with work. Any word?

I set my phone down and made a cursory flip-through of the book. It was a chronological history of the town, starting with Jonathan Chatterton's arrival. On the back page was a grainy black-and-white photo of the author, George Hart, who appeared to be in his late twenties or early thirties. Ages were difficult to decipher in older pictures, where forty-year-olds looked like today's septuagenarians. According to the bio, George had been a lifelong resident of Chattertowne.

My phone buzzed.

Most likely going to be classified a homicide.

Oh, Holden. I can't believe this.

Yeah. Please be careful. If that guy you ran into had anything to do with this...

I don't think he'd recognize me if he ran into me on the street again.

All the same.

Marcus and Renee were having problems. Maybe she had something to do with his death.

After a long pause, my phone finally buzzed with Holden's response.

How do you know they were having problems?

He sent me a message a few days ago but I didn't open it until yesterday. He said she'd kill him if she knew he'd reached out to me. You know she hates me, right?

Why didn't you mention this yesterday?

I didn't really know what to make of it. I was more focused on the fact he said he might be in trouble, and the angry parking spot thief seemed a more likely perp, but I watch a lot of crime shows. The spouse is usually the prime suspect.

I'll pass it along. Screenshot your message and text it to me. After a minute, he sent a second text. **Unless it's too personal.**

It wasn't personal.

It might be helpful information for the investigation.

Just as I was about to dig into my research, another message came through.

BTW, I hope I didn't cause problems with your boyfriend.

He's not my boyfriend. I don't know what he is yet.

I'm surprised he hasn't come up in our conversations.

Neither does your relationship with Emily.

Touché. Can we meet tonight after work? To talk.

I promised Viv I'd watch her sing at Nautilus tonight.

I could meet you there.

I'm trying to get there in time for her 8pm set.

I waited for a response, but after a few moments of silence, I set down my phone and grabbed a pen. My conversation with Holden had caused a rush of warmth to creep into my cheeks, which I slapped. *Focus, Audrey.*

I opened the book to page one.

Jonathan Chatterton was born in Newburyport, Massachusetts, in 1831. He arrived in the Washington Territory in 1858 along with his young wife Madeleine, a native of Herefordshire, England.

Jonathan believed the location of present-day Chattertowne, a pristine inland valley nestled alongside a crystal-clear river at the foothills of a lone peak, was the perfect area to build his logging empire. He'd descended from a multi-generational legacy of logging and shipbuilding along the Merrimack River and so possessed the skills and know-how to tame the land and make his mark.

I stopped reading and scowled. I was already annoyed with the book and what felt like its glorification of one white dude while completely ignoring the story of the Coast Salish, the Indigenous People who'd resided in the valley at the time of his arrival.

My ninth grade Washington State history teacher had only allotted a measly three weeks to teach us about the Coast Salish who have called this area home since long before the explorers/invaders and colonizers arrived, but it was enough for me to understand the importance of learning their history and honoring them by highlighting their story and culture whenever discussing our region and I'd read every book about the topic I could find.

I'd learned that the tribes of the Pacific Northwest had a robust economy with an extensive and competitive system of exchanging goods until it got mucked up by so-called pioneers who believed they had a better way of operating. That way was only better for the pioneers.

About three years prior to Jonathan showing up, Chief *Si'ahl* (Seattle), Territorial Governor Isaac Stevens, and representatives from the Duwamish, Suquamish, Snoqualmie, Snohomish, Lummi, Skagit, and Swinomish Nations—along with other local tribes—had met at Mukilteo to sign the Point Elliott Treaty establishing reservations and rights. No surprise, the government didn't hold up their end of the treaty. That paved the way for opportunists like Jonathan Chatterton to claim large swaths of land and then name it after themselves.

This book was turning out to be little more than Chattertowne propaganda, but I kept reading and jotting notes in hopes the unvarnished history its title promised would yield something worth discussing in my articles.

Within a few short years of stepping foot in the valley, Jonathan's vision had become a reality. The logging industry grew, particularly in the business of shingles, as did his wealth and stature in the area. Chattertowne officially came into existence in 1861. His wife Madeleine died in childbirth in 1862, leaving Jonathan with a newborn son, Michael. The midwife who'd attended her, a Flathead woman (Bitterroot-Salish) called Nettie, stayed on to care for the child after Madeleine's death.

*In 1924 Councilman Arthur Robinson led a movement to rename Chattertowne to **Swobilak**.*

"Wait. Why does it skip from his wife dying to the kerfuffle about the town's name over fifty years later? That's a lot of history to yada-yada."

I flipped back and forth. I'd been reading page thirty. The next page skipped to thirty-five.

"There are pages missing!" I yelled and then cowered when I remembered I was surrounded by coworkers and thin walls. I repeated in an excited whisper, "There are pages missing!"

The binding was still intact, but the pages were gone. Some of the others were loose, but the missing ones had been torn from the book, as evidenced by the ragged remnants of where they'd once been. I flipped backward a page and continued reading in hopes of getting context for what came before and after the missing information might reveal what should have been there.

*Mr. Robinson, a descendent of one of Chattertowne's original settler families, announced at a Council meeting he'd been informed by a Salish elder Chattertowne was originally called **Swobilak**. He asserted the woman had told him—on her death bed—**Swobilak** was a previously undocumented sub-tribe of Salish. The elder had succumbed to smallpox one year prior, so there was no way to verify the story. Robinson demanded the town be renamed in her honor and in honor of the original inhabitants. Robinson also claimed the woman had attended* *the signing of the Point Elliot Treaty.*

Truth be told, Arthur Robinson's underlying motivation for the name change was not historical accuracy but instead was a blow across the bow of his nemesis, Mayor Frank Chatterton. Political rivals who'd turned city council meetings into chaos with their bickering, Arthur begrudged the relegation of his own family's pioneering legacy to the back pages of town history, while Frank believed governing the town was his birthright as a Chatterton.

*A linguistics professor from the University of Washington was able to clarify one thing: the word wasn't **Swobilak**, as Robinson had clumsily attempted to pronounce it, but x̌ʷ**ubiləx**ʷ. It also didn't signify an unknown tribe. It was, in fact, a Lushootseed word meaning be quiet.*

My bitter laughter echoed off the thin walls.

How was I supposed to draft an accurate article about Chattertowne's history which wasn't going to upset the entire town? All I had to work with was a narcissistic city founder, displaced and ignored First Nations People, petty ego-filled arguments, and a failed crusade to rename the town the Lushootseed word for "shut up."

I leaned back and inhaled deeply, followed by an exhale I hoped would expel the stress which had overcome me.

This assignment was proving to be more complicated than I'd anticipated. What I'd thought would be a fun retrospective piece was now peppered with landmines for potential backlash.

I took another deep breath.

Regardless of what people claimed, they didn't really want their media to provide truth unless it fit with their worldview and preferred narrative.

My next cleansing breath was interrupted by a text from Holden.

See you then.

Chapter Eight

The sky was moonless, and the stars were hidden behind the fog as I approached Nautilus. The club was situated between two antique stores, already closed for the evening. A chilly wind blew from the river, so I pulled my jacket tight against my body. The bouncer, Sam, stood watch outside the entrance. He greeted me with a smile and a brief hug before he stamped an anchor on my hand with glowing ink and waved me inside.

The interior of the club was dim as well, lit by what appeared to be original Edison lightbulbs eking out their final remnants of illumination.

In its previous life, Nautilus had been a grungy fisherman's hangout, a place where men could do…well, whatever men used to do before having to slog home to the responsibilities of a wife and kids after a day (or longer) trolling the river or forging the Sound. When they weren't in the choppy seas off the coast of Alaska, many of Nautilus's former clientele commuted an hour each way to Ballard, home of the larger fishing vessels. My father claimed he encountered three of the guys from *Deadliest Catch* shortly before the bar changed ownership a couple years ago, but I'd yet to verify his story.

I'd always imagined crusty, white-bearded old salts in Ernest Hemingway-style cable-knit sweaters downing one foaming pint of ale after another while regaling the crowd with tall tales of sirens and sea monsters. More likely, it was the hiding place of guys in rubber overalls slimed with fish guts hoping to avoid dinner with their in-laws or their daughter's brutal nightly performance of "Fur Elise" on the piano.

Gentrification and new management had brought with it a much different vibe, jazzy and sophisticated with a touch of hipster. Padded orange velvet booths replaced worn barstools. In the back hall leading to the restrooms hung the last remaining vestige of a bygone era, a pay phone once used by husbands making excuses to their wives for why they'd be late for dinner.

"Hey!" I smiled as I approached the table.

Viv wore a burgundy satin dress and a long strand of pearls. Her short blond hair was accented by a twenties-era flapper-style rhinestone band strapped across her forehead. Our friend Amy and her husband Isaac were at the table with Viv.

"How'd the first set go?" I squeezed into the booth.

Amy responded on Viv's behalf. "She slayed it, as always."

Vivienne appeared pleased but embarrassed by the compliment. "I feel it went well."

Amy and Isaac had been in the middle of regaling Viv with stories of their recent honeymoon, an amazing trip to Santorini replete with food, architecture, and stunning sunsets. Eventually, however, the conversation turned to Marcus's death. I gave an update based on the latest information I'd received from Holden.

"Well, look who's here," Vivienne crowed. "Speak of the handsome devil himself. His ears must be burning!"

I peered into the inky room, but the crowd obstructed my view. "Who?"

"Mr. Dark and Sexy himself, and he looks to be alone. Left the Mrs. home tonight, hmm? Someone's on the prowl."

"She's not the Mrs.. They're still just engaged."

Vivienne assessed me with the laser focus of a sister's intuition. "Somebody's feeling defensive. What's that about?"

The dim lighting mercifully shrouded my flaming face as Holden approached.

"Evening." His teeth gleamed, and the curls on his head were damp and glistening. He wore medium-washed jeans and a quarter-zip burgundy sweater with a black t-shirt. In his left hand, he held an old-fashioned glass half-filled with an amber liquid on the rocks.

"Well, hello there, Holden. How are you this fine night? Out keeping an eye on the city? Ladies and gentlemen, I give you Chattertowne's own Bruce Wayne. Or should I call you the Dark Knight?"

I kicked Viv under the table.

"I'm good, Viv. Hey, guys." He nodded at Isaac and Amy. "Audrey, can I talk to you?"

Easing my way out of the booth, I avoided looking at my sister, who I was certain wore an expression of judgmental curiosity. I followed Holden to an unlit corner away from the crowd.

"Everything okay?"

"Yeah, I just didn't want an audience for this conversation."

He pulled out a chair for me, and I tried to play it cool, used to that sort of chivalry.

"What's going on?"

He sat across from me and took a deep breath. I held mine.

"The coroner completed her initial report. Blunt force trauma to the head prior to Marcus falling in."

"What does that mean?"

"It means he didn't purposely go for a swim."

"Well, it is February, and the water smells like the drainage runoff of a sardine cannery, so I'm not tremendously surprised by that revelation. Blunt force trauma isn't always inflicted by another person, though, right?"

"You're right, but I read over the initial police report. There wasn't anything found in the vicinity with blood on it which could've been a contact point. No stationary objects near where they think he went into the water. Whatever his head encountered must've either gone in with him or been removed from the scene. There was, however, blood spatter found on the dock in the covered area of the marina."

"So, you're saying…"

He cracked his knuckles. "CPD officially believes Marcus was murdered."

"Oh, wow."

"Yeah."

"You know, head wounds bleed a lot."

"You speaking from experience?"

"I am, actually. I once cracked my head open by standing up under a glass escalator and you would have thought…well, let's just say my poor friend who was standing next to me looked like Carrie at the prom. My point is the perp definitely would've gotten at least some blood on them."

Holden smirked. "I guess it depends on the angle the *perp* used to inflict the blow and where the spatter went as a result. There wasn't a whole lot of blood on the scene, which kind of contradicts your supposition. Some people are more likely to bleed externally, while others have more of a propensity for internal contusions and brain bleeds. From what I read in the coroner's initial report, Marcus fell into the second category. I was told a more comprehensive report with all those details is pending. I'll try to get my hands on it as soon as I can."

"There's no chance he hit his head after going into the water, even if he were pushed in? What if he accidentally bonked his head on a sailboat jib, and then stumbled around in an injured state before falling in somewhere else?"

Holden laughed, which seemed inappropriate and crass, considering our mutual friend lay cold on a slab in the morgue.

"I think that's a bit of a stretch. Based on the lack of significant water in his lungs and the condition of his skin, the coroner says he wasn't in the water more than an hour, most likely fifteen to thirty minutes. He was dead, or close to it, before he went in. Otherwise, he would've sunk instead of floated. When lungs fill with water, bodies tend to sink, ya know?"

"Dead people don't breathe."

"Not typically." He chuckled again.

Irritation warmed my cheeks. "What I mean is his lungs didn't fill with water because he wasn't breathing. And he wasn't breathing because he was already dead, which means the impact on his head must've been pretty significant for practically instant death."

"That about sums it up."

"Marcus had the temperament of a lost puppy dog. Who could have gotten so angry with him they'd want to literally bash his head in, and why? That sounds like a lot of anger for one whack."

"It does. What're you thinking?"

"It feels personal."

"I agree."

I chewed my lower lip. "The man I saw on the docks seemed angry enough to hurt someone. Do the police think he might have done it?"

"Too soon to say. They're looking at everyone right now. Including you."

"Me?" I reared back. "Why me?"

"When I told Kimball you'd heard from Marcus not long before his death and you two had a past romantic relationship, she became adamant she needed to speak with you directly, ASAP. I'm guessing you'll get a call in the morning."

"I'm a witness, not a suspect!"

"Right now, everyone's a suspect. The only thing they know for certain is the motive wasn't robbery. Marcus's wallet and phone were still in his pocket. Unfortunately, the damage to his phone rendered it inoperable, and they're unlikely to get any information from it, like who he might have messaged or called right before he died. Kimball said they're bringing in a forensic artist from Seattle to work with you sometime this week to try and identify the guy you saw since he may have seen something that could help the investigation."

"Or he's the killer."

"Audrey, you're making a pretty big leap from snarling parking spot thief to murderer." He reached out to pat my hand, treading dangerously close to the condescension zone.

"I know that, but if you'd seen him, you'd know why he freaked me out."

Holden paused. "There's one more thing I haven't told you about the crime scene."

"Do I even want to know? Don't tell me if it's going to give me nightmares. I already know I'm gonna have trouble sleeping with all this talk about cracked skulls and blood spatter."

He lowered his voice and leaned closer. "They found traces of wood in his wound. Initial comparison with wood from the dock isn't a match."

"What else could it be?"

"I dunno, maybe splinters from the handle of a wooden rake or shovel."
He cupped a handful of mixed nuts from the bowl on the table and popped
them in his mouth.

"Why would someone bring a rake to a marina?" It was my turn to be
condescending. "There aren't any leaves there. Also, if you had a shovel for
a weapon, wouldn't it make more sense to use the shovel side rather than
the handle? I'm no seasoned killer, but that seems like common sense."

"Probably. You might not want to use that argument in your interview
with Kimball, though. Besides, if we're talking about a crime of passion,
common sense rarely enters the picture. What you're talking about is pre-
meditated murder. I'm just brain-storming possible weapons. Hell, it could
be a hockey stick or a rolling pin for all I know…and, before you ask, no, I
don't have an explanation for why someone would bring those items to a
marina either." He tugged at the zipper on his sweater even though it was
already pulled down as far as it could go.

"Fifteen to thirty minutes. That means Marcus may have still been alive
when I went into the marina office."

He reached for my hand again. "There's nothing you could've done."

"It's just, to have been right there when it happened…if I'd seen him,
maybe…." My voice faltered.

"You can't think about it that way. My window overlooks the marina,
and if I had looked out, maybe I could've seen what was happening and
tried to stop it, or, maybe not, if they were inside the covered boat house.
Woulda-coulda's won't do either of us any good at this point."

"I just feel terrible." I released a weary sigh. "Speaking of terrible, has
anyone talked to his wife?" The word dripped off my tongue with a hint of
venom.

"Renee claims she was at home when it happened. Kimball said she
appeared devastated when they delivered the news."

"It doesn't mean she didn't do it, or she could've hired the parking jerk to
do it."

"You're right; it doesn't mean she didn't do it, and they'll keep her on the
shortlist as they always do with spouses. Right now, she's no more or less

in the spotlight than anyone else…including you."

"That's ridiculous."

He shrugged his shoulders. "You're the ex."

I scoffed. "From about a million years ago."

"Regardless. The blow was made at an upward angle to the back of the head. Normally that would narrow the suspect list to people shorter than the victim, but since Marcus was so tall, it doesn't eliminate very many people. That's another reason the police don't believe he accidentally hit his head and fell in, because he'd have to have been coming down toward whatever he hit his head on. Even though the spatter was in the boathouse, they've searched the edges of the boardwalk, every gangplank, and the bridge. The marina docks are splintery. Had he hit his head going in, there should be shards from the dock in his wound and blood on the dock's edge. Neither were found, bolstering the idea the initial blow was intense enough to kill and send a six-foot-six guy into the drink."

"I just can't imagine who would want to murder that sweet, dopey guy. He was a gentle giant."

"Well, yeah, but there were other sides to him than the guy you knew." Holden leaned back and folded his arms across his chest. "He had money troubles and not to speak ill of the dead, but the guy was a total flake. More than once, he borrowed money from me without paying it back. I wouldn't hear from him for months, probably because he was avoiding me from guilt or embarrassment. I don't know. Maybe he didn't want to pay me back. What if he owed money to the wrong person? Trust me, it happens, and it can get ugly. Really ugly." Holden grimaced and swigged his whisky.

"Since he owed you money, wouldn't that make you a suspect?"

He shrugged his shoulders and took another sip. "I guess technically it does. I wasn't mad at the guy about not paying me back, just disappointed he wasn't man enough, didn't value our friendship enough to talk through it. He was like my brother, ya know? We grew up together. I figured when I gave him the money, I probably wasn't going to see it again. Hell, I'd have been more surprised if he had paid me back."

"Holden, I need this to make sense. It has to be personal, because if it was a random attack, no one in Chattertowne is safe."

From behind me, someone on a microphone called Vivienne to the stage. The crowd whooped their approval. I turned to get a better view of her performance, so I didn't sense Holden leaning toward me until his breath warmed my neck.

"I'm not going to let anything happen to you, Audrey. I promise you that."

After Vivienne had finished her set, I approached to give her a hug while Holden hung back and gave a thumbs-up. Viv nodded at him but didn't return his smile. She stared pointedly at me. I shrugged my shoulders, which was as honest a response I could give her.

Once out of the club, I clinched my jacket tight against my body to ward off the frigid wind. He removed his and wrapped it around my shoulders. Two acts of chivalry in one night were practically a record for me.

"Can I walk you to your car?"

Make that three.

"Sure. I'm this way." I pointed down the street.

Our arms brushed against each other, the occasional contact seeming both accidental and intentional. "This is me."

We'd arrived at my dark gray Volvo coupe.

I rubbed my hands together and blew on them. "Thanks for coming tonight."

He grabbed my hands and rubbed them between his own. "Thank you for inviting me."

He'd invited himself, but I decided it wasn't the time for petty quibbling.

"Uh, well, good night, Holden."

He drew me close to him. The hug was longer than I expected, the embrace tighter. He enveloped my entire upper body in warmth and his soothing scent. There was an unspoken message in his lingering, but I wasn't sure what he was trying to communicate. I avoided his gaze, afraid my face would tell him more than I wanted to say.

"Audrey."

I allowed myself to look at him. He stared at me for a moment and leaned toward me. At the last moment, he turned just enough that his mouth landed on the corner of mine. We held the connection briefly, unmoving, caught in that space where we had to decide between right and wrong.

"Do, uh, do you want to get inside and warm up a bit before you walk back to your car?" I mumbled.

He sighed and pulled away with a reluctant chuckle. "I'd better not."

I nodded and fumbled with my keys until I pressed the correct button to unlock the door. "Okay, well, good night. Again."

"Good night, Audrey."

His words were barely audible over the sound of rushing blood in my head, but his conflicted tone came through loud and clear.

Chapter Nine

That night while I slept, Jonathan Chatterton entered my subconscious. In my somnolent vision, he stood on a hilltop at the valley's edge next to his horse, saddled with bags and gear.

On the other side of the valley, a white man dressed in a Halloween costume version of Native attire danced and chanted, taunting Jonathan. "*Swobilak, Kupit. Swobilak, Kupit.*"

I stood in the valley below, looking from one man to the other until my frustration grew so great, I screamed at the top of my lungs. "Would you both please *x̌ʷubiləxʷ* and tell me what I'm missing!"

The soothing jazz sounds of "Masquerade" brought me into a semi-conscious state. I flopped out of bed and shuffled into the kitchen where I fumbled through turning on the coffee maker before plopping myself onto a stool at the counter.

I pulled the book on Chattertowne and my laptop out of my bag. I flipped through the book until I reached page thirty.

Jonathan and Madeleine welcomed son Michael on the 20th of February 1862. It was a difficult birth and Madeleine did not survive. Jonathan's journals were quite revealing about this time, particularly regarding the local Flathead woman to whom he familiarly referred as Nettie. Nettie, the midwife who'd attended the birth, stayed on at the Chatterton settlement to help Jonathan care for Michael after his mother's death. It has long been rumored.

And that was it. That's where it ended. When it picked up again on page thirty-five, it was 1924 and Robinson had made his ridiculous claims about the town's original name.

Far from gaining the answers I'd been seeking, I'd instead been left with more questions. I needed to find out what those rumors were. Maybe that would explain why someone would go to the trouble of ripping pages out of a seventy-year-old book.

Forefront in my mind was how George Hart had gotten his hands on Jonathan's journal and, more importantly, who had it now?

I decided my best course of action was to take the book back to Mildred to see if she could shed any light on the situation.

For the second day in a row, I made my way back down the library stairs and through the dusty corridor into Mildred's dank domain.

"Good morning, Audrey!"

Today's cardigan was lavender.

"Morning, Mildred. How's it going?"

"Oh, fine, fine. Did you have any luck with the book last night?" She removed her glasses and let them drop until the chain caught them.

"Well, yes and no. Did you know some pages are missing?" I set it on the counter.

Mildred gasped. "What? No! Are you sure?" She flipped through the book, scowling in bewilderment. "Oh, dear. How could this have happened? I wonder if one of those darn fifth graders did this."

"I suspect it wasn't a child vandal but an adult with something to hide."

"Why do you say that?"

After showing her where page thirty left off, Mildred agreed it was possible they'd been removed because of information they contained.

"Any thoughts on what someone might want to keep under wraps?"

She shrugged her frail shoulders. "I've never heard anything other than praise for Jonathan, nothing salacious at all. My parents might've heard something, but if they did, they never told me. Jonathan is an icon around here, and I'd imagine some might go to great lengths to prevent his image from being tarnished." She tapped her cheek with her finger. "They were close with Eddie Chatterton, Jonathan's grandson. Did I mention that?"

"Your parents?"

"Yes. When I was young, my parents joined a card club. I must have been about...." Her face scrunched as she attempted to remember. "Nine. No, eight. No, it was the fall, and my birthday was in June, so nine." She huffed in frustration at her failing cognition. "Anyway, the men would play poker while the women played gin. They'd meet at a different couple's house every week, so we hosted every few months. They'd set two tables, one in our living room for the men and one in the kitchen next to the nook for the women, and there were five people at each table. I loved when it was our turn to host because my mother would go all out with the snacks." Her face turned wistful, giving a glimpse of the young girl she used to be. "My father and Eddie were always laughing and making jokes. They were probably completely inappropriate, but most of them went over my head. I loved seeing my dad in such a jovial mood."

"Did you ever see Eddie other than when your parents were hosting the card parties?"

"Oh yes, Eddie came over at least once a month with his wife for dinner. Those nights I didn't enjoy as much because I'd have to hang out with their two boys, Jimmy and Dickie. Jimmy played pranks on me."

"Jimmy? Do you mean James Chatterton, the one who committed suicide in the river?"

Her expression darkened at the mention of his untimely end. "Yes. However, Dickie..." She brightened again, smiling shyly at his name. She pronounced it with the whispered reverence reserved for a crush. "Richard was his proper name, but we all called him Dickie. He was quite the ladies' man. So handsome. All the girls wanted him to notice them."

Mildred looked to be playing a nostalgic scene in her mind. Lost in her reverie, her expressions ranged from coy to blissful. The reminiscence must have had a gloomy conclusion because a frown supplanted her smile.

"Dickie ran off at seventeen and joined the army. Everyone tried to talk him out of it, but that boy was stubborn as a mule. He wanted to get as far away as possible from this town and the people in it. He said he wanted nothing to do with the burden of carrying on the Chatterton legacy." She paused, and sadness washed over her. "He died in the Battle of Bloody Ridge, Korea."

"Oh, Mildred, I'm so sorry."

"It was a tragedy. He wasn't even a man yet, with his entire life ahead of him. All that lost potential." Her face contorted into a scowl. "Jimmy, on the other hand, wasn't a nice boy. He wasn't a nice man, either. Dickie was sweet and kind. Jimmy was cruel. Still, I know Jimmy's death broke Eddie's heart. There's only so much grief a father can bear in one lifetime."

"When was the last time you saw Eddie?"

"Oh, I'd run into him around town occasionally before he died, late eighties, if I'm not mistaken. Never again at my parents' home, though. He'd had a falling out with my father not too long before Dickie ran off and joined the service. If I recall, it had something to do with another young man in the group. Eddie and the man had a disagreement, and my father took the other man's side. At least, that was Eddie's perception."

"Do you remember what the disagreement was about?"

"I'm not sure I ever knew. What was his wife's name?" Mildred tapped her finger against her cheek again. "She was beautiful. Sarah or Sadie." She mentally sorted through eight decades of friends and acquaintances. "No, that's not it, it was more glamorous, like that famous sexy Italian actress." Her frail hands mimicked the shape of an hourglass.

I smiled at her description and hand gestures. "Sophia Loren?"

"Yes! No! Not Sophia, Sophie. That's right. George and Sophie. George and Sophie Hart."

I glanced down at the book's cover. "Mildred?"

"Yes, dear."

I held up the book.

Mildred scanned the cover until her eyes lit up. "Well, I'll be! That's right. He did write a book about Chattertowne. He had it printed at the newspaper, about ten copies and gave them to friends and family for Christmas that year. My parents had one. I don't think I ever read it, though. Well, isn't that a coincidence? Too funny!"

"So, Eddie Chatterton fell out with your father because your father didn't take his side in an argument with George Hart? *The* George Hart, who wrote a book seventy-plus years ago in which he'd discussed Eddie's ancestor Jonathan Chatterton. This book," I tapped on the book for emphasis, "which has missing pages from the portion in which potentially explosive rumors about Jonathan were discussed."

"Do you think that's what they were fighting about? This book?"

"What could George have possibly written which was damaging enough to end two friendships?"

"I have no idea. We should ask him." Mildred blinked at me expectantly.

"Ask who?"

"Why, George Hart, of course." Her thin laughter tinkled.

"George Hart...junior?"

"No, George Hart. The one and only." Mildred pointed at the book in my hand.

"He's still alive?"

"Why yes, unless you've heard otherwise."

"I haven't heard anything, Mildred. I only read his name for the first time when I found this book yesterday!"

"Oh, phew. You had me worried there for a minute." She patted her chest. "He's gotta be nearing the big triple digits, and I'm certain I'd have heard if he'd died. He lives at that nursing home over on Hughes Street. Although he's pretty much a recluse now, he was once quite the man about town and somewhat of a local celebrity. Now that I think about it, he authored several travel books. He was the Rick Steves of his day."

"Is there anything else you can recall about the Chattertons or rumors regarding Jonathan?"

She paused to consider. "No, dear, I'm sorry. Nothing comes to mind."

"I'm going right now to pay George a visit. If you remember anything, please call my cell." I wrote my number on the notepad, ripped it off, and handed it to her.

"I'll keep stewing on it. Something in this old brain is sure to break loose.

When it does, I'll text you." She picked up a flip phone and waved it in the air.

Once back in my car, I found I'd missed two calls and a text from Darren.

Call Me.

He answered on the first ring. "I was worried about you."

"Worried? Why?" I flipped down the shade visor and opened the mirror to scan my teeth for anything that didn't belong.

"Why didn't you call me back?"

"I left my phone in the car while I was in the library. I'm calling you now."

If he heard the irritation in my voice, he didn't let on. "How's the research going?"

"Fine. I'm headed to the nursing home to interview someone."

Silence.

"Hello? Darren?"

"Who are you going to see?"

"Some old dude who's been in Chattertowne his whole life. I figure he might be able to tell me some stories about back in the day. Hey, I've gotta run. I'll see you back at the office." I hung up before he could get in another word.

I didn't feel like talking to Anderson, so I called his receptionist, Laurie, and asked her to let him know I was working on the Kupit story so I wouldn't be in the office until later in the afternoon.

"I'm not going in there until he's finished his nasty knockwurst sandwich," she said. "The smell is wafting into the hallway and making me queasy."

I crinkled my nose. "Didn't that go out of culinary style with aspic and tuna noodle casserole? I didn't know anyone still ate knockwurst."

"No one should."

I drove up Sixth Street and took a left onto Parker Avenue. The nursing home was situated at the intersection of Hughes and Parker, which had always sounded to me like the name of a law firm or a mortuary. The latter wasn't far from reality.

As I stepped into the lobby, a mélange of Pine Sol and aging bodies assaulted my nostrils. Behind the reception desk, a stern-looking middle-aged woman had her face buried in a Regency romance paperback. The cover featured an ethereal nymph-like female in a white empire-waisted gown and a gentleman preening behind her wearing a ruffled blouse. Two impatient eyes glared at me over the top of the book.

"Can I help you?"

"I'm, uh, I'm here to see George Hart." My heart thumped rapidly, and my cheeks flushed.

"Is he expecting you?"

"No, not exactly. I'm…his niece. His great, great…*great* niece. I recently moved back into the area, so I thought I'd come see how Uncle George is doing. Good old great, great…." I paused. "Great Uncle George."

I attempted a convincing smile, but judging by the woman's wary expression, it fell short. On more than one occasion, I'd been told I had a terrible poker face.

"Mr. Hart's never had a family visitor in my twenty years here."

"Even more reason to let me see him."

Despite having clear reservations about my veracity, the woman blew out a long-suffering sigh. The nymph's romp with Lord Ruffleton on the fainting couch would have to wait.

"He's due for lunch in about forty-five minutes. It'll have to be a short reunion."

She led me down a long hallway that looked and smelled like Mylanta, with its pale-green shade and medicinal mint aroma.

"Mr. Hart? Your…niece is here to see you." She nearly spat the word.

A frail voice croaked from behind the beige divider curtain. "My niece?"

"Yes. Your great, great…great niece." The woman sighed with the last great, her tone heavy with derision and skepticism.

"Send her in."

On the other side of the curtain, I came face-to-face with the man whose book had captivated me for the past twenty-four hours. He looked how I'd assumed a near-centenarian might look. What remained of his hair was white except for some dark patches near his temples. Thin fluffy strands were combed from the left side of his head to the right. He wore wire-framed glasses, and the refraction from daylight peeking through the window glinted in his gray eyes. His cornflower-blue terrycloth tracksuit was not unlike the one I'd worn in my Juicy Couture phase of 2006.

"Mr. Hart?"

"Yes, dear, come sit. Is she gone? Nurse Ratched, I mean." He chuckled.

"Yes, she's gone. She seems nice enough." I didn't bother putting much conviction into my words as I eased into the chair at the foot of his bed.

"Oh, Denise is fine. A little preoccupied, but she's okay. I like to play around, I just wanted to make sure she didn't catch you in your lie." He winked one droopy eyelid.

"My lie?"

"My dear, you couldn't possibly be my niece, great or otherwise. My older brother died in the Spanish influenza epidemic of 1918 before I was even born, and my little sister joined a convent to become a different kind of sister. She's Sister Maria Ignatius now, and she turns ninety this year."

"You caught me. My name's Audrey O'Connell. I'm with the *Coastal Current* newspaper. I'd like to ask you a few questions."

"I suppose before agreeing to your request, I should inquire about what information you're looking to get out of me." He folded his thin arms across his chest in a pose of defiance belied by the hint of amusement on his face.

"Fair enough. I'm doing a series about Chattertowne for Kupit. Mildred Driscoll suggested I speak with you."

"Mildred!" His eyes became misty, and the folds surrounding them wrinkled with his smile. "That girl was a firecracker." His shoulders shook with laughter.

"She still is."

I chose not to mention the "girl" to whom he'd referred was in her ninth decade of life. People tended to get cryogenically frozen in our memories, forever in our minds and hearts as what they were when we knew them best.

"She said you used to come to her house to play cards with her parents and a few other couples."

George's face became wistful. "Yes, with my Sophie. God, I miss that woman every day. She was the social one, between the two of us. I only went along to make her happy. I never fit in with that crowd, not really. She was the buffer who made it possible. I'm quieter by nature, a bit of an introvert. If she hadn't dragged me along, I would have instead spent those evenings by the fire writing."

"Mildred mentioned you had a falling out with another member of the card club."

He tilted his head and appraised me. "Yes. I guess I'm a little surprised Mildred was aware of that. Eddie Chatterton certainly wasn't a fan of my Christmas gift to him that year."

"Funny you should mention that. I recently came across a copy of your book about Chattertowne's history in the Library's museum, but a few pages are missing. I was hoping you could tell me what they said."

"We have a museum?"

"I was surprised by that as well. Anyway, I believe they were intentionally removed by someone hoping to bury the information contained on those pages. I'd like to know what was so scandalous it caused a falling out between you and Eddie and why someone would go to the trouble to hide a secret that's at least seven decades old."

George stared at me for a long time without saying anything. I squirmed in the molded resin seat under his gaze. I tapped my pen on my notebook. I blinked several times. My confidence faltered with every passing moment of silence.

"I can't help you."

"Can't? Or won't?"

He turned to look out the window.

"Mr. Hart, you know exactly which pages are missing and why, don't you?"

He took a ragged, labored breath. "I can guess."

"Why won't you tell me?"

He turned back to face me, his expression an amalgam of pain, fatigue, and something else...resignation, maybe. "Young lady, you have no idea the depths you've waded into. The information contained in that book could have far-reaching ramifications, even today." He glanced out his window again. "It already has."

"If you could just point me in the right direction—"

He cut off my plea. "Miss O'Connell, is it?"

I nodded.

"Take some advice from a very old man. When it comes to the Chattertons, they've got more skeletons than a graveyard, literally and figuratively. If you go digging up old bones, you might not like what you find. For your sake...." He attempted to sit up. "For your safety, I suggest you leave this mystery a mystery. Now, it's nearly ten thirty. Lunchtime is at eleven, and I like to nap before I eat. You need to go."

His decrepit body slouched. He closed his eyes, indicating the conversation had ended. As I reached the hallway, a feeble voice called, "Miss O'Connell?"

I turned to look at him, but his lids remained shuttered.

"Yes?"

"Please let this matter drop. Some secrets are meant to remain submerged."

Chapter Ten

Despite George Hart's ominous warning, I returned to my office more determined than ever to uncover the potential bombshell contained in the missing pages. If George wouldn't tell me, I'd find another way.

I opened my binder and scoured my notes.

Jonathan Chatterton had settled the area in the late 1850s. His wife, Madeleine, died in childbirth in 1862. Nettie, the midwife, had stayed on to care for baby Michael and seemed to be a central figure in the mystery.

A search for Jonathan Chatterton and Nettie on Google aggregated a list of websites. Most were unrelated to my quest, but one elicited an audible gasp.

"Oh, my gawd!"

Keith, the sports reporter who worked on the other side of the partition, banged on the wall.

"Sorry!"

What had caught my attention was a blogging website called "Chatter-towne Conspiracy." At the top of the page was a photo of the site's admin. He'd called himself "The Veracitater." Not only wasn't it a real word, but the name also made him sound like an honest potato with fascist tendencies.

It was none other than Marcus Washburn.

The headlines of his blog read like a catalog of conspiracy theories, with topics ranging from the town council doping the water supply with melatonin to keep citizens compliant to Police Chief Brinks manipulating the streetlights to benefit his golfing buddies.

I clicked on the post titled "The Chatterton Family Mafia Stole My Birthright" and began reading.

Thirty years ago, my father, David Washburn, called home for what would turn out to be the last time. My mother Gayle answered the call, but she hung up on him, believing he'd been drinking. We never saw him again. The police tried to say he'd abandoned us, but my mother didn't believe them, and neither do I. They said he was a drunk deadbeat, but he never would've left his family if he could help it.

Before his disappearance, my father told my mother he'd discovered shocking information and documents to support it, which would turn the town upside down and make us rich in the process. He also told her if anything happened to him, he'd hidden a notebook containing all the dirt somewhere in the house. He told her not to trust the police or the government because they're in the pockets of the Chatterton family mafia, so when they showed at our house, my mom lied and told them she hadn't heard from him, but she believed he was in hiding or dead. They dismissed her statements as the ramblings of a woman who was in denial she'd been left by her husband.

I don't know to this day if my father is dead or alive. I fear he's at the bottom of the Jeannetta River. Unfortunately, my mom forgot where he said he'd hid his notebook. His disappearance sent her sideways. I didn't only lose my dad that day, I lost my mom too...in all the ways that mattered.

While cleaning out her house after she died last year, I finally found the notebook, and I plan to reveal its secrets little by little until the whole truth about the Chatterton family mafia has been revealed.

My dad knew things about the Chattertons, and now I know things about the Chattertons. They're murderers, criminals, and thieves. I've already been threatened to keep quiet, so if anything happens to me you know who to go looking for.

Stunned, I picked up my phone.

"Hey there. I'm glad you called." Holden's voice oozed like molasses on a warm day.

"This isn't a social call. I just found something pretty crazy related to Marcus's death."

"What's going on?"

"Did you know he was a conspiracy theorist?"

"Marcus? Yeah, everyone did. You didn't?"

"It didn't come up. So, have you read what he put on his website?"

"No, I'd hear it from him whenever we'd go out for a beer, which was about all I could take."

"Listen to this." I proceeded to read the blog post to him.

"Oh, shoot. Send me the link, I need to pass that on."

"Which Chatterton family members are still around who might have a vested interest in preventing these secrets from being revealed? What do you think Marcus meant by 'stole my birthright?' Were any Chattertons implicated at the time of Marcus's dad's disappearance?"

"Whoa, whoa. That's a lot of questions. I know Jimmy Chatterton killed himself around the time David Washburn disappeared. If I'm remembering the story correctly, Jimmy was being investigated for fraud and corruption or something. David worked as a cargo loader at the port, kinda like what Marcus does...did. Ugh, that's hard to get used to."

"I keep doing that too."

"Yeah, anyway, as for the birthright thing, I guess he could have meant losing his father's income. I know they struggled financially. Without a body, there's no life insurance, and the shipping company David worked for didn't offer any help. If it weren't for local charity, I don't know how they would've made it at all. His mom had no college degree or any job skills, and she wasn't great at keeping the jobs she did manage to get. After David went missing, she started drinking heavily, and that morphed into...harder stuff."

"He never told me that."

"He didn't tell me that stuff either. His mom did one night when she was high off her ass. Marcus was mortified. He kept telling her to shut up and go to bed."

"x̌ʷubiləx̌ʷ."

"Bless you."

"That wasn't a sneeze. It's a Lushootseed word meaning be quiet. I've never liked the phrase shut up. It's so harsh." I spun around in my office chair like a little kid on the tilt-a-whirl. "It's kind of amazing Marcus did as well in life as he did, considering his upbringing. He had a decent job, owned a home, had three cute kids and a wife."

If Holden noticed I hadn't said Marcus had a good wife, he didn't mention it.

"Marcus was an eternal optimist. He made the best with what he had."

"On another note, what do you know about Peter Chatterton? He donated an item of Jonathan's—some big knife—to the archive museum back in nineteen ninety. Is he still around?" I circled Peter's name on my notes.

There was a beat of silence. "Peter lives on the hill. Doesn't come into town much. He's sitting on dozens of prime view acres which have been passed down through the family, along with a bunch of other real estate in town and several businesses. Occasionally, the city council receives a letter from him complaining about one thing or another. We've invited him to discuss his issues at the council meetings, but he never shows."

"Is he married? Kids?"

"He's got no kids, as far as I'm aware. I know he went to college in LA on a golf scholarship, I believe, and then stayed in that area for a while. When he came back, he was married to some chick named Mandi…or Brandi…or Kandi. Whichever it was, she definitely spelled it with an I because she always dotted the I with a heart. She left town a few years back. Hooked up with her personal trainer and relocated to Miami, said she hated the climate here. Apparently, she wasn't a huge fan of old Pete either. I don't blame her; he's not the most congenial guy."

"Geez. Okay, well, I read somewhere Eddie Chatterton was an only child. Mildred over at the library told me he had two sons. James, aka Jimmy, and uh, let me look at my notes." I flipped through the notepad. "Here it is. Richard, also called Dickie. Jimmy committed suicide in the eighties. Eddie died not long after. Which one was Peter's dad? Had to be Jimmy, right? Mildred said Dickie ran off to join the military at seventeen and died in the Korean War."

"I'm almost positive Jimmy was Peter's dad."

"Are there any other Chattertons around who might want to shut Marcus up...permanently? To protect their inheritance, I mean."

"I'm not sure about siblings or cousins. Someone around here should know."

I groaned. "I know who'd know."

We spoke at the same time. "Peg."

"Dammit." He sighed. "Fine, I'll talk to her."

"Good luck. Don't forget the pastries," I sang.

"Yeah, right. Thanks."

"Hey, Holden?"

"Yup?"

"Are we going to talk about, uh, you know..."

"Can we table that conversation until things settle down? I need to get my head on straight first."

"I understand." There was a soft tap at my door. "Hey, I gotta go. I'm gonna keep digging here. Let me know what you find on your end."

"Will do."

"Come in."

The door opened, and Darren entered my office. Instead of feeling excitement at seeing him, my breathing became constricted with nerves, and my stomach felt queasy. Something had shifted in our dynamic, and I wasn't sure how to feel about him. Gone were the days of playful, flirtatious banter, now replaced with weird tension.

"Hey." I scanned his face but found nothing to indicate his mood, good or bad.

"How did it go at the nursing home?" His jaw clenched and released.

"Oh." I waved my hand in dismissal. "It was a dead end. You know how old people are. By dinnertime, they can barely remember what flavor Jell-O they had for lunch."

Darren's aqua irises bore through me. "Audrey? Wanna tell me what's going on with you?"

"What do you mean?"

"You're not acting like yourself." He placed his hands on his hips and exhaled a deep sigh.

I stood and moved toward him. "I just have a lot on my mind with my story and Marcus…."

"Shhh. It's okay." He brushed hair from my face.

Did he just…shush me?

Before I had a chance to react, he leaned closer, placed his palms on each side of my head, and gently pressed his lips to mine. He ran his hands up and down my arms.

"Audrey, I feel as though you're not being completely honest with me. You know, I saw you the other day."

"Saw me?" I was still trying to figure out how I felt about the kiss, and my brain hadn't re-engaged enough to know what he was talking about.

"You were holding his hand." He tipped his chin down and stared at me with a look of disapproval and then stroked my hair. "I know you don't owe me an explanation. I just thought we were starting something. And the guy is engaged, you know."

I opened my mouth to respond, but before I could, he pulled me face-first into his chest and kissed the top of my head.

"It's fine. It's all gonna work out the way it's supposed to," he said, answering a question I hadn't asked.

I was about to protest being treated like a child when his taut arms tensed around me. I pulled back to find him staring at my computer screen.

"I thought you said you were doing an article on the festival." His voice dipped to a quiet growl.

"I am, and Chattertowne history. There was a Native American woman named Nettie, she was Flathead, actually, and well, I was searching, and this came up."

Darren glared at the monitor.

"Turns out Marcus was a conspiracy whacko, but he might have actually been onto something. I think it's possible the Chatterton family had something to do with what happened."

Darren whipped his head to look at me. "Where'd you get that idea?"

"Why do you care? Don't you have your own stories to write?"

"I care because I'm worried about you, Audrey. Don't you get that? You're inserting yourself in the middle of a homicide. Someone already killed your friend, and now you're sticking your nose where it shouldn't be. You're going to get yourself hurt!"

"I'm a journalist. It's my job to tell the whole story."

"You're a *lifestyles* writer at a newspaper with a circulation of about seven thousand people, Audrey. Your job is to write a feel-good piece about the festival, not flip the damn town's history upside down or insert yourself into a murder investigation because you're bored writing crappy articles about Edgar and Martha Cavanaugh's freaking birdhouse collection."

His face was nearly magenta. I'd never heard him raise his voice before, and his outburst stunned me into silence.

Someone knocked on my door. "Audrey? Everything okay in there?"

"Yeah, Keith, thanks. I'm fine."

"You sure? Sounded like a riot breaking out."

"Sorry for the noise."

"Let me know if you need anything."

I turned to Darren with the most withering gaze I could muster, practically shaking with rage. "Get out of my office. If you *ever* talk to me that way again, I'll report you to Anderson."

His face morphed from frustration to dismay, to determined resignation. "I'm sorry, Audrey. It didn't have to be this way." He turned on his heel and walked out the door.

I grabbed my laptop off my desk, packed my bag, and stormed my way across the office. If anyone foolishly attempted to make eye contact with me, I didn't notice. When I pulled into my parking space at home, I had little recollection of the drive other than one long cuss-filled ranting monologue about Darren.

After pouring a glass of the Moscato I'd opened a few nights earlier, I practiced breathing techniques I'd learned from my three pathetic attempts at hot yoga.

What in the hell was going on? Sip. Deep breath. Darren was acting like Dr. Jekyll and Mr. Hyde. Sip. Deep breath. Marcus was dead. Sip. Deep breath. And, apparently, a crazy person. Sip. Deep breath. Or maybe not, since his conspiracy theories were close enough to the truth to have gotten him killed. Sip. Deep breath. Who was Nettie?

I set my wineglass on a coaster and pulled out my laptop. I'd only found Marcus's website because I'd googled Nettie, but I'd gotten sidetracked by the blog post regarding Marcus's father's disappearance and had forgotten what had led me there in the first place.

Scanning the titles, I finally hit pay dirt.

"Jonathan and Nettie: The True Story the Chatterton Family Doesn't Want You to Know."

The article was dated the day before Marcus died.

"Bingo!" I shouted into my empty apartment. "I have the smoking gun!" I clicked on the link but got an error. "File not found. That can't be." Hitting the back button, I clicked the link again and got the same result. "Well, that's freaking fantastic. What are the odds?"

I swigged my wine. What were the odds? I clicked around, but all the other articles had active links. The only dead link on the site was the Nettie post.

Someone must have deleted the article. It was the only logical explanation...unless he never wrote it. If that were the case, though, why would he have published a link with no content? Perhaps it was to taunt someone with the title itself.

"*Coastal Current.* This is Tasha."

"Hey, Tash, it's Audrey."

"Oh hey, Audrey. I thought you left already. After, uh, you know..."

"What?"

Tasha lowered her voice. "Everyone heard the fight with Darren. The walls are pretty thin around here. Keith said he thought he was gonna have to bust down the door."

I sighed. "I need to talk to Sandros. I'm at home. Otherwise, I'd go deal with this in person."

"Sandros? Is that why Darren was yelling at you for kissing Sandros at the party? Are you dumping Darren for Sandros?"

"Oh, good grief, no. I need to talk to him about computer stuff."

Tasha paused before speaking. "You know, Sandros isn't Quasimodo, Audrey. He's pretty decent, actually. Anyway, let me see if he's still there."

Tasha transferred me to Sandros's line, but after a few rings, it went to voice mail.

"Hey, Sandros, it's Audrey O'Connell. I've got a question for you, but I guess you've left for the night. I'll come find you in the morning."

I hoped I hadn't slurred my words. The last thing I needed was Sandros thinking I'd drunk-dialed him because of my fight with Darren.

Once again risking a wine-induced misunderstanding, I sent a message to Holden.

Hey. Just wanted to update you. I'm working on a couple angles. I'll let you know if they pan out. I'm also going to try to find time in the next couple days to see Peter Chatterton. I'm hoping he'll fill in some blanks for me. I got a call earlier from CPD. I'm coming in around noon tomorrow to sit with a sketch artist. I'm guessing they'll also want me to make a statement. Wish me luck. Have a good night.

Audrey

"All the rest can wait until tomorrow." I pulled a blanket over my legs and grabbed my wine, along with the TV remote. "I'm gonna relax, not think about icky stuff, drink wine, and watch a Hallmark romance movie."

Sip. Deep Breath.

Chapter Eleven

The next morning, my alarm woke me from a deep Moscato-induced slumber with the familiar opening notes of "Masquerade." After showering, I styled my hair and pulled on my favorite curve-enhancing khaki slacks paired with a butterscotch sweater, coordinating silk scarf, and leather boots. I finished the look with a shiny plum lip gloss.

Using my feminine wiles, such as they were, in order to elicit Sandros's help would be justified if Marcus's killer were caught and brought to justice. If my boss saw me, however, he might up his expectations. I'd gotten away with yoga pants and jeans at work for too long to give it up. He also wanted an update on my story, and it wasn't ready yet, so I needed to sneak in to see Sandros.

Tasha was on the phone when I arrived at the *Current*. She mouthed, "Sandros is here," and pointed to her right.

"Thank you," I mouthed back to her.

By the time I'd maneuvered past Anderson's office and rounded the partition into the IT area, I was winded and cursing my lack of cardio.

Sandros and three other guys shared the area, each with their own cubicle. None of the cubicles surrounding Sandros's were currently occupied. One domain had been plastered with posters from *Game of Thrones,* while another contained nothing but a monitor, keyboard, mouse, and a Costco-sized container of cleaning wipes. In contrast, the final cubical looked like someone had dumped their trash can all over their desk and floor following a munchie binge.

Sandros's desk was comparatively basic. His supplies were organized, although not compulsively so. He only had one item hanging on his wall, a calendar featuring ancient Greek architecture. He was freshly showered–with ringlets of wet hair and strong aftershave–and wore pressed beige slacks with a light-blue button-up shirt that nicely offset his Mediterranean skin. He was handsome in a geeky way.

He spun to face me, wearing a cat-that-ate-the-canary grin. He raised and lowered his unibrow suggestively. "Well, hello there, Audrey. I have been expecting you." He transformed from moderately handsome to outright creepy in an instant. "You seem a bit...breathless." His lascivious gaze matched his smarmy smile.

"I had to run the gauntlet to get over here without being seen."

"How excitingly clandestine." He raised and lowered his unibrow again.

Against my better judgment, I decided to play to his ego by taking on the role of damsel in distress. "I need your help, Sandros. You're the only one I can turn to."

He tsked. "To whom I can turn, Audrey. To whom I can turn. What kind of writer dangles her prepositions so...wantonly?" His slow perusal of my body felt like a violation.

"People's lives may be at stake here, Sandros."

He shifted his attention from my breasts to my face. "What do you mean?"

"May I sit here?" I gestured toward the middle cubicle.

"I wouldn't. Take Thanh's chair. Gerald goes a little psycho when people touch his stuff, and Donnie seems to be conducting biological experiments."

A glimpse at Donnie's monitor revealed several open browser windows with titles such as "Ten Ways to Cure Scalp Itch" and "Dry Scalp and You." I pulled the chair over to Sandros's desk and lowered my voice to a surreptitious whisper.

"What do you know about hacking?"

His brow furrowed into a V. "Depends on who's asking. What specifically do you want to know?"

"You heard Marcus Washburn was killed a few days ago, right?"

"Yeah." He frowned. "Rumor has it you found him."

"Not exactly. People at the docks saw him floating and fished him out. I happened upon the scene a few minutes later. Did you know Marcus?"

"Everybody knew Marcus. He was always spouting off about one crazy thing or another. He used to write a letter to the editor at least once a week. I always thought it was the most entertaining section of the paper, but then Anderson stopped publishing them. He said it was giving credence to wacky conspiracy theories."

"It seems as though I'm the only one who didn't know that side of him."

"Well, he was probably trying to make a good impression. Nobody wants to show all their crazy when trying to woo a chick."

"He wasn't trying to woo me. He's married. *Was* married."

"Well, he was a red-blooded man, and you're a beautiful woman. Anyway, what does that have to do with your hacking question?" He tented his fingertips.

"Last night, I came across Marcus's blog website. I found a link to a potentially explosive article dated the day before he was killed, but the link is dead."

Sandros's brow jumped up and down with excitement. "What's the name of his website again?" He swiveled toward his monitor. "Oh, yeah, the Veracitater." He shook his head. "He started the blog after Anderson refused to publish any more of his ramblings. I think his first post accused Anderson and *The Current* of being a part of a media cabal protecting the corrupt elite and powerful dark forces, something like that. To which post are you referring?"

I pointed to the link at the top of the homepage. He clicked it and got the same error I'd gotten the night before. A repeated attempt to open the file didn't change the results.

Sandros leaned back, tilted his head toward the ceiling, and blew out a long breath. He crooked his head in my direction. "If Marcus actually had an article on this page, it wouldn't require high-level skills to remove it. Most of your advanced gamers can break into a site like this, even mid-level."

"If you had to guess, how many guys in this general vicinity are capable of this type of hacking?"

"General vicinity? Hmm, well, everybody in this department, for starters.

Thinking about other businesses in the area, the local guys on the gaming sites, it's a lot. I mean, Seattle is a tech hub. Heck, my fourteen-year-old nephew could probably hack a site like this."

"There goes that idea."

"Yeah. They even wouldn't have to be local. That's kinda how the internet works, you know. I could hack a computer in Russia from this cubicle. Moscow, China, and North Korea have hacked computers in the U.S. Realistically, you're looking at tens of thousands who are capable, maybe more."

I grunted.

"You can eliminate most, though, because they'd have no reason to do it. Unless…"

"Unless what?"

"Unless someone hired them to do it. If I were you, I'd be looking at who *would,* because it's pretty easy to find someone who *could.*" He leaned back and crossed his arms.

"What about social media sites?"

Sandros scrunched his face in disgust. "What about social media? Other than it's a place for vapid narcissists trying to one-up each other."

"I mean, how hard is it to hack into someone's social media account?"

"Hmm. Well, that might be a little trickier. Definitely not impossible."

"Would having direct access to their computer make a difference?"

"Why do you ask?" He shifted in his chair.

"Just curious."

He narrowed his gaze but didn't challenge me. "That would definitely make it easier because you wouldn't have to hack the actual website. You could put a keystroke tracker into the system with a backdoor entrance giving a remote visual of everything typed on the computer. As for our friend, the Veracitater," he paused to chuckle over Marcus's self-given moniker. "Gimme time. I'm going to poke around here and see what I can find out. Sometimes hackers leave a trail."

"How can you see that?"

"Well, my dear Audrey, I'm going to hack his site myself."

I grabbed an open parking space three full blocks from City Hall, willing to walk the extra distance to avoid a possible repeat encounter with the parking spot thief. Also, since a ten-second office sprint had left me gasping for air, I definitely needed the exercise.

The biting wind nipped at my nose and ears. A storm was coming. I wrapped my scarf tighter around my neck, wishing I'd grabbed my wool coat before leaving home. It's been said pride comes before the fall, but they should have added vanity often comes before hypothermia.

Stinging heat slapped my frozen cheeks as I entered the lobby. I checked my phone and discovered I had about twenty-five minutes before I was scheduled to meet with the forensic artist, so I bypassed Joan for the elevator.

Once I'd arrived on the second floor, music lilted into the hallway from behind the closed door to room 204. I knocked and opened it to find Holden sitting at his desk.

"This is a welcome surprise!" He jumped from his seat to usher me into his office. "A bit chilly out there, huh, Rudolph?" He tapped my rosy nose.

"Just a bit. Not in here, though. So, this is where all my tax dollars go, keeping this building at a balmy ninety degrees in the winter."

"Exactly. Although if it were up to me, I'd keep this place at a brisk sixty-eight. I run a little hot."

I loosened my scarf at the thought of Holden's body heat. "I thought it was up to you. Don't you have any sway around here, Mr. City Manager?"

"Joan has a thyroid condition and controls the thermostat. She's right by the front door where the air comes in, so she takes the brunt. I've learned to dress in layers. In the summer, she cranks the AC, and this sauna becomes arctic."

"Poor Holden, you're probably only comfortable in May."

"May twelfth, to be exact. Hey, so, don't take this wrong because I'm happy to see you, but I'm curious why you're gracing me with the pleasure of your company this morning."

"I'm meeting with the forensic artist, but I'm early. I stopped by the paper for a bit, but I didn't want to stick around in case I ran into...anyone. I thought since I'm here, I'd check in with you, compare notes."

"I'm not sure I've got much to offer. I left Peg a voice mail. Haven't heard back."

"From what Anderson said, I'm not sure Peg even knows how to check her voicemail."

"I'll give her time to respond before I make the trek upstairs. What about you? Who are you avoiding at the office, and why?" He leaned forward and rested his elbows on the desk.

"Well, my boss, for one. I'm on a deadline and falling behind. I only went there to schmooze help from Sandros, our IT guy. I have him looking into the broken link on Marcus's website. He thinks—"

Holden's head popped up. "What broken link?"

I slapped my thigh in excitement. "Get this. Last night when I got home, I started drinking—"

Holden interrupted with a hearty laugh. "I like where this story's going already. Is that when you messaged me?"

"Hush. It was one glass of wine. I needed it to clear the cobwebs, relax me enough to let the important thoughts rise to the surface. I remembered what led me to Marcus's website in the first place. Nettie."

"Nettie?"

"Nettie was the Flathead woman Jonathan Chatterton brought in to help care for his son after his wife died. George Hart's book, the one I found in the museum archives, mentioned Nettie and rumors regarding her and Jonathan right before the missing pages."

"Whoa, whoa, back up." Holden held up both hands to pause the conversation. "What book? What missing pages? Sweetheart, you've got to start at the beginning. Explain to me what this book, the town founder who's been dead for over a hundred years, and a woman named Nettie could possibly have to do with Marcus's death."

I gave a brief summary.

"Marcus posted a link to a blog he'd written one day prior to his death mentioning this Nettie woman specifically in relation to his father's disappearance?"

"That's why I snuck in to see Sandros this morning. He's gonna help me by hacking–"

"Hold up!" Holden raised his hand again to stop me. "Don't say another word. In this case, let's go with a don't ask, don't tell policy."

"Sandros agrees it's possible someone hacked Marcus's website to take down that article. My gut says whoever's behind the hacking is connected to his death, either directly or indirectly."

"Why do you say indirectly?"

"I asked him who had the capability. With the basic website Marcus was using, the pool's pretty wide. He suggested money alone could be a motive."

"Meaning?"

"Meaning, whoever hacked the site could've been hired to do so."

"Ahh, I see. That does make it tough. Hypothetically, how could one with similar hacking ability be helpful in this scenario?"

"Hypothetically, the original hacker could've left a trail of computer-generated breadcrumbs which, depending on their sophistication level, could either lead us right to them or send us on a wild goose chase. Sandros says higher-level hackers use electronic diversionary tactics to cover their trail."

"This is crazy. You know that, right?" Holden ran his hand over his scalp.

"Yes, I know. Crazy doesn't mean untrue, though. We owe it to Marcus to find out who did this to him."

"I never took anything he said seriously. If I had…" His voice cracked with emotion.

"Hey."

I rose and went around the desk. Grabbing his shoulders, I turned him toward me. I squatted in front of him and grabbed his hand.

"You said yourself coulda-shoulda's are useless and self-defeating." My fingertips grazed the stubble on his cheek.

Staring into my eyes, he covered my hand with his. His lids fluttered shut, and he moved my palm to his mouth. Brushing his lips to my wrist, he pressed them against my skin. When his eyes reopened, they held the same conflicted desire as the night we'd gone to Nautilus.

I turned away from his pained expression. "Hoo boy."

"I don't know what to do, Audrey. This isn't me; it's not who I am. I don't do this." He threw his head back and growled his frustration.

"Look, I don't want to ruin your life. I don't want to mess up what you've built, your relationship, your career. I've come blustering back into town like a cyclone, and now everything's a mess. Whatever's here," I waved my hands in the air, "I don't want it at the expense of hurting your...Emily."

"You and I both know this has been lurking beneath the surface since you got back into town."

"You deserve more than what I have to offer. You'll have a good life with her, which is more than I can guarantee. Don't risk that for me. I'm a mess."

"Since when are relationships about guarantees, Audrey? What about you? Are you going to live happily ever after with Darren? That's the kind of man you think will make you happy?" He pulled away from me.

My hands flailed. "I'm not even sure I'm capable of a mature relationship with anyone. Here I am with you wishing..."

"Wishing what?" He searched my eyes.

"It doesn't matter." I waved my hand dismissively and rose to my feet. "You and I both know it doesn't matter. You've got too much invested in your relationship, and I'm a vortex of warped romantic instincts."

"Why do you talk about yourself that way?"

"I care too much about you to allow you to throw—"

"Allow me?" He stood. "Don't I get a say in my own life?"

His lips were so close I could practically taste them. His gaze darkened with fury and pain. It took all my self-control not to grab him and kiss him until the ache went away...his and mine.

Holden's phone rang, snapping us both out of the moment. He leaned over to grab the receiver.

"Holden Villalobos. Yeah. Yeah. Okay, I'll let her know."

"Everything okay?"

"That was Joan. She said forensics is ready for you." He rubbed his fingertips across his mouth.

"How did she know I was here?"

"She said she saw you come in and thought you might've come to see me."

"That's weird. Don't you think that's weird?"

"You have been gone a long time." Holden's laugh contained little humor. "People around here pay attention, Audrey. And they talk. A lot."

"All the more reason for us to be careful in how we interact."

"Got it."

His sudden iciness stung more than the heat slapping my frozen cheeks as I entered the building.

I took a step and stopped. I turned back to face him. "You know, this small-town busybody stuff could work in our favor."

"How so?" His mouth was set firm, except for the corners, which tipped down.

"I don't mean for us." I gestured between us. "I mean in this investigation. Someone must know something. Marcus had to have shared his theory with someone, right?"

"Probably." He exhaled. "We should talk to Renee."

I grimaced. "You mean you should talk to Renee."

"No, I mean, *we* should talk to Renee." He mimicked my gesture. "What are you afraid of? You think she's going to attack you right on her doorstep?"

"Possibly."

"You go do your thing. Come back when you're done, and we'll go together. She might be helpful. If she goes after you, I'll be there to protect you."

He patted my shoulder like a big brother, the romantic tension broken.

"Fine, but if she pulls out chunks of my hair, you're paying for me to get it fixed at the nicest salon in town."

Chapter Twelve

I passed Joan's desk and gave her the stink-eye for being a busybody, but if she saw it, she didn't let on.

The Chattertowne PD shared its waiting area with the passport office, so it was often filled with a combination of applicants, witnesses, and those wishing to file a complaint or report.

The chair behind the glass partition was vacant. Two female officers stood in the lobby cooing over a newborn baby in the arms of a third woman. I recognized one of the officers as Kimball.

"Sorry to interrupt. I'm here to work with the forensic sketch artist."

Kimball smiled at the baby once more before extricating herself from the group. "Audrey, right?"

"Yes."

"I'm Assistant Chief Kimball. I'm overseeing the investigation into Marcus Washburn's death."

"Yes, I remember."

"Why don't you follow me back to my office? We can chat before you meet with Dani." She entered a code into the keypad to the left of the door.

"Cute baby."

Kimball glanced over her shoulder. "Yeah, Charlotte's our receptionist, which is why we're a little short-staffed right now. Baby came early, and she'll be out on maternity leave for at least another month, maybe longer. If you know anyone looking for a temp gig with the potential to become permanent, send 'em my way."

"My sister Vivienne might be interested. She recently left her day job.

She waitresses at Nautilus, but she's looking to supplement her income."

Kimball led me into her office. Multiple plaques and awards hung on the wall. On the oak credenza behind the desk were two photos in coordinating frames, an 11x14 photo of a women's collegiate softball team at a tournament and an 8x10 faded photo of a large man in a navy-blue police uniform with his arm around a young brown-haired girl. The girl appeared to be about seven, wearing a bob haircut with straight-edge bangs and a giant smile minus its two front teeth.

"Is that you?" I squirmed and pointed at the photo of the child with the police officer. Her chairs seemed purposely designed to be uncomfortable.

Kimball glanced at the picture before returning her attention to me. "Yeah, me and my dad. He wanted a son. He got me. Your sister, is she the cute little blond thing with big gold eyes like a Margaret Keane painting? Sings once or twice a week also?"

"Yes, that's her."

I shouldn't have been surprised. Viv had caught the eye of many men, so it stood to reason she'd also grabbed women's attention. Kimball was apparently one of them, judging by the blush which had crept into her cheeks.

"She might be a good fit. Have her give me a call." She reached into her top desk drawer, pulled out a business card, and slid it across the desk.

I reached for the card and tucked it into my purse. "What did you want to ask me?"

Kimball pulled out a yellow writing pad and grabbed a pen from the black plastic cup on her desktop. "How long have you known Marcus Washburn?"

"We dated for a few months one summer back when I was in college. Nothing too serious, at least not on my end. We lost contact for quite a while. He recently attempted to reconnect online. I was hesitant, for obvious reasons. I didn't see him in person until...." My voice caught.

"Until the day he died?"

"Yes." I watched my hands fidgeting in my lap.

"What do you mean by obvious reasons?"

"I'm sorry?"

"You said you were hesitant to reconnect for obvious reasons."

"Oh! You know, ex-boyfriend…married…sometimes it's best to leave Pandora's Box closed."

I found myself staring at the photo of Kimball as a child. Had that little girl always wanted to follow in her father's footsteps, or had he pulled her onto his path?

"His wife seems to be under the impression something was going on between you. You sure you didn't meet recently for a little romantic reunion?"

My head jerked back to look at her face. "What?"

Kimball's gaze was hawkish. "Holden Villalobos mentioned you've got suspicions about Renee Washburn and suggested we look more closely at her. Funny thing, though, your name was the first out of her mouth."

"What…what did she say?"

"She said she believed you and her husband were involved in an emotionally inappropriate relationship, maybe even a physical one." Kimball scanned my face, like a human polygraph test.

"That's crazy!"

"Is it?" Kimball tilted her head.

"Yes! I was completely respectful of his marriage! He warned me she might be jealous of me, but accusing me of this is low, even for Renee."

"Why would she be jealous of you if nothing was going on?"

"She's hated me since the seventh grade, long before Marcus and I dated. By the time they got together, I lived in Portland."

"So, you've had no physical contact with him in the last few months?"

"I hadn't seen him in years until I saw him lying dead on the dock." Tears streamed from the corners of my eyes.

"There's something else."

"What?"

"A witness claims to have seen a woman matching your description acting suspiciously just prior to the discovery of Marcus's body."

"Meaning?"

"She says a woman with long dirty blonde hair was sneaking around the building."

I blinked at her three times. "Okay, first, that's rude. It's ash blonde. Second, I wasn't sneaking up on Marcus. I have aquaphobia."

"Aquaphobia." Her tone dripped with skepticism.

"It's a thing." I jutted my chin forward, feeling defensive.

"So, were you there to meet him? Marcus, I mean. A lover's rendezvous, perhaps?"

"You keep asking me the same thing, as if my answer will change. No, I was not meeting Marcus for a rendezvous, romantic or otherwise. I was running an errand for my boss, Nicholas Anderson. He asked me to go to the marina office to pay rent on his boat slip."

I could hear my shrieky tone and was reminded of

Hamlet's famous line "The Lady doth protest too much, methinks." Judging by Kimball's skeptical grimace, my defensive reaction wasn't doing me any favors in the credibility department.

"Mmm."

"You can call and ask him."

"I will. Nick and I are slip neighbors at the marina. I have a liveaboard sailboat near his Bayliner cabin cruiser. Before their divorce, he spent many nights on the boat when Peg and he would fight, which was quite often 'cause that broad is one unpleasant woman. We'd have a commiseration nightcap about our love lives, or lack thereof in my case."

Kimball spoke as though we were girlfriends sharing secrets at a slumber party, not interrogator and interrogatee. My befuddlement must have brought her back to the moment because she reared her head like it had been yanked. She pressed her palm against her chin to crack her neck before returning her laser-beam gaze to me.

"Villalobos said you received a message from the victim the day of the murder. Is that true?" Despite the phrasing, it wasn't a question but a thinly veiled accusation.

Still stinging from the affair allegations, I took a deep breath to regain control of my emotions before answering. "Yes, I sent a screenshot of the message to Holden. Didn't he give it to you?"

"No, he hasn't provided that yet. Could you send it to me directly, please?"

"Sure."

Kimball shifted her posture and tone. "Marcus's death must be difficult for you. How are you feeling?" Her concern seemed as fake as swap meet Louis Vuitton.

My brow arched, and my mouth pinched. "I'm fine. Like I said several times, Marcus and I hadn't seen each other in many years. What I'm feeling, Chief Kimball, is frustration his wife is making baseless allegations impugning my moral character and the Chattertowne police department seems to be buying it. Did it occur to you she's deflecting suspicion off herself and onto me because she had something to do with his death? If he and Renee were having problems, I was not one of them. If she has an issue with him messaging me, she's jealous without cause...on my part, at least. I can't speak for Marcus regarding what he was thinking or feeling. I'm happy to turn over his message because it will prove there was nothing going on between us, and I had zero motive to hurt him."

Kimball inclined her head to the left and stared for several long and uncomfortable moments. Uncomfortable for me, at least.

"Assistant Chief."

"What?"

"You called me Chief Kimball. I'm Assistant Chief. I do appreciate your candor, though, Ms. O'Connell. I'd like to see any DM or text messages between you and the victim. Saves me from having to get a court order."

I retrieved my phone and Kimball's business card from my purse. I opened the app, copied Marcus's message, and emailed it to the account listed on her card.

"Done." I shoved the phone and card back into my purse.

"Thank you. I'm not trying to be insensitive to your situation, but my job is to make sure whoever did this to Marcus is brought to justice. I can't leave any lead or allegation unexplored. I'm sure you understand. I'll take you to see Dani now." She stood and indicated for me to follow her down the hall to a small meeting room.

The petite woman sitting at the conference table smiled as I entered. She had chin-length black hair, dark almond-shaped eyes, and a friendly round face.

"You must be Audrey. I'm Dani Lim. Have a seat, and we'll get started."

Kimball hovered in the hallway for a bit until Dani got up to shut the door. I appreciated the subtle power move.

"So, from what I was told, you had a run-in with a potential witness or suspect to a murder?" Dani asked.

"Two, actually."

Her eyes widened. "Would you say you got a good look at the person either or both times?"

"I got a better look during our first encounter. I was paying more attention."

"Man or woman?" Dani wrote on the pad and entered something into her laptop.

"Man. He was short, I'd say five-foot-six at the most, probably in his sixties."

"Great. So, can you describe what you remember about him?"

Dani's serene demeanor gave space for the tension from my meeting with Kimball to fade and allowed memories to surface.

"Kinda like George Costanza. Short, stocky, and balding with a thick reddish-brown mustache. Whatever hair he had left on his head was straight and dark."

"I'd like to get more specific about his features."

Dani pulled out a spiral book of faces and asked me to indicate those which looked similar to what I remembered in terms of shape, nose structure, eyes, and mouth. After creating an initial sketch, she asked me for feedback in order to make adjustments. By the time we were done, we'd put together a reasonably accurate composite.

I returned to Holden's office and was about to knock when a conversation between Holden and a woman floated into the hallway. I stood outside the door for a few minutes debating what to do. Without warning, it opened, causing me to jump back.

While I'd never met the woman before, I'd seen enough photos online to recognize her long medium-brown hair and wide crystal-blue eyes.

"Oh! Hello. I didn't expect to see anyone standing there."

"Hi, you must be Emily." I extended my hand, and Emily tentatively shook it. "I'm Audrey O'Connell."

"I'm sorry, I don't recall where we've met."

"We haven't, but you graduated with my sister Vivienne."

Emily's face morphed into a friendlier demeanor. "Oh, right! I ran into Viv at dinner a couple months ago, and she mentioned you're back in Chattertowne. You've moved into her place, right?"

"I have, temporarily."

Her forehead creased like three seagulls flying above her brows. "Are you here to see Holden?"

He appeared in the doorway.

Had she conjured him merely by speaking his name?

If he was as nervous as me, he didn't show it.

"I am. Holden and I are working together in a semi-official, mostly unofficial capacity to try and figure out what happened to Marcus Washburn."

Emily glanced at him for confirmation. "You never mentioned that." Her mouth pulled at the corners.

"Sorry, that's my fault," I said. "I write for the *Current,* and I'm trying to keep my investigation under the radar. I need Holden's connections here at City Hall. Also, since we were on the scene right after it happened and, of course, we're both personally invested in finding Marcus's killer, being his friends from way back..." *The Lady doth protest.*

Holden remained mute, with his face tight.

Emily became somber. "Yes, it's sad, and scary. Makes you suspicious of your own neighbors. You never believe anything like this could happen in our small town. When it does, it's disturbing. You think you know people and then you find out you don't know them at all."

"I know exactly what you mean."

"Hey, I'd better get back to the school. My planning period's almost over. It was nice meeting you, Audrey. We should all go for drinks sometime soon." She turned to Holden. "Right, honey?"

"Uh, sure. Sounds good," he said.

Holden's expression was apologetic. Emily smiled radiantly.

"I'd love that," I lied.

"Great! We'll set it up soon. Good luck with whatever it is you two have going on."

I froze in the hallway until the elevator door closed behind Emily and then let out the breath I'd been holding.

Holden lowered his head. "Well, that was awkward."

"Ya think?"

"Let me get my coat and lock up. When we're done with Renee, I'm taking you out for a drink. Or two."

As I climbed into Holden's car, a black Lexus with tan leather interior parked in a reserved spot directly in front of City Hall, I called to him across the roof. "No wonder you're not in a rush to solve the parking problem downtown. You've got the primo spot."

He shook his head and smiled.

"Are you sure this is a good idea?" I asked. "Besides Renee thinking I had an affair with her husband and accusing me of being involved in his murder, aren't we interfering with an active police investigation? Could we get into trouble with Kimball?"

"Maybe."

I stared at him. "How can you be blasé about this?"

"I can only control what I can control. No use being stressed about what I can't control. I'm going to pay my respects to my friend's widow. As unpleasant as she can be, I'm not afraid of her, and you shouldn't be either." He backed onto the street, driving east on Main.

"Easy for you to say. Even if she did hate you, which she has no reason to, you could choke her out with those biceps. If she goes after me, I'm toast. Yesterday, I had to use both hands to lift a laundry detergent bottle."

Holden laughed and turned the car onto Madeleine Avenue. "First, I don't believe that. Second, I told you I'm not going to let her hurt you, and I only make promises I know I can keep."

We pulled in front of the old gray saltbox house, and my chest constricted with anxiety.

Its peeling paint and mildewed exterior indicated neglect and the need for a good pressure wash. Window boxes overflowed with dead, frozen greenery–or, more accurately, brownery–and it was difficult to discern from a distance whether they were plants or weeds.

Back when Marcus and I had dated, the house hadn't been in significantly better condition. With his father gone and his mom a hot mess, Marcus was the man of the house from a very young age. He'd mowed the lawn and performed basic handyman duties, but with little money and no help, the home was difficult to maintain. Every once in a while, his mom broke free from her fog long enough to plant flowers or rake leaves. It had never lasted, though.

"Marcus once told me this house was the original Chatterton house, the one where Jonathan lived with his wife before the officially recognized Chatterton house was built. He was adamant about it. Of course, at the time I had no idea how prone to wild speculation and wacky theories he was."

Holden looked at the house. "Interesting. It certainly looks old enough to be, but I'm sure the historical society would've been all over it if that were true." He pulled the parking brake. "Ready?"

"Nope." I gripped the door handle.

He reached over to grasp my free hand and squeezed his reassurance. "Audrey, look at me."

His kind, brown eyes warmed various parts of me.

"I'm here with you."

I managed a weak smile.

He squeezed my hand again. "How many times do I have to tell you I'm not going to let anything happen to you?"

"Probably a few more." I inhaled an exaggerated breath and opened the door. "Okay. Let's go."

Holden came around to help me out of the car. He dropped my hand, and an involuntary whimper escaped my throat in protest. When we reached the stoop, he opened the torn screen door and knocked twice.

"Did you tell her we were coming?" I whispered.

"I told her I was coming." His words came through clenched teeth.

I jerked my head to look at him with my mouth agape, but he stared straight ahead.

The door creaked open, and Renee's face appeared. Her hair was disheveled and bleached of pigment except for three inches of dark roots, either the result of neglect or a poor DIY attempt at ombre. Although she was my age, she could have passed for ten years older. Her skin sagged from her face and neck, a tell-tale sign of dramatic weight loss. She wore sweats, no makeup, and no shoes. Her sweatshirt was pistachio green accented with a coffee stain down the front.

She looked at Holden before shifting her attention to me. Her expression hardened with recognition. "What the hell is she doing here?"

I opened my mouth to speak, but Holden stepped forward to block Renee's view of me.

"Renee, Audrey, and I came to offer our sincerest condolences. Do you mind if we come in for a moment to talk?"

"I don't want that little homewrecker anywhere near me." She threw a blistering glance around him, growling her words at me.

"Please, Renee, let us in. I assure you, there's been a misunderstanding regarding Audrey's relationship with Marcus."

"I read his message to her with my own two eyes. He wanted her back, and she was going to steal my man!" She let the screen door slam in our faces.

"I wasn't!" I stood on my tippy toes and peeked over Holden's shoulder. "Renee, nothing was going on with Marcus and me. Let us in, and we'll explain everything. We're trying to find his killer, and we think you may have answers which will help us do that."

Renee contemplated briefly before reopening the door. Something I'd said had apparently penetrated her anger enough to pique her curiosity.

"You can have five minutes; then I want that hussy out of my house."

Holden motioned for me to enter. I shook my head, unwilling to go in without that strong man between my face and the woman who wanted to rip it off. He gave an exasperated sigh and entered the home.

Random junk littered every surface of the living room. Stale cigarette smoke permeated the constricted space, which was made even smaller by the volume of furniture, laundry, and toys. The place looked like an episode of *Hoarders.* My esophagus convulsed at the sight of what might've once been a bowl of oatmeal or maybe mac and cheese. On the filthy beige-ish carpet, a little boy—about four, with matted brown hair and a grimy face—played with Matchbox cars on a track.

"I've sent the other kids to stay with my mom for a little while. I'm taking this one to my sister's tonight." She flicked her hand to indicate the child. "I can't bear to have them see me such a mess."

I crouched to look the boy straight in the face. He bore a strong resemblance to his father, with his amber eyes laced with long thick lashes and freckles sprinkled across his nose. Renee's tender gaze was on her son. Her expression hardened again as soon as she looked at me.

"Five minutes." Renee crossed her arms in front of sagging breasts, obviously not supported by a bra. She turned to the boy and barked, "Xander, go play in your room."

Her harsh tone startled both Xander and me. He jumped up and scurried down the hall with three toy cars gripped in his tiny hands.

There was no space to sit on the sofa, which wasn't a disappointment. My skin crawled, imagining what inhabited the space between the cushions. Mounds of clothing were piled high. Whether clean or dirty, it was unclear. A leopard-print bra with cups large enough to cap my head hung by a strap from atop the heap. I suppressed my desire to offer it to Renee.

Everyone remained standing, an awkward circle swirling with tension amidst what looked like a tornado debris field.

"Renee, we're both deeply sorry for your loss. I know you have questions about Audrey and Marcus and their friendship. I've read his message myself, and I believe her when she says nothing was going on between them."

Renee scoffed. "Don't let her fool you. He still had a thing for her, and she was gonna take him from me, from his family." Heartbreak flashed across her face before being replaced with scorn. Her arms tightened across her chest. "Maybe she did take him away. Maybe she killed him!"

I straightened my back. "I had no interest in Marcus in any romantic way, Renee, and I definitely didn't kill him. I made every effort to be respectful of you and your family. He reached out to me for help, and I hadn't yet responded. I wish I *had* talked to him, maybe then we'd have a better idea who did this and why." I held my breath, anticipating a wrathful response. It didn't come.

Renee's skepticism faded to resignation. Her shoulders slumped, and her stance relaxed. Still, she directed her comments only to Holden. "You said you needed information from me. What do you wanna know?" The fatigue of loss showed in her eyes.

She uncrossed her arms and crumpled onto the pile of clothing at the far end of the sofa, the one with frayed terrycloth towels and washcloths permanently marred by remnants of heavy facial makeup and mascara. A mauve towel fell off the pile and onto the floor, possibly stained with rust. Or blood. I tried to draw Holden's attention to the possibly bloody towel, but my telepathy was unsuccessful.

How could I ferret the towel with the mysterious spots out of the house without Renee noticing?

"Renee, what do you know about Marcus's assertions in his blog about the Chatterton family, his dad, and his birthright?" Holden asked in a gentle tone.

"You mean all that conspiracy stuff?" She scrunched her nose in disdain. "Hell, I don't know. He'd get drunk and spout these silly things his mom told him. She was a meth head before being a meth head was a thing. How do you put stock in the ramblings of a thirty-year addict? I kept telling him he was chasing the wind. He insisted he was onto something which would change our lives forever, in a good way, for once. Promised he'd get me a big house on the hill. I wanted to believe him, but I knew deep down he was crazy."

"What if he wasn't crazy?" My words were hushed and tentative, heavy with apprehension. I feared just speaking to her might unleash a torrent of hatred.

Renee's focus cut to me like the velociraptor in *Jurassic Park*. "What do you mean?"

It was the first time since we'd arrived she'd addressed me directly.

"I'm writing a feature for Kupit. I found a connection between Marcus's blog and the story I'm investigating. Has Marcus ever mentioned a woman named Nettie?"

"Was he having an affair with *her*?"

"No. Nettie was an early Chattertowne resident. She cared for Jonathan Chatterton's son after his wife Madeleine passed away," I explained.

The only sound was the distant click-clacking of matchbox cars racing on a track.

"I guess the name's vaguely familiar, but I can't place it. He was always ranting, and it got to the point I'd tune him out." Renee's face filled with grief and regret.

"The day before his death, Marcus posted a blog about Nettie. The link seems to be broken. Is there any chance he had a backup copy somewhere in here or notes?" Holden waved his hands, indicating the chaos around us.

"I'd have to go digging through his office. It's a complete mess in there. He was such a slob. It'll take some time."

I restrained a guffaw. Had she not seen the room in which we were standing?

"It might help. If you find anything, please call me." He handed her a business card he'd pulled from his wallet. "Renee, Marcus loved you. The last time we met for drinks, he couldn't stop talking about how lucky he was."

I squinted to scan his face for evidence regarding his statement's veracity.

"We don't want to keep you," he continued. "But please give me a call if you need anything at all."

Renee nodded but didn't make eye contact with him. We all murmured our goodbyes.

Holden crooked his head toward his car. "Come on. Let's go get that drink I promised you."

Chapter Thirteen

Holden drove across the valley to a French bistro perched at the edge of diminutive Lake Camora. The hostess seated us next to a picture window with a view of the water, a man-made pond with an overly grand name.

"Are you okay to be this close to the water?" Holden asked me.

"Yeah, I don't mind looking at it through windows."

He draped his napkin in his lap. "So, how are you feeling about how today went?"

"Which part? When my ex-boyfriend's wife called me a hussy, or when I had to sit through the Spanish Inquisition by the Chattertowne PD? Or maybe you're wondering how I feel about the fiancée of a man I nearly kissed a few nights ago inviting me to hang out with them for funzies?"

Holden sharply inhaled. "Audrey, I get this isn't easy on you. Guess what? It's not easy on me, either. One." He ticked each point off on his fingers. "My friend is dead. Two, I've got responsibilities to the citizens of this town and to my family, and I feel like I'm utterly failing everyone. Three, I've got a complicated relationship with Emily, which has been made even more complicated now because of my relationship with, four, *you*. That's just the tip of the iceberg. You have no idea the stress I'm under. It's already coming from multiple sides. I don't need it from you, too."

The waitress arrived at our table with a smile, oblivious to the conversation she'd interrupted. "Bonjour. What can I get for you two this afternoon?"

Holden gestured for me to order first.

"I'll have the quiche and a Bloody Mary."

"That sounds good. I like quiche. I'll have the same, but just a water for me."

The waitress nodded at him and took our menus.

"So, we have quiche in common." Holden shrugged his shoulders.

"Quiche is a good unifier," I agreed.

"What do you think about our conversation with Renee? Anything stand out to you?" he asked.

"I don't think she knows anything. No one took what he said seriously, not even his own wife. Now, in her state of grief, to go back and try to remember something helpful or significant among all his other ramblings, it's a tough task."

I frowned, remembering how Renee used defensiveness as a shield for her pain and managed to muster some compassion for her.

"You survived the encounter." He smirked and arched his brow in an I-told-you-so manner.

"Barely. You didn't happen to notice the towel with what looked to be blood stains on it, did you?"

Holden pulled his brows together. "Bloodstains? Are you sure?"

"I mean, I guess it could have been rust or chocolate."

"Was it a lot?"

"No. I wouldn't say so."

"Then let's presume it's not blood for the time being. So, what's our next move?" He gulped his water without breaking eye contact, staring at me over the brim.

"I don't know about your next move, but I'm going to ambush Peter Chatterton. I believe he knows something."

Holden sputtered, coughing from inhaled water. "I should go with you." He wiped his chin with his napkin.

"You don't need to do that. You have a job to do, and I–" My words were cut off by my phone buzzing. I glanced at the screen.

"Who is it?"

"Darren."

"You should answer it." His blinking slowed, and his gaze bored into me.

I connected the call and put the phone to my ear. "Hello?"

"Audrey, it's Darren."

"I know. Your number's programmed into my phone."

"Listen, can you come by my house? I'd like to talk."

"I guess that would be okay. Text me your address. I'm in a meeting right now, but I could be at your place by seven thirty."

"Perfect. I'll see you in a bit."

I disconnected the call. "He wants to see me, to talk."

"I heard." There was a bite to his words.

"I'm just going to talk to him. You don't have to worry."

He shook his head. "I don't have the right to worry, even if I was worried."

I sighed. "Why won't you just tell me what you want?" My fingers toyed with the napkin draped across my lap, my gaze heavy with shame and embarrassment over the desperation in my voice.

"I just…I can't. Talking about my feelings has never been something I'm comfortable with. Not with anyone."

"What about Emily?"

"Nope."

"Never?"

"Emily and I were friends for a long time before we started seeing each other. I wasn't in a great place, and she was there for me. I wouldn't be where I am today without her support. I've just never been one for overt expression of emotion, and she's accepted that about me."

"How'd you get engaged, then?"

"She went out with her girlfriends one night. They must have gotten into her head because she came home and gave me an ultimatum to either move the relationship forward or end it. I wasn't ready to end it."

"Is it that you don't have the feelings, or you just don't like to talk about them?"

"I'm not a robot, Audrey. I have feelings, I just prefer to keep them compartmentalized and controlled."

"You think by locking up your feelings you can't ever get hurt?"

"When people let you down, a self-protective instinct kicks in. I guess somewhere along the line; I decided this was the only way to survive." His full mouth pulled further downward, and I fought the urge to leap across the table to kiss it.

"Holden, I have something to tell you, and I want you to prepare yourself, because it may come as a shock."

"What's that?"

"This entire conversation has consisted of you opening up about not being comfortable talking about your feelings. In discussing how you're incapable of being vulnerable…you've been completely vulnerable."

He smiled and shook his head. "You're right. And now I have to kill you." His smile was devilish.

"Totally inappropriate under the circumstances, but thank you for sharing with me. It means a lot."

He peeked at me from under heavy lids. "It should. I guess I feel safe with you."

"I'd never hurt you."

He gazed at me for a long time before responding. "I know you believe that, Audrey. Everyone always does."

Just before seven-thirty, I pulled my car through Darren's gate, which he'd left open for me. Long and straight, with lantern posts lining each side, the driveway curved in front of the house. I parked behind his black BMW.

With two vaulted stories, the home featured a large portico arched over solid mahogany front doors flanked by sculpted boxwood topiaries. Brick flower beds, empty for the winter, bordered an expansive lawn.

In my car, I willed my nerves to subside. I blew a stray hair from my face, fixed my makeup in the visor mirror, and checked my text messages.

Vivienne had messaged to thank me for putting in a good word for her with Kimball. They'd already spoken on the phone and done a preliminary interview which Viv felt had gone pretty well.

I looked at the house again. "Please, let this not be the final nail in the coffin of an already craptacular day." I took a deep breath and opened my car door. Snowflakes drifted down, validating my earlier winter weather prediction. That one atmospheric science class I took (but barely passed) in college was finally paying off.

Darren appeared on the front porch and ushered me into the grand foyer.

"I was starting to wonder if you were going to stay in your car all night."

"It was warm, and I was dreading the cold," I lied. "Holy moly. You can't buy this on a small-town newspaper salary. You can't even rent it."

He threw back a faux humble chuckle of the wealthy. "Family money. Come on; I have pasta and Bolognese sauce going. Hungry?"

The quiche was still digesting, and nerves had sapped the remainder of my appetite. "Uh, sure. Yeah, sounds great." White lie number two.

Darren led me into a large chef's kitchen, where a bottle of Merlot sat on the counter. He uncorked the bottle and poured the wine into a crystal decanter labeled with an Irish Waterford sticker.

"Have to let it breathe a bit."

"I don't usually drink red, so I doubt I'd notice the difference."

"Oh, you'll be able to taste the difference, even if you aren't certain why. It really opens up the flavors." He lifted the lid from the simmering pot on to cooktop. "Mmm, so good. You're going to love this."

He grabbed two glasses by their stems in one hand, and with the other, he picked up the decanter. He jerked his head. "Follow me."

"Can I help you?"

"Nope," he called over his shoulder.

We proceeded through the family room, a cozy area with overstuffed slipper chairs in blue and cream colonial striped fabric surrounding a large fireplace with a stately American cherry mantle. The next room, an atrium with large windows and tropical plants, was muggy despite fluffy snowflakes falling just on the other side of the glass. A gray wicker sofa topped with a thick smoky-blue cushion and cream linen throw pillows fringed in woven seagrass was the centerpiece, flanked by matching glass-topped wicker tables. In front of the settee was a coordinated coffee table, also in gray wicker, with a glass overlay. The only decorative items were a Wedgewood vase containing dried white hydrangeas and a coffee table book featuring lighthouses.

"This is my favorite room in the house. These door panels fully open to the backyard and pool area."

"It's beautiful."

"Sit, please, and I'll pour the wine."

I sank into the plush cushion. My inherent klutziness made red wine and white pillows a particularly bad combo. Darren poured the ruby liquid into a wide-mouthed goblet until it was about a quarter-full. He handed it to me and poured it into his own glass.

"Thank you for coming tonight, Audrey. I really didn't like the way our last conversation went, and I despise loose ends."

"I appreciate your wanting to talk and clear the air. I didn't particularly enjoy the conversation either."

He swirled his wine. "When my mom, Maddie, got sick, I felt helpless. Having money convinces a person they're insulated from tragedy, but no amount of money could've saved her. Sure, it gave us access to treatments and facilities the average person couldn't afford, but in the end, it didn't matter. Since then, I find myself constantly in a state of risk assessment and aversion." He paused to sip. "I'm sorry I got mad the other day. I know I come across as controlling. Whether you realize it or not, that's my way of trying to protect you."

"I'm pretty self-sufficient. I hope in the future you'll give me a little more credit." I pursed my lips.

"I'll try, but it's important to me you know where I'm coming from. Often the way things land, well, I know my approach can lead to my intentions being misconstrued.

"It goes to show how messed-up things can get when there's a communication failure. Like today, for example."

He crooked his head. "What happened today?"

"I went to see Renee Washburn." I drank a sip of the merlot, pulled the glass back, and swirled it. "Huh. That's surprisingly good."

His jaw clenched and released. "I thought she hated you."

"Who? Oh, Renee? She does, she did. I don't know; she's at least willing to engage in conversation with me now."

Darren blinked rapidly. "Conversation about what?"

"Holden and I–"

"Holden Villalobos?" Clench.

"Yes. We went to talk to Renee this afternoon to give our condolences and ask some questions. The Washburn place was an absolute mess, by the way, as was she. I don't think she's showered since the day Marcus died."

"What questions?" Clench.

"Questions about Marcus and who might've wanted him dead. We're hoping there's information hidden somewhere in the house, but that place was disgusting." I took a large slug of the merlot. "I really like this. It's warm and smooth, without any bitterness.

"Information on what?"

"Huh? I gotta say, I don't usually drink red wine, but this is delicious. Did I say that already? I think I did." I smiled at him. "Oh, shoot. I hope my teeth aren't purple. Are my teeth purple?" I bared my teeth.

Darren sighed and shook his head. "You said you hoped there might be information in their house. What information?"

"Whatever prompted all the wild claims Marcus made on his blog."

"Wild claims?" Clench.

"About the Chattertons. Ooh. I'm a lightweight. I'm starting to feel a little foggy." I put my fingertips to my temple.

"Do you believe there's any truth to these claims?"

His eyes had deepened to sapphire in the dim light. A shock of hair fell into his face, and I fought the urge to tuck it behind his ear.

"You're cute, you know that?"

He blinked.

"Hard to say about those whacky theories. He's dead, so there's that. By the way, Darren, this is probably the best wine I've ever had. I said that already, didn't I?"

"Were you there when I called you? Was that the meeting you were in?" He used aggressive air quotes when he said the word meeting.

"No, we'd left Renee's about forty-five minutes prior to your call." I shifted on the sofa, which wasn't as comfortable as when I'd first sat. The cushions no longer felt plush but claustrophobic. The temperature in the room rose in contrast to the snow piling on the outer windowsills. I fanned my face to cool the warmth spreading upward from my neck.

"What I meant was, were you there with Holden? When I called, were you with him?"

"We grabbed a bite to eat to discuss our conversation with Renee." I fanned my face more intensely. "It's warm in here. Does it feel warm in here to you?"

Darren glowered. "Your face does look a bit flushed. You seem... uncomfortable. Why don't you go to the powder room and grab a cool washcloth while I check on the sauce." He left without waiting for a response. It was a command, not a suggestion.

Setting my glass on the table, I struggled to hoist myself off the sofa. When I got to the living room, Darren stood at the stove glaring into the Bolognese pot. I cleared my throat to get his attention, and he lifted his head.

"Am I going the right way?"

"Keep going and turn right. It'll be down the hall on the left."

I followed his directions and found myself in a long corridor. Glossy white wainscoting lined the hallway, an elegant accent to the dusky-blue walls and precisely hung mahogany-framed family portraits.

The first photo featured Darren with his parents. About fifteen or sixteen at the time, Darren bore a striking likeness to his father, handsome and polished with those same piercing blue eyes. His mother had coloring similar to mine, although her ashy blonde hair was paired with crystal blue eyes.

The next photo was the trio at his graduation from MIT. Darren beamed with the optimistic excitement of someone ready to take on the world.

Several of the other photos appeared to have been taken at large family reunions. In the six months I'd known him, he'd never mentioned any relatives other than his parents.

Itchiness on my neck and face cut my snooping short. I clawed at my skin, which elicited nearly orgasmic relief. I opened the powder room door and turned on the light to illuminate my reflection.

111

"Oh, my gawd!"

"Audrey? What's wrong?"

Darren found me staring in horror at the mirror. Red splotches and white welts covered my neck and face.

"Hey, Audrey." His sarcasm dripped like venom. "Any chance you're allergic to red wine?"

Chapter Fourteen

Three hours and a whole lot of Benadryl later, I was released from the ER. I came out to the waiting room where my worried sister and sort-of-date were sitting.

"How are you?" Darren rubbed the back of his neck.

"Exhausted. Hey, Viv, thanks for coming."

She rose to give me a hug. "Was this payback for the drowning thing? Don't ever scare me like that again!"

My feeble laugh was lost in my sister's hair. "I'll try not to."

"What did the doctor say?" Darren's face sagged, his shoulders slumped, and his eyes were red with dark circles.

"He said I was lucky, but next time I might not be. Even though this initial reaction was hives, the second exposure can be deadly. I guess my juvenile penchant for sweet whites has been saving my life all these years." I gave a self-deprecating laugh.

Darren's frown deepened. "Audrey, I…" He struggled to find his words. "I'm sorry. If I'd known, I'd never…."

I rested my hand on his forearm. "It's not your fault."

"Your car's still at my house." He ran his hand stiffly through his hair and shuffled his feet on the tile floor.

"I'll bring her by in the morning." Viv turned to me. "Do you have your keys?"

"Yeah, they're in my purse."

"Double check."

She held out her hand like a schoolmarm who'd caught me passing notes or chewing gum. She was taking a page from my own playbook.

"Is this really necessary?"

She gestured with her fingers like Bruce Lee telling an opponent to bring it on. I sighed in resignation and dug around until I located them at the bottom, along with a foil gum wrapper, a Chapstick missing its lid, and a hairband knotted with flaxen strands. Vivienne picked through the garbage in my palm, plucked the keys, and jerked her head toward the parking lot. She was attempting to control the situation, but her petite stature tempered her ability to intimidate.

I turned to Darren. Our dinner conversation not only hadn't ended on a high note, it hadn't even included dinner.

"Thank you for all your efforts tonight, for getting me to the hospital, and for staying here to wait for me. Sorry about the Bolognese."

"I couldn't let you die of anaphylactic shock in my bathroom. Will I see you in the office tomorrow?"

"I'll be there in the morning and then I planned to go see a guy about a knife around noon." I yawned, the Benadryl taking effect.

"What guy? What knife?"

"Peter Chatterton donated a knife to the museum that was his great, great, uh great? Grandfather's. I think. Or was it great, great, great, great, great, great…" My words slurred.

"Alright, time to get you home." Vivienne placed her arm around my shoulders.

As she led me away, I feebly waved in Darren's direction.

"That was…weird," she said, opening the door for me.

The Benadryl had fully kicked in, leaving me groggy and confused. "What was weird?"

"What he just said to you. Under what circumstances would he let someone suffering an allergic reaction die in his bathroom?"

I squinted at my sister, rapidly losing the battle to stay conscious. "I don't think he meant it that way. He's a nice guy, he just has mommy issues."

Vivienne grunted. "Seems to be a pattern with you."

As I succumbed to the drowsiness, my final thought was unfortunately, she was right.

The buzzing on the nightstand was like a jackhammer to my throbbing head. I accidentally knocked the phone onto the floor and, as I stretched to grab it, toppled over the side of the bed. I answered without looking to see who it was.

"Hello?"

"What's going on over there? Are you doing jumping jacks? You sound like you're dying." It was Holden.

"Didn't you hear? I almost did."

"What do you mean?" His tone went from playful to serious.

"Turns out I'm allergic to red wine. Or something in red wine. LBT? No. LGBT? No, that's definitely not it. And I know it's not BLT." I giggled.

"Audrey!"

"Hey now, chill! I had a long night, and my head is killing me."

"I'll chill when you tell me what happened. Did Darren hurt you?"

"No! Well, not on purpose, anyway. Things were going okay at first. He talked about his mom and how losing her turned him into a control freak. He got strangely intense when I told him about going to see Renee, although it was hard to tell whether he was mad about that or you being there with me. He doesn't like you much, I don't think." I yawned and stretched my arms over my head, cradling the phone between my cheek and shoulder.

"The feeling's mutual. Tell me about the dying part, please."

I managed to lift myself off the floor and stumble into the kitchen, where I turned on the coffee maker. "Well, he opened a bottle of Merlot to go with the pasta he was making."

"Wine, huh, and he cooks?"

"Yes. Are you jealous?"

Holden laughed. "Not at all. Trust me; I can cook."

"Prove it."

"Oh, I will." His smile was nearly audible through the phone. "Audrey, for a journalist, you sure have a tough time getting to the climax." He gasped and chortled. "Of the story! I meant the climax of the story."

"You did that on purpose."

"I swear, it just came out."

"Wait! I got it. TPT! Shoot, no. LTP! I think that's it. It's a protein in grape skin. I don't react to white wine because it's made without the skins. Red wine is fermented with the skins. Anyway, the next thing I know, I'm roasting. My face is on fire. I thought I was just uncomfortable with his questioning. Nope, full-blown hives outbreak."

Holden paused a beat. "I'm not gonna lie; I'm kinda glad you had an allergic reaction to your date."

"Rude. I'm not allergic to him. Besides, it wasn't exactly a date."

"Audrey, he invited you to his house, made you dinner, and broke out the wine. It was a date."

I grabbed a mug from the cupboard, popped a cup into the machine, and pressed the brew button. "Things were already going south before my face turned the color of a stewed tomato."

"What do you think his objection might be to your talking with Renee? I understand him being unhappy about spending time with me, but she's your ex's widow who also isn't your biggest fan."

I grabbed creamer from the fridge and poured in significantly more than one serving.

"That's putting it mildly. I thought it was odd, too, but I guess my involvement in a murder case freaks him out, and he's worried about my safety. The other day he got upset because I'd left my phone in the car and had missed several calls and texts from him. Frankly, I'm surprised he didn't insist on staying here last night to keep an eye on me while I slept." Leaning against the counter, I took a tentative sip. "Although, I doubt Viv would have let him. She's not his biggest fan either."

"I knew I liked that girl." He paused. "Do you have protection?"

"Excuse me?" I sputtered and choked on my coffee.

"I swear, I'm not purposely dropping the double entendres."

"Would you care to clarify, then?"

"I meant protection, as in a gun."

"No, I don't have one, haven't ever touched a real one. I'd probably shoot myself in the foot."

I purposely neglected to mention my father had tried to teach me to shoot a BB gun when I was seven. The kick-back had caused my arms to flail, my index finger to grab the trigger, and BBs to rain upon us. That day I'd learned several curse words and experienced my first silent treatment. I'd never gone near anything resembling a gun since.

"I don't blame Benson for being worried about your safety. I'd feel a lot better if I knew you could defend yourself. Barring putting you under police protection, or having me stay with you, getting you trained to shoot is the best way. Although, it seems you're more a threat to yourself than anything."

"I'd be offended if I didn't know how true that statement is. Taking the night shift to keep an eye on me while I sleep wouldn't go over well with your fiancée, I suppose."

He ignored the bait. "What's your schedule today?"

"Viv's gonna drop me off at my car, which is still at Darren's house, then I'm headed to the office for a bit. I thought I'd drive to Peter's house around lunchtime."

"Does he know you're coming?"

"I figured catching him off-guard might give me an advantage in getting my foot in the door."

Holden grumbled to himself. "I want to go with you, but I have a meeting from ten until two. I don't like the idea of you going there alone."

"I'll be fine. He's just a grouchy old rich dude, right?"

"Call me as soon as you're done. I'll have my phone on silent, so you won't be interrupting anything. Even if I don't answer, leave me a voicemail to let me know you're okay. I'll take you to the gun range after my meeting."

"I can't imagine I'm gonna like it."

"You'll never know until you try."

"Are we still talking about guns?"

"Don't forget to call when you leave Peter's."

I gripped the steering wheel as I drove out of town under a bright midday sky. Sunlight glinted off icy patches, but a trough of artic wind blew south

117

from the Fraser River Valley, keeping temperatures well below freezing. The roads were mostly bare and wet, but I'd had enough encounters with black ice not to trust my eyes. Fresh snow blanketed cluttered yards, giving a pristine cloak to rusty vehicles which had stopped functioning long before.

After I'd gotten off the phone with Holden that morning, I'd rousted Viv out of bed so she could drive me to Darren's to pick up my car.

She was scheduled for an in-person interview that afternoon with Kimball for the temporary receptionist job. I'd contemplated telling Viv I suspected Kimball harbored a crush on her but had decided against it. If I was right, she'd figure it out on her own.

I'd spent the morning catching up on work that had fallen through the cracks. My contributions for the week were written, proofed, and emailed to Anderson. Phone calls to neglected advertisers were returned with an abundant sweet-talking. I'd missed a voicemail from the Jewish senior center requesting me to cover their widows' luncheon the following afternoon. After calling to confirm I'd be there, I entered it into *The Current's* shared online work calendar. Anderson liked to have visibility on our schedules in case something came up and he needed to get someone to cover a story.

Dani, the forensic artist, had emailed a copy of the sketch and asked me to make certain I was confident about its accuracy before it got passed on to CPD. I responded it was probably as close as we would get. I forwarded the sketch to Mildred, asking if she knew who the man was. I asked her to call me or Holden if she could identify him. I considered sending it to Holden but figured Kimball would send him the official version.

My Volvo climbed the slushy hill with little protest, and I was grateful my dad had talked me into getting all-wheel drive. "Linger" by the Cranberries lilted from my speakers, with intermittent interruptions from my nav. Dolores and I belted out the second chorus together, but I was left hanging when my phone rang.

"Hello?"

"Hi, may I speak to Audrey O'Connell, please?" The throaty voice carried a military cadence.

"Yes, Chief Kimball, it's me."

"I wanted to thank you for recommending your sister for the job. I did a phone interview with her yesterday evening, and she's coming in for a face-to-face in about an hour. It's looking promising." She sounded as giddy as a no-nonsense cop could be and didn't even correct me about calling her Chief instead of Assistant Chief.

"That's great. I'm glad it sounds like it's going to work out."

"It's against my better judgment to hire a relative of a murder suspect, but I did speak with Nick Anderson, and he verified he'd sent you down to make his slip payment. I also spoke with Gunita at the marina office, who corroborated your arrival time. Unfortunately for you, it doesn't clear you completely. The TOD could have taken place between your leaving the paper and arriving at the marina. It does, however, narrow the window enough for me to consider you unlikely to be the perpetrator."

"That's a relief, I guess. Was that the only thing you were calling about? I'm getting ready to head into a meeting."

"Dani sent over the sketch. She said you believe it's an accurate representation, is that correct?"

"As good as it can be."

"And do you recognize the man?" she asked.

"No. Hopefully, somebody does. Are you planning to send a copy to Holden?"

"Why would I do that?"

"He and I have been kind of working together on figuring all this out. He may recognize the guy. I was gonna forward him the copy I got this morning, but I figured as City Manager, he'd be getting the official version."

"Ms. O'Connell, I suggest you muster a bit of gratitude about the fact I've all but cleared you of this murder. Stay in your lane, and let me do my job."

"We're all trying to accomplish the same goal, to find Marcus's killer."

"If you interfere with or impede my investigation, it will not turn out well for you. In fact, I will take that to be a sign you have something to hide. You and Mr. Villalobos need to back off. Have I made myself clear?"

I didn't enjoy being chastised. "Gotcha."

I disconnected the call as my car neared the highest point of the hill where homes were larger and spaced farther apart. From that vantage point, the entire valley was visible, and beyond was a peekaboo view of Puget Sound.

Towering western hemlocks, pines, aspen, and a few interspersed cottonwood trees shrouded the road which still had stretches of snow and ice which had yet to melt. I turned into a lengthy steep driveway, at the end of which the sun shone upon a large single-story modern home with vaulted ceilings and an unobstructed view.

A rocky half-wall separated the front of the property from the rear yard which dropped off like an infinity edge to the snow-covered valley below. Emerald arborvitae shrubs waved their welcome, and I hoped their owner would be as hospitable. Beyond the valley, the white-topped Olympic Mountains rose high in the west while ominous storm clouds hovered above the churning Puget Sound. I reassured myself it wasn't an omen, just typical winter weather.

What must it have been like for the Coast Salish People to stand on this ridge, observing strangers infiltrate their land? Were they curious? Fearful? Angry? I turned to face the home of Jonathan's descendent. Had Peter, living in his mansion enjoying the spoils of his family's appropriation, ever thought about them? Did he care at all?

The slate path was lined with large boulders and shrubs leading to the porch. From somewhere inside, a bloodhound warbled along with the doorbell chimes. A shadow passed the frosted windows, and I prepared my most congenial face. The door opened to reveal a short, thickset man with a balding head and russet walrus-like mustache. My mouth went dry, and my blood ran cold.

Chapter Fifteen

"Y ou lost?"

As I stood face-to-face with the parking spot thief, my mind screamed "run," but my feet were leaden.

"Are you stupid?" Peter's disparagement jolted me from my daze.

"Uh, no, I'm not lost." I offered an unsteady hand. "My name is Audrey O'Connell. I apologize for arriving unannounced. I'm doing a feature on Chattertowne and the Kupit Festival for the *Coastal Current*. I was hoping you might be willing to give insight into your family's history."

My hand hung in the air. Peter's remained at his side. Both my hand and smile faltered. He brusquely gestured for me to enter. Kimball's warnings to not interfere with the investigation rang in my mind, but there was little I could do at that point other than let the scenario play itself out.

Few items adorned the walls. There was minimal color and even less warmth. The windows, however, were panoramic.

"Your view is extraordinary."

"After a while, you get used to it."

His oversized leather recliner was heavily weathered and appeared to be the only item not meticulously cared for, although perhaps he rarely got visitors, leaving the other furniture barely used.

He waved his hand at the espresso leather sectional which faced the fireplace, and I took that as an invitation to sit. Above the mantle, a framed map of St. Andrew's Golf Course hung next to a single wooden antique club mounted diagonally onto tartan plaid fabric. Hooks to mount a crosswise club were empty.

"Very cool." I indicated the showpiece.

He glanced up at it, did a double take, and grumbled an unintelligible response. Perched on the sofa's edge, I pulled my notepad from my satchel with trembling hands.

"In the library archives, I came across the knife you donated, the one which used to belong to your great grandfather Jonathan."

"My three-times great grandfather."

"Right. The Chattertons have an amazing legacy, and I could write about your family based on previously published documents. However, I was hoping to get an insider perspective. Say, for example, if there are any untold stories."

Peter's scowl deepened, his face more clearly resembling the man who'd nearly knocked me down on the docks. "Are you trying to dig up dirt on my family? Is that what this is, a hit piece? Another shakedown?" His voice rose an octave and several decibels. He leaned forward, his stubby hairy index finger pointing at me. At least his fingernails looked clean. "You workin' with that Veracitater or whatever the hell he calls himself?"

My eyes widened at his mention of Marcus. "No, like I said, I'm a feature writer for the *Coastal Current*." Digging through my bag for ID and locating it at the bottom, I thrust it toward him, my hands trembling. Adhered to the back was a neon pink reminder to buy tampons. I yanked the note and crumpled it.

He snatched the lanyard from my outstretched hand, examined both sides and raised his head to look at me. "What do you want? What are you after?"

"Marcus Washburn, er, uh, the Veracitater. Did he contact you?"

Peter's features were so tight his face practically collapsed in upon itself. "Yeah, he called me a while back after that tweaker mom of his died. He was ramblin' on about some garbage that woman told him. I told him she was crazy, and so was he for believing her, but he wouldn't drop it."

"Is that what you meant by another shakedown? Was he attempting to blackmail you?"

"He wasn't blackmailin' me, but he was makin' outrageous claims about what he believed he was owed from me and my family, and there were threats involved."

"I'm pretty sure that's the exact definition of extortion."

"It's all rubbish! Whatever proof he thought he had woulda never held up in court."

"Did he—" I hesitated, but at that point, I had nothing to lose. "Did he ask you about Nettie?"

Peter's hooded eyes sharpened like a falcon eying its prey. "What'd you say your name was again?"

"Audrey O'Connell." My voice came out strong despite my fear, instilling just enough bravado in me to believe I might be able to make it out of there...and not on a gurney.

"You from around these parts? Is your family?"

He was probing, but for what I couldn't determine.

"I was raised in Chattertowne. My dad came to the area for college, met my mom, and never left. My mom's family's been here for...well, forever, I guess. Probably since not long after Jonathan arrived."

"What's your mom's name? Who are her people? Tell me their names."

"I don't see what that has to do with—"

"Humor me."

"My mom's maiden name was Bristow."

Bristow," he repeated. "And?"

"And what?"

"Who else?"

"I don't know. What is this, an episode of *Finding Your Roots*?"

He stared, unblinking, and I squirmed.

"There are some Harrises in there, and I think my great-great grandmother Aunt Fanny was a Dedeaux."

A flicker of recognition crossed his face.

"What difference does it make?" I asked. "Can we please talk about Nettie?"

After a long silence, Peter answered with eerie calm. "What do *you* know about Nettie?"

"If I knew about Nettie, I wouldn't be here."

"What did he tell you? Marcus, I mean. Did he offer to cut you in if you wrote an article spreadin' his theories?" He leaned toward me, his forearms resting on his thighs. "How much money did he promise you'd get after he squeezed it outta me?"

If Peter had uttered the words "an offer you can't refuse," it wouldn't have been surprising. My survival instincts were kicking in, my fight-or-flight response screamed flight, and I wanted to get out of there as quickly as possible. It would take a finesse I wasn't sure I possessed but was determined to try and muster.

"Nothing. He told me nothing. He promised me nothing. I'm not here to blackmail you, Peter. I want to tell the authentic story of Chattertowne and your family, not the legends we've been fed year after year. I was researching leads for my article, and Marcus's Veracitater website came up. Unfortunately, the link to his blog about Nettie seems to be dead."

"Like Marcus himself." Peter gave a mirthless chuckle and slapped his thighs. "Well, that's the end of that, then, huh? Can't stir trouble when you're six feet under, now, can you?"

I jumped from the sofa, startling us both. "Very true. Hey, sorry to cut and run. I've got another appointment...with, uh, Assistant Police Chief Kimball at City Hall. Wouldn't want to keep her waiting. She might send someone out looking for me."

Peter rose. "Kimball can wait. If you'd like, I can make a call and let her know you'll be late to your appointment. You didn't get what you came for yet, what you really came to find out," he taunted. "Come on, Audrey, don't you wanna know if I killed Marcus Washburn?"

I hesitated before responding. "Did you? Never mind. Don't tell me anything. Let's pretend this conversation never happened."

His laugh sounded hollow. "Don't work like that, Miss O'Connell. You're really somethin', ya know that? You think it's that easy? You ask a question like that, and you think I'm just gonna spill my guts?"

"Ah, yes, well, so sorry, I guess I mismanaged my time. I wish I could stay and play whatever game this is, but I've got somewhere to be." I gave a look of faux chagrin mixed with equally false indignation. I reached down to snag my bag.

"Why don't you sit so we can finish our conversation, Audrey. Kimball will wait."

It wasn't a request. The gun in his hand pointed at me, indicated he either didn't believe my excuses or didn't care.

Chapter Sixteen

I was at least twenty minutes from town. A few people knew where I was, but by the time anyone got there, it would be too late. Peter jerked his head and the gun toward the sofa. Holden had been right. I shouldn't have gone alone, and I needed protection. Unfortunately, those revelations were useless to me now. Easing back onto the sectional, I stared across the coffee table and postured my body to give off what I hoped was an aura of self-assurance. My sole goal at that point was survival.

"Let's start at the beginning, shall we?"

"The beginning of what?" I asked. "The beginning of Chattertowne?"

"If you'd like. Tell me what your research has revealed so far. What do you think you know about my family? What do you think you know about Nettie?" He slouched and crossed his arms over his round belly. The gun hung loosely in his right hand.

"Well, I came across a book…"

"Lemme guess. George Hart's book."

"How did you know?"

"I shoulda dealt with him years ago. He swore to my father he'd keep his yap shut. The only reason my father didn't chuck him into the river with a cement block was because my grandfather begged him not to."

"I don't mean to be insensitive, but that seems cruelly ironic considering your father took his own life in the river."

"If you believe that, I got a bridge to sell ya."

"What do you mean?" If I was gonna die, I might as well go knowing the truth.

"My father was murdered. Nobody commits suicide in the river, 'specially not in December. If they do, they jump from a bridge. They tried to make it look like his guilty conscience got the better of 'im, but I know better. He wouldn't do himself that way."

"Who benefitted from killing Jimmy but staging it as a suicide?"

"Are you daft?"

I recognized a rhetorical question when I heard one.

"He was connected. A Chatterton family legacy, I guess you could say. He was about to be indicted and they killed him to shut him up, keep him from testifying. They made it look like a suicide to keep the heat off everybody else."

I leaned forward, momentarily forgetting I had a gun aimed in my general direction. "Who killed him?"

"Let's just say there are lotsa people in this town who don't got clean hands. They knew my pops could take 'em all down. He possessed enough… insurance, shall we say, to burn this city to the ground. Metaphorically speaking, o'course." His unfocused gaze darted around the room.

"Did Jimmy throw David Washburn into the Jeannetta River with a cinder block tied to his ankle?"

Peter looked at me with amusement. "Look, I'm not sayin' he killed him. I'm not sayin' he didn't. David Washburn was a troublemaker, and his son was an apple off the same tree. David saw things he shouldn't have, got his hands on information that shoulda stayed buried in the past, and, also like his son, he thought he could make a quick buck by shakin' my family tree. You wanna swim with sharks, there's a good chance you'll end up sleepin' with the fishes instead." He chuckled at his own joke.

"So, was that what Marcus was attempting to hold over you? Your father's crimes and involvement with David's disappearance?"

"Nah, I mean, he asked about his dad, but I didn't have the answers he was lookin' for. Besides, he was more focused on the other story. The one you were fishing around about."

"About Nettie?" I asked.

"That damn Nettie. Couldn't keep her legs shut. Took advantage of the poor man while he was still grievin' his dead wife."

"I find it difficult to believe Nettie was in any position to take advantage of a white man in the mid-1800s, but you're saying she and Jonathan were in a romantic relationship?" I did my best to control the eagerness in my voice. It was the type of information I'd been hoping to get from the meeting... minus the hostage part.

"No. I'm sayin' he was screwin' her, wasn't no romance about it."

"Maybe they were in love." Why was I arguing with a man holding a gun on me?

"He mighta been. No accountin' for taste, 'specially when your options are limited. She was just a gold digger who got herself knocked up, probably on purpose to trap him."

"Peter."

"What?" he grumbled, presumably distracted by angry thoughts of Nettie.

"Why are you pointing a gun at me? You're not going to kill me...like you killed Marcus."

He stared at the gun like he'd forgotten he held it. "Insurance."

"Insurance for what?"

"That you keep your big fat mouth shut about all this Veracitater crap, and about Nettie. First, it was Marcus, then his wife. Now you. I'm getting real sick o' this."

"Renee Washburn? Did she call you?"

"This mornin'. Found somethin' interestin' of her husband's, she says. Wants to make a deal, she says. Oh, I got a deal for her, all right. Same deal I got for you." He waved the gun haphazardly in my general direction.

"Threatening me with a weapon has only made this situation worse. I'll have to report it, you know." I jutted my chin with false bluster.

"*Or*...I could shoot you and bury you on my property." He waved the gun side to side to emphasize each word. "How long do you suppose it takes to find a body on dozens of acres?"

The doorbell rang, startling us both. I said a prayer it was the police and not a Girl Scout selling cookies.

"You stay right here. Keep your trap shut, ya hear me? Don't you move offa that couch." He jolted the gun at me to emphasize his command.

As soon as he was out of sight, I grabbed my bag, jumped off the sofa, and ran for the door leading to the back deck. Despite shaky fingers, I managed to flip the latch to unlock it. Peeking in the direction Peter went, I couldn't see him or whoever was at the door. It was difficult to tell if the arguing voices, both male, were on the porch or in the foyer and what they were arguing about. I had no intention of waiting to find out.

I slid the glass open, barely enough to squeeze through. The button on my jeans caught on the frame, and I cursed myself again for skipping the gym. With my butt, I pushed the door open a tiny bit more until I popped out the other side. Without bothering to slide it shut, I tiptoed across the deck toward the stairs.

Fear of calling attention to my escape prevented me from clomping down the steps as fast as possible. Willing myself to be light as a feather, I hopped the last five steps onto the grass. It was another terrible miscalculation. I landed wonky on my right ankle. Pain shot up and down my leg. Hobbling to the side of the house and flattening myself against it I shimmied along the wall. The voices at the front of the house grew louder and angrier, but the words remained muffled and unintelligible. My car was in view, however, the distance seemed insurmountable with an unreliable ankle.

As I contemplated army crawling on my belly across the yard, two consecutive shots rang out. Covering my mouth to stifle a scream, I dropped to a squatting position and suppressed another shriek from the searing pain it caused in my ankle. My heart fluttered like a hummingbird, and I started to feel light-headed.

The sudden stillness was eerie. The only sound for miles was the wind rustling through the pines.

A disembodied voice broke through the silence, bellowing my name. "Audrey!"

It was barely audible over the pulsing beat of blood flowing inside my head.

"Audrey! Are you out here? Dammit, where are you? Audrey!"

"Darren? I'm over here!" My voice sounded feeble, lost in the chilly breeze.

Darren rushed around the corner. He scooped me into his arms which sent a sharp spike of pain through my leg. Wincing, I cried out in agony. He carefully set me down and leaned me against the house.

"Did he hurt you?" He touched my face, my hands, and my arms, looking for signs of injury.

"Darren, we have to get out of here! Peter Chatterton is the parking spot thief! He murdered Marcus!"

"Whoa, Audrey, slow down." He petted my hair like a Siamese cat. "Deep breaths. You're okay now. I'm here with you, and I'm not going to let anything happen to you, I promise."

"I can't be calm, Darren! Peter wants to kill me!"

"You don't have to worry about Peter Chatterton anymore. He's dead."

His voice was as stony as his face, and his words echoed. Darkness filled the corners of my eyes, threatening to overtake the light. An aching anguish overwhelmed my senses. Somewhere in the distance, sirens wailed as it all faded to black.

Chapter Seventeen

Kimball hovered over me, staring into my face. Her breath smelled like strawberries and I wondered if her skin looked so good because she never wore makeup.

"My skin looks good because I sleep with a clear conscience."

I blinked into awareness. "Oh, shoot, I said that out loud?"

"Yup. How're you feeling there, Audrey?"

I attempted to sit up, but Kimball eased me back onto…onto what? What was I lying on? Craning my neck to look below my body, I found I was, after all, going out on a gurney. At least I was alive to experience it.

"What's wrong with me?"

"Judging by the swelling and the fact it's already blue, green, and purple, you've likely broken your ankle. According to the witness, you went limp as a noodle when he told you he shot Peter Chatterton." She barely contained her smirk.

"Where is Darren? He was with me after–"

"He's giving his statement." Her poker face was fully engaged.

"Peter Chatterton's dead."

"Yes." She nodded. "Darren says he shot him in a struggle. Peter was deceased before we arrived."

My head and ankle throbbed, making it difficult to process Kimball's words. There was a struggle? I'd heard an argument and then shots.

"How….why was Darren here? And how'd you know to come? I heard sirens right before I blacked out."

"He says he got concerned when you didn't answer his texts. He knew

131

you were coming here and was in the vicinity."

Did I tell him that?

"He also said something about listening to a police scanner app. We can talk about this later after you've had a chance to get fixed up. You've been through an ordeal. We can sort the details later when you give your statement."

A dark sedan pulled into the driveway, and someone jumped out. As the figure got closer, Holden's worried expression came into focus.

"Are you okay?" His normally smooth face sported a deep wrinkle between his dark brows.

"I hurt my ankle jumping off the deck."

Taking a deep breath so as, I assumed, not to wring my neck in frustration, his words were measured and strained through gritted teeth.

"Why were you jumping off the deck?"

"Long story. Holden, Peter Chatterton is dead."

He nodded his head, his gaze filled with warmth and concern. "I know, I got the call." He glanced at the paramedics. "You ready for her?" He looked back at me. "I'll follow right behind." He squeezed my hand and stalked toward his car with his shoulders tilted forward and his fists clenched at his side.

One of the paramedics tapped my non-injured leg. "Ready?"

A rolling stretcher wheeled out of Peter's house carrying a large black body bag and a shiver came over me.

"Ready as I'll ever be."

Following a series of x-rays and examinations by doctors in the emergency room, along with an unpleasant re-breaking of my ankle, I was casted (booted) and resting (drugged) by the time Vivienne and Holden came in to see me.

"Hey." I mustered a smile.

"Hey. How're you feeling?" It was rare for Vivienne to be so subdued.

"I'm good now. They gave me happy pills."

"You look like the Joker."

I caught a glimpse of my lopsided grin reflected in the monitor. She wasn't wrong.

"They're waiting for the doctor to sign off on your paperwork, and then you can go home." Viv smirked. "The nurse said if you keep coming here, they're going to designate a room for you."

"I should get a frequent customer discount."

Vivienne chuckled. Holden didn't.

"Are you mad at me?" I asked him.

"No, I'm not mad at you," he said.

"Could you tell that to your face?"

He didn't crack a smile.

"I'll tell them you're ready for the release papers." Viv made a swift exit through the curtain.

I reached for his hand. He studied my fingers in his palm.

"I should've been there."

"This isn't your fault," I said.

"I knew it was a bad idea for you to go alone. I told myself I was being irrational."

"I had no idea who I was dealing with until he opened the door. It wasn't until he said something about Marcus not causing any more trouble now that he's dead, like it was no big deal, that I got really worried for my safety and decided that was my cue to leave. He had other ideas."

Holden squeezed my hand. "How in the hell did Benson get out there before the rest of us?"

"I'm still trying to figure out how any of you knew to come. I thought I was a goner, especially after I got hurt. A gimp doesn't stand a chance against a guy with a gun."

"It was the sketch. I was in my meeting when I kept getting calls from an unknown number. It turned out to be Mildred. She said you'd sent her the sketch, and she knew right away who it was. I would have, if you'd sent it to me."

"I'd planned to, but I assumed Kimball would send it to you."

"She didn't." His mouth tightened.

"Yeah, I talked to her on the way up to Peter's, and she got irritated with me when I asked. So, what happened next?" I asked.

"I guess Mildred tried to call you first, but it went straight to voice mail. That's when she called me. I called my buddy over at CPD, Tony Bianchi, as soon as Mildred told me what was going on, and he put out an APB. I'd tried Lacey first, but she didn't answer."

"Lacey?" I cocked my head.

"Kimball."

"Huh. Wouldn't have guessed that."

"Life is full of ironies, Audrey."

"Did you know Alanis Morrissette's song 'Ironic' doesn't contain a single irony? Now that's ironic." I yawned.

"Looks like those painkillers are kicking in."

My eyelids sagged. "I don't think I can walk. How will you get me out of here if I'm unconscious?"

"I'll get you home. I'm not leaving your side until I know you're safe and sound."

"I like the sound of that. Promise you won't ever leave me?"

He sighed. "You know I can't promise that."

Chapter Eighteen

I stood in Peter Chatterton's living room holding a wooden golf club. Blood dripped from the wedged metal head. I was desperate to escape but couldn't get my right leg to budge, like it was encased in cement. Mustering all my strength, I lugged my right foot across the living room floor. The club dragged behind me, leaving a crimson trail. I stumbled down to my knees. Rather than trying to get upright, I pulled myself using my forearms. When I reached the foyer, a man lay motionless across the threshold. My heart raced as I crawled onto the bloody body. Expecting to see Peter, I screamed when I looked into the eyes-wide-open but completely dead face of Holden Villalobos.

"Audrey? You okay?" The voice whispered into the darkness.

"Holden? What time is it?"

His silhouette moved toward the bed. "It's about midnight." He brushed a stray hair from my face. "Viv had to go to work. Are you okay? You screamed my name."

"I had a nightmare. I was at Peter's house, and someone was dead. When I went to look, I realized it wasn't Peter. It was you." I felt a tear stream down my cheek.

He pulled me in for a hug. "I'm okay, and you're safe. It's all over."

He rubbed my back, and I exhaled in exhaustion and relief.

"How's your ankle? Do you need another pain pill? I think you're about due."

"It's throbbing pretty bad. I think that contributed to my nightmare because in my dream, my foot weighed like a hundred pounds."

"I'll grab your pill and more water." He stood and picked up an empty glass from the nightstand. "Are you hungry? You haven't eaten anything for hours."

"No, the pills make me queasy."

"I'll bring you a couple crackers to go with it. You shouldn't take it on an empty stomach."

"How does Emily feel about your spending the night here?"

He stopped in the doorway but didn't turn around, his figure silhouetted by the glow coming from the living room. He heaved a weary sigh. "I'm leaving as soon as your sister gets home."

The next morning, I hobbled into the kitchen, unable to sleep. It was about six a.m., and the pain in my ankle was excruciating. I turned on the coffee maker, grabbed myself a glass, filled it with water, and searched for the pain pills. On the counter, tucked underneath the prescription bottle, was a piece of paper with Holden's handwriting.

Good morning, I hope you slept well. Call me when you wake up. -H

I assumed he didn't mean at the crack of dawn on a Saturday morning.

I chased a pill with the water. I filled the coffee mug before grabbing my phone and the note from Holden. I placed my crutches under my armpits and eyed the sofa. The task ahead was daunting. Leaning on my left foot and crutch, I reached to place the mug on the side table. I shoved the note and phone into the waistband of my never-been-to-yoga pants.

Using my crutch, I pivoted toward the sofa and swung my body until my rear made it to the edge, just barely. Holding onto the armrest, I made a full stretch to snag the coffee. I felt proud of my accomplishment, even though no one had been there to witness it.

I turned on the morning TV news but set the volume low. Although I couldn't make out the anchor's words, there was no need for sound. Peter Chatterton's photo in the upper right-hand corner with the caption "SHOT DEAD" told me all I needed to know.

The camera switched from the newsroom to a field reporter named Sharon standing at the entrance to Peter's driveway. She wore a bright yellow rain slicker like the guy on the fish sticks package. I turned up the volume.

"Police say Mr. Chatterton, a prominent resident in the Chattertowne community and direct descendent of the city's founder and namesake Jonathan Chatterton, was shot dead Friday afternoon in the foyer of his hilltop home. Few details have been released. Sources tell me the alleged shooter claims he acted in self-defense and on behalf of a woman being held against her will inside the residence. Peter Chatterton had no prior criminal record. He had no known children and was unmarried at the time of his death. No word yet on when or if services will be held. We're expecting an official statement from the police later today or tomorrow. Back to you, Boyd."

The camera returned to the anchor, who moved on to a story about a transportation bill stalled in the state legislature.

Despite being under the haze of pain medication, a multitude of questions came to mind. Why was Darren at Peter's house? What were Darren and Peter arguing about? What would've happened if Darren hadn't shown up?

The last question was one I wasn't ready to think about.

I grabbed my phone off the table. It showed several unread messages. My mother's text was a terse demand to call ASAP. I planned to call her after I'd talked to Holden...and drank another cup of coffee...and popped another pain pill...or two.

I woke to someone in the kitchen.

"Viv?"

"Hey, happy Saturday. Well, maybe not *happy* Saturday, more like I'm relieved you're alive Saturday. Can I get you anything?"

I wriggled into a sitting position on the sofa and adjusted the pillow under my foot. "What time is it?"

"Eight-thirty."

"Geez, I guess my pain pill kicked in and knocked me out again."

I'd missed four calls. One was from my mother, one from my boss; one was from Holden, and one from Darren. I didn't really want to talk to any of them.

"What's your plan for the day?"

Color tinged Viv's cheeks. "Remember, I went in for that receptionist interview yesterday afternoon? Well, I got hired and I start this morning. We were in the middle of my interview when Holden left a message for Lace, uh, Assistant Chief Kimball, saying Mildred had identified the man in the sketch as Peter Chatterton and you'd gone to Peter's house not knowing who he was."

"I'm surprised you didn't ride up to Peter's with Kimball."

"She didn't check the message until after I'd left. Once she got to Peter's and had assessed the situation, she called to tell me what was going on. She said it was best for me to wait for you at the hospital, because you'd be headed back down the hill before I could get up there. She was quite sweet about it."

Sweet wasn't how I would've described my encounters with Kimball.

"So, do you think this job will be a good fit?" I asked.

"It's only temporary, until the regular admin lady comes back from maternity leave. Unless, of course, she changes her mind and decides to stay home full time."

"When do you have to be there?"

"I'm supposed to start my training at nine, but I don't like leaving you alone in this condition. I'm sure under the circumstances, Lacey would be okay with me starting Monday instead. As it is, she's coming in on her day off to train me."

"Hey, I managed to get myself and my coffee over to the sofa with no help this morning. I don't have any place to be and several phone calls to make. Don't worry about me. If I get desperate, I'll call Mom and have her come over."

"If you're sure…" Her words were hesitant, but the way she was backing toward the door said otherwise. "Call me if you need anything." She grabbed her purse off the counter and her jacket from the kitchen barstool.

"I won't."

Viv took a deep breath. "Okay, I'm off!"

138

"Good luck!"

Her response was faint as the door closed behind her. "You too."

I started with the easiest callback on my list. Anderson expressed appropriate concern for my well-being coupled with not-so-subtle hints about meeting my deadline.

"I'm not trying to pressure you, but I need your first Kupit segment."

"I can't just do a puff piece and ignore everything I've discovered. I don't want to get into too many specifics, but after talking with Peter Chatterton yesterday, I'm more convinced than ever there's a huge scandal waiting to be salvaged from the depths of Chattertowne's history, and it's linked to Marcus's murder."

"That's a pretty strong statement. Got anything to back it up?"

"Peter got furious yesterday when I mentioned Nettie, the Flathead woman who helped raise Michael Chatterton after his mother Madeleine died. He made a derogatory comment about Nettie getting herself knocked up on purpose, basically admitting they'd had a love child."

"Michael and the woman who raised him?"

"No, Nettie and Jonathan. So, that means Michael had a sibling." My statement was met with silence. "Hello?"

"I'm thinking," came the gruff reply. "If what Peter said is true, if they had a child, did that child have children?"

"I have no idea. What are you getting at?"

"Audrey, think. Why would it matter if Jonathan had an affair with an Indian woman resulting in a child? What would motivate a hundred- and fifty-year cover-up?"

"His reputation? I don't know." Being semi-sedated wasn't conducive to connecting dots.

"His wife had died; he needed someone to help take care of the kid. He was probably lonely. I doubt anyone would care about him getting companionship to endure the harsh winters and help raise his kid. Even the Puritans in this town would chalk it up to necessity." He paused. "If they had a child together, however, that child would not only be Michael's sibling, but would also be a legal co-heir with him, as would that child's descendants."

"You're right, and I just realized something else! Marcus Washburn's final blog called out the Chattertons for stealing his birthright. I'd assumed he meant Jimmy was somehow responsible for his father's disappearance. Now I'm wondering…do you think Marcus Washburn is…was…a descendent of Jonathan Chatterton and Nettie?"

"That's a mighty big leap, my dear, although not out of the realm of possibility," he said.

"You wouldn't happen to know where Jonathan's original house was, would you?" I asked.

"It's over on Main. There's a historic marker."

"I know about that one. They took us there for a field trip in the fourth grade. Is it the original homestead, though?"

"I've always assumed it was. Why?"

"A long time ago, Marcus told me his house, the one where he spent his childhood and moved back into after his mother passed away, was Jonathan's original home, the one he lived in before the one on Main was built. It's a saltbox on Madeleine Avenue. What if Marcus's family lived there because they were descendants of the original owner, Jonathan? Is that possible?"

"Audrey, I don't mean to speak ill of the dead, but you know that young man was prone to exaggeration, right?"

"Yes, I've heard. I just thought if it were true, it could tie this whole thing together in a pretty little bow."

"Unfortunately, in journalism, as in life, rarely will you discover convenient resolutions with no loose ends. It's often messy and complicated and not pretty," he said.

"So, you think it's a dead end?"

"Not necessarily. It's worth investigating. At the very least, I think you've stumbled upon one hell of a story. I don't know where it will lead, but if what you're saying is true, it could turn the town's history upside down."

"It's not only about history, though. If Marcus had proof he'd descended from Nettie and Jonathan, Peter might have worried his assets were at risk," I said. "Have you seen Peter's house? I can't begin to imagine its worth, not to mention the dozens of acres and any other business holdings which were passed down to him through the official Chatterton line. That's a strong motive for Peter to kill Marcus and put an end to any inheritance claims."

"I knew Peter," Mr. Anderson said. "Not well, but we were acquaintances. Sure, he talked like Al Capone, but I never took it seriously. I just can't imagine him killing anyone."

"I can. I had his gun in my face. And I'd say it was more Whitey Bulger than Capone."

Anderson sighed. "I suppose you're right."

"Not only that, but Peter also admitted his dad, Jimmy, was involved in organized crime. He said it was a Chatterton family legacy, which makes me think Peter was carrying on that legacy. I need to find out if anyone else might have a claim to that fortune now Peter's gone. It's the least I can do for Marcus and his children, if they're the rightful heirs."

"I'm giving you permission to follow the story, but please be careful. We don't know what the organized crime angle is about, and that's a dangerous world. As for putting Chattertowne's history in a new light, don't worry about how it'll be received. Seems to me this community has been in denial long enough. In the meantime, can you finish your other projects? Also, do I need to find you a replacement for the widows' luncheon this afternoon? I checked your calendar to see if anything needed to be covered during your recuperation and spotted the notation."

I smacked my forehead. "I forgot about the widows' luncheon. Do you have anyone who can go in my place?"

"I'll send one of the twerps from the high school and have them email you their notes. I'd still like you to write it up. I don't have the patience to deal with their grammatical errors and casual style."

"Okay, sounds good. I'll get you the mock-ups for my section and keep you updated on anything I find."

"I'm glad you're okay, Audrey. No story is worth risking your life, you know that, right?"

"There was a time when Marcus was the most important person in my life. If he died trying to discover the truth about what happened to his father, the best way I can honor him is by completing the mission on his behalf."

"Take care of yourself…and watch your back. Feather ruffling can have pretty rough consequences."

The phone hadn't even completed a full ring on my next call before the tirade began.

"Audrey Jeanne O'Connell, what in the world have you gotten yourself into?"

"Morning, Mom."

"Dad and I were so worried, but Vivienne told us not to come to the hospital."

"I was treated and released. There was no time for visitors, and when I got home, the pain pills knocked me out for the night."

She shifted from chastisement to motherly clucking. "What can we do for you, honey? Do you want me to bring you soup? I can make a pie if you'd like."

"Thanks, Mom. It's okay. The pain pills have robbed my appetite."

"Well, I guess losing weight's a nice, unexpected benefit to nearly getting yourself killed. Did Vivienne tell you she's starting a real job today at the CPD?"

"Waitressing is a real job, and singing is her passion."

She tsked. "Waitressing is what you do while searching for a real job, and singing at a nightclub is a hobby."

I choked down my reply like the lima beans she'd forced me to eat as a child and feigned a yawn. "Sorry, Mom, meds are kicking in. I'll call you later."

I hung up the phone, and my fake yawn led to a real yawn and then another. Fatigue and painkillers overtook me once more.

Chapter Nineteen

A buzzing sound had woken me up, but my phone showed no call coming in. I was confused and discombobulated until a second buzz came from the front door, accompanied by a knock.

"Just a minute!"

A brief self-evaluation left me dissatisfied. I wore no bra, no makeup, no deodorant, and my hair and teeth were fuzzy. Sliding my booted foot off the pillow and onto the floor, the doorbell buzzed again.

"I said, hold on!" Using my crutches, I pulled myself up from the sofa. "Who is it?" I bellowed my deepest, most threatening voice.

"You're not fooling anyone. Open the door."

Shoot, it was Holden. I attempted to smooth my hair which caused me to lose balance and fall against the door with a thud.

"You okay in there?" His voice held an equal amount of concern and amusement.

"Hold on. I'm trying to figure out how to open the door without falling over."

Hopping back a half-step, I unlocked the deadbolt. I turned and pulled the knob until the crack widened enough to reveal Holden's smirking face.

"You gonna let me in?"

"I'm trying." Pivoting to swing the door open, I lost my balance again and fell into Holden's broad chest. "You smell so good you give me the collywobbles," I moaned, my words muffled by his shirt.

His chest rumbled with laughter. "What did you say?"

"Nothing. I said nothing. You heard nothing."

With one hand, he stabilized me. With the other, he reached for my crutches and positioned them under my armpits. Stepping back, he put his hands out to steady me in case I fell again.

"You good?"

"I'm good." I staggered across the room and thrust myself onto the sofa.

"Whoa! Careful." He lowered himself onto the armchair.

"I'm fine. I hate these stupid things." I threw the crutches onto the ground.

"It's day one." He clasped his hands and rested them on his stomach.

"Yeah, well, one day is about all I'm willing to give it."

"You want me to get you a wheelchair?"

"I'm gonna hobble around on this boot. Can't be any worse."

"The doctor said you shouldn't put any weight on it for a while."

"Doctor-schmockter." I waved my hand dismissively.

"I've gotta ask you something."

"What?"

"What in the hell's a collywobble?" He smiled broadly, his white teeth gleaming.

I buried my face into a pillow. "It means you give me butterflies."

"I'll keep that in mind." He chuckled, clearly enjoying my discomfort.

"So, did you just come to say hi? Because I don't see you've brought me chocolate or booze to help me cope."

"There's something you should know."

His shift to a serious tone caught my attention. Maybe he'd say I gave him the collywobbles, too. He looked somber. Definitely wasn't that. I raised my left eyebrow for him to continue.

"Renee Washburn's missing."

"Missing? Missing how? When?"

"An officer went by this morning to let her know the primary suspect in her husband's murder is dead. Her car was in the driveway, but no one answered when he rang the doorbell. The neighbor said she'd seen Renee getting the mail yesterday morning in her nightgown but never saw her leave the house otherwise. I guess she's got a *Rear Window* thing going on. She's disabled...sets herself in her front room with a view of both the television and the street so she can watch her neighbors' comings and goings."

"Do you have any idea how much it turns me on you just made a Hitchcock reference?" As soon as the words escaped my mouth, I covered it. "Ack! These pills have not only stolen my appetite, they've taken my verbal filter." I waved my hand. "Disregard. Sorry, go on."

"The neighbor never saw Renee leave, but she did see a man, a big guy, show up around ten thirty, sometime during *The Price Is Right*. At first, she thought it was Marcus. Then she remembered...it couldn't be. Anyway, the dude knocked, and Renee let him in," Holden said.

"Maybe Renee has a boyfriend. That would explain her accusations about Marcus and me. Cheaters like to point fingers to redirect from their own misdeeds."

"The neighbor gave him the sister's number. The sister said she hadn't heard from Renee since she dropped the little boy off at her house. When the officer went back to Renee's, he knocked instead of ringing the bell, and the door swung open. He called out to her, but there was no response. When he saw how disheveled the living room was, he'd assumed there'd been a home invasion or at least a struggle."

"Did anyone tell him that's the normal condition of her house?" I asked.

"Yeah, but the whole thing smells rotten."

"That house smelled rotten. Kind of like what emanated from the backside of my old dog Gunther after he'd eaten from the garbage can."

"Renee wouldn't take off without her car or her kids, would she?"

I shrugged my shoulders. "I don't know; I wouldn't think so. Did I mention Peter told me Renee called him?"

"When?"

"Yesterday morning."

"About what?"

"He accused me of working with Renee and Marcus to extort him. He said Renee had called earlier that morning to make a deal. After we visited her, she must've gone through Marcus's stuff and found the notes or proof of his claims. Peter said I got a deal for her, same deal I got for you. Real *Godfather*-like. Do you think he meant he killed her? Because I know he had bad intentions toward me."

Holden rubbed the side of his nose. "Anything's possible. Sounds like he was a real thug."

"He talked like every stereotypical gangster character from every mafia movie I've ever watched, playing a role, trying to be like his father...who, by the way, probably had David Washburn killed. He made references to cement blocks and sleeping with the fishes. People don't disappear, never to be heard from again without something bad happening to them. I'm guessing Marcus's dad saw shady stuff at the port, and he may have tried to use that and what he'd discovered about Nettie's baby as leverage to blackmail Jimmy. I think that was only part—"

"Audrey!" Holden barked.

"What?"

"Why do I feel like I'm missing half the story...again?"

"Sorry, I get confused about what I've said and to whom. I spoke with Anderson this morning, and he picked up on things Peter said, which I hadn't yet finished processing. When Nettie's name was mentioned, Peter went completely sideways. He told me she got pregnant because she was a gold digger, which means she had a baby with Jonathan Chatterton! I'd been looking at the cover-up from a scandal perspective, but Anderson pointed out—"

"If there was a baby, there was another heir, possibly several by now." Holden brought his tented index fingers against his mouth.

I lost focus watching him bounce his fingers off his lips. "Yeah. I, uh," I cleared my throat. "I didn't catch that when he said it."

"You were under duress. You had a cool enough head to escape, which is pretty impressive."

"Survival instincts kicked in. I saw an opportunity to get out and took it."

"I know you'll give a complete statement about what happened to the police, but if we talk through it, maybe we'll discover something."

"Well, I can tell you, when he first opened the door, I almost peed my pants."

Holden smiled. "That would've been quite a shock, your parking thief standing right in front of you."

"I tried to play it off, but I think he sensed something from the get-go. When I started asking questions, he got defensive. No, defensive isn't the word. Hostile."

"At what point did he pull the gun?"

"We'd been talking about Marcus, and things took a dark turn, almost gloating over Marcus's death. I made an excuse and got up to leave, but the next thing I knew, he was directing me back onto the sofa with a gun in his hand. I tried to ignore the weapon pointed at me and got him talking, partly as a stall tactic, partly curiosity. I asked about his dad. He told me he absolutely did not believe Jimmy killed himself. He said his father was on the verge of being indicted and had dirt on lots of people, which he could use as leverage. Insurance, he called it. Peter said those people he had the dirt on made sure Jimmy stayed quiet by shutting his mouth permanently and then making it look like suicide. Anyway, if there *were* a secret heir to the Chatterton fortune, and Marcus blackmailed Peter because he believed he was descended from that heir, that would explain everything."

"Maybe." Holden looked over at my foot. "I'm not sure your toes should be that color."

I craned my neck. Purple piggies peeked out from the boot. "They do look a little like stuffed eggplant."

Holden got up, lifted my foot, removed the pillows, and slid himself underneath my leg. He gently rested it in his lap and began rubbing my toes.

"You don't have to do that. I'm sure my feet smell. I haven't showered since yesterday morning, and this boot's sweaty."

"I'm fine. You're fine. Keep talking."

He caressed each toe to get the circulation moving, which caused all the blood to leave my brain and rush to my feet…and other places.

"Uh. Where was I?"

"You said that would explain everything."

I blinked three times. "Oh, yeah, so, get this. Marcus is a weirdo…*was* a weirdo." I sighed. "Anyway, he's poking around, digging into conspiracy theories, generally pissing people off. Most of the time, he's way off base, which makes him a nuisance, not a threat. According to his blog, Marcus believed his dad had hidden documents that were supposed to be financially beneficial in some way, but his mom had forgotten where he'd stashed them. She'd also told him David had warned her she wasn't to trust anyone because corruption had infiltrated even the highest levels of law enforcement and city government. Then, supposedly while cleaning out the house after his mom died, he found the documents."

"When did Jimmy die?"

"Mid- to late-eighties, I think. Why?"

"I'm trying to remember who the mayor was back then."

I held up my index finger and grabbed my phone. It rang several times before the call connected.

"Hello?"

"Mildred, hi, it's Audrey O'Connell. Are you okay? You sound breathless."

"Audrey! Yes, I'm fine. I was just out back doing some gardening when I heard the phone ring. How are you, honey?"

"I'm okay, thanks to you. If you hadn't gotten word to Holden about Peter, I'm not sure I would be."

"I'm so glad you're okay."

"Me too. Hey, I'm sorry to bug you on a Saturday at home with this random question."

"No problem, dear. How can I help?"

"Do you happen to remember who was Chattertowne's mayor in the mid-eighties?"

"Hmm. That would have been Harold King. He was mayor for quite a while, at least ten to twelve years."

"Wow, that's a pretty long time. Did he retire?"

"Not by choice. Within days of each other, Jimmy was found dead in the river, and David Washburn went missing under suspicious circumstances. Rumors were rampant around town about unsavory happenings at the port. Chattertowne lost some of its naiveté, and Mayor King paid the political price. Not to mention, his family had moved here from Los Angeles in the nineteen sixties, and you know how Chattertowne feels about outsiders. He lost his re-election bid to Nick Robinson."

"Do you think it's possible Mayor King was corrupt?" I cocked my eyebrow and smirked at Holden.

"I find it quite plausible. We're a small community. If illegal activities were happening, I'd think the man overseeing it all would have at least some knowledge." She paused before adding, "Not to mention his cousin Andy was Chief of Police."

I widened my eyes. Holden tilted his head and raised his brows.

"Mayor King's cousin Andy was the Police Chief," I whispered.

"What was that? Speak up, dear. I'm having trouble hearing you."

"Sorry, Mildred, I was relaying what you said to Holden Villalobos. He's here with me."

"Ahhh. He's a handsome fella. Back in my day, he'd have been off-limits, but good for you, sweetie."

"We're just friends. We're working together."

"I suppose if you've got to put in long hours, it may as well be in the company of a fine-looking man."

I laughed. "Thanks for the information and again, for the whole saving my life thing. I owe you dinner, at least."

"I'd love that, dear. Bring Holden along too. We'll have a grand time!"

"I'll ask him. I'll be in touch."

"Bye, now."

There were several beeps, mumbling, and what sounded like cursing under her breath before Mildred disconnected the call.

"What's that grin for?" Holden asked.

"She's adorable."

"What did you need to ask me?"

"Mildred wants us to join her for dinner sometime this week."

"Even though we're just friends?"

"What was I supposed to say? It's complicated?"

"That would be more accurate, but I hear what you're saying. No need bringing anyone else into this convoluted situation. Except your sister, of course."

"What about my sister?"

"I assume you've told her what's going on between us. Don't sisters share everything?"

"First of all, no. Second, how could I tell her what's going on between us when I don't even know what's going on between us?"

"Good point. Let's table that discussion for another time. Or never. Tell me what Mildred said. I was trying to discern from your side of the conversation, but I think I missed a few things."

"Basically, Mayor King and his cousin Police Chief Andy ran Chattertowne together for about a dozen years leading up to and including Jimmy Chatterton's death and David Washburn's disappearance. As a result of the turmoil, Mayor King lost his job. There were rumors about criminal activity, and she surmises the mayor and chief must've had an inkling of what was going on, either by directly taking part or turning a blind eye. If David Washburn went to either of them to report suspicious activity he'd witnessed, and they were part of the corruption, there's a good chance they tipped off Jimmy Chatterton or one of his nefarious associates to deal with him. Wait. Didn't David go missing after Jimmy died?"

"I'm not sure. Honestly, I don't know how you're keeping all this straight. These stories are so tangled, my brain feels like a pretzel," Holden said.

"I find it's helpful to look at it like a timeline rather than an interrelated web of people and incidents. First, we have Jonathan and Madeleine. She dies in childbirth, so Nettie comes on the scene. Nettie and Jonathan fall in love, or lust, or whatever, and maybe, probably, have a baby. Jonathan died when Michael was nineteen. The hypothetical baby might have been a teenager also, assuming he or she survived. The infant mortality rate was high back then. I believe the missing pages in the Hart book describe what happened to Nettie and the rumored baby, so therefore, the person most adversely affected by the revelations had the greatest motive to remove the pages."

"Or…"

"Or, what?"

"Well, if we're talking recently, the person most likely to be affected in a negative way would be Peter, and now he's dead. I finally heard from Peg, who told me Peter had a sister, but she died a few years ago. She wasn't sure if the sister had any kids. I guess she didn't want to have anything to do with her brother or Chattertowne. Peg had the impression she'd left for college and never looked back."

"So, like I said, it's likely Peter removed the pages to protect his fortune. What else makes sense?"

"What if David Washburn stole the pages back in the eighties to blackmail Jimmy Chatterton?"

He ran a finger across my toes, eliciting a shiver.

"Ah! That tickles. So, why not steal the whole book? George made about ten copies and gave them to friends and family as a Christmas gift, including Eddie. They may still be floating around town."

"As his son, Jimmy would've had access to Eddie's copy if he still had it, so if David approached Jimmy and said he had pages from the book, Jimmy would've known exactly what that meant and what was at stake."

"I guess it's possible David stole the pages, and that's what Marcus, and subsequently Renee, used to extort Peter. Based on my experience, that's definitely something Peter would kill over. It also means anyone in possession of a copy would have been in danger."

"Thankfully, that harrowing chapter has come to an end," Holden said. "It's crazy to think the information on those pages possibly contributed to David Washburn's disappearance and/or death, Marcus's death, Peter's death, and Renee's disappearance."

"That's a lot of collateral damage from one book. No wonder George tried to warn me off."

"And yet…"

"What was I supposed to do? Sit on my hands while Marcus's killer got away with it?"

"I'm not blaming you. If Peter really was responsible for Marcus's death, then he deserved to die. The question is, what did David discover, and what did he do with that information?

I shrugged my shoulders. "David must've figured out there was another heir to the Chatterton fortune, and perhaps he had reason to believe he was a descendant, plus he'd already witnessed illegal activity at his job and, according to Marcus's blog, it was connected to Jimmy. After his plan to blackmail Jimmy failed because you can't blackmail a dead guy, but you sure can piss off his co-conspirators, he probably ended up either at the bottom of the river or on the run."

"Who goes on the run, but never comes back?"

"I know he's probably dead, but let me hang on to this little shred of hope, will ya? So, Jimmy was under investigation for corruption and, according to Peter, was killed by his cohorts before he could testify against them and bring the entire system down. Let's say Marcus somehow came across the info about Nettie and the baby, along with whatever proof David had accumulated that Jimmy was dirty. Like a dummy, God rest his soul, Marcus threatens to reveal the information on his public blog, but maybe he also privately contacts Peter hoping to extort hush money. Instead, Peter kills him to shut him up. Then, we alert Renee to the fact there's likely blackmail-worthy material somewhere in Marcus's office. She tears the place apart until she finds it–"

"Or…" Holden interrupted. "She tries to bluff. She hasn't found the info but tries to scam Peter into thinking she knows something she doesn't, and it backfires."

"I don't like the woman, but I don't want her dead. She's all those kids have left. We have to figure out what happened to her."

Holden patted my boot. "No, you're going to stay here and recuperate like an obedient patient and let the police handle it. I got an earful from Kimball about your meddling."

"Our meddling."

"Can I get you anything before I go?" He removed my foot from his lap and placed the pillow underneath it.

"Yeah, I'll take that bottle of pain meds on the counter. I have one more phone call to make before I go down for the count."

Holden tossed the bottle. "Nice catch. Who you gonna call?"

"Ghostbusters." I gave him a lopsided grin, popped a pill in my mouth, and gulped my cold coffee. "I have to call Darren back. It's the polite thing to do."

"Audrey, you don't have to justify anything to me. If you wanna talk to the guy, that's your business, but there's something about him I don't trust." He'd reached the door, his fingers resting on the handle.

"I have conflicted feelings about him too. He did save me from Peter yesterday, so he gets props for that. I still can't figure out how he got to the house before everyone else, though. Kimball said he told her he was in the area and heard it on his police scanner app."

"He said that same thing the day of Marcus's murder. Don't you find it strange a financial reporter listens to a police scanner?"

"Sure, but my dad listens to the same app for entertainment. God knows why garbled, static-y conversations between dispatch and patrol are interesting to people." I shrugged my shoulders.

Holden crossed the room and planted a kiss on my forehead.

"What's that for?"

"I'm just really glad you're okay."

I smiled. "Thanks."

"I'll call to check in on you later."

"Let me know if you hear anything about Renee." I waited for the door to shut before picking up my phone. "Please let it go to voice mail. Please let it go to voice mail. Ple–"

"I was wondering when I'd hear from you." Darren's voice was calm.

"Sorry, I've been out of it." It was only a partial lie.

"Understandable. How're you feeling?"

"My ankle hurts like a bitch, but I'm alive, thanks to you."

"I told you I'd do everything in my power to keep you safe." His tone was defensive, as if his integrity were in question.

"I appreciate that. How are you? I'd imagine shooting someone, even in self-defense, would be traumatic. The police aren't giving you trouble, are they? You didn't have a choice. I'll tell them that myself."

"They didn't arrest me, but they held me for a good long while. Let's just say I spent enough time in interrogation I could describe every aspect of the room in detail. As for the shooting, I'm going to need time to process it. I don't regret doing it, for your sake as well as my own. However, one doesn't easily get over taking a life, even if there was no choice."

"Something keeps bothering me. How did you get there before everyone else? Kimball said you were in the area. What reason could you have for being way out in the sticks?"

"I don't regret what I did."

I lowered my chin. "You don't regret what?"

"I followed you there."

Chills ran down my arms and legs. "Why...why were you following me?"

"With all the craziness going on, I wanted to keep an eye on you. I parked down the road from Peter's house, and when the APB came over the scanner, I knew you could be in real danger."

"I guess I can't be too mad, considering I *was* in real danger."

"I'm glad you see it that way," he said.

"What happened when you got there? The doorbell rang, but I couldn't hear the conversation. I was too busy trying to make my escape."

"When he opened the door, I asked for you. He tried to play it off like he didn't know what I was talking about. I told him I'd seen your car and knew you were there. That's when I spotted his gun. I didn't stop to ask why he had it, I just lunged for it. In our struggle, it went off."

I shuddered. "It's a relief to know this ordeal's over. Mostly."

"What do you mean, mostly?"

"You haven't heard?"

"Heard what?"

"Renee Washburn's disappeared."

"Disappeared?"

"An officer went to notify her of Peter's death. When he got there, her door was ajar, her house torn apart. She was gone, but her car's still there."

He scoffed. "That house was a mess to begin with."

"How did you know her house was a mess?"

He paused. "You told me. The night you came over for dinner. You'd been at her house and commented about the mess. Don't you remember?"

"I guess I didn't realize you paid such close attention to my ramblings."

"I pay attention to everything you say. Hey, I'm gonna let you get back to recuperating. I'll check on you later, okay?"

"I'll be here. If I don't answer, it's because I've turned my ringer off, and I'm sleeping."

"Rest easy."

Grabbing the brown bottle from the coffee table, I popped a pill into my mouth, followed by the remainder of my coffee. In the distance, a truck rumbled, and the wind whipped a tree branch against the window. I was overcome by the strangest sensation, an unsettled yet eerie calm. Then it hit me.

I'd already taken a pill.

Chapter Twenty

I opened my eyes just before dawn on Sunday. Nearly eighteen hours had passed, and during my hibernation, Viv had placed my laptop on the coffee table next to me. Crisscrossing my left leg under my right to adjust to a comfortable sitting position, I checked my email. A kid named Geoff had sent a message regarding the widow's luncheon.

Miss Audrey,

Mr. Anderson asked me to send you my notes.

There were 14 ladies at the widow's luncheon, plus Rabbi Silver. They ate crustless triangle sandwiches filled with a "cream cheese schmear and vegetables." I'm pretty sure the only vegetable in there was cucumber. I can't tell you if they were good because I didn't eat them.

Someone made raspberry lemonade and someone else made carrot cake. A lady named Liza complained there wasn't lemon in the frosting and another lady wearing a purple hat choked on a pecan while eating the cake. Or a walnut. It was a nut of some kind. She was okay after she got whacked on the back a couple times and spit it out.

There was a dramatic reading of the 23rd Psalm, the one about walking through the valley of death or whatever, and then an Elvis impersonator sang "Are You Lonesome Tonight?" Several people cried.

I overheard one lady tell her friend as they left she hoped it was a one-and-done. The raspberry lemonade was good, though. It had whole raspberries floating in it and ice cubes with mint frozen inside. Hope that helps.

Geoff

I laughed as I responded to his email.

> *Geoff,*
>
> *I'm disappointed I missed the event. Sounds like quite the time. I wonder who thought it was a good idea for an Elvis impersonator to sing "Are You Lonesome Tonight" at a luncheon for widows? Anyway, thanks for filling in, and for the notes.*
>
> *Audrey*

Weeding through the rest of my emails, nothing appeared so pressing it couldn't wait until Monday, so I made another stab at getting information about Nettie. The last time I'd searched online, I'd gotten sidetracked by Marcus's website.

It had been nearly a week since his murder, and although Peter had practically admitted his guilt, I still had many unanswered questions, both about Marcus's death and the Nettie story which I'd come to believe had precipitated it.

I scrolled past links I'd already reviewed. Toward the bottom of the second page, there was a listing for an online copy of an out-of-print travel book about Chattertowne, the Skagit Valley, and the Cascade Mountain Loop. The author was none other than George Hart.

"Alright, George, if you're not gonna talk to me, maybe your books will speak for you."

A library had scanned the complete manuscript into a searchable document, so I typed "Nettie" into the search bar, and a page appeared with Nettie highlighted in yellow. I skimmed the preceding paragraphs for context.

"Travelers to Chattertowne will be no less than stunned by its beauty, with an expansive valley blanketed in glistening snow as far as the eye can see throughout December, January, February, and March."

The book had to have been written pre-climate change. Throughout my childhood, there'd been only one to two minor snow events per year, most of which were melted by the next day.

"In early April, verdant rolling hills emerge, and wildflowers awaken from winter slumber. Summer brings fresh ocean breezes to cool the warm days while miles of corn fields grow under the blue, sunny skies. Finally, in the fall, what each visitor dreams of seeing, an eye-popping mélange of ochre and rust-colored trees blanket the area, leaving even the most jaded traveler speechless. From the hills, there is a panoramic view of the vale all the way to Puget Sound and the Salish Sea. From Eddie Chatterton's hilltop estate, one can experience unobstructed vistas of the sparkling Jeannetta River, named by his grandfather, original settler Jonathan Chatterton, for his Franco-Indian bride Nettie. Nettie was the progeny of a Bitterroot-Salish woman and a French Jesuit missionary."

I bounced on the sofa. "The Jeannetta River was named for Nettie," I whispered. "The Jeannetta River was named for Nettie!" My volume increased as my excitement grew.

Vivienne's bedroom door creaked open. "What's happening out here?" Her voice was froggy, and her hair was matted on one side. "Have you lost your mind? It's six thirty in the morning!" She leaned against the doorjamb.

"I'd think I was crazy too if I hadn't seen this with my own eyes! I'm sorry, I just..." I took a deep breath. "Nettie is Jeannetta! Jeannetta is Nettie! I can't believe I never saw it."

Vivienne closed her eyes for a long moment before reopening them. "Say again?"

"The Jeannetta River was named for Jonathan Chatterton's Flathead lover, or wife. This says she was his wife."

"So, what?"

"So, he loved her!" I clapped my hands together. "It means the rumors of their relationship, and probably their love child, are true! She wasn't just his son's nanny, she was his wife! And that means Marcus was right!"

Vivienne shuffled over and plopped onto the sofa. She scrunched her face. "I still don't understand. How does this help you?"

"There's so much I haven't told you, but believe me when I say, this is huge. Jonathan's first wife Madeleine died giving birth to Michael, who's always been thought to be his sole heir, but I've come to believe he wasn't. Marcus believed it too, which is probably what got him killed."

"Hold up, let me make sure I understand this. Ol' Johnnie-boy comes out here with his pasty little wife Maddie to settle the area. She dies giving birth. He hooks up with the woman who's been taking care of his kid and has a baby with her, but no one's ever heard this before? In more than a hundred years? Yet somehow, not-so-bright conspiracy theorist Marcus figures this whole thing out? Doesn't that sound crazy to you?"

"Wait, what did you say?"

"I said, doesn't it all sound crazy to you? I'm sorry, I don't mean to hurt your feelings since you dated the guy and all, but let's be brutally honest here...Marcus Washburn was no genius. He was the *only* person to figure out this secret? Well, until you, that is."

"Yes, of course, it sounds crazy. The whole thing is crazy...and you don't even know the half of it. Organized crime, a love child, murder, and now Renee's gone missing."

"Renee's missing?"

"I'm surprised you didn't hear that during your training at the station yesterday."

Vivienne's cheeks darkened. "I was busy. My job is to answer the phone, direct calls, and file paperwork. She–they don't keep me up to date on their investigations."

I studied my sister's face. "You know you can tell me anything."

Viv brushed away my statement with her hand. "There's nothing to tell." After a beat, she added, "At least not yet. I don't know." She buried her face in her hands. After a moment, she pulled her hands away, dragging her fingertips down her cheeks and pulling her lower eyelids with them until she looked like Droopy, the cartoon dog. "I need some time to wrap my brain around what's happening."

"Okay. I'll leave it alone. For now."

"Thank you. So, what are you going to do with this latest information?"

"I'm going to the source."

"Which is?"

"George Hart. I went to see him last week after I discovered his book about Chattertowne had missing pages, but at the time, I had no idea the information in it was connected to Marcus's murder."

"You're not leaving the house today."

"Viv, I have to. George stonewalled me last time. I'm not letting him off the hook so easily this time."

"You can't drive on pain medication."

"I'll call an Uber."

Her sigh was heavy with resignation. "Do you want me to take you over there?"

"You don't have to do that."

"Actually, I do."

"I hate to put you out, but you're right. I shouldn't be driving," I said.

"So, where are we going?"

"He's at the assisted living facility on Hughes and Parker. Sunset Hills, or something like that."

"Sounds depressing," she said.

"Well, it smells like old people mixed with school cafeteria, but it's not terrible. I need to take a shower before we leave."

"Do you need help showering with your boot?" she asked.

"I'll be fine. I'll just wrap the dang thing in a trash bag and work around it."

At a quarter to nine, Vivienne and I pulled in front of the nursing home. The sign read "Sunrise Peak." Close enough, although a tad less ominous. I thrust myself from the passenger seat, grunting and wincing as I maneuvered my crutches into position.

Viv rushed around the car. "If you were patient enough to wait five seconds, I could've helped you." She pursed her lips and shut the door once I was out of the way.

"I hate relying on other people."

"Independence can be a lonely virtue."

"Thanks, Confucius. I'll take that under advisement," I said.

Once inside, we approached the reception desk with the click-clack of my crutches announcing our arrival. The formidable Denise had been replaced by a teenage girl whose nametag read "Britney."

"Hello." Unlike Denise, Britney greeted us with a warm smile. "Are you here for Family Day? It's not supposed to start 'til nine-thirty."

"We're here to see George Hart. He's, uh, our great uncle." The lie didn't come out easier the second time around.

"Can you sign the family day visitor's log?" She handed me a clipboard.

I scanned the log. As I was about to sign it, I stopped cold.

"Britney?"

The girl glanced up from her desk. "Yes, Ma'am."

"It says here George already had a visitor today, about an hour and a half ago."

"Oh, yeah, he did. I really wasn't supposed to let him in that early, but it was his nephew, and he was hot. Oh! He must be your cousin!" Britney wore a dreamy look of infatuation.

"His nephew?" My mouth went dry. "I can't read this. What did he say his name was?"

"Marcus."

"He said…" Swallowing didn't come easily. "He said his name was Marcus? What did he look like?"

"Like someone who should be in a boy band." A goofy grin crossed her face.

"Could you be more specific?" I asked.

Britney scrunched her pretty face. "Well, uh, he had the eyes of Niall and the lips of Justin Bieber. I couldn't see his hair because he was wearing a baseball hat. If he had Justin Timberlake's curls under that hat, he'd be all my fantasies."

I immediately turned and headed toward George's room. The frantic sound of my bounding crutches, followed by the slapping of Vivienne's flip-flops, echoed through the hallway.

Britney called after us. "Don't forget to sign out when you leave!"

"Audrey! What's wrong? Be careful, or you're going to hurt yourself even worse! What happened?"

"George doesn't have a nephew."

Using my crutches to vault my body several feet at a time, I rounded the corner into his room and skidded to a stop at the privacy curtain shrouding his bed. I stood rooted to the spot.

Vivienne whispered in my ear. "What are you doing?"

"I'm afraid of what I'm going to find on the other side of that curtain."

I strained to hear a sound, any sound, coming from the other side. I pulled back the drape. George appeared to be sleeping peacefully. I took another step closer, my heart pounding in my throat. His chest was still, devoid of the reassuring rise and fall indicating breathing. His face was placid, no eyelid flutter caused by dreaming. I stretched my fingers toward his bony arm and touched his skin. I quickly retracted my hand. It wasn't ice-cold, but not warm either.

"Is he...." Vivienne choked on her sentence.

I gulped and nodded. "I think so. Will you please tell Britney we have a situation here? She needs to call the police."

"What are you going to do?"

"I'm gonna sit before I pass out. Then I'm going to call Holden."

"Those are both good ideas. You sit, and I'll be right back." Viv rushed from the room.

I attempted to calm myself in the presence of my third dead body that week. Not my favorite kind of trifecta. Leaning my crutches against the wall, I slumped into the molded plastic chair and pressed the button to dial Holden. It rang four times before a female voice answered.

"Hello?"

"Emily?"

"Mm-hmm." She croaked.

"I'm sorry to bother you. I wouldn't have called this early if it weren't an emergency. I'm trying to reach Holden."

"Who's this?" A rustling sound came through the phone. "Oh, Audrey. Holden's in the shower. Can I help you with something?"

"Could you please let him know I'm at Sunrise Peak Assisted Living and

George Hart is dead?"

"Wait. Who's dead?"

"George Hart."

"Is that the old guy who wrote travel books?"

"Yes, how did you know?"

"I teach ninth-grade Washington State history. He brought in a book he'd written for our short unit on Chattertowne. He was old but he knew his stuff, and he was able to give historical accounts of events he'd lived through. He was a spunky little man, and the kids really enjoyed him. I was going to make it an annual thing, but the following year his health had deteriorated too much for him to be exposed to a bunch of germy teenagers. It's a shame he passed away, although having lived nearly a century is a pretty amazing accomplishment."

"Emily, the book he brought in, do you still have it?"

"No, sorry, he said it was one of the last surviving copies, and he needed to keep it safe."

Did that mean it was somewhere in his room? Had someone killed him and stolen his copy?

"Oh wait, hold on, Audrey. He's coming out now."

After a pause and muffled conversation, Holden's voice boomed through the phone. "George died? That's too bad."

"Why are you so calm about this?" My irritation with his lackadaisical attitude about George's death was magnified as I pictured him standing naked next to Emily.

"Well, he *was* a hundred…."

"Ninety-nine, but I'm not sure this was natural causes. Someone got here before me."

"What do you mean?"

"I discovered something in my research this morning, so I wanted another go at getting George to open up. When we got here, the logbook showed someone else had been here around seven. The girl at the front desk said he was a cute boy-band type, wearing a baseball hat. He told her he was George's nephew. Holden, he said his name was Marcus."

"You think George's nephew Marcus wasn't a Marcus or his nephew?"

"I *know* he wasn't George's nephew. Last time I was here, I pretended to be his great-niece. He told me his brother died as a child from the Spanish flu, and his sister was a nun. George had no family."

"Stay there. I'm calling it in, and I'm headed that way."

Vivienne appeared in the doorway with a man wearing burgundy scrubs. He rushed to George and lifted his wrist to check for a pulse. After getting none, he replaced it gently and patted his hand.

"I don't think you have to call it in; it's already been done." I looked to Viv for confirmation, and she nodded her head.

The next several minutes were a whirlwind. The medical staff ushered Viv and me into the hallway so they could examine George. Soon after, the CPD and CFD arrived, followed by a grim-faced Daphne Pierce.

As Daphne prepared to enter the room, she was stopped by the officer who stood watch at the doorway.

Daphne held up her coroner's badge. "Is Kimball here?"

The officer shook his head.

A few minutes later, Holden arrived wearing a sorrowful expression. His hair was still damp, and the smell of his freshly applied spicy aftershave preceded him. "Fancy meeting you here, at another suspicious death. This is starting to become a regular unpleasant occurrence."

Tears began to spill down my face.

"Hey, hey, I was teasing. This isn't your fault." He pulled me into an embrace.

"George was just a month shy of his centennial birthday. He deserved a big celebration."

Holden stroked my hair while I sobbed into his chest like a brokenhearted child for the second time in a week.

"The police won't tell us anything. Will you go in and see what you can find out?" My voice was ragged.

"Of course."

He released me, grimaced at Viv, and entered George's room.

"When are you planning to tell me what's going on between you and

Holden? That vibe definitely doesn't feel like a platonic working relationship."

I sighed. "Nothing's going on because we've decided nothing can go on."

"Judging by the chemistry I've witnessed between you, I'm not sure your hearts and hormones have gotten the memo."

"I can't do anything about that. We're doing the best we can to honor his commitments, under difficult circumstances."

"Commitments? Plural?"

"To Emily. To Chattertowne. The last thing we need right now is a scandal in the mayoral office on top of three deaths and a possible kidnapping."

Before Vivienne could respond, Holden re-entered the hallway.

"Anything?" I asked.

"They'll do an autopsy. Daphne's inclined to call it death by old age, which it still could be. I explained to her that George was a witness in the Marcus Washburn case and also that someone falsely claiming to be a relative had been in the room around seven. Her initial time of death estimate of three to seven this morning coincides with the visitor's arrival. She believes, however, he passed away closer to the early or middle portion of that range, around four or five. Rigor has started to set in, which takes anywhere from two to six hours following death. The visitor was here during that T.O.D. range, so they'll give it a more comprehensive look. My guess is we won't have any definitive answers on cause of death before Monday late in the day."

Vivienne turned to me. "We should get you home. You shouldn't be on your feet this much."

"I'm only supposed to be off one foot."

She huffed. "Funny."

"Vivienne's right. You're doing too much in your condition."

I wanted to punch Holden for siding with my sister, who seemed to be taking advantage of the situation to shift our power dynamic. Also, the last thing I wanted to do was go home and be stuck on the sofa all day, helpless and useless, while a killer skulked around.

"My condition is, I'm starving. Are you guys hungry?"

I placed my hand on Holden's forearm but withdrew it when a zip of electricity passed between us.

"Let's all go to breakfast," I said. "Who doesn't love breakfast? Everyone loves breakfast. I can tell you all about it at breakfast. How about Sandpiper Café over on Thirteenth?"

Holden shrugged. "Fine by me."

"After that, you have to put your foot up," Viv said.

"I'll put it up at the restaurant."

The three of us plodded toward the entrance, with me hobbling on my crutches and dragging my booted foot behind me like a zombie. I gave an apologetic wave to Britney, white-faced at her desk.

Wind and an icy rain/snow mix pelted us as we made our way through the parking lot. A black BMW with Massachusetts plates was parked next to Vivienne's car. As we got closer, the driver-side window came down.

"Hey."

"Darren?"

"Police scanner." He held up his phone.

Holden came behind me. "Benson? What are you doing here?"

"I could ask you both the same thing. Again. Audrey, you seem to be making a habit of finding yourself smack dab in the middle of crime scenes."

I sighed. "We're going to breakfast. Would you like to join us?"

Holden cleared his throat. I ignored him and his unspoken disapproval.

"Sure. I'll follow you." Darren gave Holden a victorious glance as he raised his window.

Turning to face the man grumbling to himself behind me, I sang through smiling, gritted teeth. "Trust me."

He grunted but didn't argue. "Sandpiper's."

I eased into Viv's front passenger seat.

"This should be interesting." Viv shifted the car into reverse.

"I know! How'd I get myself into this position?"

"You mean the position where you're sandwiched between two attractive guys vying for your attention?"

"When you put it that way, it doesn't sound all that terrible."

Viv pulled into the parking lot at the strip mall where Sandpiper Café was situated between a dry cleaner and a sip-n-paint studio. Before I'd had a chance to open the door, Darren stood at the ready to help me like an attentive golden retriever.

"It's okay. I'm not gonna fall over again. I'm getting the hang of it."

"When did you fall over previously?"

"Oh, here and there over the past couple days. The boot throws off my balance. My ankle's fine, though, it doesn't hurt. The drugs are stellar."

Holden watched with blazing scrutiny as Darren assisted me. I returned his look with my brow raised in challenge, and he gave a scowl in response. None of this was lost on Darren, whose head was on a swivel, his attention bouncing between us.

Holden opened the door for me to pass through, with Viv and Darren following close behind. Although the restaurant was busy, the waitress took pity on my condition and escorted us to a booth in the back.

Propping my crutches against the booth, I slid in first, followed by Vivienne, leaving Darren and Holden to have to sit next to each other. Darren gave a flourishing *after you* motion to Holden, who frowned as he squeezed in.

Holden reached under the table and, cupping my calf, pulled my boot onto his lap. I became flushed and flustered by the pressure of his thighs on either side of my leg and his hands on my toes. He was visibly cheered by my reaction.

Darren studied me. "Audrey, are you alright? Did you eat or drink anything unusual today?"

"What…what makes you ask that?"

"Because your face looks like it did the night at my house when you had your allergic reaction."

I suspected Darren mentioned my being at his house to get under Holden's skin, but whether the dig elicited its desired effect, Holden's mild expression gave nothing away. He had no tells, unlike Darren's jaw clench. He dragged his fingers seductively across the top of my toes to send me the message he wasn't intimidated when it came to Darren.

"I'm good," I squeaked. "It's just warm in here." I used the menu to fan my cheeks.

Darren slapped his menu onto the table. "I think I'll have the crepes." His declaration rhymed crepes with steps.

"I prefer quiche." Holden winked at me.

The waitress arrived at the table with a coffee carafe and four mugs. She poured a cup for each of us, took our orders, and dashed off to the next table.

"So, am I to understand the mafia's operating in Chattertowne?" Viv dropped the question like a bomb.

Darren dropped the spoon he'd been using to stir his coffee and clenched his jaw.

"Nothing official." Holden gave both Vivienne and me a warning look.

"Unofficially, though..." I returned Holden's stare with a defiant one of my own. "During my chat with Peter prior to his untimely, albeit necessary, death–"

I paused when I saw Darren's face pale.

"It's okay," he said. "Continue."

"Peter heavily alluded to organized criminal activity in Chattertowne. Not just back in Jimmy's day, but ongoing to this day."

"Was he specific?" Darren's mouth tightened.

Holden interrupted before I could respond. "I think it's unwise to speculate about an ongoing investigation, especially considering Darren's involvement."

He squeezed my big toe.

"I disagree," I said. "I believe someone killed George Hart this morning to keep him quiet, maybe even to steal his copy of the Chattertowne book. Obviously, it wasn't Peter Chatterton. If what Peter told me was true, there must still be either an active syndicate working with a new generation of criminals, or at least remnants who don't want to spend their sunset years in federal prison."

Holden laughed. "You think a seventy or eighty-year-old man murdered a hundred-year-old man to steal a book and bury a thirty-year-old secret?"

"No." I bristled at his condescension. "Britney said the guy looked young. He could've been sent on behalf of someone, or some*ones.*"

"Holden's right," Darren said.

His statement surprised everyone at the table. Holden choked on his coffee, Viv stared at Darren with wide eyes, and my mouth dropped open.

"Excuse me?" I asked.

"This is like your insinuations about Marcus being murdered by bad guys, Audrey." Darren's laugh was haughty, and his patronizing tone did not ingratiate him to me any more than Holden's vise grip on my toe.

I scowled at both men sitting across the table. "Believe whatever you want, but my gut's telling me it's all connected. Maybe Peter killed Marcus, or maybe he had someone in his organization do it. We'll probably never know. With Marcus and Peter dead, Renee missing, and now with George out of the way, there's no one left to tell the story."

Holden's countenance shifted from mockery to one of grave concern. "There is. You. You're the one who's been reconstructing the story from the ground up, amassing all the information and putting the pieces of the puzzle back together."

Silence filled the table at the implication of his statement. If someone believed I possessed the information for which Marcus and George were killed to keep them silent, I was still a threat to them and, therefore, in danger.

"That's it." Holden slapped his hands on the table. "I'm taking you to the range, and you're going to learn how to shoot. Today."

Chapter Twenty-One

"I'm telling you, this is a bad idea," I said.

Holden pulled up to the industrial complex where the gun range was located. "And I'm telling *you*, you're gonna give me an ulcer. I can't keep an eye on you twenty-four-seven. I need to know you can protect yourself."

He opened the back door to retrieve the crutches.

"Don't you want to know what I found out this morning that had me all hot to trot to Shady Meadows?" I asked.

He shut the door in response. When he opened the passenger door, he failed to fully suppress his smile.

"I do. And it isn't Shady Meadows; it's Sunrise Peak. Your version sounds like where has-been gangsters go to die."

"Probably not too far from the truth," I said. "That's basically what an assisted living facility is. People get sent there to die. Did you know I was the first family member to visit George in like twenty years?"

Holden blinked. "You're not family. You lied about being his niece." He grabbed a large black bag from the trunk.

"Great, great, great niece. And you know what I mean. Family as far as they know."

Leaning on my crutches, I took in the front of the range. Two large windows and a glass door were fortified with bars like a pawn shop in a seedy strip mall.

"This is it?"

I'd anticipated a more clandestine vibe, but instead, the lobby had the bright sterility of a shopping mall dental office. The man behind the counter looked like every Eagle Scout I'd ever known. He wore the beigest of beige pants with a blue checkered shirt reminiscent of a picnic tablecloth.

He greeted Holden with a salute. "Well, hello, sir. Good to see you again, Mr. Mayor."

"Cliff, man, I keep telling you I'm the city manager, not the mayor."

Cliff gave a conspiratorial wink. "We all know who's the brains of that operation, who's really in charge over there."

It was an open secret in town that Holden spent his days trying to do damage control for his mercurial boss Mayor Quincy. He'd once told me he didn't mind doing the heavy lifting and was grateful the mayor was more interested in being the facade of the operation because it allowed Holden to do his job without interference, but he would never admit that publicly.

"My girl Audrey here needs to practice shooting."

"Are you wanting her to have lessons? Or just a pass?" Cliff asked.

Holden pulled his membership card from his wallet and placed it on the counter. "Just a pass. I'll work with her."

Cliff scrutinized me. "Do you think it's a good idea for her to shoot in her condition?"

Holden must've sensed I was about to bail because he placed a firm hand on my back. "Yeah, she's good. I'll hold her steady."

Cliff eyeballed me up and down. "Lucky you." He raised his eyebrows twice. "She'll need to watch the training video."

Something wasn't quite right about Cliff's eyes. They were sort of...cross-eyed, but not exactly. Was that...was that a glass eye? I jerked to look at Holden. He cocked his head and leaned in so I could whisper into his ear.

"I think he has a glass eye."

Holden's brows and forehead furrowed. "What?" He hadn't even tried to keep his voice down.

I glared at him and spoke through gritted teeth, "He has a *glass eye!*"

Cliff turned to stare at me, and I was horrified I might've said it loud enough to be heard. Judging by the confused look on Holden's face, Cliff would've had to have above-average hearing if he'd heard what I'd said since the man right next to me hadn't. Although, it was said when one sense was diminished, the others increased.

"Does she need to use the bathroom?"

He directed the question to Holden.

Like I was incapable of answering for myself.

"No, she's fine. Let's get her set up on the video."

Cliff directed me to an area where several vending machines lined the walls, and six pub tables were positioned in the middle with stools tucked underneath. A faded poster showed a camouflaged Sarah Palin holding a rifle to advertise her (at the time) upcoming show with the phrase, "She's coming with a full heart and a full magazine."

Hanging above the poster was an old TV with a VCR mounted below it. Cliff pulled a remote from his pocket and aimed it at the player. The machine hummed as it rewound. I glanced back toward the lobby and made an exaggerated face of concern at Holden. He chuckled and returned to filling out paperwork.

For the next eight and a half minutes of warped, garbled video, Firearm Fred, Safety Expert, explained why I should never point a gun—loaded or unloaded—at anyone, to always assume it was loaded, to stay behind the firing line (to avoid getting shot), to keep the safety on when not shooting, to keep my finger off the trigger until ready to shoot, and to be aware of my surroundings so I didn't trip and accidentally set off the weapon. That last one was of greatest concern to me.

When the video finished, I returned to the lobby, where Holden had donned clear plastic safety glasses and ear protection. He handed me the equipment, and I struggled to position them properly.

"These earmuffs don't feel right." I shifted them back and forth, trying to get them to sit comfortably on my head.

Cliff snickered. "They're sound blockers, not earmuffs. Earmuffs are for building a snowman." His voice sounded muffled and far away, but the condescension came through crystal clear.

Holden leaned close, pulled the padded cover off my ear, and whispered, "They're earmuffs. Ignore him; he's always heckling me about things he thinks he's an expert on. He's not."

"I hope one of you is an expert. My life's in your hands."

Holden adjusted my ear protection device, whatever it was called, and straightened my safety glasses. "You're cute." He mouthed the words emphatically before grabbing the bag containing his gear off the counter.

Cliff buzzed us through the first of two sets of doors, momentarily trapping us in the middle.

"We're alone," Holden yelled, raising his eyebrows suggestively. His grin was mischievous.

I shook my head and laughed. "You're incorrigible."

He held up his hands in mock surrender. "I kid, I kid."

The second buzz unlocked the forward doors, and I followed him into the shooting range.

"For a place where it's important to see what you're doing, it's awfully dark in here," I said.

"There are lights at each station and on the targets."

He led me to a bay with a small shelf that separated us from the abyss into which we'd be shooting.

I craned my neck to look downrange, but everything appeared tar black. "What's back there?"

Holden squatted and pulled a rifle from the bag in sections. "There's a rubber berm trap. It absorbs the bullets, so they don't ricochet all over the range." He stood and faced me. "We'll begin with the rifle. I think it'll be easiest for you to start. It has less kickback, a smaller muzzle flash, and is easier to control. Have you ever played the duck hunting video game?"

"I think so, a long time ago."

"How about target games at the carnival?"

"Not really. Oh, wait! I did try the one where you shoot water into the mouth of a clown until his balloon pops. Does that count?"

"Not really. So, you're a true beginner. I can work with this." He inhaled an exaggerated breath.

"Such a martyr."

"I don't want to assume you know things you don't or forget to tell you something important." He assembled the weapon and loaded what appeared to be enormous bullets, checked the safety, and placed it on the counter facing away from us. Pulling out a target sheet with concentric circles, he attached it to the clips. A button to the left of the cubicle sent the target out into the dark. "I'm going to have you start here, at about thirty feet."

"Seems far."

"It shouldn't be for this type of weapon. If it's too far, we can pull it in. Do you think you can stand on your boot, or do you need your crutches? It'll fit in the crook of your arm better if you don't have them."

"I'm a little worried about losing my balance and shooting you in the face."

"I'm not going to let that happen. Here, I'll stand right behind you and keep my hands on your hips to hold you steady. I'll be too close for you to shoot me in the face. First, I need you to look and make sure the safety's on. When the safety's on, it's pushed in here." He pointed to the mechanism. "Is it on?"

"Yes, it's on."

"Okay, lift the rifle to your shoulder and hold the barrel here with your left hand. You want the butt to nestle right in here. You don't want it too high, and you don't want it loose. This is called your shoulder pocket. It needs to be pressed tight against it." He touched me just above my armpit, below my right shoulder, to indicate where to place it. "Good. Do you feel how that sits in there?"

"Yes, I think so."

"Now, rest your right cheek here and look through the scope. It might be easier to close your left eye."

"Is that why Cliff only needs one eye?"

I sensed Holden freeze behind me, and then his entire body began shaking with laughter.

"What? It's a reasonable question. The man works at a gun range with only one functional eyeball." I placed the rifle back on the counter and turned around to look at him. "That doesn't give me a whole lot of confidence in this operation."

"Jeez, you kill me." He wheezed with laughter, and a tear formed in the corner of his eye.

"I'm trying to figure out how *not* to kill you."

Holden took a shuddered breath. "Okay. Where were we?"

He wiped the stray tear before turning me around and pressing into my back. He placed his hands on my waist. It felt very intimate, despite the weaponry.

I picked up the rifle and positioned it against my shoulder. I rested my cheek on the stock and closed my left eye. "I can see the target."

"Do you see how there's a cross in the scope?"

"Yes."

"You want the center of that cross to line up with the center of the target. Can you do that?"

"Yeah." Squinting to see it, I closed my right eye, switched to my left, and then my right again. "It's hard to focus. This is heavier than I expected and hard to hold in place."

"You'll get used to it. Okay, make sure your index finger's straight and not on the trigger before you release the safety. You want your fingertip to pull the trigger."

I tried to hold the rifle steady despite my shaking arms. "I don't know if I can do this. I'm scared. There's a real bullet in here."

Holden's breath warmed the back of my neck, and his voice rumbled, "Breathe. Shooting's as much about breathing as anything. Spread your legs shoulder-width apart, maybe a little less, and lean forward. There you go. Now, release the safety. Take a deep breath, about three-fourths full, hold for a respiratory pause, then pull the trigger."

The trigger required more pressure than I'd anticipated. The gun fired, and I yelped. I re-set the safety and placed it down with trembling hands. A hole had appeared in the white space to the right of the center target.

"You did it! How did it feel?"

I turned to face him. "Truthfully? Terrifying."

He leaned toward me before pulling himself back like a puppy who'd reached the end of his leash. "I'm proud of you."

"That was the scariest thing I've ever done in my life."

He placed his hands on my shoulders. "You're shaking."

"It's not like on TV. I could feel the power I held and then the adrenaline rush afterwards."

"You ready to try again?"

"I don't know."

"The best way to get over timidity is to keep practicing."

Taking a deep breath, I nodded and picked up the rifle again.

"See that circle in the upper left? Aim for the middle."

"I'll be lucky if I hit the circle at all." Releasing the safety, I took a breath and fired three shots in a row. Once again, as soon as the shots were taken, I engaged the safety and put down the gun.

"How was that? You hit the target. A little low and to the right, but you were in the general vicinity."

"About the same, maybe a little better. I'm not sure how this will help me if someone tries to come after me, though. By the time I got myself into position, they'd have the advantage."

"I agree. I wanted you to practice with the rifle first to get the feel of shooting. Now we're going to move on to the pistol. Let me fire off what's left in here. Move back a little." Holden picked up the rifle, disengaged the safety, and decimated the bullseye of each target.

"Show-off. Do we need to clean up the shell casings?"

"No, they're past the line. Remember? Never go past the line."

He broke the rifle into sections and placed it back into the bag before pulling out a weapon that was tiny in comparison.

"What's that, a lady gun? Did you bring me a lady gun?"

"This lady gun, as you call it, is a Glock Nineteen. It's used by Israeli Special Forces, along with many U.S. law enforcement agencies. Its compact size makes it perfect for concealment; it's lightweight, has good capacity. Shooting a pistol is different than a rifle. For one thing, you'll have both hands together. With your strong hand, you want to grip it high to give you the best control."

He wrapped his arms around me from behind, holding the handgun in front of me. He rubbed between my thumb and forefinger, and I felt my neck and chest grow warm. "This webbed part of your hand should fit right in here." He placed the gun in my hand and positioned it accordingly. "Your trigger finger needs to be pointed straight, and these lower fingers need to be here under the trigger. Your left hand will wrap around them with your right thumb over your left."

"This is awkward and uncomfortable."

"It takes time to get used to the positioning. Eventually, it feels natural and becomes second nature."

"You seem to be under the impression this is going to become a hobby. It's not. I'm only doing it to make you feel better. What you should be doing is teaching me how to use my crutches for self-defense."

"Ease a bit on your grip. Your knuckles are white as a ghost."

"I'm afraid if I loosen my hands, I'll drop it and shoot one or both of us in the foot. I've got decent protection with this boot. You've got nothing but nylon and rubber between a stray bullet and your toes."

"Relax a bit. Not completely, just enough so your hands don't fatigue. You're gonna feel a decent kickback compared to the rifle. Make sure you're leaning slightly forward. You're going to take a deep breath, let out half, fire, then exhale fully. Let's practice a few breaths."

He breathed in and out, and I began to sync my breathing with his. As our chests rose and fell together, I closed my eyes, lulled by his warm breath on my neck and the rhythm of our bodies moving in coordination with each other. For a moment, I forgot where we were.

The door buzzed, breaking me from my trance and causing my eyelids to fly open.

A large gentleman passed behind us with a case the size of a tuba.

"What the hell does he have in there, a cannon?" I asked.

"I'm guessing that's a pretty large weapon, and it's gonna make a lot of noise. It'll be harder for you to shoot if his blasts make you jumpy. Let's have you fire off a couple shots and get out of here before he gets set up. We don't need you becoming even more skittish."

After a few additional directions from Holden, I fired the Glock. It exploded like a bomb going off in my hands. I engaged the safety and set it down.

"Whoa! That flash was much brighter! And the shot was much louder!" I said.

"Yeah, I tried to warn you. Let's do one more."

"Nah, I'm good."

He evaluated me for a moment and then shrugged his shoulders. Picking up the Glock, he fired off the remaining rounds. He roped in the target paper and handed it to me.

"Souvenir."

"Thanks. I think I smell like gunpowder."

He smiled. "You have a shell casing sticking out of the hood of your sweatshirt."

Reaching around, I pulled it out as the first blast came from the cubicle on the end. I threw my hands in the air, causing the casing to fly. "Aanndd, I'm done."

As we passed the video viewing area, the tables were filled with about a dozen giggly twenty-somethings on a group date. One guy made a gun with his hands and said, "Pew! Pew!" to the delight of his female companion.

The comfortable rapport which had developed between us diminished into tension once we were back in the car and on our way to my apartment. I fidgeted and fought the urge to babble. I couldn't stop thinking about what it felt like to have his arms around me.

Holden gave me a sidelong glance. "You wanna tell me what's on your mind?"

"Who says anything's on my mind?"

He turned to look at me with a *who do you think you're fooling?* expression. "How about we start with what precipitated your early morning visit to George?"

I breathed out my relief. If there was one thing Holden and I shared, it was a mutual desire to avoid uncomfortable conversations.

"So, get this…they were married!" I clapped my hands.

"Who was married?"

"Jonathan and Nettie."

"How do you know?"

"These days, many resource libraries scan entire books, especially out-of-print and hard-to-find copies, and they upload them to their websites. When I searched for Nettie, a link to a book came up. It was a local travel guide written by none other than George Hart. In it, he asserts the Jeannetta River was named by Jonathan for his French-Indian bride Nettie!"

"I guess if they were married, that lends credence to the rumors about an heir. So, you went to see George hoping to get more info?"

I sighed. "Yeah, George was being stubborn last time I went to see him. He said it was because he was protecting me. I feel like I'd have been better off knowing what dangers I was dealing with. Maybe I could've saved his life."

"It's important we separate fact from supposition. We don't know George was murdered. Yes, we know his visitor was lying about who he was, and he used Marcus's name, which is fishy, but George was ninety-nine. That's really old, Audrey. He was living on borrowed time and then some. Any secrets he knew about the Chattertons, he'd known for decades, so he wasn't an imminent threat to anyone. We also don't know Renee's been kidnapped, only that she's missing. Not to mention, we don't know for certain Peter killed Marcus."

"He practically admitted it to me!"

"He was playing a game of cat and mouse with you. From everything you've told me, I think he was fishing to find out what you know and what you think you know. Did he ever outright say he killed Marcus?"

"No, he didn't say," I scrunched my face and lowered my voice. "'I killed Marcus.' Not in those exact words."

"That was actually a pretty good impression of Peter." He laughed. "Maybe he did it, maybe he didn't. I don't know. I just don't think we're doing ourselves any favors making assumptions."

"I get it."

"Can I count on you to behave yourself?"

"Define behave." I fluttered my eyelashes.

"Nice try, but I'm immune to the eyelash flutter. You're recovering from an injury you sustained while escaping a man who threatened to kill you. If George was murdered and our Justin Bieber/Timberlake look-alike is somehow connected to Marcus's death, someone's still out there with bad intentions...probably toward you. I'd offer to give you my gun for protection, but after what I just witnessed, that's not a good idea. The city doesn't have the manpower to position an officer at your apartment, especially not this week, but I can call in a favor and get a patrol car to drive by your place a few extra times per day just to be on the safe side."

"You won't hear any protesting from me."

Holden pulled into a parking spot in front of my apartment complex, turned off the car, and unbuckled his seat belt.

"You don't have to come in."

He crooked his head to look at me. "Do you not want me to come in?"

"I don't want you to feel obligated. I'm pretty self-sufficient."

"You're also too stubborn for your own good. So, what's your plan for the rest of the day?"

"I'm gonna take it easy."

He gave me a skeptical look.

"I am. I have a small story to write about a disastrous widows' luncheon, and I need to get my notes into a cohesive form to write my first piece for the Kupit Festival. If I get organized, maybe something I've missed will pop out at me. What about you?"

"I've got some groveling to do at home. I was supposed to spend the day with Emily, but that obviously didn't turn out as planned. We have dinner tonight at my sister's, and I need to have a talk with Noah." At this last statement, his expression darkened.

"Ah, yes, Sunday family dinner."

Holden's younger sister Harper hosted a monthly dinner with their parents, two brothers, and their families. His middle brother Liam lived in Seattle and sold insurance, while his youngest brother Noah lived with his wife and three young kids just around the corner from Holden and Emily.

"Everything okay with Noah?"

Holden frowned. "You know, I love the guy. I'd do almost anything for him, but sometimes, he makes his life hard for no damn reason at all and without thinking about how it affects the rest of the family."

"I get it. When Viv nearly drowned, my mom blamed me, so I blamed myself. I swore from that day forward I would be her protector. I was seven. I've always felt a responsibility to chart the course and make it safe for her. Sometimes, though, I get a little resentful because she never stops to consider how her reckless choices affect me. I've been so terrified of water for twenty-five years I don't even own a swimsuit. Meanwhile, she's got no problem cliff diving in Mexico or snorkeling in Hawaii. How's that fair?"

"We resent them for choices we're making on their behalf, which isn't fair either. We aren't their parents. We gave ourselves a responsibility no one asked us to take on. I've gotten involved in all sorts of shenanigans trying to clean up my baby brother's messes. You came back to Chattertowne the instant Viv was in trouble. You gave up your job, your apartment, your friends…why?"

My shoulders slumped. "If I didn't, who would?"

"I doubt your mom intended for you to carry this burden. Just because Viv almost lost her life when you were kids doesn't mean you're supposed to perpetually give up yours in tribute."

I studied Holden's face. "It's nice to have someone to talk to about this who understands. Most of the time, I keep these feelings bottled inside me because of all the guilt."

"Trust me when I tell you this. I understand more than you could possibly know." His mouth tightened. "Hey, are you sure you don't need my help getting upstairs?"

"There's an elevator." I opened the door and climbed out. I thrust my head back into the car. "Uh, I might need help after all. My crutches are in the back seat."

"Gimme a sec."

He hopped out and came around to my side. I held on to the passenger door for support. He handed the crutches to me and stood by while I wrangled them under my arms.

"Got it?"

"Yep."

He studied me. "What's that look?"

"What look?"

"That grimace. The puckered lips, like you just took a swig of lemon juice."

"Nothing." I swayed, shifting my body weight from one crutch to the other.

He placed his large hands on my shoulders, stopping me from rocking side-to-side.

"It's all gonna sort itself out, eventually. We just gotta be patient."

"Patience isn't my strong suit."

"I've gathered. Now go upstairs and lock your door. Don't open it for anyone."

After flipping the deadbolt to the locked position, I took a pain pill from the bottle on the kitchen counter, popped it into the back of my throat, and drank straight from the tap to wash it down. En route to the bedroom, I grabbed my laptop. Once in bed, I adjusted the pillows to support my back, put one under my booted foot, and propped the laptop on another. With my phone, I snapped a picture of my leg and sent it to Holden with the caption,

Snug as a bug in a rug.

Three dots appeared. After a minute, the dots disappeared. When they reappeared, all he sent was a thumbs-up emoji.

Chapter Twenty-Two

My **Good Monday morning!** text to Holden received a phone call in response.

"Hey. You couldn't just text me back?" I asked.

"Morning…and I prefer the phone. Less chance of miscommunication that way. How are you feeling?"

"Decent. I don't even think I'll need a pain pill today."

"What's on the docket?"

"I've got to dig deeper into this whole Nettie component. I know she's significant, maybe even the lynchpin at the center of everything. I've been going through the *Current's* archives. This area's history didn't start when Jonathan showed up, but you'd never know it by reading past Kupit articles. It's been the same thing year after year, a celebration of colonizers' stories. Other than a few random references, there's been minimal mention of the Coast Salish People. I refuse to do that with my articles."

"You're gonna upset a lot of people."

"Anderson told me to write the articles my conscience compels me to tell. Who's been served by whitewashing the truth all these years? Not Marcus. Not his dad. Certainly not Nettie. It's like ripping off a bandage. It may be painful for this town to face its complete history, but some wounds must be laid bare in order to heal."

"I wonder how the more set-in-their-ways folks like Peg are gonna respond."

"She may outweigh me, but I can outrun her if need be."

Holden didn't join my laughter. "Keep what you're working on close to the vest for now, even with Darren. Maybe especially with Darren."

"That's not gonna be a problem. I don't think he's thrilled I left with you after breakfast to go to the gun range."

"Perfect. Keep it that way. So, you're determined to go to work today? I don't think anyone would blame you for taking more time to recover."

"Too much to do. Tasha offered to take me. Once I get to the office, I need to check in with Sandros, see if he's discovered anything about the hacking stuff. Any leads yet on Renee?"

"I think I'd have heard if there were. I'll let you know what I find out."

My phone buzzed. "Can you hold for one sec? Mildred's calling."

"I have to go anyway. I'll call you later to see how it's going."

I clicked over to answer. "Good morning, Mildred!"

"Oh, hello, Audrey! I hope I'm not calling too early."

"Not at all. I was just finishing a call with Holden."

"Well, dear, that's why I'm calling. I want to invite you both over for supper tonight. I make a to-die-for butternut squash ravioli in cream sauce, and it's been ages since I had a reason to make it."

"Sounds wonderful, Mildred. I'm available, but I need to check with Holden. What time are you thinking?"

"How about five-thirty?"

"Okay, five thirty it is, unless Holden can't make it."

I passed along the invitation to Holden via text message, and he accepted, so I sent a text to Mildred confirming the plan.

I climbed into Tasha's car. "Thanks so much for picking me up."

"No problem. I'm surprised Anderson didn't just tell you to work remotely."

"I have been, and I don't plan on staying long, but I really need to talk to Sandros in person."

Tasha stiffened.

"Did I say something wrong?" I asked.

"No." She gripped the steering wheel and stared straight ahead, her mouth in a firm line.

"You know there's nothing going on between Sandros and me, right?" I said.

"It's none of my business. It's just…."

"It's just what?"

Tasha took a deep breath. "After all these months of flirty banter with Darren, you don't even seem to like him anymore. You're clearly not interested in Sandros, yet you kissed him at my party…when someone who really likes him could have been kissing him instead!"

"Oh, Tasha, I'm sorry. I…I didn't know. That night at the party I was feeling bad about Darren's hot and cold attitude, and I wanted to make him jealous. Sandros was willing to give me attention, and I used him without consideration for anyone else. There's no excuse for my behavior, and I'm sorry."

Tasha's shoulders slumped. "Sandros doesn't even notice me when you're in the room. I laugh at his stupid jokes, I smile like an idiot every time he walks in the office, and I hand-deliver his messages when I could make him pick them up like everyone else. I'm making a fool of myself over a guy who barely knows I exist!"

"Sandros is a guy, which means by nature he's a little clueless. I'll bet if you invite him to lunch, his response will surprise you, in a good way."

She gasped. "Come right out and ask him? I couldn't!"

"Sure, you can. While I'm talking to him today, you should come in. I'll help you wrangle a date."

"You…you'd do that?" She blushed from her chest through her ginger scalp.

"Sandros may not be my type, but I think you two are a great match. I'd be happy to help."

Tasha's tight face eased into a hopeful smile.

Once settled into my office with my boot propped on an empty overturned trash bin, I finished editing the copy for the widows' luncheon and updated my ads before sending everything to Anderson for review. I had a few minutes to spare before I planned to go talk to Sandros, so I made a call.

"Chattertowne Police Department, how may I direct you?" My sister's familiar voice answered in an unfamiliarly formal tone.

"Oh my gosh, I almost forgot you work there! It's so weird!"

"If you're not calling to talk to me, why are you calling, Audrey? It's busy around here." Her voice was prim and clipped.

"I need to talk to Kimball. I'm hoping to find out if there's anything new on Marcus's case or Renee's disappearance."

"I don't think she can comment on active police investigation. I'm not even sure she's cleared you as a suspect." She lowered her voice. "I need this job, Audrey."

"Viv, please just put me through. I need to ask her some questions for my article."

A sharp exhale came through the phone. "Fine. Hold, please."

After ten seconds of "What's Going On" by Marvin Gaye, Kimball's voice boomed through the receiver.

"Good morning, Ms. O'Connell. How can I help you?"

"I'm checking to see if there are any developments on the Washburn cases, particularly Renee."

"Is this on the record or off the record?"

"Whichever you'd prefer."

"On the record, there are no new developments. Peter Chatterton is the prime suspect in Marcus Washburn's murder. We have yet to officially rule out others, including you. Renee Washburn's still missing. Off the record, and I'm only telling you this because I know anything I tell Villalobos he'll share with you…as a matter of fact, you may have already heard this from him because I spoke with him a half hour ago."

"I haven't talked to him. What's going on?" Marvin's song echoed in my mind after I uttered the words.

"There's a theory emerging Renee's somehow involved in Marcus's death, and she's on the run."

I gasped. "Really."

"You sound surprised. You're the one who posited the theory in the first place," said Kimball.

"Well, yeah, but I was told she'd given a credible interview, and when Holden and I went to the house she did seem like a grieving woman. She was a mess, as was the house, although it was difficult to tell whether she'd let the house go after he died or if it was like that before."

"We've got staff sifting through their sh-…junk as we speak, looking for evidence connected to her possible kidnapping as well as any indication of collusion with Peter."

"Need help?"

"You wanna dig through her garbage?" Her tone was skeptical.

"Not particularly, but Peter mentioned Renee called him the day she went missing. Holden and I had told her the day before that Marcus may have had evidence of the claims on his blog about his stolen birthright, Nettie, and the Chattertons. Something's got to be lurking in Marcus's mess of an office. I want to solve this thing. If it'll move the investigation along, and clear me once and for all in the process, well then…"

Kimball muttered to herself. "I must be crazy. This is completely against my better judgment, but we're short on manpower. Two of our officers are at a training in Seattle all this week. I doubt you'll be effective in your condition, but I'll let Sergeant Bianchi know you'll be coming by and to keep an eye on you. About what time do you think?"

"I've got some work to finish here at the paper, and before I leave, I need to speak with a colleague. I'll have to Uber it over there, so about one, I'd say."

"Alright. If you do discover anything, at the Washburn house or otherwise, please call me right away."

"Will do. By the way, how's Viv working out?" I asked.

"She's great. She takes her job seriously, very professional."

"Yeah, I gathered. She was playing gatekeeper when I called."

Kimball chuckled. "I told her I wasn't to be disturbed."

"Well, I'm glad she's a good fit. Between you and me, I think she's hoping the receptionist decides to take permanent maternity leave."

"She won't have to worry about staying on, I'll find a spot for her."

"I'm sure that'll make her feel better. Hey, thanks for taking the time. I know you've got a lot going on. I appreciate the courtesy."

"No problem, Audrey. I'll be in touch."

"Likewise."

For the second time in about a week, I entered the IT den. This time all the cubicles were filled. Thanh was a clean-cut Vietnamese kid wearing an outfit similar to Sandros's. Khaki pants and button-up shirts appeared to be standard-issue computer geek uniform. Gerald wore a variation on the same thing; only the dangerously sharp creases on his pants and shirt indicated compulsive perfectionism.

Donnie, on the other hand, wore a too-tight black t-shirt with a giant green and blue eyeball which, as evidenced by the new poster on his cubicle wall, was the logo of a YouTube gamer. Donnie had feathered hair and a chain wallet attached to his Levi's. His accessories said tough guy, but his dadbod said he spent his free time playing *World of Warcraft*. He occasionally paused typing to scratch his head, so apparently, none of the ten remedies for scalp itch had proven effective.

The potpourri of drugstore colognes made my eyes water. My own perfume or pheromonal signal must have created a disturbance in their atmosphere because they all turned around to stare at me.

Sandros preened like a peacock. "Audrey! Good to see you again. Couldn't stay away, huh?" He waggled his unibrow.

"You know me," was all I could muster, which was enough to satisfy Sandros and his compadres, who stared at him like he was a god. Sandros pointed at Thanh, indicating he wanted him to get up. With nowhere to sit, Thanh leaned awkwardly against the wall.

"Audrey and I need to discuss something private," Sandros announced to the room. "I'm going to need you all to put on headphones for a few minutes."

I suspected their compliance had less to do with established respect for their supervisor and more with newfound esteem for his perceived ways with women…well, woman. Thanh looked around with uncertainty before leaving the room altogether.

"I feel bad. He can't do his work because I took his chair."

"He's fine; he wasn't working anyway. He was mining Bitcoin."

I rolled closer to Sandros. "So, did you find anything?"

His smugness gave him a Cheshire Cat-like appearance. "Of course, I did. Let's start with Marcus's blog. Whoever hacked into it knew what they were doing. My first clue was they used a VPN to hide their IP."

"English, please, Sandros. I don't speak techy."

"A VPN is a virtual private network. ISPs, internet service providers, usually have visibility of their users' IP addresses. VPNs block visibility by sending your activity onto a private network. IP stands for internet protocol, and it's the system operating the internet. It determines how things are transmitted on several layers, depending on the scope of networking involved. Your devices, your computer, laptop, phone, etc., each have a virtual address attached to them, an identifier. While you may be browsing in the privacy of your home or office, your activity isn't private…unless you use a VPN. Our hacker used one to hide his IP and his identity, but he did more than that."

"What do you mean?"

"He used a proxy chain."

When I didn't react, he sighed like I was unable to figure out one plus one equaled two.

"A proxy chain consists of multiple IPs linked together. Our hacker used it to hide his trail. When he got to Marcus's site, he left the breadcrumbs I told you about, but his breadcrumbs were not from his loaf, so to speak. They were from a proxy server and crumbs were left there. Those breadcrumbs led to another proxy server, and so on."

"You were able to track them back to our hacker?"

"Nope."

"Well, then, why do you look so self-satisfied?" I asked.

"You have no idea how complicated and difficult it was to even get as far as I did. Marcus's website didn't require much expertise to crack and yet the hacker was highly skilled and used unnecessarily complex techniques to do so. What does that tell you?"

Once again, my bafflement caused him to roll his eyes in frustration.

"It tells you," he paused for dramatic effect, "we aren't dealing with a kid who took a couple programming classes at the community college. This is high-level three-one-three-three-seven stuff. The person who did it's no lackey."

"What in the heck is three-one-three-three-seven?"

"Elite-level hacking. In the hacking world, numbers are used to cloak groups and interactions from search engines. I'd try to explain to you what I saw while I was digging around, but you wouldn't understand it. Heck, I thought I'd dumbed down the explanation enough. You still seem completely lost."

"I'm not lost. I understand what you're saying. I just don't know all the terminology." I pursed my lips and twisted them to the left. "So, the most intriguing part of all this *isn't* someone hacking into Marcus's blog to delete his post or why, but that whoever did so was highly skilled at masking their identity?"

"Yes, but not only because of their technical ability. Don't you get it?"

"I guess not."

"We're talking about one of two groups. The government, well, *a* government, or the upper echelon of hacking, the top two to three percenters. If I had to place bets, my money would be on a government agency."

My mouth formed an O. "Like the FBI?"

Sandros gave a solemn nod. "Like the FBI."

"Oh wow. So, now I need to figure out why the FBI might want to take down Marcus's stupid conspiracy blog. It must have something to do with what got him killed. Dang, Sandros, you did come through for me. I'm impressed."

Sandros smiled. It wasn't his usual violating smile, but one of affection. Someone whimpered behind me, causing his attention to shift upward and over my shoulder. I spun around and came face to face with a crestfallen Tasha.

"Tasha, I'm so glad you're here," I said.

She turned to leave but stopped when she saw my pleading expression.

"You won't believe what Sandros was able to figure out. Sit, you've gotta hear this. He was just explaining it all to me. Fascinating stuff."

I stood and placed my arm around Tasha's shoulder, led her over to the chair, eased her into it, and spun her to face Sandros. Since the estrogen in the room had doubled, Gerald and Donnie turned to ogle Sandros's new guest. Sandros scowled and pointed at their monitors in a nonverbal command to mind their own business.

"Audrey, this is supposed to be on the down-low." He lowered his unibrow until it hovered just above his dark eyes.

"You can tell her the cool stuff you did without going into too much detail. It's okay, I trust Tasha."

Sandros appraised Tasha as if for the first time. His expression softened when his gaze reached her face.

"Audrey asked me to investigate potential hacking, and I was able to determine it had to have been done by a high-level hacker related to a group like Anonymous or the FBI."

"Crazy, right?" I took a step back. "Hey, I gotta go. You two should go to lunch. My treat for all your hard work, Sandros."

His head raised to look at me. "Wait, don't you want to hear the rest?"

"The rest?"

"Remember that question you asked me about how someone might access social media?"

"Yeah."

He wiggled his eyebrow, and I gasped.

"Someone did hack into my account?"

"Not exactly. It's pretty much what I suspected. Someone installed a keystroke tracking device. I'll spare us both the technical explanation. There was something installed on your computer sending all keystroke activity through a kernel. It logged it, allowed access to your system, and could've been used as a device driver. For however long it's been installed, someone's had access to your computer and all its content."

I placed my hands on the back of the chair to steady myself.

Tasha's gaze widened. "Are you okay?"

"Nope."

"I've been asking myself why someone would want to search the computer of a low-level writer working at a mediocre small-town newspaper. It makes no sense." Sandros shook his head.

"Sandros, I'd be insulted if I weren't so freaked out right now. Unfortunately, I have a good idea who. I just don't know why."

Chapter Twenty-Three

I leaned on my crutches and made several futile attempts to keep my brown leather satchel slung over my shoulder while waiting on the sidewalk for my scheduled ride. The self-pity had set in. My armpits were chafed, my left hip ached from overcompensating for my useless right side, and I'd just discovered someone had been spying on me via my computer.

It wasn't that I didn't trust Sandros, but I had a feeling if I were to tell him I suspected Darren was the one keeping tabs on me, he might not be able to keep his thoughts about it to himself. The last thing I needed was Sandros tipping Darren off before I'd had a chance to figure out the reason for the espionage.

My phone buzzed with a text message from Mildred.

No time for squash. Pub in Kirkland?

I responded to say we'd pick her up around five fifteen from the library. In return Mildred sent a cat emoji with heart eyes, which I took as agreement. I sent a text to Holden letting him know our plans with Mildred had changed and I asked him to grab me from the Washburn house around five.

Do I even want to know?

Probably not.

A silver Prius pulled up next to the curb. Music poured from the stereo when a slight man with dark skin and darker hair hopped out of the car.

"Ms. O'Connell?" His accent was thick like his mustache.

"Yes, that's me. Do you think I'll be able to fit? I've got this bum ankle and crutches. I forgot to mention it when I scheduled the ride."

Because we were similar height, I looked straight into his deep brown eyes. They twinkled below dark bushy brows and feathered bangs. His mustache was peppered with gray hair, but his cleft chin was clean-shaven.

"We will make this work. I am Kashif, by the way."

He opened the door and held his hand out for me to give him the crutches. Flinging my satchel onto the floor, I eased into the back of the car, right leg first, and dragged my rear across the black neoprene seat cover. The fabric was like a diver's wetsuit and wasn't conducive to smooth sliding. My left leg was angled out, and my hip flexed awkwardly. Kashif carefully shut the door and skittered back into the driver's seat, shoving the crutches into the space next to him.

"How are you today?" He lowered the volume on the sitars.

Tree-shaped cinnamon and blackberry-clove air fresheners hung from the rearview mirror. Adjusting my body to give my leg room to stretch in hopes of relieving the pressure from my hip, I was distinctly *un*comfortable despite the comforting aroma. Discomfort was a feeling I was becoming increasingly familiar with.

"Do you really wanna know?"

"I do."

"I'm headed to the home of my dead ex-boyfriend to try and figure out if his wife is a kidnapping victim or is somehow involved with his murder."

He was quiet long enough for me to begin to wonder if he was contemplating kicking me out of the car.

"It is interesting how when we perceive a person upon first impression, that is not necessarily the truth about them. I had assumed your greatest current struggle is your injured leg, but I was mistaken. I am sorry about your friend."

"Thank you."

"May I ask you a question?" His kind espresso-colored eyes looked at me through the mirror.

"Sure."

"You say you are trying to discover if your former love's wife is responsible for his death."

"Yes."

"I have found often what we tell ourselves we are seeking and for what purpose is only a partial reason. What do you hope to learn? About yourself, I mean."

Caught off guard by the question, I pondered it for a few minutes. "I guess I feel like I have a lot to prove…to my mother, to my boss, but mostly to myself. Marcus–my ex–represents many of my regrets and failures."

"How so? If you don't mind my prying."

"When we dated, we were only nineteen, but he was already pretty broken and wounded. I found his neediness exhausting. I know that must sound selfish, but I had enough on my plate with trying to keep an eye on my younger sister."

"I do not think that sounds selfish. I think it sounds like you made the choice you felt was best for you at the time."

"Recently, Marcus reached out to me for help, and I ignored him. Now he's dead. I know I couldn't have saved him, but somehow I still feel guilty."

"What will you do with these feelings?"

"I know it won't bring him back to his family, but if I can find his killer and figure out why this happened, it might give them some closure while also relieving some of my guilt. If I solve this case, I'll also prove I'm capable of being an investigative journalist, and I'm not a failure just because I scampered home with my tail between my legs." I paused. "I'm sorry. I didn't mean to turn this ride into a therapy session."

"Please do not apologize. I was professor of sociology in Pakistan before coming here ten years ago, and I miss deep conversations. I have never been a fan of small talk. I see each passenger who rides in my car as a chance to connect with another human being. If you had left having only talked about the weather, I would have regretted a missed opportunity. It sounds to me as though you needed to get much off your heart but haven't had an opportunity to do so. Purging one's thoughts can be cathartic, clearing the path to see our next steps. Sometimes that is easier to do with a stranger. Many people have never learned how to deal with either their emotions or others' emotions. I have a theory this is the reason behind most road rage incidents I witness. So much frustration and so many unexamined feelings."

He pulled in front of the battered saltbox house, and my stomach churned with unease.

"I wish you great luck, Ms. O'Connell."

"Thank you, Kashif."

"Allow me to assist you."

He retrieved my crutches from the passenger seat before opening the rear door to help me out of the car. I slung my satchel over my left shoulder, which swung around and hit the back of my head.

"Do you need me to accompany you to the house?" he asked.

"I'm good, thank you. I appreciate the offer, though."

I gave a smile and a slight wave as he drove away and trudged to the front stoop. Both the screen door and front door were open. Inside, two women were cross-legged on the floor, digging through piles of paper and junk. Their progress was difficult to measure, considering the enormity of the task.

A man peeked out from Marcus's office. "Hey. You must be Audrey. I'm Sergeant Bianchi. Tony."

About forty, with silver strands streaking his jet-black hair, Tony was average height with a muscular build, medium complexion, and brown hooded eyes. His thick ebony mustache was of a shade found only in a tin of shoe polish or a bottle of Just for Men. His five o'clock shadow at one o'clock in the afternoon likely resulted from strong Southern Italian genes.

"Did the crutches give me away?"

"Definitely a clue. Kimball called and said you'd be coming. Mentioned something about you being a glutton for punishment, subjecting yourself to this disaster. Why don't you join me in here?"

He beckoned for me to follow him, and the women gave a *better you than me* look. Navigating through the mess would have been tricky, even without crutches and a heavy boot. I made several apologies as I maneuvered through the landmines of Renee's living room, my bag swaying haphazardly and bumping over piles of laundry and mail. By the time I'd reached the doorway to Marcus's office and saw what was inside, it was obvious why

CHAPTER TWENTY-THREE

Kimball had allowed me to help.

"Hoo-boy," I breathed.

My reaction elicited a chuckle from Tony. Lofty stacks of multi-colored file folders balanced precariously amid overstuffed bookshelves.

"Have you found a method to the madness?"

"I have," he said. "The blue folders are documents related to city activity, like anything pertaining to council meetings, statutes passed, city budgets, and property tax records. It looks as though he'd been tracking the taxes and assessments of all his neighbors. For what purpose, I'm not sure. The red folders are bios and research on nearly every city official and employee from the mayor down to the facilities supervisor."

"That's a little creepy."

"Imagine finding a bio on yourself." He waved a thick red folder. "He documented my income to the penny, kept notes on major purchases like the minivan I bought for my wife last year. Also, he clipped and saved any newspaper articles mentioning my name."

"I had no idea the depth of his paranoia. What about the green files?"

"Those are the ones I find most interesting. They're his notes and research on all his conspiracy theories about his dad and the Chattertons. I've been goin' through those today 'cause I think that's where we're gonna get to the root of what mighta gotten him killed. My theory is, amid all the kooky off-based conspiracy theories, he got a little too close to the truth on one of 'em, and someone didn't want him getting any closer or blowin' the lid off it."

"You're probably right. Any sign of a printed copy of his last blog, the deleted one?"

"Not yet. You're welcome to grab a stack and start searchin'." His hand waved dismissively at the piles. "Anything that looks like garbage, toss it in one of them black bags."

"Do you mind if I start with the red folders?"

"Be my guest." He plopped into the black pleather office chair.

I grabbed several red files from the stack on top of the cabinet before settling into the green paisley armchair in the corner and propping my boot on the matching ottoman.

The first folder was a profile for Councilwoman Margot Hennepin. Marcus had listed all her known affiliates, her council votes, as well as her salary and financial information about her notary business. There was a star next to her name at the top of the first page, drawn in silver Sharpie.

The second file contained information on Mayor Quincy. His name didn't have a silver star. It had a red circle with a slash through it. Mayor Quincy's records included every document he'd made public while running for office, including personal tax returns. A few articles Marcus had included from *The Current* alluded to the possibility Mayor Quincy had a drinking problem, although no specific allegations were made. Despite a drunken outburst at a holiday party two years ago, he'd been re-elected to a second term in the fall.

Next was Port Commissioner Armand DiLupo's file. Marcus had drawn a silver star next to his name. The report included a family tree. None of the names rang a bell except one: Frank DiLupo. This also happened to be the only name circled in red on the genealogy report.

Frank DiLupo was a notorious Seattle mob boss indicted for a bribery scandal in 1988 which had also entangled several high-ranking state officials. It had never occurred to me that Armand could possibly have been related to Frank.

"Um." I fixed my gaze on Tony.

He looked up from the file in his lap. "Find somethin'?"

"I'm not sure."

Tony reached for the file. "What am I lookin' at here?" He thumbed through the pages.

"This is the file on Port Commissioner DiLupo. Marcus included a family tree for him. So far, it's the only file containing one, so I assume it has something to do with making a connection to the name circled in red."

Tony scanned the page and chuckled. "Well, would ya look at that?"

"This isn't the first time organized crime in Chattertowne has come up. Back in the mid-eighties, when Jimmy Chatterton was found floating in the marina, there were rumors about corruption and smuggling at the port.

There's a possibility the mayor and police chief at the time were involved or at least looked the other way. Before he died, Peter Chatterton told me his father was *connected*, if you know what I mean, and others in town were involved. He believed they killed Jimmy to keep him quiet because he was about to be indicted on federal charges and feared he'd agree to testify in exchange for a deal with the U.S. Attorney's office. Official word was he committed suicide to avoid prison, but Peter was adamant it was all a setup."

"That's a lot of conjecture. Got any evidence to back it up?" he asked.

"I'm working on it."

"You know most Italians aren't in the mafia, right? And in that vein, not all mafias are Italian." He folded his arms and sneered.

"Of course, but that doesn't mean the connection between Port Commissioner DiLupo and a convicted mobster isn't important. I can't shake the feeling it all goes deep into Chattertowne's past."

"You're overthinking this. I've been in law enforcement for over fifteen years. In my experience, homicides tend to be committed for one of just a handful of reasons." He checked them off on his fingers. "Domestic violence, money, and substances elevating a conflict to the point someone loses control. Other than that, you got your occasional psychopath. Rarely, and I mean hardly never, is it the result of old grudges. People who hold grudges for a long time typically keep holdin' those grudges. They don't decide one day to take revenge after years of bein' angry."

"What if dormant grudges are resurrected because someone starts bringing things back to the surface or threatens to expose their secrets?"

"I suppose that's possible, but you're losin' sight of the fact most situations follow Newton's Third Law. For every action, there's an equal and opposite reaction. If X, then Y. People's actions, as complicated by emotions as they can be, tend to be linear."

"That's a lot of math. I'm a writer. I don't do math."

"Let the facts lead the story, not the other way around." He picked up a new file. "I'm not sayin' the Port Commissioner being distantly related to a criminal isn't somethin' to keep in mind, but I think we should focus on direct links to Marcus and not get caught up in his crazy theories. Nine times outta ten, it's the spouse."

"I thought we were supposed to let the facts tell the story. Isn't assuming Renee's guilt letting the story guide the facts?"

"Touché." He smiled with his mouth but not his eyes.

The room was silent for what seemed like hours, save for the shuffling of papers. Each folder revealed random bits of information about various city employees and officials that were both job-related and personal. I felt voyeuristic reading some of the profiles he'd generated. How had Marcus justified such invasions of privacy?

Some folders had been designated with the red-slashed circles, some with silver stars. It was difficult to determine which symbol indicated guilt and whether it was Marcus's personal biases or legitimate facts which had led him to his conclusions.

Peg's folder had a red circle and hand-written notes such as "crazy bitch" and "eyes and ears of City Hall," which were both accurate assessments, in my opinion.

Holden's profile had a silver star. I felt like doxing a close friend was icky, but Marcus must have believed no investigation was complete without vetting all players. Their friendship had been somewhat estranged because of the unpaid loan, but Holden had said he didn't hold a grudge, so why would Marcus?

The first page of Holden's file appeared to be some sort of financial accounting record. His home was modest for the area, with an appraised value of about $600,000. The other numbers listed, however, were a whole lot bigger than I'd have expected for a city manager in a small town. Several entries were unidentified except for a date next to them. I assumed they were banking deposits, and they totaled nearly $700,000. Holden's salary wasn't even six figures, so unless he'd inherited money from a rich uncle, there wasn't an obvious explanation for how he'd amassed that kind of money or how Marcus had obtained those figures.

Tears pricked my eyes at the sight of the next item in the file. It was a photograph of the three of us taken more than a decade ago. A looming Marcus stood on the left with a cat-that-ate-the-canary full-toothed grin.

I was next to him, wearing a blue blouse with coral flowers coordinated to match my coral shorts and coral bandana in my hair. The camera had caught me mid-laugh, my head tipped backwards. Holden beamed at me. There was something more than amusement in his expression. It looked like…longing. I'd never seen the photo before, and Holden had never given any indication he might have seen me as anything more than Marcus's girlfriend.

"Hey, Tony?"

"Yup?"

"Do you mind if I take this picture? It's from our college days, and I can't imagine it pertains to the case in any way." I held it up for him to see.

He glanced at the photo. "Yeah, sure, I can't see the harm. Nice bandanner, by the way."

I set the picture aside and turned to the next item, a list of dates and names. The names were incomplete with nothing to identify whether they were first names, last names, or both. Alanna, Dakota, Bradford, Marianna Lee. Underneath each name were four letters followed by six numbers, a space, and four more numbers. There were no notes of explanation, and I could only speculate why Marcus had felt they were significant enough to include.

I glanced at Tony, who was staring at the file on his lap. I slipped my phone from my coat pocket and snapped a picture of the strange list.

A cocktail napkin fluttered into my lap. On it was written one sentence: I O U Holden Villalobos $500. It had been signed by Marcus Washburn.

There was an article dated the week Holden had started his job as city manager. In the accompanying photo, he was seated behind his desk with hands clasped in front of him and a huge smile on his face.

I stared at the photo until a tap on the office door caused me to raise my head and be greeted by the real-life, in-person smile of Holden Villalobos.

Chapter Twenty-Four

"Find anything interesting?" Holden asked.

"Hey. You're a little early, aren't you? We don't need to be at the library for another," I checked the time on my phone, "hour and forty-five minutes."

"I thought I'd come see what's happening here, if you need a hand." Holden's indigo shirt was open at the collar, revealing his sinewy neck.

Tony glanced at him and gave a head bob. "Hey, man."

Holden nodded back. "'Sup, Tony?"

"Same old. You?"

"Can't complain. Taking a couple hot chicks out to dinner tonight," Holden said.

I guffawed.

"I sure hope for your sake one of them is your *fee*-an-cée." Tony smirked.

"Not this time. Tonight, I get to squire this invalid," he tipped his head toward me, "and her elderly friend."

"So, this date's some sort of community service?" Tony's chuckle was low and rumbled in his barrel chest.

"Hey!" I protested. "I'll have you know I'm a ton of fun, even with limited mobility, and Mildred has more personality in her little finger than most people have in their whole body. Her stories are fascinating, and anyone would be lucky to spend the evening with us."

I narrowed my gaze at them. Holden raised his hands in mock surrender.

"You comin' out for softball this spring?" Tony asked him. "I've been going to the batting cages a couple times a week gettin' ready, makin' the most of this mild winter."

"You know it. I'm going for MVP this year."

"Yeah, yeah, whatever." Tony laughed. "Since you're here, how about you go ask those broads in there if they need help."

"Gah, Tony. I told you before, you can't call women broads." Holden shook his head and walked into the living room.

After he left, Tony lowered his voice. "Keep your wits about you, Audrey." He jerked his head toward the living room.

I began to open my mouth to make a joke in response, but his serious expression caused me to shut it and nod my assent.

Having finished the files in my lap, I returned to the pile of folders on the table. Tony's words and demeanor had rattled me, but I didn't want to leave without finding something to help solve Marcus's murder.

On the bookshelf behind the stack, a red book with a wide spine labeled *The New English Dictionary* caught my eye. It wasn't a dictionary. Just as Anderson's globe hid his booze, so did one of his "dictionaries." I'd seen him shoving a flask inside it on more than one occasion.

I pulled the book off the shelf and opened the cover. Sure enough, the center of the book was cut out, and nestled within was a small safe. I tugged on the lock to no avail. I grabbed a few of the red files to camouflage it, hobbled back to the corner with the book, and slid it underneath the photo Tony had agreed to let me take home. Any guilt I felt about not handing the safe over to the police was assuaged by the fact I had every intention to give it to them...eventually.

A while later, Holden ambled back into the room. "Anything?"

"Nope." My voice rose an octave and about twenty-five decibels.

Holden gave me a curious expression.

Tony sighed. "So far, I'm not seeing much of anything to get excited about."

"You ready to get out of here?" Holden asked me.

"Yep. Gimme one sec."

He moved to help, but I waved him off.

"So damn stubborn." He turned on his heel and walked out the door.

I figured he'd assumed my resistance was due to fierce independence, not that I was attempting to smuggle evidence from a secondary crime scene.

Tucking the book into my satchel, I swung the bag over my shoulder and held it close to my body. I placed the crutches under each armpit.

Tony glanced up from what he'd been reading. "See ya."

"Bye." I gave a tiny wave with one of my free fingers.

Outside, Holden leaned against his car. I kept a tight grip on the bag and its hidden contents as I handed him my crutches and climbed inside. He threw the crutches in the back, behind his seat, and slid behind the wheel.

"So, we're grabbing Mildred from the library?"

"Yeah, she wants to take us to a pub in Kirkland. I'm not sure which one."

I pulled my hair back and to the side, and he stared at my bare neck.

"Kirkland." He blinked several times. "Do you think she's trying to prevent gossip by taking us out of town?" he asked, pulling away from the curb.

"Maybe she just wants to get out of Chattertowne for the night."

I studied his face while he drove.

"So, you and Tony are friends?"

He glanced at me before returning his attention to the road. "Bianchi? We're friendly enough, run in the same circles. Why do you ask?"

"Well," I hedged, fiddling with my shirt. "He gave me a warning about you, like he thinks you might be, I don't know, someone I need to be careful with."

Holden guffawed. "That's rich."

"What does that mean?"

"Nothing."

When we arrived at the library, I called Mildred to let her know we were parked out front. She appeared at the entrance wearing a pale blue cardigan. Holden hopped out and opened the rear door for her. My parents had taught me elders should always ride in front, but my injury precluded good manners.

Mildred slid into the back seat. "I'm delighted we're doing this! I haven't had a night out in ages."

"You know Holden, right?" I gestured to him.

"Of course, I know Mildred! How could I not know the celebrated historian of Chattertowne?" His voice boomed. "If it weren't for your tenacity in trying to let me know about Peter, Audrey might not be in as good of shape as she is."

A blush appeared on Mildred's crepey cheeks. "Glad I could help. Also, it's easy to be a historian when you've been alive for much of the history. So, Holden, I hear you're running the town these days."

"I'm just around to lighten the load for Mayor Quincy and make him look good."

"Talk about impossible tasks."

Holden chuckled. "He's not so bad." His attempt to downplay his boss's well-known inadequacies was unconvincing.

The drive to Kirkland passed quickly. Mildred regaled us with stories of Chattertowne's bygone days. She described when her family had purchased their first television, how she'd been voted homecoming princess, and experienced her first kiss with Gordy Hoffman on the Ferris wheel at the Kupit Festival on her eighteenth birthday. I begged Mildred to allow me to include that story in my article, and she agreed.

At Pauper's Pub, we were led to a brown leather booth in a dim corner. Mildred sat in the middle, with Holden and me flanking her on each side. The waiter took our drink orders, and before Mildred had finished removing her coat, he'd arrived with three glasses of foaming amber ale straight from the tap.

"Holden, I'm not sure if you're aware, but I know your grandmother," Mildred said. "We play bridge together at the Senior Center. Lovely woman. Portuguese, if I'm not mistaken."

"She is, and my grandfather's side was from the Azores and Cape Verde."

Mildred got a far-away look. "Sometimes I wonder whatever happened to Rafael."

"Rafael?" I asked.

"Oh!" She was flustered. "I hadn't meant to say that aloud. He was a sailor whose family had moved here from Portugal when he was a baby. We met at a USO dance. It was practically love at first sight, but I was young, only fifteen, and my father wasn't a tolerant man. He forbade me to see Rafael."

"Oh, Mildred, I'm sorry."

She shrugged her frail shoulders, but her face was deeply sad. "It wasn't meant to be, I guess. Speaking of grandmothers, Audrey." She sipped her beer. "I knew your grandmother, too, before she passed away. Your mother's mother, Allie."

"You did? She died from a heart attack a year and a half after I was born, so I never knew her. My mom never talks about her side of the family. My dad thinks she's ashamed about growing up poor with an unmarried mother."

"Mmm," Mildred murmured.

"My Great Gramma May was also tight-lipped about Grandma Allie. Whenever I'd broach the subject, she'd only say, 'No one should have to outlive their child.'"

"Losing a child brings deep grief," Mildred agreed.

"How did you know my grandmother? What was she like?"

"We both went to First Presbyterian church. Allie had the most beautiful dark hair. Shiny, like the mane of an Arabian mare. I was so jealous, with my frizzy mousy nest." Mildred scowled and fluffed her hair. "Her eyes were hazel, like yours."

"My mom has hazel eyes, and Viv has gold eyes."

"They probably came from your grandmother. I didn't spend a lot of time with her socially, but I know she made the most beautiful woven blankets. She sold them during the summer market and at the Christmas bazaar."

"I have one of her blankets, a baby blanket. It's yellow with blue stripes around the edges and an orange sun with a tree embroidered in the middle. I think it had a matching yellow hat, but I've lost track of it. I used to wrap my doll in it."

"She donated blankets and hats to the closest hospitals for each and every newborn. It sounds like yours was extra special, though."

"Wow, that's cool. I wonder why my mom never told me she did that. That's a heritage she should have been proud to pass on to her daughters. All I got were warnings about not adding to my family's already tarnished reputation."

"I can't speak for your mother. I know Allie struggled with both personal and familial shame. Times were different back then. Certain things weren't done, and if they were done, they were either done in secret or accompanied by tremendous public disgrace."

"You mean like illegitimate pregnancies."

Mildred shifted in her seat. "Mm."

"Mildred?"

"Yes, dear." She fixated on her glass as she rotated it.

"If you know something about my family that might shed some light on why there's this sense of disgrace hanging over us, please don't hold out on me. It's been shrouded in secrecy my whole life, but I could feel its effects nonetheless."

"I don't want to resurrect old wounds or stir the pot. I don't think your mother would appreciate that." Mildred's mouth twisted.

The stories demanded to be told, but her lips refused.

"You know the phrase about those who don't know history being prone to repeat it?" I asked.

Mildred nodded warily.

"This is my history too, and I have the right to know."

She took a deep breath and pointed her index finger at me. "You didn't hear it from me, got it?"

Chapter Twenty-Five

"You're aware your Grandma Allie was unmarried when your mama was born," Mildred began.

"Yes, that's why her birth certificate says Claudine Bristow, with no father listed," I said. "None of that is news."

"Similarly, Allie's father was born Verne Dedeaux, with his mother Fanny's maiden name."

"You must be mistaken. My mom's middle name is Dedeaux, so I know that's a family name, but I'm positive Great Grandpa Verne's last name was Bristow, and his father was Elmer Bristow."

She shook her head.

"What do you mean, no? If Verne wasn't born a Bristow but a Dedeaux…."

Holden gave me a pitying smile.

"Mildred, you're not saying…are you saying Elmer *wasn't* Verne's father?"

She nodded.

I slumped into the curve of the booth. The clash of a metal pan dropping onto the kitchen floor echoed the cacophony of my thoughts.

"I'm just…I…I don't understand. Why lie about who Grandpa Verne's father was? Why so many secrets?"

"Most secrets are meant to protect either the secret keeper or the one most adversely affected by the secret. Sometimes, it's both. I have a feeling that might be the case here."

"So, then, how did *you* know this secret about my family that even my mother didn't know?"

"I said I knew Allie from church, but that's only part of the story. I met her when I was leading a support group for unwed mothers. I myself had been in trouble at sixteen."

"Rafael?" Holden asked.

Mildred nodded. "My parents sent me to a Pennsylvania home for girls in my situation. After my son was born, I was told I had no choice but to give him away and come home like nothing ever happened." Her face clouded with grief. "It was the most difficult thing I've ever done in my life. I didn't want to do it, but my parents insisted all our reputations depended on it. Scandal isn't easy to live down, especially in small towns."

Mildred fiddled with her napkin, wringing it through her hands.

"When the pastor's wife announced they were going to start the group, many were upset, saying it condoned hanky-panky outside of marriage. I was the first to volunteer because I'd been there and didn't want the girls to feel alone, as I had. My mother was horrified, said I was airing our dirty laundry. Stan, my husband Stan, God rest his soul, he knew about my sweet baby boy and encouraged me to participate. He didn't care what those old biddies thought about me, and he certainly didn't care what they thought about him. He'd known part of me broke the day I gave Tomas away. That's what I called him...Tomas. I don't know what his adoptive parents named him, probably Jason or Steve." She grimaced. "Anyway, Stan thought it would help heal my heart to walk the hard road with those girls, especially since I wasn't able to have more children."

I placed my hand over Mildred's. It was soft and frail. "I'm sorry, that must have been difficult. I'm grateful you were willing to share your own pain to help others in similar circumstances."

"Allie was a formidable young woman, and she was not about to let convention rob her of the opportunity to raise her own child. One night, after everyone had left the meeting, she pulled me aside to talk. She said her grandmother Fanny had confided in her that she'd gone through a similar experience when she found herself pregnant with Allie's father, Verne. Fanny said her neighbor Elmer, who'd held long-standing affection for her, had offered to marry her. Elmer didn't care he'd be raising another man's child, and he promised to raise the boy like his own. Which he did, until Fanny grew bored and discarded him for her next paramour, of course."

"Thus, beginning our family legacy of dysfunctional relationships. Fanny had four husbands. Four. Did you know she made everyone call her *Aunt* Fanny because she didn't want her boyfriends to know she was a grandmother?"

"Fanny had her issues," Mildred rebuked me. "But I'll give her this, she was there for your grandmother when she needed her most." She stabbed the table with her bony fingertip. "She told Allie strength was in her bloodline, and that gave her the confidence and determination to make choices on her own terms, not anyone else's. Your family's story may stray a bit from conventional norms, but that doesn't mean it isn't still a legacy of which you can be proud. You should feel grateful to come from a line of women who may not have always made the right choices, but they faced their consequences head-on. If I may be so bold, the stubborn and determined apple didn't fall far from the tree."

Holden cleared his throat. "Damn straight."

I swatted in his direction but addressed my comments to Mildred. "You're right. I should be proud to be from a line of ardent women. So, what do you think Fanny meant about strength being in Allie's bloodline?" I took a swig of beer.

"Probably because she was Flathead. Bitterroot-Salish. A tenacious bunch, like you. Survivors."

I sputtered, spraying my beer. "What?"

Holden wiped his face with his napkin.

Mildred frowned. "You didn't know you have Native ancestry?"

"No! I was told I'm English and Irish on my father's side, the O'Connell side, and my mother said she's part French. Never once has she said we were…Flathead."

"Maybe she doesn't know."

"Mildred, why didn't you mention any of this to me when we were talking about Chattertowne's history?"

"My mind isn't what it used to be. I've seen a lot of things, known a lot of people. After our first meeting, memories surfaced of my time with your grandmother. As with the stories about Eddie and George and my parents, everything's in there somewhere. Regarding your grandmother, well, I wasn't sure the story was one I had the right to tell."

"I knew Fanny had a sordid love life. She's always been a legendary character in our family lore, what with her complicated romantic entanglements, dispassionate discarding of husbands when they no longer suited her purposes, and a flagrant disregard for societal norms. Lying about her son's father, that's pretty messed up, but I will say I'm grateful she was willing to share her story with my grandmother. Giving empathy and revealing private details about her life…from what I've heard, that was uncharacteristic of Fanny. I'm sure it must have been what Allie needed in that moment."

"I know it was. Allie told me that conversation gave her the strength to make the decision to keep your mother instead of giving her up for adoption, which her mother had pressured her to do."

"It's hard to believe Gramma May wanted my mother given up for adoption."

"It's never an easy decision for anyone under those circumstances, but especially in that era."

"You'd think Grandpa Verne, knowing his mother had been in similar circumstances when she was pregnant with him, would have supported his daughter in keeping her baby. Unless he didn't know Elmer wasn't his biological father." I paused. "If Elmer wasn't Verne's dad, who was?"

"I have no idea. Allie didn't know either."

"I wonder who I could talk to who might have insight about the Dedeauxs and our family connection to the Bitterroot-Salish? I'd really like to learn more about that side of my family, for my own curiosity but also for my articles."

"I have a childhood friend, Marie Journet, who might be just the person. She's part Flathead. She lives in Ellensburg now and doesn't cross the pass during the winter if she can avoid it, but I'll bet if you were willing to make the drive, she'd meet with you."

"I'm anxious to get some answers. I guess I could call, but I'd rather meet in person. Do you think she'd be available tomorrow?"

Holden scoffed. "You planning on driving a hundred miles per hour? Because if you put that boot on the gas pedal, your car will be moving fast as a rocket."

"Eh, I forgot about that. Will you drive me, pretty please?" I fluttered my lashes.

He ignored me. "Mildred, do you think it's too late to call and ask Marie if she's available tomorrow? I have a busy week, and it's the only day I'm free to drive Audrey."

"I can certainly find out."

Mildred plopped her bag onto the table. More tote than purse, her short arms barely reached over the top. She pulled out a hairbrush, a case for reading glasses, and a bottle of Pepto Bismol. Eventually, she located her phone and an address book that had been around since the Nixon Administration. Combing through pages filled with blue, black, and red inks, with some names and addresses scribbled out, she landed on surnames starting with J. Her fingertip dragged halfway down the page and stopped.

"Here she is!"

She flipped open her phone and slowly pressed each button with as much force as she could muster. Putting the phone to her ear, her face lit up when her friend answered.

"Marie! It's me, Mildred!" She paused. "Yes! I'm out to dinner with friends. Marie, I've got a favor to ask. My friends would like to come see you tomorrow. Audrey's a reporter who's just discovered she has Flathead heritage. She'd like to know more about that, and I told her you're just the one she should speak with." Mildred winked at me. "Wonderful! I have the address from your Christmas card. Is that the best place to meet?"

I couldn't make out her words, but Marie's volume matched, if not surpassed, Mildred's.

"Perfect, I'll have them meet you there at eleven." After a moment, she responded, "I wish I could. I'm still a working woman, you know. I'll try to schedule time for a visit when the weather improves. I don't like driving in snow and ice."

The meeting was set for the next day at a diner in Ellensburg.

Chapter Twenty-Six

The ride back from Kirkland was subdued. With no conversation to stimulate her and the dulcet tones of D'Angelo playing on the stereo, Mildred fell asleep. Sitting at my feet, the safe's presence was palpable. Did Holden sense it, too, like the tell-tale heart?

He stared straight ahead with a grave expression on his face.

I touched his arm. "You okay?"

He glanced over at me and returned his attention to the road. "Just thinking about everything that's happened, everything that's changed."

"Could you be more specific?"

He breathed out a long sigh. "Not long ago, my life was moving at a normal pace, and I felt in control of my world. I'm not saying I didn't have challenges, but I felt like I had a grip on things. Then Marcus died, and I had to face the fact control is just an illusion. Now I just feel cornered."

"That sounds like an existential crisis."

He gripped the steering wheel. "Everyone starts out with good intentions, you know, trying to do the right thing. Then life happens, and choices get made...or they don't get made, and soon you're looking at where you are, who you're with, and what you're doing, and you can't figure out how the hell you got there. Know what I mean?"

"I think so. There've definitely been times these past few months I've questioned a lot of things. My faith in humanity's been shaken pretty hard after dealing with Peter, coming to grips with what was going on with Marcus, and discovering the corruption throughout Chattertowne's history. I hate the fact it isn't the place I believed it to be."

"You really have been in denial. You haven't had to face any of the ugly, but that doesn't mean it didn't exist."

"I know I have some pretty big blind spots. It's just that when someone I trust or admire turns out to be other than who I thought they were, it messes with my head. I can deal with flawed humans because I need grace as much as the next guy, maybe even more, but I don't know what to do with the paradox of my perceptions and beliefs about a place or a person and the reality of who they are if those two things are markedly different. I may be a disaster, but at least what you see is what you get. I need the people in my life to operate the same way."

"People aren't one-dimensional. No one's all good or all bad, except for Jesus and Hitler, and even Hitler must have had his moments." Apparently sensing my horror through the darkness, he scoffed, "I'm not defending Hitler. Geez, Audrey. I'm saying we all begin life with the potential to do both good and evil. We all make mistakes. We all make selfish choices. We are often dually motivated. Things that seemed like a good idea in the moment later become our biggest regrets. Most of us try to do what we think is best, not only for ourselves but those we love."

"Love makes self-*less* choices when the self*ish* choices would be easier, feel better, or benefit us more. It's doing the hard stuff, including walking away when it's the right thing to do."

"Are we talking about us now?"

The headlights of a passing car highlighted his clenched jaw.

"Maybe. I've been spending all this time with you with little or no regard for your relationship and what flirting with crossing lines does to my dignity and self-respect."

"I'm sorry our moments of weakness have left you feeling like your dignity's been compromised, but no offense, Audrey, an illicit near-kiss is the least of my problems." His expression hardened, and his full lips tightened.

A heavy silence filled the car.

"I think it's best you don't drive me to Ellensburg tomorrow."

Holden adjusted his grip on the steering wheel. "You can't drive." His words hissed through gritted teeth.

"I'll figure it out, or Darren can take me."

I mustered enough courage for a sidelong glance. Holden's wounded expression provided the payoff I'd been looking for, proof of a direct hit to his pride or his ego. It was too much to wish for jealousy.

"You do that, Audrey."

A chasm of unspoken hurt, irritation, and weariness over the hopelessness of the situation filled the space between us all the way to Mildred's house. Holden accompanied her to the doorstep, where she placed her hand on his forearm and said something to him. He shook his head, and his shoulders slumped.

He waited for her to unlock the door, and when she opened it, they both threw their arms in the air.

I opened the car door and leaned out to yell, "Everything okay?"

Holden turned to look at me and grimly shook his head.

I felt my chest constrict with fear. Wrangling my crutches from the back seat, I managed to get myself upright. I hobbled up the pathway to her house. Holden was holding his cell phone up to his ear with one hand and had the other on his hip.

"What happened?" I whispered to a shaken Mildred.

She didn't say anything, only pointed into her house. I peeked my head inside and gasped. The place had been tossed. Mail was all over the floor, a bookcase had been turned over, and several pieces of what used to be a blue and white ceramic vase were scattered on the ground.

I reached out to pull Mildred into a hug. She felt tiny and frail in my arms. Her body trembled.

"Just get someone over here as soon as possible, will ya? Thanks." Holden ended his call and exhaled. "I think we should wait out here. We don't want to mess up the crime scene. I think I have an extra blanket in my trunk for emergencies." He headed toward his car.

I turned to Mildred. "It's going to be okay."

"My home...my sanctuary...the place of all my memories with my beloved Stan. It's been violated. How can I ever feel safe here again?"

"The police will do a thorough investigation, and whoever did this will be dealt with."

Holden wrapped the blanket around Mildred. She was shivering, but I suspected it was as much from shock as it was from the cold.

He turned to me. "Sorry, I only had one."

"I'm fine."

A police car pulled up with lights flashing, but no siren. Sergeant Tony Bianchi hauled himself out of the driver's side and slammed the door.

As he ambled toward the house, Tony said, "Twice in one day, Villalobos. How lucky am I? Luckier than you, I guess. I see your date didn't go as well as you'd hoped."

"Very Amusing," said Holden.

"Anyone been inside yet?"

"Nope. We picked Mildred up from the library and headed down to Kirkland. I walked her to the door and waited for her to get safely inside. When she opened the door, she immediately knew something was wrong, so we didn't go in."

Tony turned to Mildred. "Was the door locked?"

"Of course. I'm a woman who lives alone. Do you really think I'd leave my house unlocked?" She jutted her chin in defiance.

"I watched her unlock it with the key," Holden said.

Tony turned on his flashlight and shone it around Mildred's dark living room.

He whistled. "You generally a tidy person?"

"Yes."

I got the distinct impression Mildred wasn't a fan of Tony.

"I'm just sayin', I've been over at the Washburn house all day, and it looked quite similar. Apparently, that was their typical way of livin'."

Mildred huffed with indignation. "Well, not me."

"Hey, Bianchi," Holden said. "Mind if we chat for just a minute?"

They walked a few feet away on the grass and huddled together. Their voices rumbled, but I wasn't able to make out what they were saying. Holden made a few hand gestures, and Tony listened. Then they both chuckled.

An SUV with the CPD insignia parked on the opposite side of the street, and Kimball got out. Tony's posture immediately stiffened.

"Villalobos," Kimball called as she came up the sidewalk. "You'd better have a good reason for telling dispatch my presence was required during my off-hours at the scene of a minor break-in."

"I'm not sure I'd consider it minor," Holden said. "Assistant Chief Kimball, this is Mildred Driscoll. She works in Chattertowne's archive and records department. She's been helping Audrey with her research. We were at dinner in Kirkland all evening, and when we got here, found the place trashed."

Kimball's expression was placid. "What was taken?"

"We don't know yet. No one's been inside, but from what I saw, someone was in there looking for something. It doesn't look like a robbery to me."

"Oh, I hadn't realized you were a crime scene expert. When did you graduate from the academy, *Detective* Villalobos? Or have you just watched a lot of *Magnum PI*? Ms. Driscoll, I'd like you to follow me into the home so you can point out anything which might be missing. Please don't touch anything."

Mildred followed Kimball inside.

Tony gave an uncomfortable chuckle.

"What are you so smug about?" Holden asked.

"I'm just enjoying someone else being on the receiving end of her wrath for once."

"What's Kimball's deal, anyway?" I asked. "My sister seems to think she's super nice and sweet, but my experience hasn't been so warm and fuzzy."

Holden shrugged his shoulders. "Who knows? Maybe because she's a woman doing a historically man's job, she feels the need to prove she's tough as nails."

"I got the feelin' her old man puts a lot of pressure on her," Tony said.

"Wha—"

I didn't get a chance to ask him to clarify because, at that moment, Kimball appeared in the doorway.

"Bianchi, come look over the scene with me."

Tony twisted his mouth and raised his brows at us before following her into the house.

Holden and I stood awkwardly on the stoop, not making eye contact.

Finally, I said, "What was Mildred saying to you when you walked her to her door?"

He heaved a sigh. "She told me you were too special for me to be playing games and that I needed to figure out what kind of man I was going to be."

"What does that even mean?"

"I think she overheard some of our conversation."

"How do you feel about what she said?" I asked.

"I think she's one hundred percent correct."

Tony peeked his head out. "Kimball suggested you two head home. By suggested, I mean she wants you to go. No use in staying here while we process the scene since it could take a while. We'll get Mildred buttoned up and settled in before we leave and set up an hourly patrol for the night."

"Any indication what was behind the break-in?"

"The back door was busted. Kimball seems to think it was just some druggy looking for something easy to sell. So far, Mildred hasn't discovered anything missing, but she doesn't have many things that would pull a lot of scratch at the pawn shop."

"Interesting. Well, tell her goodnight for us," Holden said.

"And let her know if she needs me, she can call or text," I added.

"Will do."

Bianchi went back inside, leaving Holden and me alone.

"C'mon, Audrey. Let's get you home. You've been on your feet way too long tonight."

Chapter Twenty-Seven

Once we arrived at my apartment complex, Holden opened the door to help me out of the car. My bag, heavy with the book safe, swung from my left wrist like a pendulum. He came alongside me as we entered the lobby. Standing at the elevator, he sighed and pulled me toward him, enveloping me in a full-bodied hug. I groaned as the crutches dug into my ribs, and he released me.

"You okay?" His voice was husky.

"It's all just so much, but I'm okay. You?"

"I will be."

The elevator doors opened. I entered with my head down and raised it only once the doors had shut. The only thing keeping me from bursting into sobs was knowing they would echo down the shaft for him to hear.

Pulling the book safe from my bag, I gripped it in my right hand along with the crutch handle. Turning my gaze to the ceiling, I exhaled a ragged breath.

The elevator door opened, and I leveled my gaze. I yipped with surprise at the sight of a man standing there.

"Darren! What are you doing here?"

"I came to check on you, make sure you're okay. I haven't seen you since Sunday morning after George...."

"I was out to dinner."

Darren kept pace with me as I limped down the hallway toward my apartment.

"With Holden and Mildred," I added.

"That's an interesting combination. How was it?" Clench. Release. Exhale.

I struggled to grip the safe and my bag while dragging my boot and maneuvering the crutches down the hallway. The gray utilitarian carpet had come unglued, creating an obstacle course of ripples.

"Interesting." I stumbled over a ripple.

"Hey, can I carry something for you?" he asked.

We were almost to my apartment door, and despite the strain of the satchel, I didn't want to hand over my contraband.

"No, I've got it, thanks, but in my left jacket pocket, you'll find my keys."

He took the keys and unlocked the door. I clunked over the threshold, placed the book on the kitchen counter, and hurtled my exhausted body toward the sofa. I flung the detested crutches onto the floor. Darren slowly shut the door and placed the keys on the fake dictionary. He didn't give it a second glance, and I exhaled with relief that my secret cache hadn't caught his attention. He sat next to me, graceful in his repose.

"Not that I'm not glad to see you…."

I looked for an indication he realized I wasn't claiming I was glad to see him either.

"But I must admit I'm a little surprised. I kinda figured I was *persona non-grata* with you."

Darren slanted his head. "Why would you say that?"

"Maybe because the last time I saw you, you were less than pleased I was headed to the shooting range with Holden."

"Audrey, I need you to understand something. Regardless how it may appear, this…." He waved his hands in the air, indicating whatever non-specific *this* was. "Isn't about jealousy. It isn't even about you."

I gave him my most skeptical look.

"There's a lot more going on than you know," he said.

I waited for him to elaborate. He didn't.

"So, if it's not about Holden—"

He interrupted. "That's not what I said. I said it isn't about jealousy."

"So, it *is* about Holden, but not because you're jealous. Is it that you don't trust him? Because, frankly, the feeling's mutual."

Darren leaned forward. He rested his forearms on his thighs and clasped his hands in front of him. A wisp of sand-colored hair fell onto his forehead from its coiffed position above his left ear. Blowing the stray lock from in front of his eye, he shook his hands like they held a rattle.

"I don't trust him, and I have good reason. You're just going to have to take my word for it." He stopped to watch me for a moment. "You're adorable when you cock your left eyebrow. I'm not sure if you know this, but you do it a lot."

"Only when I'm with you." My mouth twisted into a smirk.

"So, dinner was interesting, you said?"

"For a number of reasons, not the least of which was dropping Mildred off at her home, only to discover it had been ransacked," I said.

"Ransacked!"

"Yes. That's why I'm home so late. We had to wait for the cops."

"Did they determine what had happened?" he asked.

"Eh. Kimball thinks it was a tweaker looking for something to sell. I'm not so sure."

"Why else would someone break into an old lady's house?"

"I have a theory," I said.

"Would you like to share it?"

"I haven't decided yet."

Darren laughed. "Why's that?"

"I'm not sure I can trust you."

He appeared slightly wounded by my statement.

"I have to ask you something, and I need you to be honest."

He slanted his chin toward me. "If I can."

My words came out in an anxious whoosh. "Someone's been tracking my online activity through my computer at work. I think it's you, and I wanna know why." I folded my arms.

I expected him to react with defensiveness or remorse, but he just blinked at me.

"I guess that's my answer."

He opened his mouth to speak and stopped. When he tried again, he struggled to find words. "Audrey, I…I know none of this makes sense to you right now, but I promise, it will."

"Seriously? You're admitting to cyberstalking me, and I'm supposed to just accept there's a valid and justifiable explanation, a rational reason for this egregious invasion of privacy, but I can't know the reason?" I squeezed my arms tighter against my chest.

My concerns and reservations about him had been suddenly usurped by a desire to bonk his pretty head against the wall.

Darren pursed his lips as he formulated his response. "I know it seems unreasonable, but at least I'm being honest with you. Doesn't that count for something?"

"It might, if it weren't for the fact you haven't really been honest since the day we met."

"That's unfair."

"Is it? Tell me how this sounds. You're a financial and computer whiz who went to one of the most prestigious universities in the world, but you've relocated across the country to work for peanuts at a small-town newspaper. You live in a mansion on the previously mentioned salary of peanuts…and we're not even talking name-brand peanuts, but the off-brand dollar store version. No top hat, no monocle, just the word peanuts in black letters on the front. Peanutz with a *z*. You say you've got no family other than your dad, but the photographs in your hallway say otherwise. Did your mother really die of breast cancer, or was that a lie too?"

His face contorted, and my stomach dropped.

"Darren, I'm sorry. I shouldn't have said that."

He composed himself before speaking in a hushed tone. "Yes, my mother died from breast cancer. I donate my entire pathetic *Current* salary to the Maddie Benson Foundation, which my mom created after her diagnosis to help other women. Yes, I'm overqualified. Yes, I invaded your privacy, and no, I haven't been forthcoming with you about many things. I'd apologize for tracking your computer, but it would be disingenuous for me to do so because I'm not sorry. I had a very good reason."

"One you can't tell me."

It was unseemly for a grown woman to sulk, but his fractional honesty infuriated and confused me.

"Yes, one I cannot tell you, at least not yet."

"When?" I pouted.

"At the pace things have been moving lately, not long."

"Ominous. Can't you give me something? Anything? If you can't tell me why you tapped into my computer, can you at least tell me why you can't tell me why?"

Darren smiled. "You're a persistent one."

"Don't patronize me."

"Here's what I can tell you. my lack of transparency—"

"You mean your dishonesty," I said.

"I mean my lack of transparency. It's not without purpose. When you know it, all will be forgiven, I've no doubt. You've got every reason to withhold your trust from me, but I want you to know I do care about you and would never do anything to hurt you."

"You think lying to me and sneaking around behind my back, snooping into my life, doesn't hurt me?" I asked.

"You're just going to have to take me at my word. I'm doing it to protect you. In fact, that's why I'm here now. I know you're going to meet with someone in Ellensburg tomorrow, and I want to go with you."

"I literally made those plans tonight at dinner. Do you have a bug in my purse? Did you tap my phone? You've got a lot of nerve. How do you know I don't already have company for the trip?"

"Mildred sent you an email with the details of the meeting and Marie Journet's contact information. I haven't tapped your phone, nor have I eavesdropped on your apartment. Also, I hadn't considered you might've already asked someone to take you."

"Lucky for you, I've disinvited him, so I guess you'll be an acceptable alternative."

"I'm flattered."

"You don't get to be offended right now." I poked his chest. "Got it?"

He nodded.

"I'm tired. Pick me up at nine-thirty." I glanced between Darren and the door waiting for him to catch the hint.

"Alright. I'll be here at nine fifteen. Want me to bring coffee?"

"Nine thirty. Drip with cream, two stevia. I'm not gonna deprive myself just to punish you, but don't think for one second I am over this." I yawned. "Oh, and a big dollop of whip on top."

I locked the door behind him and glanced at the counter. My bed beckoned me, but so did the safe. I opened the faux cover and stared at the three-digit lock with the small black knob. It was an obstinate barrier to a potentially significant breakthrough—maybe even the smoking gun—in Marcus's murder, Chattertowne's history, or both.

I yanked on the knob, but it refused to budge. I scrolled each wheel of the combination lock to zero and pulled again to no avail. In my next attempt, I set it to one, two, three, but the rudimentary code proved fruitless. I wasn't a quitter, but fatigue and dismay overtook my enthusiasm. I slid the book under my right armpit and clunked to my waiting bed.

Chapter Twenty-Eight

When my morning alarm sounded, I flung a pillow at my phone. I would have hit snooze, but I was too excited for the day's adventure and what I might discover, or I would be once the caffeine Darren was bringing hit my veins.

My body creaked and cracked as my arms stretched, and I rolled off the mattress until my good foot hit the floor. I reached for the crutches, glared at them, and threw them down.

It wasn't pain that made walking on my injured ankle difficult, but the heaviness of the boot. Dragging the boot without the support of crutches put pressure on my other leg, which created hip and knee discomfort, but my chafed armpits cried out for a break. Since much of the day would be spent in the car, I decided to ditch the sticks, grabbed the safe from the nightstand, and hobbled into the living room.

After her late night at work, I'd expected Viv to be sound asleep. She was not only awake, but also dressed and about to walk out the front door.

"You're up early," I said.

"I have to be at the station by nine."

"How are you functioning on so little sleep?"

"It's rough, but I have a feeling it's temporary."

"Which part is temporary?"

"Hopefully, the late nights. If this gig at the station turns into a regular thing, I'll tell Leon I'm done waitressing, and I'm only available to sing on the weekends. What do you have going on today?"

"Darren's taking me to Ellensburg to meet with a woman about her

Flathead heritage. Viv, I have so much to tell you. Mildred told me some crazy stuff last night at dinner about Gramma Allie and Aunt Fanny."

Viv wrinkled her forehead. "I'm not sure if I'm more curious about that or the fact you're spending the day with Darren. Sounds like we do indeed have a lot of catching up to do. I'm only working at the station until noon today, so maybe we can talk before I have to leave for Nautilus."

After Viv left, I returned my attention to Marcus's safe, which taunted me from the coffee table. I glared back at it.

I started with Marcus's birthday, June seventeenth. Six-one-seven, twist. Nothing.

I stomped to the bedroom Quasimodo-style to get my phone, which had a text from Darren reminding me of our designated pick-up time.

Leaning against the edge of the bed for support, I opened Facebook and searched for Renee Washburn. We had several mutual friends. Renee's profile picture was of Tom Brady, which didn't help my already-low opinion of her. That was considered blasphemy in Seahawks country.

A scan of her bio revealed Renee's birthday to be November third. A Scorpio.

Hobbling back to the living room, I rotated the dials into position for Renee's birthday. One-one-three. Again, the knob resisted. I tried their children's birthdates, which I pieced together from Marcus's postings. No luck.

On a whim, I maneuvered the gears into a code I was certain would prove futile. I twisted the knob. It made a full revolution, and the metal plate sealing the safe lifted.

The code he'd chosen was my birthday. I could hardly believe it, but the unlocked safe spoke for itself.

My hands shook with anticipation as I removed the torn piece of paper on top, and my chest constricted at the sight of my name in Marcus's handwriting.

Audrey,
I know you'll find this, and I know you'll know what to do with

it.

Marcus

The bulky item underneath the note was enveloped in animal hide and bound by leather ribbon. The front flap had a slit, with a leather button poking through. I carefully lifted the item as if removing a baby bird from its nest and brought it to my nostrils. The musty smell reminded me of all the downtown Chattertowne antique stores my Gramma May used to frequent, often with Viv and me in tow.

I placed it in my lap and began opening it. With each unraveling of the strap, I came closer to revealing the cocooned prize.

At last, when I reached the end of the labyrinth of trim, I slid the button through the hole and lifted the flap to find a bundle of fragile yellowed papers. My fingertips caught the edge of the first sheet and turned it on its face to reveal the next one. I loosely held each page and cursorily examined paragraphs of faded sepia cursive writing, lists, maps, and drawings.

It didn't take an expert to know the papers were old.

I was holding Jonathan Chatterton's journal. I'd believed the safe contained something important, but never in my dreams had I imagined it to be a nineteenth-century historical record from the town's founder.

I glanced at the clock on the microwave. If I didn't hop in the shower right away, Darren would arrive to find me wearing pajamas.

Still, I couldn't resist letting my index finger trace over the soft cover one more time.

The promised hot cup of coffee warmed my hands as Darren merged onto the interstate. If it weren't for the chilly temperatures, I'd have rolled my window down to inhale the scent of pine. After my shower, I'd slid the diary into a plastic Ziploc bag and into the satchel, which now rested at my feet. It was a delicious secret, one I didn't think I could keep to myself for long, but I still wasn't sure if Darren could be trusted with such an important revelation.

On the east side of Snoqualmie Summit, the forest began to give way to plains, and soon we took the exit for Ellensburg.

Marie had asked to meet at an old-school diner near Central Washington University. A red and white sign reading "Gary's" hung over the door of a tan building with oil-rubbed bronze street lanterns flanking each side. The interior was cluttered with memorabilia such as tin signs, classic car and iconic celebrity posters, retro neon logos, and advertisements for everything from soda to soap to automotive oils. The booths were red leather, the counter stools were red leather, as was the waitress's skin. Not really, but she'd seen a lot of sun and/or indoor tanning beds. Her hair was a platinum bouffant straight out of 1962.

"Seat yourselves, darlin's!" Her raspy greeting completed the scene.

In the corner was a woman with braided silver hair so long it rested on the table in front of her. She wore a cobalt cowl-necked sweater patterned with beige zigzags, dream-catcher earrings, and beaded necklaces which adorned her wrinkled décolletage. In contrast, her bisque face was smooth and serene. She could've been anywhere from sixty to a hundred.

Upon our approach, she considered us, and whatever she'd observed must've passed scrutiny because she nodded her assent for us to join her.

"You must be Audrey." Marie extended her thin, frail hand in greeting. Her skin was cold but not clammy, supple without being slick.

"Yes, hi, Marie. Thank you for agreeing to talk with us this morning. This is my, uh, coworker Darren."

Instead of a normal handshake, Darren cradled her hand like he was holding a valuable antiquity. "So lovely to meet you."

"So, how do you know Mildred?" I asked, scooting into the booth across from Marie.

"Mildred and I have known each other since we were girls. She used to babysit me and my little sister on the nights our parents played bridge."

I leaned forward. "She told me about those bridge nights. She said the couples were tight until Eddie Chatterton and George Hart had a falling out. Do you remember anything about that?"

"I wasn't very interested in what was happening with the grown-ups. I was enamored with Mildred in the way little girls admire older girls who seem far more mature and sophisticated. I do, however, remember very clearly Mr. Chatterton's boys were brats."

"That's what Mildred said, with regard to Jimmy more than Dickie. Speaking of Mildred, did she explain why I wanted to meet with you?"

Marie played with the bead necklaces. "She said something about you writing about Chattertowne's inception for the newspaper, but also, you're on a personal quest to understand your own heritage."

"Until recently, I thought those were two separate things, but now I believe they're connected. I've seen evidence Jonathan Chatterton was romantically involved with, maybe even married to, a Flathead woman named Nettie and I'm almost positive they had a child together. Then last night Mildred dropped a couple bombshells about Aunt Fanny and my Grandma Allie having Flathead heritage."

"Aunt Fanny?"

"You might have known her as Frances Dedeaux…or Frances Bristow…or Lundquist…Littlejohn…or Doughty. None of the men who gave her those names stuck around for long, although I suspect Aunt Fanny was the one who ended the relationships."

"Oh! Mrs. Doughty, yes, I do remember her and her granddaughter Allie Bristow as well, although she was younger than me." Marie tapped her lips with a long arthritic finger. Her nail was painted fuchsia. "I recall hearing rumors about a Flathead connection to the Chatterton family, but always disregarded them. People tend to romanticize Native history. They want to claim the perceived benefits of tribal heritage while exempting themselves from the biases, racism, and persecution Indigenous People experience. They love the idea of Indigenous culture but couldn't tell you the difference between the Bitterroot-Salish and the neighboring Blackfeet Nation."

"So, you think the rumors are false?" I couldn't hide my disappointment.

"Not necessarily. Mrs. Doughty likely had Salish roots because she was good friends with my grandmother, and my grandmother rarely associated with anyone outside her social circle."

"What can you tell me about the Flathead People? Or should I call them Bitterroot-Salish? Flathead sounds like it might be a derogatory term."

"No one knows for certain how the name came to be. There were tribes who participated in the flattening of heads, but the Salish did not. We believe it was likely the result of a misunderstanding. This is the sign language used to identify our People." Marie pressed a hand to each side of her head. "It means *we the people*."

"Fanny's maiden name, Dedeaux, sounds French, which fits with what my mother always told me about that part of my heritage. She never mentioned any Indigenous relatives, though. Was intermarriage common between the French and the local tribes?"

"It wasn't uncommon. A lot of traders came through, not to mention the Black Robes."

"Black Robes?" I asked.

"The Jesuits. One of my ancestors was a French Jesuit priest, Henri Journet, who fell in love with my three times great grandmother, a Salish woman named Sulee. Family lore is they met while building St. Mary's Mission. Sulee helped in the hewing of the timber. We are from the Billings area, so I am also part Crow," Marie said.

Darren leaned forward. "This is fascinating stuff. So, if Audrey's descended from any of these groups, how would she go about establishing her connection?"

Marie shook her head. "She likely cannot, and, truthfully, she probably should not. She can take a DNA test, but if she is even ten percent North American Indigenous, I would be surprised. The blood-quantum issue is a sticky one." She glanced at me. "You could try to reconstruct your lineage, but records are spotty. All I have are my family's oral history and traditions, along with some artifacts I have inherited. My skin is pale. My eyes are light. I have only my father's and my grandfather's word. For me, that is enough. For others, maybe not. As the Cherokee Nation has stated, using a DNA test or family stories to imply a connection to any tribe is wholly inappropriate and wrong. What defines a member of a tribe is not easily quantified. This is an area everyone must tread carefully."

The waitress brought our food, which created a lull in the conversation. I surprised even myself when the next words flew out of my mouth.

CHAPTER TWENTY-EIGHT

"I have Jonathan Chatterton's journal!"

Darren's brows furrowed. "What?"

Marie's eyes widened. "*The* Jonathan Chatterton?"

"Yes. *The* Jonathan Chatterton."

Darren's scowl intensified. "Audrey, what are you talking about?"

"I just found it this morning, but I haven't read it yet."

Darren took a deep breath, pacing its release. "You tend to start conversations where you left off in your own mind. Could you bring the rest of us up to speed?"

I pulled out the Ziploc bag. "Yesterday, I was at Marcus's house going through stacks of files, trying to find a possible motive for his murder and Renee's disappearance. I figured Marcus got his hands on something which fed his blog posts about the Chatterton family, like the pages missing from George Hart's book. I also couldn't discount the possibility he was paranoid and delusional. Okay, not a possibility, he definitely was, but not necessarily about this." I tapped the table with my fingertips. "When I was in his office yesterday looking through the files he'd compiled, I noticed a book on his shelf identical to one my boss keeps in his office for hiding his whiskey flask. It looks like a dictionary but has a locking safe inside. I didn't tell Sergeant Bianchi I found it because I didn't want him to take it before I'd had a chance to see what was inside. I shoved it in my bag."

"That's a crime." Darren crossed his arms.

"When I got home last night, I was planning on busting into the safe, but—"

"I was standing there waiting for you," Darren said. "I sensed you were agitated, but I figured it was about me."

I pursed my lips. "You're not totally wrong about that. My reservations about you have been growing by the day."

Marie looked between the two of us with fascination.

Darren raised and lowered his left brow. "Understandable. So, after I left, did you look at it?"

"Marcus prided himself in being able to sniff out corruption and conspiracies," I said. "He considered himself brighter than the average guy. He wasn't, so I figured he'd have used a basic code like triple zero or one-two-three."

"What did the magic number turn out to be?" Marie shoveled a caramelized banana from her Jamaican French toast into her mouth. "Excuse my manners. I'm starving, and this is delicious."

I shifted in my seat. "By all means, please eat."

Darren's gaze narrowed at me. "You're acting squirrelly."

My cheeks warmed. "It's embarrassing, but I swear it's not what it sounds like."

"Spit it out."

"He used my birthday."

Darren's left eyebrow shot up again, and this time it stayed there. "Wow, he must've still carried a torch for you after all these years."

"See, that's what I thought at first, but then I found a note inside addressed to me. I think he reached out to me knowing if anything happened to him, I'd pursue the story until eventually I found the safe."

Marie's expression brightened. "You're in possession of an artifact that could change Chattertowne's historical narrative significantly. After we're done here, I'll have you two follow me to my house, and we can lay it out on my dining room table to take a look."

Darren gestured toward my plate. "Go on, then. Chow down. I wanna see what old Johnny boy has to say for himself."

Chapter Twenty-Nine

27 September 1863

Chattertowne, Territory of Washington

I am a coward and a sinner. I have sent Nettie away to my former home to lie-in until such time she can birth my child. I have given her neither the dignity of my last name, nor the defense of her reputation.

She was there for my beloved wife Madeleine as she brought our son Michael into the world, and as she took her last breaths. She has raised Michael as her own, she has been a helpmate to me, and I have rewarded her by denying her in the public square.

I have lain with her, and loved her, and impregnated her, and now have abandoned her. Instead of honoring her and making her my wife, I have bastardized our child, never to be legitimate, and sentenced her to life as a Jezebel. I am no better than her Jesuit father, Phillipe Dedeaux, who never claimed her and raised her as an orphan instead of as his own after her mother passed.

Whispers and innuendo abound, but Nettie has promised to remain steadfast in her denials. Tis a cruel world in which we live, and I am complicit in its cruelty. I am ashamed and embarrassed and find myself contemplating what Madeleine might think of such matters. No doubt she would be ashamed on my behalf.

Tis a sign of my deep abiding cowardice that legitimacy for my child shall come only when I can no longer be held to accompt for my iniquities.

24 April 1864

Chattertowne, Territory of Washington

The Lord hast blessed me with another son, and Nettie has given him the virile name of Jacob Philippe. Her accompt is he has black hair and hazel-gray eyes with brown skin, markedly different from his fair-haired light-eyed brother. Tis unlikely anyone in Chattertowne will match him to me.

When Nettie comes home, we shall have a ceremony between the two of us to unite in Spiritual Matrimony. I love her, and I want her to be my wife, even if in secret.

In the Name of God, Amen. The Seventeenth Day of July in the Year of our Lord One Thousand Eight Hundred and Seventy-Two, I, Jonathan Chatterton, of Chattertowne Township, Territory of Washington, being of sound body and mind, thanks be to God Almighty, do hereby enter this document, my last will, and testament. At the time of my death, will I commit my Spirit unto the Heavenly Realm and into the waiting arms of my Savior, the Lord Jesus Christ, upon whom my faith rests. I authorize the disposal of my estate, land, and belongings in the following manner.

To my firstborn son Michael Jonathan Chatterton, I bequeath half my land, as designated at the incorporation of the Chattertowne Charter. I bequeath my current home and all of its contents. I hereby request he be made executor of my will and testament. May he use wisdom, disposing of my Earthly possessions according to my desires listed herein.

To my son Jacob Philippe Dedeaux, I bequeath half my land, as designated at the incorporation of the Chattertowne Charter. Bearing the surname of his mother has both protected him and robbed him of his birthright. I pray one day, he shall freely use my name.

To my love Nettie, my wife in the Eyes of Almighty, I give and bequeath the remainder of my belongings and my original homestead for her to live in until I am face to face with her again at the Pearly Gates.

On this, I hereunto set my hand and seal,

Jonathan Chatterton

Signed, Sealed, and Acknowledged by Jonathan Chatterton in our presence and witnessed thusly,

Aaron Grimes

Hugh Shropshire, Attorney

Chapter Thirty

I gasped as the parchment, wrinkled and worn soft with time, fell from my fingertips. Marie was on the verge of tears. Darren's skin was sallow, and his expression was filled with horror.

Dedeaux. Jacob Dedeaux. His mother's name. His mother, Nettie. Jeannetta. Jeannetta Dedeaux. Daughter of French priest Philippe Dedeaux.

Could it be? Could I really be?

I looked again at Darren. "Are you okay? You look like you might vomit."

He shook his head no. I wasn't sure if he meant no, *I'm not okay* or no, *I'm not going to vomit.*

After a prolonged silence, Marie clapped her hands. "Well, isn't that just… something! Do you suppose there is a connection between your Dedeaux ancestors and Nettie and Jacob?"

"The rumors of Salish heritage, the same French last name, the sense of illegitimacy and shame hanging over my family, passed from generation to generation through our DNA…if it is true, and if we are descendants of Jonathan—"

"Then you are rightful heirs and blood-related.…" Darren began but stopped, grimacing as he swallowed. He stared at the documents on Marie's kitchen table like they carried the plague.

His pallor was reminiscent of my Uncle Burt a few years ago on the Fourth of July when he'd had to be rushed to the hospital for a perforated appendix. I eyed him with both curiosity as well as concern he might need medical attention.

Marie went to her cupboard to retrieve a Stella Artois glass, filled it with water, shuffled back to the table, and set it in front of him. "You look like you could use a beer. This will have to do for now."

He nodded, slurping the water.

My instincts said the journal, the will, and Marcus's death were all connected somehow, but I didn't feel any closer to solving the puzzle.

"Peter!" It came out of my mouth neither as a whisper nor a shout but more like the hushed exclamation one might emit following a discovery in a sacred location.

Darren spat his water. "What about Peter?"

"Peter?" Marie echoed.

"Peter Chatterton. He was…." I hesitated.

"I killed him this week." Darren's stark tone belied the magnitude of his words.

Marie's gaze widened. She looked to me for confirmation, so I nodded my head.

"Long story," I said. "Peter wasn't a good dude. He was holding me hostage at gunpoint when Darren showed up."

"Oh my! How frightening."

I nodded at her. "It was."

Darren's face remained impassive.

"It just occurred to me a DNA sample from Peter could prove my connection to the Chattertons. That is, if he hasn't already been, uh, disposed of in whichever way he requested." I grimaced. "I guess I could get it from his hairbrush, although that Friar Tuck hairstyle he had going on was severely lacking in follicles. I'll bet his toothbrush could be used. As far as I know, there are no other Chattertons. I heard Peter had a sister, but she's dead too."

A whimper emanated from Darren, who took another swig of water.

"I'm not intent on contesting Peter's will or making a claim on his estate," I continued. "But I'm not necessarily opposed to it either. I mean, who wouldn't want dozens of hilltop acres? I'd probably feel pretty gross inheriting Peter's dirty money, so I'd want to donate a good portion just to get rid of the bad juju."

Darren shifted again, his posture upright and tense. "If his money was gained through corruption or illegal activity, the Feds will be all over it. You don't want to get caught up. I promise you."

"At this point, it's all conjecture anyway. Dedeaux could just be a coincidence." I shrugged my shoulders.

Darren guffawed. "You know it isn't, Audrey. Name another person with the last name Dedeaux."

"Rod Dedeaux," Marie said. "Rod Dedeaux was the head baseball coach for the University of Southern California for forty-five years. He's considered one of, if not the greatest college baseball coaches of all time." She looked at our surprised expressions. "What, you think an old lady can't know about sports? I'll have you know I could hold my own in any sporting conversation with anybody."

"I played baseball," Darren said. "So, I should've remembered Rod Dedeaux. Other than *that* Dedeaux, it's not a common name, so there's a high probability you're related, but, Audrey, you need to be careful pulling these threads because, on the other end may be an unwelcome and dangerous surprise. This info needs to stay between us. It's very likely Peter had a mole inside the Chattertowne P.D. and also at City Hall." He gazed intently at me.

"You think Mayor Quincy's on the take?"

He blew out a sigh of frustration and shook his head. "Just be careful, and discreet."

On our trip back over the pass, I pondered several things, not least of which was what it meant for my mother, sister, and me to be directly descended from Jonathan and Nettie.

I was angry at Jonathan for the way he'd treated the woman he'd claimed to love, and their child, who'd probably never felt legitimate. I was also frustrated with Nettie for not demanding more for herself and her son but I realized that was unreasonable considering the era and her circumstances.

Meanwhile, Darren quietly stewed and ruminated on...well, whatever Darren tended to ruminate on.

Rather than taking me to my apartment when we got back into town, he instead ascended the long driveway to his own house. He put the car in park and turned to face me.

"Audrey, we need to talk. Will you please come inside?"

It was clear from his serious tone and expression romance wasn't on his mind. My last visit to his house hadn't ended well. I hoped this one would have a more pleasant and less itchy outcome.

"Okay, but only for a little while. I'm beat, and I'm overdue for a pain pill."

After the long drive, I needed to use the toilet. I paused in the dim hallway, once again drawn to his family photographs. One of the older snapshots was a portrait of about twenty people at Founder's Park, which was surprising considering Darren hadn't grown up in Chattertowne.

I recognized him as the toddler in the arms of his father, Brian. Next to them was his mother, Maddie. Both parents were laughing at a squirmy towheaded Darren, who appeared to wriggle in his dad's embrace.

The woman next to them didn't appear to be enjoying the moment. Her posture was wooden, and her mouth was pulled tight from excessive plastic surgery and a bad attitude. Her bleach-blond hair, tanned skin, and enormous perky breasts were unnatural and contrasted with Maddie's sandy hair, makeup-free face, and trim athletic figure. The woman wore a beaded tank dress while Maddie sported khaki shorts and a flowy sleeveless mauve blouse.

Entranced by Maddie's joyful expression, I didn't notice Darren standing at the end of the hallway until he turned on the light.

"Oh! You startled me."

"What are you looking at?"

I returned my gaze to the portrait on the wall.

Standing next to fake-and-bake Barbie was a familiar face, the face of my nightmares, a stout man with dark hair, a thick bristly mustache, and a menacing glare. He'd been in front of me all along, but somehow, I'd missed it.

There was no missing it anymore.

"Peter," I whispered.

My head jerked to look at Darren, and I was suddenly filled with panic.

"Why…how…I don't—" I pleaded for any explanation for why Peter Chatterton was in a family picture hanging in the hallway of Darren's home other than the most obvious one.

His face softened. "Audrey, it's not what you think."

I took a large gulp of air and hiccupped. I slapped a hand over my mouth to quell the sound. The next hiccup was muffled. "I don't know what (hiccup) to think! Why is Peter Chatterton in a picture on your (hiccup) wall?"

He stepped toward me, and I stepped back, stumbling over my boot.

"Please don't come near me. Tell me why the man who almost killed me, the man you killed, is in your family portrait standing next to your mother?"

Darren's shoulders slumped. His chest rose and fell, his breathing laborious. "He's standing next to my mother Madeleine because he is, he *was*…"

Madeleine.

Vivienne's words from the day George died came rushing back to me. Johnnie showed up with his pasty little wife, Maddie, to settle the area. Maddie. Madeleine. Peter had a sister who died a few years ago, around the time Darren lost his mom. The dots connected one by one in my mind until he drew the definitive line between the final two.

"He was her brother." Darren sighed. "Peter Chatterton was my uncle."

Chapter Thirty-One

Darren's proclamation had me on the verge of fainting. I steadied myself with my left hand and focused on inhaling and exhaling, so I didn't hyperventilate.

His back was pressed against the wall, and his hands covered his face.

Impulsively I opted for escape rather than waiting to hear his explanation. With my physical limitations, I hoped the element of surprise would work in my favor. Bolting down the hall, I flung the door wide open. I hopped foot to boot down the steps like a Gibbon monkey running on its hind legs.

"Audrey, please come back. Let me explain."

I glanced over my shoulder without stopping. Darren stood at the top of the steps.

Despite the risk of further injuring my ankle, I kept hobbling, adrenaline masking any pain. Unfortunately, my lack of cardio training kicked in somewhere around the fourth block, so I juked into an alley to hide behind a rhododendron bush and called my sister.

"Wanna enlighten me about the *Secret Squirrel* routine?" Vivienne asked when she pulled into the alley and rolled down her window. She shook her head at the sight of me crouched next to the shrub.

I hobbled to the car and slumped into the passenger seat so only the very top of my head was visible through the window.

"I don't even know where to start. So much has happened today. My head's going to implode. Or explode. Either or both are possible at this point." I rested my forehead against the cool glass, my breath fogging the window.

I began by regaling Viv with the events of my dinner with Holden and Mildred, how she'd told me our Great Grandpa Verne was not Elmer Bristow's biological son and Aunt Fanny most likely had Native American ancestry. Next, I recounted the discovery of Jonathan's journal and his will, which had confirmed his love child with Nettie, a boy named Jacob Dedeaux. Dedeaux, as in Aunt Fanny's maiden name. That meant we were possibly the unknown illegitimate descendants of Jonathan Chatterton. I ended with what I'd discovered at Darren's house about Peter being his uncle.

The final pieces of the puzzle had started to fall into place and a picture had emerged of family secrets and lies spanning more than one hundred fifty years which had culminated in the intersection of my story with Darren's. Our connection no longer appeared coincidental but instead a calculated plan on his part.

"How he knew about the information Marcus possessed," I mused, "I can only speculate. He must have caught wind of the Veracitater blog from Peter. With his degree from MIT in Computer Science, his admission of spying on my email and social media accounts, and the job he acquired, for which he's underpaid and overqualified, they all point to motive, opportunity, and means to infiltrate Chattertowne with the purpose of putting a stop to Marcus. Darren was able to be so stealthy because no one knew he and Peter were related. He's a Benson, not a Chatterton."

Once inside our apartment, I flopped onto the sofa and flung my boot onto a pillow.

Vivienne froze in the middle of the living room with an alarmed expression.

"What's wrong?" I asked.

"I've just had the most repulsive realization." She gagged like she'd tasted or smelled something terrible. "He's our cousin."

"Who's our cousin?"

"Darren. Darren is our cousin." She closed her eyes.

"He's our cousin," I repeated.

She sunk to the floor and leaned her head against the sofa. "Distant cousin, but still. Please tell me you didn't...you know...with him."

"No, thank goodness, but we did kiss once." I groaned. "That's why he acted the way he did at Marie's house! I swear, his face turned the color of split pea soup after we discovered Jacob's last name was Dedeaux. He must've realized we're related. Although, if he didn't already know, why'd he cozy up to me in the first place?"

"Probably a combination of romantic interest and your Kupit project. Two birds, one stone. He enjoyed being with you, was attracted to you." Viv grimaced and gave an exaggerated shiver. "But also, he could keep tabs on your research."

"Remember how I brushed aside the idea he was reading my direct messages? He was. He admitted it to me last night. Marcus sent me a message over the weekend and on Monday is when Darren came to see me in my office, first thing in the morning, as a matter of fact, and then later he asked me to lunch. He must have already been tracking my computer. The timing's too convenient to be coincidental."

Viv nodded. "Agreed."

"He insisted I not tell anyone about us being Chatterton heirs because there could be moles connected to Peter—maybe even the mob—in the CPD and City Hall."

"Turns out Darren was the one connected to Peter, so we obviously can't trust him," Viv said.

"Darren probably whacked Marcus over the head with an antique golf club. When I was at Peter's house, I noticed one was missing. Or maybe Peter did it, but Darren told him to do it. Or–" I raised my index finger in the air. "Maybe Darren did it with a baseball bat! Did you know he was a scholarship baseball player at MIT?"

"I didn't." Viv twirled her hair. "It's hard to believe there's a mole in the police department who leaked information to Peter. Everyone seems great so far."

"What about Kimball? Should we talk to her about this?"

At the mention of her boss, color crept into Viv's cheeks. "I can talk to her. I'm seeing her tonight after work. I'm only doing the early show."

She let her head fall back onto the edge of the sofa. I stroked her hair the way I had when we were kids snuggling and watching cartoons on Saturday mornings.

A wistful expression crossed her face. "I've never connected to someone so quickly on so many levels. I really didn't see this coming."

"I'm happy for you, Viv. You deserve to be well-loved."

"I'm finally starting to believe that."

"It does surprise me a bit, not just because she's...well, she's a she, and you've never dated a woman before, but also she's super intimidating."

Viv laughed. "Not when you get to know her. She's actually pretty sensitive under that tough exterior. She's got one of those push-me-pull-me types of relationships with her dad. She feels like nothing is enough for him, and he'll never fully be proud of her. He dangles his affection and approval like a carrot. Even being assistant chief isn't good enough. He wants her to be chief of police, like he was."

"Speaking of police, when I was sorting through files at Marcus's house, Sergeant Bianchi warned me to be wary of Holden. When I told Holden, he said, 'that's rich' like it was a hypocritical statement. What's your take on Tony?"

"Hmm." She emitted a soft grunt. "He does have a slight Italian mobster vibe going on, but that doesn't mean he's actually a mobster."

"I know that."

"What about Holden? You said there was a suspicious ledger in his file indicating he's got more money than he should for his salary."

"I haven't had a chance to investigate it. The numbers don't match Holden's standard of living. You'd think if he were up to no good, laundering money or embezzling or whatever, he wouldn't be living in an old house and driving a five-year-old car."

"Was there anything else in his file?" Viv asked.

"There was a list of partial names followed by letters and numbers, but they could mean anything." I let out a frustrated groan. "I can't see him hurting Marcus or doing anything illegal, but I don't know what to think anymore."

"It sucks not knowing who to trust, huh? Story of my life." Vivienne pouted. "I always wanna believe people are who they present themselves to be, but that's usually left me feeling foolish and disappointed."

I lay my head back on the pillow. "I know exactly what you mean."

I began to relax, but then a submerged thought bobbed to the surface. Bolting upright, I swatted Vivienne's shoulder again.

"I think I know what those names and numbers in Holden's file are! Can you drive me to the marina?"

She stared at me like I'd grown two heads. "You hate the marina."

"Yes, but it's the only way to verify my theory. Maybe there'll be a life vest I can wear."

"You really should see someone about this fear of yours, sis. I'm the one who almost drowned, and yet I have no problem being near water."

"That's because you were two, and you don't even remember it. I was seven, and I was supposed to be keeping an eye on you."

"Audrey, look at me."

I tilted my head toward her but didn't make direct eye contact.

"I'm serious. Look in my eyes."

We locked gazes.

"You were a child yourself. You should've never been given the responsibility of watching a toddler near the water. It wasn't your fault. You can let yourself off the hook. I'd say twenty-five years of self-punishment is more than enough for the mistake of turning your head for thirty seconds."

"You could have died."

"But I didn't. I'm right here. And you know what else? You've more than made up for that day by rescuing me a dozen times since then. I'm an adult now. I'm officially releasing you from your duties."

I exhaled a soul-weary sigh. Tears flowed down my cheeks. "I wish it were that easy."

"It is that easy. Now," Viv clapped her hands. "I've got to be at Nautilus by six fifteen for my set. It's four o'clock now. Is that enough time?"

Chapter Thirty-Two

Vivienne grabbed my hand and tucked it under her arm, clutching it tightly. "You can do this."

I took a deep breath and nodded.

We trudged around the corner of City Hall to the edge of the gangplank at the entrance of the marina. The last time I'd been there, I was treading behind the somber processional of Marcus's body.

We passed the marina office and the Port Authority building. Ahead large vessels were anchored in the widest portion of the river. A shiver came over me from the frigid salty wind, nerves, and the exhilaration of impending discovery.

As we got closer to the edge of the dock, I gripped her arm like my life depended on it.

I pointed to the name on the hull along the port side of the giant iron ship, Dakota, and then to the containers on top.

"Do you see it?"

"What am I looking for?" Viv cupped her right hand against her forehead to shield the sun.

"That container ship out there, the gray one with all the metal crates on top?"

Viv nodded.

"The day Marcus died, I sat on this dock and stared out at another ship anchored there. I knew there was something familiar about the list when I saw it, but I didn't know what. Look at what's written on the side of the containers."

Vivienne gasped. "The numbers and the letters are cargo container identifiers! Does that mean the names listed are ships?"

I held up the picture I'd taken of Holden's file and the chronicle of names and numbers to compare with the ship in the harbor. Dakota was third on the list.

"It's a match," I whispered.

Heavy footsteps on the pier caused us both to whip our heads around. A tall, thin man with white hair, a white turtleneck, and a gray suit marched in our direction.

He was unnaturally tan for the Pacific Northwest in any season, much less winter. His cheeks were flushed with anger. His neck was long, exacerbated by the turtleneck, and his egg-shaped head atop it like a lightbulb on a streetlamp.

Despite walking with authority, the man didn't belong. Everything about him was out of place, from his light Italian suit to his expensive tan leather loafers.

Instead of coming farther toward us, he rounded the corner of the City Hall building. The creak of a door opening was followed by the sound of it slamming shut.

Viv and I exchanged stunned glances.

"Did you know that door was there?" she asked.

"I didn't."

I'd already started hobbling toward the back entrance with Vivienne close behind. The metal door was cream-colored with chipped paint along the bottom and no window.

"What's the plan?"

I shrugged my shoulders and jerked my head toward the door. I crossed my fingers for luck. Viv didn't protest beyond a groan of reluctant acquiescence.

I twisted the aluminum knob and pulled the heavy door about four inches which created a gap wide enough to peek my head inside. The man's footsteps stopped, and I held my breath until the opening and slamming of another door echoed above me. I opened the door further and wriggled through with Viv tailing me like a shadow.

I attempted to be light on my feet while dragging my boot up two flights of cement steps. I struggled to catch my breath on the landing between the first flight and the second. I bent over, panting, my hands on my thighs for support. I squared my shoulders with determination for the rest of the ascent, preparing to climb the equivalent of Kilimanjaro.

Using my shoulder to leverage the weight of the door once we'd gotten to the second floor, I poked my head through the opening. The corridor was empty. I motioned for Viv to go through and allowed the door to bounce off my rear in order to avoid it slamming shut.

A beam of light streamed from under the crack of Holden's doorway. Viv tilted her head with unspoken questions. I raised my brows and grimaced. We scampered down the hall and ducked into the alcove by the women's restroom.

The argument coming from his office was muffled but clear enough to distinguish two male voices. Holden's was lower and steadier in contrast to his visitor, whose tenor verged on shrill. I craned my head around the corner in hopes of better making out what they were saying.

The man in the gray suit thrust through the door, and I jerked back just enough to be out of sight while still having a tiny glimpse of what was happening.

The man paused at the threshold and pointed menacingly. "Handle it, Mr. Villalobos–now–or I will!" He stomped down the hall, yanked the stairwell door open, and disappeared. It slammed behind him.

"Whoa. Holden's involved with some scary dudes. Do you think it has something to do with the money Marcus listed in his file?" Viv whispered.

"I'd stake my life on it."

"Hopefully, you won't have to. So, what should we do? Should we confront him?"

I chewed a hangnail on my thumb. "Lemme think for a sec."

The fact Holden had skeletons—possibly even fresh corpses—in his closet was unnerving. While the idea he had motive or was capable of murdering his longtime friend seemed absurd on its face, I needed to be objective when considering the aspect of opportunity.

"About thirty minutes before Marcus's body was discovered, I ran into Holden. He was wearing workout clothes and carrying a duffle bag with what looked to be black polo. He left because he got a call that seemed to put him in a bad mood. When he showed up at the docks, his shirt was dark blue. I'd assumed it was the same shirt that looked different in the light, but maybe he changed."

"Who called?" Viv asked.

"No clue. I headed to the marina office. I was there fifteen or twenty minutes, give or take, and by the time I stepped out again, a crowd had already gathered around Marcus's body. I texted Holden, who showed about ten minutes later. He'd come from an angle which at the time had confused me, but with everything else going on, I'd dismissed it as unimportant. I didn't know about that side entrance, which would've given him twenty to thirty minutes to go down the back stairwell, have an altercation with Marcus, knock him into the water, and get back up the stairs to his office without anyone seeing. He could have cleaned any trace of blood from his skin in his private bathroom and changed his black shirt to a navy one."

"So where does that leave us?"

I frowned. "Holden had enough time to kill Marcus. What I can't figure out is motive. If Marcus threatened to expose the source of Holden's money, and it was illegal, would he have murdered his longtime friend just to keep him quiet?"

"Hmm. You'd know better than me. I never knew either of them well, but in my experience, when people feel cornered, they're capable of all sorts of things."

I slapped a hand over my mouth. "Last night on the way home from dinner, Holden said he felt cornered. He used those exact words."

"Okay, Holden may have had motive but what about Darren? He's the one who stands to lose the most if the Chatterton family secrets are revealed. He's the one you know has been outright lying to you and cyberstalking you. He had to kill Marcus to protect his inheritance. I'll bet he killed Peter for the same reason."

I was about to respond when a door opened, followed by the jarring thud of it closing and brisk footsteps on the tile floor. We froze. A single breath might have given away our presence. Vivienne looked like a wax figure of herself. The footsteps ceased just short of our hideout. I snatched a peek of muscular golden-brown biceps bulging under a lavender polo as they entered the elevator.

I exhaled. "He's gone."

"Holden?"

I nodded.

"I was gonna pee my pants if he came down here!" Viv squealed.

"You and me both. Here's what I'm thinking. I need you to go downstairs and find him. Stall him however you can."

"What are you planning?" Her forehead wrinkled with worry.

"I'm going to snoop. If he walks in, I'll improvise."

Viv was skeptical. "Improvise?"

"I may have to use my feminine wiles."

"Do you even have feminine wiles?" She laughed.

"I'll have you know lots of guys find me feminine…enough. And I can be wily as a coyote." I crossed my arms across my chest in offense, but Viv was unfazed by my mock outrage. "Look, Holden and I…there's something there, Viv. We almost kissed."

"You kissed Holden too?" she hissed. "When did this happen?"

"We didn't kiss. We almost kissed. The other night at Nautilus when he escorted me to my car."

"I knew it!" Vivienne poked her finger at my shoulder. "I knew something was going on between you two. Look, I'm the absolute last person with any right to judge, but geez, Audrey…this isn't like you. Have I finally rubbed off on you? Tainted you with my poor judgment and low morals like Mom always worried I would?"

Although Viv had attempted a joke, the hurt behind her statement came through loud and clear.

"First, you're human. Your mistakes have tended to be more public than others, but, Viv, you're one of the kindest and most compassionate people

I've ever known. Second, I'm thirty-three years old, and my choices are my own. You aren't responsible for me."

"But you're responsible for me, right?" She gave me a pointed look.

"We need to have a long talk, and we will. Right now, though, I need you to find Holden and stall him long enough for me to look around his office."

"Please be careful."

"I'll be in and out in less than ten minutes. I just need to see if there's anything to explain the large sums of money listed in Holden's file…or the scary-looking dude making not-so-veiled threats against him."

"Because you think Holden's innocent and Darren's the killer, right?"

"Right now, Viv, everyone's a suspect."

Chapter Thirty-Three

Holden's office was unlocked, an homage to small-town ways. Leaving the door ajar, I began looking for evidence of nefarious activity. At first glance, nothing appeared out of place.

I scanned the room. Near the door, something caught my attention. More accurately, the lack of something. Beneath Holden's diploma was a shelf holding his fraternity keepsake box, and below that were four empty clips. I'd noticed it when I'd last visited his office but hadn't given much thought to what was supposed to be there. This time, Charlie Jacobs's story about Holden breaking into the cheese and ice cream shop in college floated to the forefront of my mind. My stomach dropped.

Holden's wooden fraternity paddle.

I was certain it was the missing item. With its handle designed for easy grip in the commission of all manner of fraternity shenanigans, Holden and his massive biceps could have used the paddle to strike Marcus with the upward force described in the coroner's report.

Holden had means, motive, and opportunity.

I eyed the cherry wardrobe which stood in the corner.

When I was a little girl, my Great Gramma May had a similar piece. I liked to play Narnia with it, imagining the back led to a wintery land full of magic and an endless bounty of Turkish Delight candy. My Uncle Trevor had once traveled to London and returned with a package of rosewater Turkish Delight for me, but after tasting the gelatinous nougat confection for the first time, the wardrobe fantasy had lost its luster.

I pulled the brass handles, and the cabinet opened. From a horizontal pole hung several button-up dress shirts, suits, and polos. On the floor of the chest, a mesh laundry bag was stuffed with wadded clothing. I pulled out the top item, a navy cashmere sweater, and ran my hand over its soft surface. I couldn't resist nuzzling it into my face to catch a whiff of Holden's musky scent. Underneath the sweater was a pair of gray slacks, and at the bottom, a black pique knit.

I stared at the shirt with dread.

My trembling fingers hooked the collar of the polo, and my stomach lurched as I pulled it out. A dark reddish-brown splatter was visible on the front.

"Audrey?"

I spun around in surprise, fear, and mortification, along with a bit of relief Holden hadn't caught me smelling his dirty laundry, which I still held in my hand.

"Why are you digging through my dry-cleaning bag?"

I thrust the shirt at him without comment.

He took it and examined it before looking back at me. "What about it?"

"That's the shirt you were wearing when you—"

"This is the shirt I was wearing when I did what?"

"There's blood on it! You wore it the day Marcus was killed. Holden, did you kill him?"

The accusation hung in the air between us.

He shut the door and put his hands on his hips. "Audrey, what in the hell are you talking about?"

"When I ran into you outside City Hall just before Marcus died, you had your gym bag with your street clothes. I saw a black polo. When you got to the docks, though, your shirt was navy blue. At the time, I thought the lighting had made the color look different, but the proof is there." I pointed to the shirt hanging from his fingertips. "Hidden at the bottom of your laundry bag. Marcus's blood is on it. That's why you changed, isn't it? You beat him upside the head, knocked him into the water, and ran up the back steps to change into a clean shirt without anyone realizing you'd left your office."

Instead of becoming defensive or breaking down in an admission of guilt, Holden threw his head back and laughed. Bewildered by his response, I waited for him to regain his composure.

"I should be hurt and angry and offended. Eventually, when I've allowed myself to absorb what's just happened, I will be. Right now, though, I'm too stunned to be angry at your accusation that I murdered my friend." His tone sharpened. "You wanna know why I changed my shirt, Miss Marple?"

He held the shirt out for inspection. When I didn't take it, he pulled it back and opened it to display the front.

"I spilled barbeque sauce on it. That's not blood, Audrey. It's Carolina Sweet and Spicy. Smell it."

Once again, he thrust the shirt into the space between us. This time I reluctantly grasped it. Bringing it to my face, I inhaled the familiar notes of his cologne and something else…a rich, smoky scent tinged with tanginess and sweet molasses.

I raised my gaze to meet his, a showcase of fiery indignation alternating with wounded heartbreak. I swallowed a cantaloupe-sized dose of chagrin.

"Holden, I…I'm so, so sorry. I didn't want to believe—"

"If you didn't want to believe it, why are you standing in my private office, which you've just been violating, accusing me of murder? How could you? Do you not even know me at all?" His hands remained on his hips, but his shoulders sagged.

A panting wide-eyed Vivienne burst through the door. "Oh, hey again, Holden! I forgot I had one more question to ask you. Audrey! What are you doing here?"

Her performance had all the subtlety of Al Pacino in *Heat*.

"Cut the BS, Viv. I know you were trying to keep me out of here so your sister could snoop. You may be a great singer, but you're a terrible actress."

"It's okay, Viv, I think I've been reading this situation wrong," I said.

"What about the old guy who looked like a James Bond villain?" Viv asked.

Holden crooked his head. "Bond villain?"

"The man who just left, the one who looks like a gray alien mated with Peter Graves," I said.

Holden frowned. "What in the hell are you prattling on about?"

"The guy in the gray suit and stupid white turtleneck and expensive loafers who was yelling at you." I grabbed my throat to mimic the turtleneck. "Clearly, he's not from around here, and he gave off serious bad guy vibes like a character from *Kojak* or the *Rockford Files*. What are you mixed up in, Holden?"

He swiped his palm across the back of his head, trying to rub the pain out of his neck. I suspected I might be the source of that pain.

"Vivienne, could you please shut my door?"

He sat in his overstuffed leather swivel chair. Folding his hands, he placed them on the ink blotter pad covering the surface of the desk.

"First, I just have to say, you both have the pop culture vernacular of eighty-year-old women."

Viv snickered.

"What I'm about to tell you cannot leave this room. Do you ladies understand?"

We bobbed our heads in assent.

"Your instincts about the man who was here earlier aren't wrong. He's not a good dude. His name is Mickey Whelan, and he's part of an Irish crime family out of L.A. with a tangential affiliation to a small faction in the greater Seattle area. My younger brother Noah has a wife, three little kids, and a severe gambling addiction. I didn't know this until he came to me a couple years ago, terrified and crying because he was in debt for tens of thousands of dollars. Whelan had shown up at his house with a warning. He said by not repaying his debts, Noah had not only jeopardized his own life, he'd also risked the safety of his wife and children. Whelan proposed what he called a mutually beneficial solution."

"Lemme guess," I interjected. "In exchange for your looking the other way or providing assistance for these guys to use the Port of Chattertowne to transport illegal substances or smuggle whatever contraband they're moving, they'd wipe out your brother's debts?"

"That was the general idea, only now we're two years in. It's worked so well they've gotten their money and then some. They're using my past complicity as leverage to force me to continue."

Viv leaned forward. "The money in Marcus's ledgers isn't money you've been compiling for yourself but debts you've been paying on your brother's behalf! That's messed up, but kinda sweet."

Holden's eyes widened. "Marcus had ledgers listing my debts?"

"Marcus compiled bios on everyone, including you. When I saw those numbers, I thought he was trying to prove you were on the take. In addition to the financial info, he also had identifying info on cargo ships and the containers he suspected were being used for criminal activity. I didn't realize what I was looking at until today. That's why I had Viv drive me down here to double-check."

Holden leaned back. "How in the hell did he figure all that out?"

"Marcus wasn't the smartest, but he also wasn't the sanest person in the world either. He was obsessive about his theories. Once he got ahold of an idea, no matter how bonkers, he was like a dog with a bone. Here's the thing, though, he wasn't completely bonkers. He was right about you even if he had the details wrong, and he was also mostly right about Jonathan Chatterton."

"How so?"

"I've got the lowdown on his so-called stolen birthright. Turns out Viv and I may be descendants of the long-lost heir."

"Oh!" Vivienne laughed and clapped her hands. "And wait 'til you hear this! Darren is our cousin!"

Holden blinked at her. "Pardon?"

"Distant, but still." I shuddered.

"When all this is over, Audrey," Holden spoke through gritted teeth, "you and I are going to set some ground rules for communication. I saw you last night. You said nothing about this."

"I didn't know until today. Yesterday I found a small safe hidden in Marcus's office. Inside were portions of Jonathan's journal and his will. He talked about his wife Madeleine dying in childbirth and the Flathead woman, Nettie, who helped raise his son and bore him another, named Jacob. Because of the circumstances–her being Native and him being the prominent widowed, uh, widowered? Whatever, he was the widowered town leader–they gave Jacob Nettie's last name, Dedeaux, to avoid scandal. Remember, Mildred told us my Great Grandpa Verne was born a Dedeaux, not a Bristow. Based on my conversation with Marie Journet earlier today and what I read in the journal, I now believe Aunt Fanny descended from Jonathan Chatterton and Nettie. She might even be their granddaughter! Which," I took a deep gasping breath to sustain my oration to its climactic conclusion, "if true, also makes Darren our cousin! Oh, and one more thing. Nettie's given name was Jeannetta, as in the river, and my middle name is Jeanne, spelled J-e-a-n-n-e. All I'm missing is the t-t-a."

"I still don't get how your being related to Jonathan makes you cousins with your boyfriend." He smirked.

"It's not nice to gloat over others' unfortunate and accidental dating of relatives," I scowled. "After reading the will, which spelled out the child's existence, his name, and the concern over his technical or perceived illegitimacy, Darren's face went puce."

"He was angry?" Holden asked.

"No, he was nauseated. Puce, like the color of snot."

Holden arched his brow. "Audrey, puce is a reddish-purplish color."

"No way, it's a pale green."

Vivienne pulled out her phone. "Sorry, sis. Holden's right. I guess it's a common mistake, people thinking it's green. Says here it comes from the French word for flea, and when used to describe a color, it's referring to dried blood left on sheets after you've gotten a flea bite. Super gross."

"Told ya. It could also describe the color of dried barbeque sauce." Holden's smirk morphed into a full grin.

"Okay, not puce. Anyway, there's an old family reunion photo hanging in his hallway. Peter was in the picture, standing next to Darren's mom Maddie, aka Madeleine, who was named for her ancestor Madeleine Chatterton. She was Peter's sister. I was so freaked out about him being related to Peter that I didn't put together the next piece of the equation. The connection makes us like third or fourth cousins. Or is it half-first cousins, four times removed?"

"It was me who figured out the cousin part." Viv lightly patted herself on the back.

"Oh! That reminds me, where's your fraternity paddle, Holden? That is what was hanging there, right?" I indicated the empty space beneath his diploma and keepsake box.

He looked at me, startled, and then at the empty clips. He tilted his head with a bewildered expression.

"I don't know. I didn't realize it was gone. You don't think whoever killed Marcus used my…oh, this looks bad, doesn't it? Where in the hell could it have gone?"

"You leave your office unlocked."

"I lock it when I leave for extended periods. I wander a lot, going up and down the stairs, visiting various departments. I haven't felt the need to lock the door during the day when I'm in and out. Apparently, I should have." He directed a pointed look at me. "Damn, I wish I noticed when it went missing." He rubbed his head.

"The day I met with Kimball and the forensic artist, I noticed the empty clips."

"I hate to break up this party 'cause you two are about as fun as a migraine at an EDM concert, but I've gotta go do this show." Vivienne jumped up like a spring toy. "Remember, Audrey, I'll be out late because I have a date afterwards. Don't wait up." She winked. "And if I were you, Holden, I'd be looking square at Cousin Darren. I'll bet he has your paddle."

He nodded. "Agreed."

"Can you give Audrey a ride home? I'm worried Darren might be waiting for her at our apartment as he did last night."

His expression darkened. "I'll get her home safely."

"You'd better, or I'll send Lacey after you." She turned to me. "I know you want to figure this out, but please be careful."

"I will."

Viv closed the door behind her.

"I don't think it could be Darren who took the paddle. I mean, how could he have gotten in here without anyone seeing him?" I said.

CHAPTER THIRTY-THREE

"I don't know. He's sneaky, just like his Uncle Pete," Holden said.

"Maybe Peter snuck in through the side door and grabbed the paddle."

"Maybe. Or maybe Darren wasn't nearby listening to a police scanner."

I blinked at Holden.

"I didn't kill him, Audrey."

I gave a soul-weary sigh. "Remember last night when I told you I need my villains to be villains and my heroes to be heroes? How difficult it is for me when people turn out to be other than who I believe them to be?"

He grimaced.

"Imagine how it might be, then, to find out all at once my family story is a lie, my sort-of crush is my cousin, not to mention a big fat liar, and my other…whatever you are, whatever we are…." I waved my hands in the air. "You're entangled with shady people. I've discovered so much deception lately, I'm having trouble discerning truth from fiction. Can you see how someone like me, who takes everyone at face value, might feel now as though I can't trust *anyone*? You're not clean, Holden. Even if you didn't kill Marcus, you've used your position as an elected official to satisfy gambling debts to the Irish mob."

"Sometimes people have to make tough choices between the lesser of two evils. I chose compromising my values and the risk of prison to protect my brother and his family. I won't apologize for that. Family means everything to me. Loyalty to family means everything. That doesn't make me a killer. We've gotta figure this out, Audrey, or I could be in big trouble." He stared at me with a penetrating intensity. "If you, of all people, someone I've opened myself up to in ways I rarely do, if you suspected me of Marcus's murder, who's going to believe I had nothing to do with this?"

"There's so much conflicting evidence," I said.

"It's gotta be your cousin-boyfriend…or is it boyfriend-cousin?"

I scowled and scanned the room for something to throw at him.

"Come on, Audrey, he's been deceptive about his relationship to Peter. Doesn't that make him a prime suspect? Maybe he shot Peter to cover his connection, and he killed Marcus because he thought he'd have to share the Chatterton fortune with him. Maybe Marcus figured out who Darren really is. Darren has motive for Peter's death, which we already know he's responsible for, motive and opportunity for Marcus's death, and George Hart's also. You and I both know he fits the description of the guy who visited George right before his death. Then, surprise! Who do we find in the parking lot of the nursing home?"

"Darren," I whispered.

"Darren."

I shrugged. "I've considered everything you're saying. He went to MIT, but he's a part-time financial reporter for a small-town newspaper. He's got so much money I don't think he even needs a job. Have you seen his house?"

"No, and I'm not thrilled you have either. I'd prefer you to stay away from him."

"We work together."

"I'm worried about you, Audrey. If he's already killed two, maybe three people, including one who was family, he's capable of anything."

Holden's skin was smooth, save for three laugh lines along the outer corner of each eye and the two parallel lines between his furrowed brows.

"Darren could've stopped me today when I ran out of his house. He didn't. He looked more sad than angry. If he wants to explain, I'm willing to hear him out. I've gotta do what I think is best. I have a story to write, and it turns out Darren knows more about the Chatterton family than anyone else in this town."

Holden sighed with resignation.

My phone buzzed in my pocket. "Speak of the Devil. He just texted me."

"What's he saying?"

"'We need to talk. Woodmark Hotel at Carillon Point eight p.m. Woodmark Suite. Bring Holden.'" I raised my left eyebrow. "What do you think?"

"I think either he's invited me because he's got nothing to hide, or he's planning on killing us both."

Chapter Thirty-Four

As we drove Lake Washington Boulevard past the white cupola of Locke Pavilion at Kirkland's Waterfront Park, streetlamps began to illuminate one by one in anticipation of darkness on the cool late-winter evening. Holden pulled into the Woodmark Hotel's circular driveway and stopped in front of the valet stand.

The hotel had a subtle sophistication, with its three stories oriented to maximize unobstructed views of the lake and marina. Inside the lobby, gray marble floors and deep-blue walls accented by white coffered ceilings and crown molding. It bore a touch of nautical design without being kitschy.

As we entered the elevator, I inhaled an apprehensive breath. Holden grabbed my hand, his grip warm and encompassing. He rubbed his thumb against my palm as we rode to the third floor, which had the paradoxical effect of both calming my nerves and making my heart flutter.

Holden led a half-step ahead while still holding my hand, shielding me from whatever or whoever might appear. With his other hand, he made a fist and pounded the door twice. Darren opened it and nodded a somber greeting. He made a barely perceptible wince at the sight of us tethered to each other. Voices bubbled into the hallway, indicating he wasn't alone.

We followed him into the spacious living room, where a wall of windows gave an unobstructed view of the lake. Perpendicular to the fireplace, two sofas faced each other, with a large coffee table between them. Two people, a man, and a woman, sat next to each other on one of the sofas with their backs to the entryway.

An imposing man in a dark-blue suit stood near the kitchen. He bore a striking resemblance to Vin Diesel, if Vin Diesel were Filipino. He wore an earpiece and sunglasses, despite being indoors.

The woman turned her head. At the sight of me, her nose scrunched like she'd caught a whiff of something rotten. I mumbled an expletive.

It was Renee Washburn.

The man next to Renee rose from the sofa. He was broad-shouldered and stood at least six and a half feet tall, looming over everyone in the room, including the man in sunglasses. Although I didn't recognize him, something about him was familiar.

He reached out to shake Holden's hand before cradling mine, patting it, and smiling like we were long-lost best friends.

Renee emitted an angry gurgling sound.

"Audrey, I presume. It's nice to finally meet you." His deep, gravelly voice was accompanied by a twinkle in his dark eyes.

"I'm sorry, who are you?"

The man looked at Darren, confused. "You haven't told her?"

"Haven't told me what?"

The man released my hand and rocked back on his heels. His black Nikes looked to be about a size twenty-five if that were a thing.

"My name is David Washburn."

After my sharp intake of air and Holden's "What the—" silence fell across the room. Renee smirked, enjoying the fallout from the bombshell revelation. Darren's expression remained stolid.

The room was a swirling mixture of light gray walls, linen pillows with blue concentric designs, crystal and silver accents, dark cherry wood, and about a million of my scattered thoughts.

David directed me toward the sofa. "You look like you need to sit, young lady."

I nodded and eased onto the sofa opposite Renee, who was shooting daggers in my direction. Holden sat next to me while Darren took the spot facing Holden.

On the coffee table was a handful of aged paper with ragged edges along the left side. I leaned forward and gasped. They were the missing pages from George's book. I looked around the circle with incredulity, wanting to yell at someone, but unsure where to start.

David pulled a chair from the dining table and situated it across from the fireplace. "I'm sure you have questions."

Holden glared at Darren, who appeared to be focusing his attention solely on David.

"I'll start." I slapped my thighs. "Let's do a recap, shall we? David Washburn isn't dead, despite having been absent from his son's life for more than thirty years. Renee Washburn wasn't kidnapped, but has been hiding out with David in a posh hotel suite, apparently in possession of the missing pages I've been trying to locate, all the while enabled by faux reporter, Chatterton heir, and liar extraordinaire Darren Benson, the nephew of Peter Chatterton, the man he shot and killed. Did I miss anything?"

Holden shook his head. "I'm curious about David and Renee, but I want an explanation of how Darren ties into this."

Darren turned to face Holden, whose level stare was neither unemotional nor calm but an indicator of his white-hot rage. The intensity of their interaction had me squirming in my seat.

"I am responsible for Peter's death, but not Marcus's, and certainly not George's." Darren glanced at me. "Yes, Peter was my uncle, but he wasn't a good guy, and neither was my grandfather. That's why my mom avoided Chattertowne and the family. Her father, Jimmy, was involved with a syndicate out of Seattle and Los Angeles that used the Port of Chattertowne to smuggle cocaine back in the eighties. After Jimmy was killed—and he was killed, it wasn't suicide–the FBI contacted my mom. Apparently, he'd decided to cooperate with their investigation but had been killed before he had a chance to do so. Because it was a sensitive situation, they allowed the public to believe the suicide story." He indicated David. "You wanna chime in here?"

David leaned forward, bowed his head, and wrung his hands. His sizable frame made the chair look like it had been constructed for a child. With his close-cut curly salt-and-pepper hair, bronze skin, and baleful tobacco-colored eyes gazing at me, it was like seeing a future version of Marcus he'd never become.

"It was you the neighbor saw the day Renee disappeared, wasn't it?" I asked.

Surprise crossed David's face. "I suppose. And I suppose you must think I'm a terrible dad, having left my little boy and his mom. Every night for the past thirty-plus years, I've beat myself up over it, and I'm gonna have to live with guilt for the rest of my life. I stand by my decision, though, 'cause who knows what might've happened if I'd stayed. I did what I thought was best at the time."

David's voice caught. He took a ragged breath and continued. "Back then, I was working as a longshoreman. I've always been the kinda guy to mind my own business, and I'm not sayin' I'm an angel, but I was startin' to see stuff that wasn't right. Armand, the dock foreman, was a shifty SOB. I hear he's Port Commissioner now. Figures. He always looked like he was up to somethin'. I'd see him slinkin' around, meetin' with guys in expensive suits and I-talian shoes. When I asked about it, I was told to stop with the questions. Armand had lots of meetin's with Mayor King, Jimmy Chatterton, and Chief Andy. I went to the library and researched everything I could. That's when I discovered I was livin' in the original Chatterton house."

"I told you!" I pointed triumphantly at Holden.

David nodded. "I found records saying Jonathan first built a saltbox house outside of town limits. I guess he'd initially wanted to live separate from the townsfolk for privacy, and 'cause he was kinda hoity-toity. That turned out to be a big mistake with life-threatening consequences."

"Madeleine," I murmured.

David looked at me. "You've seen the diary, then?"

I nodded.

He frowned and shook his head. "Yeah, his ego killed his wife."

"I don't know, from what I read, I think she hemorrhaged," I said. "I'm not sure being in town and having others there to help would've made much difference."

"Maybe. Anyway, the house's description and location sounded like mine. I bought that house from George Hart. Agent Benson told me he had passed away. I'm sorry to hear that."

"Agent Benson?" I jerked my head to look at Darren.

He blankly stared back at me.

"You really didn't tell her anything, did you? Yeah, so, anyway, I went home and scoured the place. I found the papers hidden in the attic, the pages from George Hart's book, the journal, and the will."

"Wait. George stole pages from his own book in the library archives?"

"I guess so, because all the items were together. For a couple days, I sat on the information, trying to figure out what to do with it. I'm no dummy. I knew it was valuable, and I thought if I could squeeze Jimmy for a little cash, I'd be able to give my kid a decent life. So, I confronted him with the information I'd accumulated in a notebook about the smuggling and Jonathan's love child. He didn't take too kindly to it, as you might imagine, threatening to unleash all his minions on me. That's why I hid the journal. I knew Marcus had found it when he mentioned it in his blog."

"You know about Marcus's blog?" Holden spoke for the first time since David's monologue had begun.

"I've been keeping track of Marcus this whole time. I've had a subscription to the *Current*. I created a fake Myspace account and later a fake Facebook account in order to see pictures of his family. Then I found his blog. It was a bit...."

"Whackadoodle?" I supplied.

David laughed heartily. "Yeah, I suppose you could say that. He had a creative way of looking at things. I guess the apple don't fall far from the tree. Discovering that journal was the worst thing that ever happened to me. It cost me my family, and I didn't want him to do anything stupid like I had. Unfortunately, he took my stupidity to the next level, and it really cost him...." David's voice caught again, grief overwhelming his ability to get the words out.

Despite her zombie-like appearance, a whimper escaped Renee.

"I wonder why George didn't take the journal and the pages with him when he sold the house," I said.

"I'm not sure. Maybe he forgot where he'd hidden them. Maybe he didn't want to carry that burden anymore." David cleared his throat. "Back to Jimmy Chatterton. I confronted him. Days later, he was floating in the river, and I got scared. Scared for me and scared for Marcus and my wife, Gayle. I called the FBI and told 'em what I knew. There was a suggestion made..." He formed quotation marks with his fingers to indicate the suggestion was more an order. "For me to enter witness protection. I knew if I testified, even if they put us into WITSEC, my family would be looking over our shoulders until the day we died. I didn't want that life for them. I thought it would be easier if they thought I was dead. So, I took off. I went to Cleveland, got a fake passport and a cheap Toyota from my cousin Ricky, crossed the border into Canada at Detroit-Windsor Tunnel, and settled in Toronto. Sometimes I'd get drunk and call home, but I'd hang up soon as I heard Gayle's voice. Eventually, I stopped calling." He swiped under both eyes.

Holden returned his attention to Darren. "I still don't understand how you fit into all this, besides being a Chatterton with everything to lose from Marcus's exposure of your family secrets."

Darren ignored him, instead choosing to address me. "I'm sorry I've been withholding information from you, but I had a job to do."

"I'm guessing that job isn't financial reporter for a small-town periodical, *Agent* Benson." I folded my arms.

He had the decency to appear contrite. "I was recruited out of MIT by the FBI's Criminal Investigative Division to work financial crimes with an emphasis on cyber-activity. My superiors were well aware of my family connections. When things heated up again in Chattertowne with Peter heavy in the mix–smuggling, money laundering, corruption–it was decided I should come back, set up residence, reconnect with my uncle, and try to infiltrate his organization. Unfortunately, Peter got suspicious when I tried to talk to him about the so-called family business. He'd heard from his mole or moles at City Hall I was nosing around, and he didn't trust anybody, family or not. He knew my mom had never approved of his activities. He figured she'd turned me against him. He was right on all counts."

"So, you planned to use my research for your investigation?"

"That, and I needed to make sure you didn't reveal my identity. You're a relentless pursuer of truth, Audrey. Tenacious. Even with the lightweight topics Anderson assigned, you didn't miss a detail. I had no doubt you'd uncover something about the missing Chatterton heir and the history of corruption. I began monitoring your email and social media accounts when I heard you'd been given the story. I'd already been observing Marcus because of his blog posts. Audrey, I did...I do...care for you. That wasn't an act. Yes, getting close to you gave me access, but I could've monitored your activity without doing so in such an intimate manner."

Holden grunted. David observed the entire scene with enthrallment. Renee looked like she wanted to punch me or vomit...or both.

"Tell me about Peter." I gritted my teeth.

"Peter was a short man with a Napoleon complex and an affinity for Francis Ford Coppola movies. He had daddy issues because Jimmy was unkind to him, always making him feel like a screw-up. His wife was an awful woman who, although I'm sure he was no picnic to live with, shattered what was left of his fragile manhood. His own sister, my mother, wanted nothing to do with him. All he had was a twisted legacy of his father's connections with the Whelan Crime Family. So, even though they were responsible for Jimmy's murder, he reached out to Mickey Whelan to restore what he viewed as the heyday of the Chattertowne Port. He already had DiLupo in at Port Commissioner. The Whelans and DiLupos have a tentative alliance dating back at least fifty years. Peter had at least one insider within the police department...and he had you at City Hall." Darren glared at Holden and crossed his legs.

Holden returned Darren's stare with a smirk and a cock of his eyebrow. "She already knows everything."

Darren blinked, glanced at me, and returned to his showdown with Holden.

David blew out a long breath, still consumed in his reverie and oblivious to their ego battle. "After Marcus was killed, I hightailed it down here and got ahold of Renee. Unfortunately, she'd found these pages," he pointed at the papers on the table, "mentioning Nettie. They were stuffed under

Marcus's side of the mattress. She put it together with what you and Holden had said. By the time I showed up, she'd already contacted Peter to try and shake the tree a bit, see if she could get cash out of him. Peter threatened to unleash holy hell on her. I convinced her to call the FBI. They sent Darren, and he put us here with Mr. Clean over there." He indicated the man in sunglasses.

"So, it's settled, then. Peter killed Marcus," I said.

"Not so fast, Audrey," Darren interjected. "I talked to Peter about Marcus. I'd just left his house when I passed you on the road. I'd asked him about the port operation, about the lost heir, and if he'd killed Marcus because he was getting too close to the truth about either or both. I mentioned he was missing one of his antique wooden golf clubs from St. Andrew's. He said it was in the shop being refinished, and he had people to take care of the situation without getting his own hands dirty. He refused to give specifics when pressed for details. That doesn't mean he wasn't responsible for Marcus's death, but I don't think he administered the death blow."

David flinched. Renee looked stoned.

"When you ran into Peter on the docks, he'd been there to confront Marcus," Darren continued. "Peter had seen the blogs and had sent Marcus messages warning he'd take legal action, or worse. Marcus responded by threatening to expose what he knew if Peter didn't pay him five hundred thousand dollars. One reason I was shocked to discover you and Vivienne are the long-lost Chatterton heirs, besides the fact we were sort-of dating…."

A collective groan echoed across the room.

"Marcus gave Peter the impression *he* was the heir. I don't know if he actually believed it or if he thought he could con Peter into handing over the money. Renee, do you know?" Darren asked.

Renee's placid face turned sour. It was her go-to expression whenever she was forced to acknowledge my existence.

"Like I told these two when he dragged *this* one to my house uninvited." She pointed at Holden and me. "I knew nothin'. He told me nothin'. If I woulda known, I woulda figured out a better plan."

I chose not to argue the point that Renee's approach had nearly gotten her killed.

"If not Peter, then who?" I asked.

Darren rubbed the back of his neck. "The running theory is someone in the City Hall building killed Marcus. Peter's mole, someone he could've ordered to handle Marcus after the confrontation, who had the ability to get to the docks right away." He turned again to Holden. "Any thoughts? In addition to yourself, I mean."

Holden grimaced. "I didn't kill him. Like I told Audrey earlier today when she also accused me of murdering Marcus, I was in my office eating barbeque brisket. I sent several emails during that time, in between bites. You can check my records if you haven't already, which I'm guessing you have, otherwise, you would've arrested me."

"What about Tony?" I asked.

"Bianchi? Why do you think Bianchi's dirty?" Holden sounded surprised.

"Tony told me Marcus had a file on him, and you said Tony was being hypocritical when he warned me about you."

"He meant you should be wary of getting romantically involved with me. That's why I was giving him grief at Mildred's the other night. I said, 'that's rich,' because Bianchi's got a reputation for crossing those very lines, even though he's married. Besides, Marcus had a file on everyone, including me, and that doesn't make me a gangster. Despite," Holden glared at Darren, "what some people may think."

"What about George Hart?" I asked.

"You think a hundred-year-old man killed Marcus?" Darren scoffed.

His condescension had irritated me when we were sort-of dating. Now we were family, it was insufferable.

"Ninety-nine. I mean, who killed George? The receptionist said the fake nephew who came to visit him right before Viv, and I arrived looked like a boy band member. Darren, you could pass for a One Direction guy with a baseball cap on."

He laughed. "Boy band, huh? Yeah, that was me. Unfortunately, George had passed by the time I got there. The coroner confirmed it was a heart attack in his sleep. I'd hoped to find out what he'd told you, since you were cagey about your visit. I couldn't report his death because I'd have to be there when the police arrived, and I didn't want to jeopardize my case. I'd recently been questioned regarding Peter's death, and it was tough enough pulling strings to get out of the Police Station the first time without blowing my cover. My presence at two suspicious deaths in as many days didn't bode well. I promise you, Audrey, George wasn't murdered. He died of old age."

Tears spilled down my cheeks. "I had visions of him being suffocated. He was a sweet man, and I was hoping he'd make it to his hundredth birthday. I'm going to feature him in my Kupit Festival articles, if I still have a job after all this."

I observed the gathered ensemble.

Marcus's missing dad, back from the dead.

His hostile wife, also no longer missing.

Darren, my cousin/FBI agent, no longer of romantic interest, as I had a strict policy against dating people with whom I shared DNA.

Then there was Holden.

Holden remained unclassified, unavailable, and off-limits.

Finally, Darren broke the silence. "You and Holden never saw David and Renee. As far as you're concerned, they're still missing persons. We don't know what Peter told Whelan, and we don't know the identity of Peter's mole. My only clue is something Peter told me the morning he died about alliances being multi-generational legacies. I assumed he was referring to a previous connection of Jimmy's."

"The King cousins!" I yelled.

Darren looked at me with bewilderment.

"Mildred told me Jimmy was running his operation while Mayor Harold King and his cousin, Andy, the Police Chief, looked the other way," I said. "Maybe it's someone related to them. What about Peg? She's got such a nasty disposition. Is she related to Mayor King or Chief King?"

Holden shook his head. "After her divorce, she changed her name from Anderson back to her maiden name. She goes by Peg Hoffmueller now."

My shoulders sagged. "Well, it was worth a shot. I don't see Tony being related to the Kings, so it can't be him. I saw a photo of Mayor King in the archives, and he's the WASPy-ist of WASPs. He doesn't look Italian at all."

"You're on the wrong track anyway," David mused. "They aren't related through their dads, but through their moms. Andy isn't a King. He's a Kimball."

Chapter Thirty-Five

David's off-the-cuff declaration that Police Chief Andy's last name was Kimball fell like a lead weight onto my chest.

A flashback to photos on the credenza behind Kimball's desk connected the final dots. Kimball, playing college softball. Kimball and her dad, Chief Andy Kimball, the one she could never please.

I doubled over, gasping for air. Each attempt to fill my lungs was accompanied by a yip. Holden and Darren both looked at me with alarm. They jumped up and hovered over me.

"Audrey, breathe in through your nose and out through your mouth," Holden ordered, placing his hand on my shoulder.

"K-k-k…"

"Her sister works for Assistant Chief Lacey Kimball. Must be Andy's daughter," Holden said.

"I know," Darren snapped.

"N-n-no!" I wheezed. "V-v Viv- Vivienne. She's on a date!"

"I was with you when she said she had a date after work, remember?" Holden said. "We'll make sure she doesn't go into the station until we figure out if Kimball's the mole."

I didn't enjoy the feeling of being handled and pacified like a child. The only thing missing was a placating pat on my hand.

"No! Listen to me! She's on. A. Date. With. Kimball. Right. Now!" I clapped my hands between each word for emphasis.

"Oh shoot," said Holden.

Darren called to the agent standing guard. "D'Almada! Get Agent

Shalhoub on the radio. Let him know we need an APB on Lacey Kimball, white female approximately thirty-five to forty. Short crew-cut hairstyle. She may be at one of the bars in Chattertowne in the company of Vivienne O'Connell." He turned to me. "How old's your sister?"

"Twenty-seven. S-short blond hair and big golden eyes. She's f-five two, about one hundred fifteen pounds."

Darren nodded at D'Almada, who scuttled into the other room.

"Wait! You can't put out an APB! Kimball's a cop; she'll either get the alert or someone from the force will let her know!"

"She's right, Benson." Holden grimaced.

Darren grunted and went into the bedroom.

A cold hand enveloped mine. Renee had reached out to comfort me. Closing my eyes briefly, I squeezed her hand in gratitude and released it. It was an unexpected act of compassion.

A moment later, Darren returned to stand in the middle of the living room with his arms folded across his chest. "We need to go."

"Audrey." Holden's hand still gripped my shoulder. "I think you should stay here with David and Renee."

Breaking his grip by jumping from the sofa, I waved my arms in protest. "No! I'm going with you. She's my sister!"

Darren shook his head. "I agree with Holden."

I gave a maniacal laugh. "Oh, isn't that sweet? Now you wanna play nice with Holden? Now you pick his side? Are you freaking kidding me?"

I was primed to unleash all my frustrations of the past several months upon those two infuriating men. Giving up my life in Portland, working for less than a living wage at a small-town newspaper, pining over an ambivalent Darren only to discover we were related, and Holden, Mr. Hot-and-Cold who couldn't decide how he felt about anything in his life, including me. Throwing in the antagonistic wife of an ex, his father who'd abandoned him, three dead bodies in less than two weeks, and the cherry on top, my sister dating a homicidal cop, I'd finally reached my limit.

I closed my eyes. When I reopened them, I'd harnessed so much chill the blood running through my veins felt ice cold. "I can ride with Holden or

Darren, or I can call a freaking Uber. Regardless, I'm going to help my sister. *Capiche*? Or whatever the Irish word is for *Capiche*."

Hands on my hips in defiance, I dared any of them to argue. I held my ground and my breath, waiting for the onslaught. It didn't come.

Holden sighed in resignation. "You can ride with me."

Darren's jaw clenched, but he didn't protest. "Any ideas where they might be on this date?"

He grabbed his jacket and gave a nod to Filipino Vin before jerking his head toward the door. Renee and David murmured good luck wishes as Holden and I followed Darren into the hallway.

"They could still be at Nautilus. Normally Viv sings at six-thirty and eight, but she only had the early show tonight," I said. "She should have finished her set within the last fifteen minutes."

Holden pushed the button when we reached the elevator. "You should call her, say you're checking in. Be careful, though. You don't want to alert Lacey."

I glanced at my phone and grumbled. "No service."

"Give it a minute."

As we stepped into the lobby, a half bar appeared in the upper left of my phone screen. I attempted the call again, with the same result. By the time we'd reached the valet stand, I had full service. I redialed, and at the sound of Vivienne's voice mail, tears streamed down my face. Holden put his arms around me. Darren watched us, stone-faced.

"Hey, Viv, it's me. Holden and I just finished dinner and are headed back to Chattertowne. We were hoping to grab a drink after your shift. Not sure if you're still at Nautilus. When you get this message, could you—" My voice caught. I cleared my throat and continued. "Could you give me a call? Love you."

As soon as I hung up, my body was wracked with sobs. Holden tightened his grip before releasing me when his car arrived.

Darren put his hand on my shoulder. "I'll be right behind you. I just need to stop for gas."

I nodded, unable to speak for fear a whimper would escape my throat.

Holden clutched the steering wheel. I gnawed my fingernails and cuticles. The radio was off, so the only sound was tires rolling rhythmically over the asphalt. Outside my window, fog swirled like dry ice in a bowl.

"Where do you think they might go if they aren't at Nautilus?" he asked.

"I've been wracking my brain trying to figure that out. I knew from my initial meeting with Kimball, that farce of an interview after Marcus's death," I spit the words, "that she was interested in Viv, but I didn't expect Viv would reciprocate her feelings because she's only dated men. I sensed something was going on, though, because I know my sister, and I can tell when she's smitten. I asked her about it, and she said when or if there was something to tell, she would. Today she referred to it as a relationship, but it wasn't until we were at your office that she mentioned the date."

"That's a difficult conversation for her to have, I imagine. She might not yet have come to terms with her feelings or what that means. You never know how people will respond, even those who love you."

"I don't judge her for falling in love with a woman! Leave it to Viv, though, to pick a woman who's a killer. She's really got a gift for seeking out destructive relationships with any gender."

Holden's laugh was bitter. "Do you hear yourself? You contradicted yourself between one breath and the next. You're all about judgment, Audrey. If you're not judging others, you're judging yourself. I'd go so far as to say it's your superpower."

I pouted for a full minute, feeling defensive. The worst part was even though his words stung, they rang true.

"You're right. I know you're right."

"None of that matters right now. The only thing that matters is finding your sister."

"We should start at Nautilus. Even if they aren't there, they might have told someone where they were going."

A bouncer and red velvet rope were the only barriers between Nautilus's heavy ornate oak doors and about a dozen millennials trying to enter the club for open mic slam poetry. The large bald man checking IDs smiled at us as we approached. His tough exterior was used for intimidation when needed, but in my experience, he was a big teddy bear.

"Holden! Audrey! Fancy seeing you two here together."

"Hey, Sam. We're looking for Viv. Have you seen her?" My teeth chattered.

"Sure did. She was here until about a half hour or forty-five minutes ago, something like that. Left with a *friend*." His smirk and raised eyebrow said everything.

"Would that friend be Lacey Kimball?" I asked.

"Why yes, yes it would." His round face split into a wide smile, revealing a gap between his two front teeth. "I think they'd already had a drink or two. They were pretty giggly."

Imagining a giggling Kimball was difficult. Prior to that night, I'd never have imagined her a cold-blooded killer, either.

Holden flopped his arm around my shoulder. "We were hoping to catch 'em for a drink. Any clue which way they were headed?"

Sam scrunched his face. "I wasn't payin' too much attention. I think they went that way." He pointed across the street.

"The marina," I murmured into Holden's neck.

"Sounds like we should go check it out, then. Thanks, man."

The two men performed some sort of slap/grip/fist bump routine instead of a handshake.

Holden grabbed my left hand and looked both ways. We jogged across the street, a cumbersome task with my boot bringing up the rear. The frigid air created such stiffness in my back I feared a strong shiver might shatter me like an ice sculpture.

"Kimball's got a liveaboard sailboat in the marina," I said. "She told me Anderson is moored in a slip near hers."

"Stay here, Audrey." Holden's voice was firm. "The last thing we need is you in all your graceful glory, stumbling around on a sailboat with a killer. Besides, I know this isn't your favorite place."

I stopped, yanking him backwards. "Uh, no, I'm going with you."

"Audrey." He gave an impatient sigh. Worry clouded his expression. "You're more a liability than an asset. No offense, but even if you didn't have a debilitating fear of water and a propensity for injuring yourself, which you verifiably do, clunking that boot down the dock will not make for a stealthy approach."

I didn't like that he was right. Fear, common sense, and my compulsive need to rescue my sister were at a standoff. Holden cast the deciding vote with another order to stay put. I watched his shadow descend to dock B, maneuvering the gangplank as furtively a man of his bulk was able.

I texted Darren an update and put my phone in my pocket before drawing my jacket closed to buffer against the cold marine air. My nose stung from the biting wind, winter's last gasp. Rubbing my arms to create friction for warmth and to give my hands something to do, my head whipped back and forth between the area where Holden had disappeared into the inky blackness and the street in front of Nautilus where Darren was supposed to appear at any moment.

With each passing car, my fear grew, and my heart raced faster until eventually anxiety and restlessness got the best of me. I pulled out my phone.

"Hello?"

"Mildred, it's Audrey. I'm sorry to call so late."

"That's okay, dear. Are you alright?"

"Not really. Do you remember our conversation about Mayor King and his cousin Andy?"

"Yes, of course. Why?"

"I need to know anything else about them that you can remember. Anything at all might help."

"Audrey, you're frightening me."

"I'm sorry, it's just that my sister's life is at stake."

"Oh, my. Well, let me see. The King and Kimball families moved to Chattertowne from Los Angeles in the nineteen sixties. Harold and Andy were still young enough to be babysat, which I did on occasion when their grandmother was out of town. She split her time between California and Washington because her sons lived in Los Angeles and her daughters were here."

"Were you friends?"

Mildred paused. "She wasn't the warmest of women, and that's putting it kindly. No, Lottie Whelan and I were *not* friends."

"Mildred, I gotta go!"

I hung up the phone and contemplated my strategy on how to get to my sister, because I wasn't leaving her with the mafia princess for one minute longer.

Hopping down the dock would create a ruckus like a herd of kangaroos. If I dragged my boot, it would scrape across the grate like fingernails on a chalkboard. I settled on a vaulting motion, hoping I could travel more ground with fewer steps without also flinging myself into the water.

The din of the club quieted the further I got from the street. The marina light posts put forth a dim glow through the fog, just enough to see a few feet in front of me. The gangplank's grated metal teeth provided much-needed traction, since fog had dampened its surface, and my ability to stay upright under even the best circumstances was a crapshoot.

The water was still and dark. A wave of anxious nausea passed over me. I forced myself to pretend it was solid ground. I ignored the whisper of *Danger!* inside my mind, which grew louder with each step. The only thing that kept me moving was my determination to rescue my sister.

Most of the vessels were buttoned up for the winter. Up ahead, however, bits of conversation and a beam of light spilled onto the dock from one of the boats.

I figured the deepest voice had to be Holden, although Kimball's wasn't much higher.

There was no third voice.

I paused next to a white boat with navy-blue writing: Peg's Castaway. The rear entrance of the cabin cruiser was dim except for the glow of a table lamp. A figure passed in front of the light. The door slid open, and Anderson's familiar voice called out through the shadows.

"Audrey? Is that you?" He wasn't yelling, but he also wasn't quiet.

"Shh."

I climbed down to his swim platform.

CHAPTER THIRTY-FIVE

"Mr. Anderson," I whispered. "I need your help, but we've got to be quiet."

The sound of a door sliding open caused me to duck onto my haunches, a position becoming quite familiar.

A throaty female voice called out, "Hey, Nick, how's it going? Everything okay?"

"Sure thing, Lacey. How's your night been? You up for a whisky?"

"I've got company. Thanks, though. Hope we aren't keeping you up."

"Oh no, I came out to catch some fresh air before bed. Early riser, you know. Another time, then," he bellowed.

"You got it." Kimball's disembodied voice sounded strange, skipping across the water.

I stared at Anderson, waiting for the all-clear signal.

"She's gone. Is this about your sister?"

"How'd you know?" I used a handle on the back of the boat to pull myself into a standing position.

"Well, I've seen her around here a few times recently. I hope you're not trying to break them up. Everyone deserves love and happiness, Audrey. In whichever form it takes."

"I'm not spying because of that. It's because Kimball murdered Marcus Washburn!"

His face twisted with shock and disbelief. He crooked his head and squinted at me. "What're you talking about? Kimball's been a cop for over fifteen years. Her dad used to be Chief of Police. Her uncle was Mayor. She comes from a long legacy of public servants, men of renown in this city."

"Actually, Mayor King and Chief Andy are cousins which makes Mayor King her, uh, second cousin. No, first cousin, once removed. Something like that. Not that it matters. That's what I'm trying to tell you. She comes from a long legacy, all right, a legacy of corruption and murder. King and Kimball allowed the Port of Chattertowne to be used for smuggling because they're related to the Whelan crime family out of Los Angeles."

"Whoa."

"I believe they offed Jimmy, or at least had someone take him out so he couldn't testify against them, and that King and Kimball are still overseeing the local operation with Lacey as their inside man, er, woman. Holden's trying to get Viv off Kimball's boat so when the FBI shows up–"

"FBI! The FBI is involved?"

I eyed him with skepticism. "Darren Benson's an FBI agent. You didn't know that?"

"How in the hell would I know that? He presented himself as an overqualified finance expert looking to decompress from the frenzy of corporate America following his mother's untimely death. That's the story he sold me, and dangnabbit, I bought it." He grimaced.

"None of us knew. Well, I knew something was off. I didn't know it was that…or the fact he's my cousin."

My loaded remark elicited the expected stunned expression, but I didn't have time or inclination to explain.

"Speaking of Darren, he's on his way here," I said. "In the meantime, I'm gonna see if I can get closer to the boat to figure out what's happening and why Holden hasn't gotten Viv out of there yet. Will you text Darren the slip number and location of Kimball's boat?" Grabbing a cleat drilled into a wood beam, I hoisted myself up and flopped onto the dock like a flounder.

"Audrey, don't do this. You should go home and let the police handle it. Honestly, I can't even believe you're out here, what with your phobia—"

"It's a little late for that now," I hissed. "You sent me down here to pay your slip rental the day Marcus was killed, which is when I saw Peter, which is why I had to give a statement to Kimball, which is how she got connected to Viv, who is currently being held captive on her boat. I gotta go. Let Darren know what's happening. Please."

Still on my hands and knees, crawling seemed as viable an option as any, despite the rough, splintery planks. My fingers were numb from cold and full of wooden slivers, but I persisted, undeterred, for my sister's sake…and Holden's.

My final approach to the boat was made slithering on my belly. Water lapped against the pylons below, and a bolt of fear ran through me. I peeked over the edge.

The sliding glass cabin door was ajar. Holden leaned against a counter inside, arms hugging his broad chest. His casual air and lack of urgency confused me, and I began to wonder if he might be more involved than I previously thought.

As I contemplated my next move, I was startled by a squawk above me. Two seagulls circled overhead. One of the birds dive-bombed mere feet from me, his target a white paper bag with blue and white checks. The words "Chuck's Chowder Grotto" were printed in blue across the middle. He swooped away, and his buddy made a play for the bounty.

I was a frequent customer of Chuck's and friends with the owner, Dave. He'd named it for his favorite former Seahawks coach, Chuck Knox. Considering Chuck's had the best chowder in town, it was no wonder the gulls were going nuts over what might be inside the discarded bag.

This was, however, an unfortunate turn of events and hampered my ability to remain unnoticed.

I waved my arm to shoo them away, and in return, they seemed to think I was playing a game. One of the gulls did a screeching fly-by. With one hand covering my hair and the other swatting wildly, my activity caught Holden's attention. He made a casual glance in my direction, followed by a double take. Even in the dark, his eye roll was visible. He looked annoyed but also like he was struggling not to laugh at the mayhem of the scene out on the dock.

Kimball's voice rumbled with unintelligible murmurs. Holden stepped in front of the gap, blocking me from her sightline. I found this a reassuring sign he was still on my side and that I could trust him…in the current situation, at least.

Why hadn't he overpowered Kimball and dragged Vivienne out? And where was Darren?

A ruckus in the cabin was followed by breaking glass. Holden was no longer visible in the doorway.

On the right side of the slip was a dock box for storage of extra life vests, cleaning supplies, and maintenance items. I considered opening the lid and crawling inside, but not wanting to encounter spiders or rats, I instead postured myself behind it. Cobwebs blew into my face and mouth.

The cabin door slid fully open, and Kimball staggered out with a gash on her forehead. She grabbed a side rail for support, and she seemed winded and distressed. Her left hand held herself steady while her right swiped at her brow. She winced and held out her fingers for inspection. They were covered in dark liquid.

There was no movement or noise coming from within the boat, and there was still no sign of Darren. I was the last line of defense. If Kimball escaped before Darren showed up, she could disappear forever.

A rope ladder hung from the left dock. Kimball grunted with each grasp of the next rung, leaving marks as she went. In the pitch-blackness of the late-winter's night, with no moon to cast its glow upon the scene there was no red or blue or purple, but I knew it was blood.

Kimball reached the platform and began her getaway. She ambled in my direction. Her galloping footsteps vibrated the dock.

I inhaled deeply, filling my lungs, and thrust my boot into her path. Her fulsome backside lurched forward, and the toe lip of her thick-soled Doc Martens boots caught on a metal cleat.

With no railing to stop her, she disappeared over the edge. The hollow thump of some portion of her body hitting wood was accompanied by a yelp followed by a splashing plop.

I pulled myself with my forearms, and my stomach dragged across the rough-hewn planks. An aggressive lunge pitched me too far forward, causing me to roll onto my back like a pill bug with feet in the air.

Of course, it was at that very moment Holden appeared, towering over me. His expression was a mix of amusement and concern.

Darren ran the gangplank toward us. "Where are they?"

Behind him were five men in windbreakers with gleaming yellow FBI logos printed on the left side.

"Where's Kimball?"

Still lying on my back, I pointed over my head in the direction of Kimball's launch. The men rushed over. Two of them jumped onto the platform below, and judging by the spray hitting my face, one jumped into the water. Darren,

Holden, and the other two agents looked on while they attempted to locate Kimball.

"Got her!"

Everyone scrambled to help lift her onto the dock. Everyone except me. I wasn't worried about Kimball. I couldn't have cared less if she lived or died. All I cared about was finding my sister.

Chapter Thirty-Six

While the crowd, including Anderson, hovered over Kimball's wet, grayed face, one of them, a tall thin man with a bald spot and a goatee, performed CPR and mouth-to-mouth. My ankle throbbed inside my boot. Tripping Kimball had been one stress too many.

I remained determined to get to Vivienne. Using the dock box for leverage, I grabbed the handle and drew upon what little upper body strength I possessed to maneuver into a semi-upright position. Hunched over, I hobbled over to Kimball's ladder.

The boat listed away from the dock. One of the mooring ropes was untied. Holden spotted me and jogged over.

"Audrey, what are you doing? You're gonna hurt yourself."

He reached for me, but I swatted at his hand.

"I have to help Vivienne."

Gripping the cleat, I slid my left leg onto the first rung. My booted right foot slipped. I swung around, hanging two feet above the aft of the sailboat.

Holden dropped to his stomach, grabbed my right hand, and clasped the left, which still had a shaky hold on the cleat.

"If you aren't the most obstinate woman I have ever—" He gently lowered me onto the boat.

I stumbled backward into the giant steering wheel.

My first thought was that the sailboat should've been a clue to anyone who'd visited that something didn't add up about Kimball's life. Somehow, Anderson had spent several evenings downing cocktails on the beautiful teak deck with its shiny brass railings but had never suspected she was on the take.

I slid the door open to go inside. Holden landed on the platform behind me with a thump.

"Audrey, wait."

I ignored him.

The interior was even more luxurious, with striped teak flooring, teak cabinets, tables, and molding surround. Cobalt teardrop lampshades, gray paisley pillows, and velvet cushions made the seating area both elegant and comfortable. White wainscoted walls sported glossy teak railings, which led into the galley. Amidst the refined and tidy style was evidence of a struggle: remnants of a broken lamp, a crystal glass knocked over with its contents pooled on the table next to it, a dining chair upside down.

Down the hall was a door which I assumed led to the bedroom. I tentatively turned the knob, filled with trepidation about what I might find.

Vivienne lay on the round bed, her cheeks pink in contrast to her pale skin. Her eyes were closed but fluttering.

Holden came in behind me and rested his hands on my shoulders.

"How can she sleep through all this chaos?" I whispered.

"She's sedated. When I got here, she was already unconscious, and Lacey was preparing to set sail. I assumed she knew about my association with Whelan even though I hadn't known about hers, so I bluffed. I told her he'd contacted me and wanted us to come up with a plan because the FBI was onto her about killing Marcus. She was rattled by my accusation but didn't deny it. She mumbled something about her father, Whelan being her cousin, and did I understand what family pressure was like? When I asked what was wrong with Viv, she told me to mind my own business. I pressed her further, and she told me Viv played your voicemail over speakerphone. Kimball got spooked."

My chest heaved with a shuddering breath. "So, this is my fault."

"Nope, it's not. Your sister came here of her own volition. You tried to warn her. You couldn't know she'd let Kimball listen to the voicemail."

He squeezed my shoulders, and his warm breath brushed my ear, both comforting and unnerving at the same time.

"What happened after that?" A tear slid down my cheek.

"Apparently, Kimball spiked her drink. She must've figured she could explain it all to Viv once they were out at sea, call it a spontaneous romantic getaway or something. I'm not sure she thought it all the way through. When I told her you wouldn't stop until you located your sister, she said she'd already dropped both of their phones in the water so we couldn't track them. Eventually, they would've had to stop somewhere, though, and Viv would've found a way to reach out to you."

Starting to feel lightheaded, my legs buckled. Holden caught me and lifted me onto the bed.

"Do you think she would've killed her?"

Holden grimaced in response. It wasn't reassuring.

"I don't know. I don't think so. She was desperate, but I believe she's in love with her. When I said I didn't care what she did, but she wasn't taking Viv with her, she said leaving her behind was unimaginable. That's when I made my move toward the bedroom. Lacey jumped on my back, and we wrestled. I grabbed a tall wooden saltshaker off the table and whacked her in the head. She nailed me with something from behind. I think I blacked out."

"My guess is it was that lamp over there." I indicated the ceramic shards. "You couldn't have been unconscious long, though, because you were standing over me pretty soon after I knocked her into the water."

"I heard the scuffle. I should've known you could take care of yourself, even with your boot. I'm pretty damn proud of you, not just for figuring out this whole thing and stopping Kimball, but the way you were able to overcome your deepest fear to make it happen."

I stared into his tender, crinkled eyes. He came closer. My breath became ragged in anticipation of his lips meeting mine.

"Hello? Everyone okay?" Darren called from the living room.

Holden sighed and pulled away from me. "Back here."

I responded to Holden's eye roll with a wry smile. "Be nice to him. He's family."

We both groaned and laughed.

"Is she okay?" Darren stood in the doorway. His forehead was creased with concern.

Holden nodded. "She will be. Kimball gave her something to knock her out, but she's breathing okay. Speaking of, how is Lacey?"

"She's stable. When she went in, she got tangled in a fender line. She wasn't too deep, and we were able to revive her. She had water in her lungs but was able to cough it out after we rolled her onto her side. The gash on her head was bleeding profusely. Head wounds tend to do that."

"Karma's a bitch."

Both men looked at me.

"What, you don't see the great Karmic comeuppance in that she nearly suffered the exact fate she inflicted on Marcus?"

I had no empathy for Kimball at that point, not even in my reserve tank.

"Yeah, I guess she got what she had coming to her." Holden rubbed the back of his neck.

Darren–Mr. Straight-and-Narrow, Mr. Law-and-Order–looked uncomfortable. He shrugged his shoulders and nodded reluctantly. "I'm not a fan of revenge, but I can live with the universe bringing justice to deserving parties. With regard to a person getting what they deserve, Mr. Villalobos, we will need to have a conversation regarding your involvement."

"I'm prepared to face the consequences."

My heart sank imagining what lay ahead for Holden, who'd admitted to having done some pretty sketchy stuff.

"Darren, you can vouch for him! He's been helping us. He can testify as a cooperating witness."

"I'll do what I can. There are extenuating circumstances, and your testimony regarding Kimball, Whelan, and my Uncle Peter will go a long way toward convincing the U.S. Attorney overseeing the case some leniency is warranted, but you've committed some pretty serious crimes."

Vivienne began to stir. I didn't bother wiping away the tear of relief which fell down my cheek. I brushed platinum silken curls from my sister's forehead.

"Wh- Audrey, what are you doing here? Where's Lacey?" She squinted at her surroundings.

"Kimball…Lacey…she isn't the woman you, we, any of us thought she was. She's a dirty cop. Really dirty. She killed Marcus."

Vivienne pushed me to get off the bed.

"No, that's not true. She's been helping us."

"What do you mean, she's been helping us?" Darren asked, his eyes wide.

Vivienne, still woozy from whatever cocktail Kimball had given her, leaned against the edge of the bed.

"We've had several conversations over the past couple weeks brainstorming about what happened to Marcus. I told her everything Audrey's discovered. She said she suspected Darren killed Peter on purpose, not on accident, and I should be careful about what I say in front of him. For good reason, right, Audrey?" She looked to me for confirmation. "Darren is Peter's nephew, and he lied to you. He's the one behind all this. He has to be!" Tears filled her eyes.

Darren muttered, "That explains why she's been a half step ahead this whole time."

I glared at him for his insensitivity, and he had the temerity to look affronted. Placing my hand over Vivienne's, my voice was firm but compassionate.

"No, Viv. Darren's with the FBI. He's been investigating organized crime in Chattertowne, including his uncle's involvement. Everything Holden said earlier–the smuggling, Whelan, the blackmail—Lacey was the go-between, and she was Peter's mole at City Hall. She's been following in her dad's footsteps, Police Chief Andy Kimball, and his cousin Mayor King, who we think are still operating the local syndicate of the Whelan Crime Family. We'd assumed Chief Andy was a King, but he was a Kimball. When I found out, I knew you were in trouble."

"I told her you thought the Kings might've been involved in Jimmy's death and David Washburn's disappearance. She said you were way off base." Vivienne buried her face in her hands.

"That must have spooked her, knowing how close Audrey really was to the truth," Holden said.

"She also told me she thought Renee wasn't kidnapped. She was on the run because she was involved with Marcus's death, and it was nothing more than a domestic dispute."

"Speaking of, guess who I saw tonight, alive and well in a hotel room in Kirkland?" I said.

Viv removed her hands to look at me. "Renee?"

"Oh yes, Renee, but she wasn't even the most shocking appearance. David was there."

"David Washburn's alive? Where's he been all this time?" she asked.

"Canada," I said. "Anyway, he's the one who keyed us into the fact Andy's last name is Kimball. I guess Lacey got nervous after hearing the voicemail I left for you. If you told her about Holden's confession of involvement with Whelan and Darren's newly-discovered connection to the Chattertons, she must've felt the walls were closing in."

"Cornered." Holden nodded.

We exchanged knowing glances.

"I remember her pouring me a shot of whiskey, then everything gets a little hazy...." The truth of what happened dawned across Vivienne's heartbroken face.

"She laced your drink. No pun intended."

Holden chuckled at his own lame joke, and I swatted at him.

"She was getting ready to leave the marina," I said. "She'd already untied one of the lines when Holden arrived. If we hadn't gotten here when we did, you two could be well on your way to Mexico or Canada by now."

I didn't want to think about the idea that any resistance from Viv once she'd regained consciousness could have put her in grave danger.

"Holden, you stopped her?" Viv asked.

"I wish I could take the credit. All I did was stall her long enough for your sister to take her down like a ninja."

"Less like a ninja, more like Maxwell Smart," I laughed.

Viv managed a sad smile in recognition of the bumbling secret agent from nineteen-sixties TV.

Holden threw his hands in the air. "For the love of all things holy, would you two please bring your pop culture references into this millennium!"

"So, what...what happened to Lacey? Is she okay?" Vivienne looked conflicted and ashamed to still care for her attempted kidnapper.

"She went into the river. They were able to pull her out and resuscitate her. She's been taken to the hospital with an FBI escort." Darren relayed the information as if he were giving a traffic report.

His demeanor made a lot more sense since his identity as an FBI agent had been revealed. All those frustrating encounters I'd taken personally where he'd seemed stand-offish and sometimes a little harsh were merely the result of his training and agenda.

Viv glared at Darren. "I want to see her tomorrow. Can you make that happen? I think you owe me that." Her eyes were bloodshot, and her lip trembled, but her jaw was set firm.

He nodded. "I'll do my best."

After the medic examined Viv and gave the all-clear, Darren accompanied the three of us to Holden's car. He promised to keep us apprised of any developments. Another agent would be assigned to interview each of us individually. He gave Holden a regretful smile, an indication his interview would not be pleasant.

I fluffed Viv's pillows, cocooned her with the comforter, and kissed her on the forehead.

The drab, whitish room in our boring, basic apartment had become a haven from a scary, chaotic world. The notoriously unreliable furnace provided warmth in contrast to the frigid winds which howled outside, and the dowdy vertical drapes acted like metaphorical insulation from people with bad intentions. Compared to the jagged wood shards I'd crawled across earlier, the coarse Berber carpet felt like a soft mink pelt on my feet, although it still smelled like rodent.

As my sister drifted off to sleep, tears of relief and sorrow flooded my eyes. I'd cried more in the past three weeks than I had in the previous three years. I was grateful Viv was safe but devastated her heart had been broken.

I texted my mother that we needed to plan a lunch date so I could update her with everything I'd learned about our family history. She responded that she would love that.

I returned to the living room to find Holden standing near the sofa. He motioned me closer and wrapped his arms around me. I reveled in his warmth and inhaled his spiced skin. Tension seeped from my body like a leaky tire. After several minutes, he broke our embrace. He nestled me under a blanket on Viv's sugar-daddy sofa and kissed my forehead.

With his hand resting on the doorknob, he turned to look at me. His gaze intensified. His broad shoulders rose and fell with each breath. His beautiful mouth hung, weighted with sadness. Slow blinks became more rapid until his lashes fluttered like the wings of a hummingbird. He jerked his head to look away.

Then he was gone.

Sitting by myself in the quiet room, my internal cacophony of fear, doubt, insecurity, self-judgment, and second-guessing swelled like a tidal wave, deluging my mind and heart. I'd spent my life avoiding those moments by filling noiseless spaces with music, TV, work, and friends. Social media had become a great and terrible mechanism to avoid having to confront my inner monologue.

Long-submerged thoughts and feelings floated to the surface where they could no longer be ignored. I grabbed a notebook and pen from the coffee table and began to write.

Eventually, we must stop blaming and forgive those who came before us for passing down their inadequacies and insecurities to us. Only then can we take responsibility for our own stuff while learning to love and forgive ourselves.

Eventually, we must look ourselves in the mirror and decide what to do with our thoughts, figure out how we feel about ourselves, our lives, the choices we make, the relationships we form, and the relationships we abandon.

Eventually, we must either choose to fight for a new way of living and thinking or surrender to dysfunctional legacies as our preordained destiny.

I refuse to accept I'm destined to follow in the footsteps of Aunt Fanny, who used and discarded men in order to feel desirable and worthy, was embarrassed by her heritage, and too prideful to be called grandmother.

I will not live like Nettie, who seemed to have accepted living in secret shame rather than as a legitimate wife because she fell in love with a coward and wanted at all costs to protect a man who was unwilling to do the same for her.

I have no right to judge them. They did the best they could with the circumstances they faced and the tools they possessed.

That doesn't mean I have to become them.

When navigating seas, the calmest waters are often in the center of the wake created by the ships which have already sailed through the channel. Leaving that path can be daunting. It requires forging through rough ripples and swells to get out onto the open sea.

However, of one thing, I'm certain. If I never escape their wake, if I stay on their course, I'll end up at their destination, not mine.

I want to set my own course. I *must* set my own course.

Chapter Thirty-Seven

Chattertowne Coastal Current
Kupit Special Edition
By Audrey O'Connell

Welcome Spring!

In two weeks, Chattertowne will celebrate the annual Kupit Festival. When first given this assignment, my intention was to honor tradition while also bringing a fresh perspective on Kupit, on Chattertowne, and on all the people who've called this place home.

What I found was quite surprising.

Beneath the surface of our idyllic community were long-submerged stories anchored in shame, pride, fear, greed, and prejudice.

They say a family's as sick as its secrets. The citizens of Chattertowne are family, and the truth is, we've been fighting these secret cancers since our town's inception. We've propagated a charade of unblemished heroes while exercising purposeful ignorance of our whitewashed history.

I was warned against dredging secrets and casting our town or its founders in an unfavorable light as if my intentions in seeking truth were to destroy our legacy in the process.

I love this place and my childhood memories of Kupit. My identity was molded on these streets, in Chattertowne's parks, within its schools, by its leaders, teachers, and coaches. The person I am, because I was raised here, can never be satisfied with less than an authentic account.

We all claim to love Chattertowne, but can we be genuine in our love for it without knowing and accepting its entirety...the good, the bad, and the ugly?

We've never appropriately honored the People who called this valley home prior to Jonathan staking his claim a hundred and fifty years ago. One tepid effort to rename Chattertowne was fueled by hatred of the Chatterton family, not a sincere desire to pay respect to the Coast Salish.

How many residents even know about the woman for whom the Jeannetta River was named? I'd never given it a second thought and was stunned to discover it was in tribute to a Flathead woman called Nettie, who Jonathan Chatterton was too ashamed to publicly declare his wife, despite a spiritual and physical union resulting in a son. Had he possessed the courage to assign her rightful place by his side and the respect she deserved, her story would have been known.

Over the next two weeks, in a series of feature articles, I'll be sharing the history of this valley, its people, its heroes, its villains, and its unsung contributors, along with Nettie's story and a more complete version of Jonathan's. The truth is, he was both a brave man and a coward. It's okay for us to be honest because that makes him human, not legendary.

It's well past time to take a candid look in the mirror and decide what legacy we want to leave, one of unvarnished truth or one crafted and molded from cherry-picked facts. I posit the greater is the one which values honest appraisals of history and spurns false narratives designed to highlight certain aspects while ignoring others.

Recent developments leading to the arrest of former Mayor Harold King, former Chief of Police Andy Kimball, Assistant

Police Chief Lacey Kimball, and others have exposed an underbelly of corruption and affiliation with organized crime. Assistant Chief Kimball has agreed to plead guilty in the death of Marcus Washburn, which she claims was committed under the duress and direction of her father and his cousin. The weapon, reportedly lying at the bottom of the Jeannetta River, has yet to be located. In exchange for a reduced charge, Kimball has chosen to testify against her father and others involved in the conspiracy. (Full disclosure: my sister Vivienne has chosen to remain in a relationship with Lacey Kimball and plans to support her through her upcoming legal battle.)

Port Commissioner Armand DiLupo has been indicted under the RICO statute (Racketeer Influenced and Corrupt Organizations Act). Councilwoman Margot Hennepin has been charged with fraud for using her notary business to legitimize altered cargo manifests and various legal documents.

Former City Manager Holden Villalobos has also agreed to a cooperation agreement in exchange for a reduced sentence on the guilty plea he entered last week for his part in the illegal operations at the Port of Chattertowne. His testimony is sure to bring other unpleasant revelations into the public purview.

I believe we are strong enough to confront our flaws as a community, and this cleansing, while painful, will lead to a brighter future for Chattertowne, one of which we can all be proud.

Delving below the surface of this town has been both unsettling and affirming for me. I feel more connected than ever before, more invested in its potential, and more cognizant of how our collective past has shaped us. Discovering my own family's story has changed how I see myself in relation to Chattertowne and the people from whom this land was taken. My goal isn't to undermine good feelings or nostalgia about our history but to give a comprehensive picture to celebrate the whole story and honor all the people who have contributed to making this place what it is today.

My upcoming series will feature excerpts from Jonathan's will and diary entries, George Hart's biography and his accounting of the history of Chattertowne, a preview of festival events and participants, along with a multifaceted discussion of the Coast Salish, their traditions, art, and culture and the mark they left on this region largely ignored in previous Kupit retrospectives.

My hope is you'll fall in love with this place all over again.

I have.

Knowledge is power. It creates a clean slate from which we can all move forward to make this town everything it can be.

So, here's to Chattertowne and the best Kupit Festival yet!

Acknowledgements

I cry every time I write my acknowledgments. The further I go in this journey, the more people I get to thank who have helped me along the way.

In what may be a literary first, I'd like to start by shouting out my therapist T.R., without whom I wouldn't have finished this book in the first place. Our work together has changed my life and enabled me to stretch and grow beyond what I ever thought was possible.

Thank you to my extraordinary husband, who, after three decades together, is enjoying his new role as my plus one. You make great arm candy.

There aren't enough words to express my love and admiration for the four stellar humans that call me mom. I love watching each of you thrive on your chosen paths, and I can't wait to see where life takes you. Also, thanks for helping me come up with the title, Parker!

Thanks to my parents, whose unwavering support has given me the courage to put myself out there and try scary things.

For my siblings, I love you and am so grateful to have you guys in my corner.

To my family and friends, thank you for celebrating with me and for encouraging me.

Lisa Everett-Rector, my earliest beta reader who saw the potential in this book when it was twice as long as it needed to be, your friendship and support mean so much to me.

To my friend and first editor, Holly, your role in the formation of this book and in my career will never be forgotten.

Thank you to my fantastic editor Shawn for bringing this nearly 20-year project to fruition. I love working with you!

For my agent Dawn Dowdle, from our first phone call, I knew I was in good hands. Thank you for your tireless advocacy, your friendship, and your mentorship.

No acknowledgment would be complete without my Writing Sisters, a wonderful, eclectic, talented group of women I'm blessed to know.

About the Author

Kate B Jackson is an alumnus of the University of Washington. A blogger turned author, in addition to her mystery series, she's written rom-com and mystery screenplays as well as a middle-grade mystery/adventure series. She's a member of the Pacific Northwest Writers Association, Sisters in Crime, Northwest Screenwriters Guild, Crime Writers Association, and Mystery Writers of America. She lives in the Pacific Northwest with her husband and has four grown children. She's represented by Dawn Dowdle of Blue Ridge Literary Agency.

SOCIAL MEDIA HANDLES:
  FB: @KBJacksonAuthor
  Twitter: @KateBJackson
  Pinterest: Katebjacksonauthor
  LinkedIn: KateBJacksonauthor
  IG: @kbjacksonauthor

AUTHOR WEBSITE:
  https://KBJackson.com

Also by K. B. Jackson

The Sasquatch of Hawthorne Elementary, part of the Sasquatch Hunters of Washington, Inc. series (Reycraft Books)

"Flip Flop," short story in *Hurricane Review Literary Anthology*

Printed in the USA
CPSIA information can be obtained
at www.ICGtesting.com
LVHW091054211223
766988LV00063B/1861